THE AMISH BONNET SISTERS BOX SET VOLUME 9

A SEASON FOR CHANGE, AMISH FARM MAYHEM, THE STOLEN AMISH WEDDING

SAMANTHA PRICE

A SEASON FOR CHANGE

BOOK #25 THE AMISH BONNET SISTERS

CHAPTER 1

Cherish was feeding her dog outside when she looked up and saw Ada and Samuel approaching the house in their buggy. It was so early in the morning that she was surprised to see them. Hoping Matthew would be with them, she walked over.

Ada stepped down from the buggy. Then she pulled out a box from the back.

Matthew wasn't with them. "Hello. Where's Matthew?"

"He's working at Mark's saddlery store today."

"That's right. I forgot he was doing that."

Ada smiled at the box in her hands and then looked up at Cherish. "I brought chocolate cake and those chocolate cookies you love."

That made up for Matthew not being there. "Thank you."

Ada started walking to the house. "Simon left yesterday. I suppose you know that."

"He left?"

Ada nodded.

"Left for home?" Cherish asked.

"Yes." Ada stopped walking when Levi passed them and said hello. Then he got into the buggy and left with Samuel.

Cherish just stood there, staring at Ada.

"So he didn't tell you?" Ada asked.

Cherish shook her head. "No."

"I thought you and Simon were closer than that. I must've been mistaken." Ada left her and walked into the house.

Cherish was frozen to the spot. She had hoped Simon would come and say goodbye and then they'd plan something for when she went to her farm since he lived close by. What was the point? He clearly wasn't interested. Now Ada knew it too. Cherish could see it in her eyes the way she'd stared at her just now.

Bliss came out of the house. "Hey, Cherish, *Mamm* wants to know..."

"I'll be back later. I forgot to do something." Cherish ran into the orchard and when she was far enough away from the house, she slumped to the ground and allowed some tears to escape her eyes and fall down her cheeks. She hated being weak and crying was weak, but she couldn't stop.

The orchard was so barren and lifeless in the winter. The rows of leafless, tangled branches reaching up to a cold, gray sky emanated a certain eeriness. The frozen ground also did nothing to lift her mood.

It was such a shock that Simon had left without telling her. He'd said he'd stayed longer than he had meant to and she thought that was for her. Maybe he'd stayed for some other reason. Just when she'd started to see a future for herself, she'd fallen flat on her face. Was this a sign that nothing in her life would run smoothly?

Then her mind started to wander as she looked up at the clouds. What had ever gone right for her?

Dat had died and then her oldest sister, Florence, who was like a second mother, abandoned her whole family to marry an outsider. Then she got close to Aunt Dagmar and then she died too. Cherish sobbed at all the people who'd left her. It didn't matter that *Dat* and Aunt Dagmar couldn't help dying, the pain was just the same as if they'd walked out the door and kept going.

Simon leaving without a word felt just like all the other disappointments she'd suffered.

"Cherish, what's wrong?"

Cherish scrambled to her feet, wiping her eyes when she saw Bliss had found her. She didn't want her or anyone else to see her crying on the ground. "I'm okay."

"It doesn't look like it. What's upset you?"

Cherish brushed down her dress with her hands. She trusted that she could tell Bliss the truth. After all, Bliss was no stranger to life's cruel disappointments. "I'm just upset that Simon left and he didn't even say goodbye."

Bliss produced a letter from beneath her black coat. "Maybe he did."

Cherish stared at the envelope in her stepsister's hand. It didn't even have a stamp. It simply said, 'Cherish.' "Is that from...?"

"Yes. I got it from the letter box just now. I was hoping Adam might have written a note explaining his feelings and telling me why he doesn't want anything to do with me. There was something there, but it wasn't for me and it wasn't from Adam. It has Cherish written on the front and on the back it's got Simon. He must have put it in there himself. It's not been sent through the postal service."

Cherish sniffed. "It's really from him?"

"Yes. I guess so, unless you know any other Simon?"

"I wonder why he did this." Cherish started feeling a little better. He'd left, but he was thinking about her.

"Open the letter and find out. I'll be back at the house if you want to talk."

"No, stay in case it's bad news." Cherish couldn't take her eyes off the envelope. "No, go. I'll be okay. No, stay."

Bliss smiled. "Am I going or staying?"

"You go. If it's bad news, you'll hear me screaming and you can come back."

"I've got a feeling it'll be good news."

"Really?"

Bliss nodded.

"Did you read it already?" Cherish asked.

The smile left Bliss's face. "Of course not. I'd never do anything like that."

"Okay. Sorry. I didn't mean to say you would."

Cherish watched Bliss walk away. She was sad for Bliss, how she checked the letter box, hoping to hear from Adam. It didn't make sense that Adam would leave her a note, but it seemed Bliss was grasping onto any, even the smallest, hopes.

CHAPTER 2

*O*nce Bliss was in the distance, Cherish propped herself against a tree, opened the envelope and pulled out the letter.

Hi Cherish,

I've left as you know by now if you're reading this.

I didn't want to say goodbye, because I am awful at goodbyes.

Let me know when you're at the farm and I'll come and see you. Since it's too far to go back and forth by buggy every day, maybe I can make the journey there and stay for a couple of days. I could help out at the farm and do whatever you need me to do.

I'm glad I got to know you. It would've been nice if I could've stayed longer.

We've got a phone in our barn and I've written the number and our address at the bottom of this page.

Call me as soon as you know when you'll be at the farm.

FAITHFULLY,
Simon

ALL CHERISH'S fears had been washed away. He did like her. He even signed the note, 'faithfully.' What did that mean? It had to be good. He didn't say 'yours faithfully.' That had to mean something. Maybe it meant he'd be faithful to her and not date anyone until she moved to the farm so they could continue their relationship.

Looking down at the letter, she saw how neat his handwriting was and there were no misspelled words. He was like Malachi, her farm manager, but a better version.

She held the letter to her heart. He'd given her his number and his address. Could this be the man she'd eventually marry? She'd never given much thought to the kind of man she wanted, but Simon seemed very nice. Besides that, he didn't live far from the farm she'd inherited from Aunt Dagmar. It was totally perfect.

Cherish decided to share her news with one person. That was Bliss. It would cheer her up. Cherish walked back to the house, feeling a whole lot better.

She opened the back door and then walked through to the kitchen looking for Bliss. *Mamm* and Ada were the only ones there.

Mamm glared at Cherish. "Well, where is it?"

"What?" Cherish asked.

"I sent Bliss out to find you to ask where you put the cookie jar."

"It's on the top shelf."

"What's that you've got there?" With one swoop, *Mamm* stretched out her arm and plucked the letter out of her hands.

"Nee, Mamm. That's private."

Mamm turned the envelope over, looking at the back and the front. "While you're under my roof, nothing is private."

"That's right, Wilma. That's what I used to tell my *kinner.*" Ada chortled.

"And that's probably why they moved out," Cherish quipped, as she made a grab for the envelope while *Mamm* held it out of reach.

"I think you were rude just now, Cherish," Ada sneered. "My children moved out when they married and not before."

"Sorry. I know I was rude." It was easier to admit it and agree with Ada. She'd learned that the hard way. Finally out of exasperation, Cherish told her mother, "It's from Simon."

"I can see that. So what's he got to say that I can't see, hmm?"

"Nothing."

Mamm said, "I'm reading it, so sit down while I have a look at what he's saying to my youngest daughter who is not of marrying age. I thought he seemed too keen to spend time with you. I didn't like it when he asked if he could go for a walk with you after dinner the other night."

"I thought you liked him, Wilma," Ada said.

"I do as a person, but I didn't like it when he asked in front of everyone if he and Cherish could walk outside—alone. He did that deliberately so Levi and I wouldn't say no. It was too cold out, and a storm was brewing so his decision wasn't wise. They would've been better to talk on the porch, but oh no. He knew best. Now sit down, Cherish, while I read this."

Ada sipped on her cup of hot tea while Cherish sat down. "Sure, *Mamm,* read it, but I will be old enough to marry soon. And I can even marry now with your permission."

Mamm made a mocking sound from the back of her throat. It was a cross between a laugh and a croak. "Permission? You won't get that. You'll marry when you're mature enough and not before. For some, that's eighteen and for some it could be twenty-eight. I'd say you'd fall in the group who will marry at twenty-eight." *Mamm* pulled the letter out of the envelope.

"What happened to mail being private?" Cherish grumbled.

"Oh, you can have private mail when you're no longer living in this house under my roof."

Ada smiled. "You tell her, Wilma."

Cherish suddenly thought of something. As per the agreement after they found her father's will, the orchard belonged to the shareholders. And just like that, Cherish realized that she was more of an owner of this house than her mother was. But, she'd get nowhere pointing that out and could very well get sent to her room. Or worse, she wouldn't get to visit the farm for a very long time.

Mamm started reading. "Hmm. Seems he's invited himself to your farm. That's quite rude. I'm a little shocked. He's got no manners at all if he thinks it's okay to invite himself somewhere. It's typical, not unlike the way he thought we wouldn't mind him talking to Cherish away from us. What did he have to say that he couldn't say in front of us.?"

"I said he could come to the farm, *Mamm*. He didn't invite himself."

Ada said, "Yes, Wilma, he's not a rude boy. I told you I'm good friends with his parents and Melvin and Harriet have raised him well. "

"He's not a boy, he's a man," Cherish pointed out.

Ada continued, "He's been taught right from wrong. He's a good young man. You really should trust my judgement more, Wilma. Look how well I matched Mercy and Stephen. Then I was able to match your second oldest daughter as well. I have a gift for this kind of thing."

Cherish sat there in silence, keeping her lips closed. Ada didn't match Honor at all. Honor matched herself and now Ada was taking the credit for it. But wait, did Ada have anything to do with Simon turning up on her doorstep the day after Hope's wedding? "Did you tell Simon about me, Ada?"

CHAPTER 3

*A*da shook her head. "No. I never said two words about you. I thought you met him at the wedding."

Cherish was relieved. Ada said she hadn't match-made them, and Ada would never lie. "I did."

Wilma gulped as she stared at Simon's letter. Her last visit with Mercy played through her mind. Mercy hadn't been getting along that well with Stephen, and Wilma couldn't help wondering if that was a result of the marriage being hasty. If they'd taken longer to get to know each other, Mercy would've probably realized that Stephen got on her nerves most of the time. Still, Stephen was a good person and a good father to their two children. Mercy would have to learn to adjust.

The last thing Wilma wanted was for Cherish or any of her girls to suffer a similar fate. It was so hard to tell the young they didn't have to rush into something when rushing in was all they wanted to do. Mercy had only been eighteen when she married and so too was Honor. There was no need for Cherish to repeat that pattern.

Then and there, Wilma decided she was going to prevent Cherish and Favor, her two youngest daughters, from marrying until they were well into their twenties. "There's only one thing for it."

"What's that, *Mamm?*" Cherish asked.

"I'll have to go to the farm with you next time."

"You will?" Cherish jumped to her feet and ran around the other side of the table to hug her mother.

Wilma put up her hand. "Not so fast. I will, but I never said when."

"Well… when?" Ada asked. "Now that you've said that much, you have to give her a time."

Wilma handed Cherish the letter while she stared up at the ceiling. "We can't go at harvest time. No, that wouldn't do. We'll go in January, in the new year just after Christmas. It's coming up soon, but it's the time of year when we don't have many commitments."

Cherish was delighted to hear that since it was only weeks away. "Okay." Cherish folded her letter and held it tightly in her hand.

"Just remember this." *Mamm* shook a finger at her. "If you rush into marriage, you might spend your lifetime regretting it."

"What's that got to do with going to the farm?" Cherish asked.

Ada busied herself cutting the chocolate cake that was in the center of the table.

Mamm looked down at the letter in Cherish's hand. "I think you know. Just remember this, you are special. Just wait. You'll have your choice of men when you're older. Don't jump on the first train that comes to the station. There's always another train, always a better train. Maybe there's already a train that's been waiting at the station and you haven't noticed it yet. When the time's right, you'll see that train and all will be well."

"Oh, that's confusing." Cherish saw how serious her mother was and did her best to hold in her laughter. "How will I know which train is the right one?"

"You'll just know."

"But what if I don't?" Cherish asked.

"You will."

"But how?"

Wilma threw her hands in the air. "All these questions. You haven't changed since you were three-years-old. 'Why,' 'how,' and 'what for' were your favorite words."

"You're the one who brought up the trains. Now I'm confused."

Wilma explained, "Sometimes it's the ones who are overlooked who make the best husbands. Just because someone is loud and makes their feelings known, doesn't mean that man will make a good husband. That's why you have to wait and make sure you've considered all your options."

Ada looked up from the large slab of chocolate cake she'd served herself. "Samuel was quiet. I had my choice of men, but there was just something about Samuel. One day, we were both helping out at an auction and then he started talking to me. I liked what he said and then we were together every Sunday from there. We got married three months later."

Cherish nodded at Ada's story, pretending she was listening, but she was too excited about going to the farm. Cherish looked at her mother. "I'll make sure I consider the quiet trains as well as the rattling, noisy ones—also the ones that aren't moving to go anywhere. Although, that does sound uninspiring."

"Good."

Ada's brow furrowed. "Wait a minute. Who's catching a train and where is that person going?"

"No one. I just told Cherish I'd take her back to the farm," Wilma said.

"I heard that, but there are no trains that go to the farm."

"I know. I just told Cherish I'll take her to the farm just after Christmas. Weren't you listening?"

"I was thinking about something else, and I was cutting the cake. I can do two things at once but I can't do three!" Ada stared at Wilma.

"We might even see if Favor wants to go with us. It'll be a little getaway for both my girls. Bliss and Debbie can be in charge of the *haus*. I won't tell Favor just yet. I'll make it a surprise."

Cherish hoped Bliss wasn't anywhere close enough to overhear what Wilma just said. It would make her feel ten times worse. Bliss considered Wilma as her mother, but it was clear Wilma didn't quite return that feeling.

"When did you say you were going?" Ada asked.

"In a few weeks. Just after Christmas and into the new year," Wilma repeated.

"That's *wunderbaar*, Cherish. You'll be able to see Simon again."

Mamm turned away, picked up the teakettle and filled it with water while Ada and Cherish talked about Simon.

When they were all sitting, drinking a second pot of tea, Ada broke some very different news. "Just this morning I got some news right from the bishop's wife's mouth."

CHAPTER 4

"What's that?" Wilma stared at Ada. Ada always got interesting information from the bishop's wife.

"John Bontrager's parents are coming to stay with them for a couple of days."

"Staying with the bishop?" *Mamm* asked.

"Correct. They're coming here to see Debbie. Does she know this?"

"No. When are they arriving?" *Mamm* wriggled in her chair.

"They asked to stay with the bishop for two nights. Starting from tomorrow night. They'll want to see Jared."

Mamm nodded. "Of course. That's why they're coming."

Cherish said, "She knew they were coming but they didn't say exactly when. All they said in their letter was they were coming after Hope's wedding."

"And it's after Hope's wedding now." Ada put the teacup up to her lips and took a sip.

"I just hope they don't upset Debbie." *Mamm* looked down at the table.

Cherish bit her lip, worried about how easily Debbie could be pushed around. She had allowed her late husband to push her around and, he had talked her into the secret marriage in the first place. "Of course they will upset her. They want her to live with them and they're very persuasive, and Debbie is fragile at the moment. I'm worried she'll cave."

"Cave?" Ada asked. "What does that mean?"

"Give in to them. She might. She likes to keep everyone happy even if it disadvantages herself."

Ada and Wilma looked at one another. "This isn't good, Wilma. Is Cherish right?"

"I hope not. We don't want to lose her and little Jared." Wilma sighed. "They've only been here for a few months and now I can't imagine them being gone."

"Me either," said Ada. "We've grown so close with her. We'd be losing a good friend. Oh, I don't want to even think about it."

"Cherish, go upstairs and have Debbie come down here."

"Okay." Cherish headed up the stairs. She knew better than to deliver the news Ada had just given her. Ada or *Mamm* would want to tell her themselves. Cherish heard noises coming from the sewing room that had been converted to a nursery. She pushed the door open slightly to see Debbie changing Jared's diaper.

"Hi, Cherish."

"Good morning. Ada is here."

"I know. I saw her out the window. I'm coming down after I change him. Everything okay?"

"Yes." Cherish moved further into the room. "Can I help you with anything?"

"No, but thanks. All done." Debbie lifted Jared up, settled him on one hip, and started walking out the door. Cherish followed them down the stairs.

When Ada saw Jared in Debbie's arms, she immediately got off her chair and stretched her arms out for him. Debbie handed him over.

"Cherish, make some tea for Debbie," *Mamm* said.

"Which tea would you like?" Cherish asked.

"Just some of my rose tea please."

"Rose tea for a rose." Ada smiled as she sat down with the baby. "He's getting so big. Every day I see him, he's bigger."

"Really? I don't notice it except his clothes seem to be getting smaller."

Then Ada and Wilma looked at one another.

"What's going on?" Debbie asked.

Ada spoke. "There's no easy way to say this. I heard from Hannah, the bishop's wife. She told me that John's parents are coming. They've asked to stay there for a couple of nights starting from tomorrow night."

Debbie slumped back in her chair, totally deflated. "I hoped it would be too far for them to come."

Cherish put the teacup and saucer down in front of Debbie and then sat next to her.

"Oh, Cherish. I brought cookies as well as the cake. Would you be a dear and put a few of them on a plate?" Ada asked.

"Sure." Cherish didn't mind doing that. She loved Ada's cookies. Besides, she could eat one or two of the cookies while she was doing it. That way, *Mamm* wouldn't be able to count how many she had. *Mamm* always tried to stop her at three.

Debbie sighed. "I hoped they wouldn't come. You know when people say they'll do something someday, and then they never do it? That's what I was hoping for."

"They want her to move in with them," Cherish said with crumbs flying out of her mouth.

Ada looked up at her. "We know this and don't talk with cookies in your mouth."

"Sorry."

"Be sure to do what *you* want to do, Debbie," Wilma said.

"I want to stay here."

"Don't get bullied into going with them then," Ada told her.

"That's what I'm worried about. I don't want to, but I can't help feeling sorry for them. Now that I've had Jared, it makes me feel how awful it is for them to have lost John."

"They haven't lost him. He's in the Lord's *haus*. They know where he is," Ada said.

Wilma continued, "Life has hardships, but sometimes we can make things harder for ourselves for no good reason. Sometimes in life you have to do what *you* want, especially where there's a child involved. Jared will be happiest where you are happiest."

"Do you think so?" Debbie asked Wilma.

"I do. It makes sense."

Debbie held her head. "I can't help feeling guilty. They live so far away they'll hardly ever get to see him."

"With how they raised John, it's probably a good thing." Cherish placed the plate of cookies into the center of the table and sat down. When she noticed it was quiet, she looked around to see everyone looking at her. "What? It's the truth."

Wilma said, "Debbie doesn't want to hear his name all the time."

Ada added, "They can't be responsible for what their son did, just as Wilma can't be responsible for all the stupid things you girls do."

Cherish kept quiet and reached for another cookie, thinking about what stupid things Ada was talking about. She didn't think about that for long because she was too busy enjoying how the chocolate pieces melted in her mouth and how the cookie part was all buttery and smooth. This batch was well-done on the edges as though Ada had left them in the oven for a little too long. For Cherish, that made them even more tasty.

"I'll just have to get through it and get past it. I know it will be unpleasant for them and for me. I wonder why they didn't write and tell me the date and the day they were coming."

"Maybe they were going to surprise you," Wilma said.

Ada took another sip of tea. "If they're staying at the bishops' tomorrow night, that means they'll be traveling tomorrow and then they'll come here the day after that."

"That makes sense. I'll have to prepare what I'm going to say to them. I'm glad I got some warning. Thanks, Ada."

"Aren't you seeing Peter today?" Ada asked.

"I am. I nearly forgot. I remembered when I woke up, but forgot just now with the news of John's parents."

"Go out and enjoy yourself. We'll look after Jared," Wilma said.

"Thanks, but I'll take him with me this time. Peter said he wants to get to know him."

Cherish swallowed her mouthful of cookie. "That'll be the first time you've gone out together, just the three of you."

"I know."

"And how is Bliss doing?" Ada asked.

"She's in her room, totally depressed about the breakup with Adam," *Mamm* said.

"Totally," Debbie agreed. "I wish there was some way we could make her feel better."

"After your chores, Cherish, why don't you take one of the buggies and get her out of the house?"

"Okay. Where should we go?"

"That's between you and her."

"*Denke, Mamm.* I think she needs to think about something else."

After Wilma told Cherish that three cookies were enough, Cherish walked upstairs smiling about her mother not noticing the cookie she'd eaten before setting the plate on the table.

CHAPTER 5

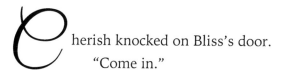herish knocked on Bliss's door.

"Come in."

Cherish pushed the door open. Bliss was lying there, looking up at the ceiling.

"I would've come up sooner, but *Mamm* grabbed the letter and read it. Then we found out Debbie's parents are most likely coming here tomorrow."

Bliss sat up. "Was the letter good news?"

Cherish sat down next to her. "Yes." She handed the letter over to let Bliss read it.

"That's great. I'm happy for you." Bliss smiled and handed it back to her. "I'm glad things are going well for one of us."

"Not only that, *Mamm* is taking me to the farm just after Christmas. Well, in early January, she said."

"Truly?"

"Yes, she was the one who said it. She said it just now in front of Ada, so she won't go back on it."

"You'll be able to see Simon much sooner than you thought."

"And I've got some good news for you."

Bliss's face lit up. "About Adam?"

"No, about today. *Mamm* said we could go into town after our chores. Wait, no. She said I could take you somewhere. I just added that bit about town because I thought that's where you'd want to go."

"Really? We get to go out?" Bliss looked happier.

"Yes. Where do you want to go?"

"Anywhere," Bliss said. "You choose. I'm having trouble concentrating. It hurts my head to think."

"Let's get ice-cream."

Bliss laughed. "It's freezing outside. Are you sure you want ice-cream?"

"Maybe not. We'll drive around until we see some nice food. Food that will make you feel better."

"Okay. Thanks, Cherish. I'd really like that."

"I have to do chores first. I think *Mamm's* letting you off chores for the day."

"It's all right. I can't leave everyone else to do everything. I'll come down and help."

"Okay. If you want."

The two girls headed downstairs.

After they spent a couple of hours doing chores, Wilma allowed Cherish and Favor to take Bliss out for the rest of the day. Bliss insisted on driving the horse and buggy, and Favor insisted on sitting next to her so Cherish was relegated to the back seat.

A few minutes into the drive, Favor announced, "I know a great hamburger place."

"That sounds good. I'm so hungry," Cherish said.

"I'm not." Bliss shook her head. "I haven't had any appetite since Adam dumped me."

"As soon as you smell these burgers, you'll be hungry. They're sooo good."

"Okay. I'm willing to give it a try. Where is this burger place?"

"It's right in the center of town."

"Really? Oh no. I don't want to see anyone. I probably should've stayed at home." Bliss rubbed her face with her hands, taking her hands off the reins.

"No. You have to get out and forget about Adam. I find that when I'm unhappy, I feel better if I make myself smile," Favor suggested.

Bliss sighed again. She'd been doing a lot of that lately. "I'll need more than a fake smile to feel better, Favor."

"It's not fake. It is when you start, but pretty soon it becomes a real smile."

From the back seat, Cherish rolled her eyes at Favor. She wasn't helping at all.

Then Favor had an even worse suggestion. "Maybe after our burgers we can visit Krystal."

Cherish leaned over to the front. "No. This outing is for Bliss. We're trying to make her feel better. We're not going to do things that you want."

"The thing is, I don't know what I want anymore, Cherish. Going out was a mistake. I can't be around people. I'm going to turn around."

"No, Bliss. You have to force yourself or you'll end up a cranky and lonely old lady."

Bliss said nothing and pretty soon, Cherish noticed Bliss wiping her cheeks.

"Nice one, Cherish." Favor turned around and glared at her.

"I thought I'd be married to Adam next year. Now, I'm alone and I will die alone."

Favor patted Bliss's arm. "That's what we all thought about Florence, but even she found someone."

"Pull over, Bliss. You're in no state to drive." They hadn't gotten into town just yet. Bliss did what Cherish said and then both Bliss and Favor got into the back seat. Cherish moved the buggy forward. "I didn't mean to upset you, Bliss. I just want you to be happy. If you don't marry Adam, you'll marry someone else. If he doesn't know what a wonderful woman you are, he doesn't deserve you. Don't you agree?"

"I guess it's just that he's got standards and I failed to meet them."

"Everyone makes mistakes though," Favor told Bliss. "He's got to see that and when he does, he'll be back."

"Favor's right. Are you telling me he's never made one mistake?"

"He wouldn't have. He's perfect and so honorable, that's why he's so disappointed in me. He needs someone just as good as he is. I failed."

Cherish silently agreed with Bliss about Adam being perfect. As far as she could tell, Adam was perfect in every way, but... Hmm. Maybe that 'perfection' was his flaw? Who was really that perfect? Surely he'd made one mistake, and maybe if she could find out about it, she could point out to him how hypocritical he was being. Talking to him hadn't worked, so she had nothing to lose by trying something different. "Come on, he can't be perfect. Has he made a mistake that you know about?"

"No. He hasn't. He doesn't make mistakes," Bliss said. "Everything he does is carefully thought out, in his business and his relationships."

The rest of the trip was spent in silence.

CHAPTER 6

When they got into town, Favor directed Cherish where to park the buggy. They ended up in a side-street not far from the hamburger destination.

Once they were out of the buggy and walking up the street, Cherish asked, "How do you know about this place, Favor? I've never been here before."

"I've been here a couple of times with Krystal."

They walked in and immediately the smell of the hamburgers hit their nostrils. "See, Bliss? What did I tell you?"

"I'm still not hungry."

"You will be once you taste them. I'll get them. You two sit down. What does everyone want?"

"Nothing. I'll just have an orange juice."

"Boring. I'll order for you. What about you, Cherish?"

"Surprise me. Get me what you're getting."

"Okay. Three burgers with the works and three chocolate shakes."

As Favor walked off to the counter to order, Bliss and Cherish sat down in a booth.

"It's so nice here, don't you think?"

Bliss's gaze lowered to the black and white checkered floor and then went up the pastel colored walls to the old-fashioned stamped metal ceiling. "Yes. It's nice."

"And aren't you glad to be out of the house?" Cherish asked.

"I am."

Cherish was determined to get Bliss to smile before the day was out. No, to laugh. She hadn't done that in ages. "I just want to say this. Adam is great, sure he is, but there are a lot of other great men. He's not the only one who's nice."

Bliss looked down. "He was the only one for me."

Cherish swallowed hard. This wasn't going in the right direction. She thought about what her mother said. "Men are like trains. There will always be another one coming to the station."

Bliss's eyebrows drew together. "What? Stop it, Cherish. How is a man like a train?"

Cherish shrugged. "I don't know. It didn't make much sense to me either. It was something *Mamm* said. She doesn't want me to rush into a relationship. I don't think she wants me to like Simon, or something."

"She just doesn't want you and Favor to marry and leave her alone, but she doesn't have to worry about that because I'll be there forever to keep her company. I'll be living at the apple orchard forever. Until I'm an old lady. I'll die alone under an apple tree, a sad and lonely old wretch."

Favor sat down. "Why are you both looking so weird?"

"Nothing," Cherish said.

"It's coming to the end of the year. Why don't we say what new things we're going to do next year? I'll start. I'm going to have a break from writing to my pen pals. Your turn, Cherish."

"Why are you doing that?" Cherish asked.

"So I'll have time to do other things. Don't ask dumb questions. It's your turn, just say something."

Cherish announced, "I'm going to go back to the farm."

Favor frowned. "It's not something you're going to do. You have to say your intention for the whole year. It's a change in habit or a change of attitude."

"It's too far off. How will I know what I'm going to do?"

"You're so stupid, Cherish. You set an intention so you can follow through."

The waitress brought over their milkshakes.

When she left, Favor turned to Bliss. "What about you?"

"Next year, I'll do my best to stop thinking about Adam."

Favor picked up her milkshake. "I'll say cheers to that."

Bliss picked up her milkshake and they clicked the glasses together.

Cherish guessed that was something Favor picked up from being around Krystal too much. Their mother wouldn't approve. But there was a glimmer of a smile around Bliss's lips, so that was a good thing.

"I want to get better at sewing. Will that do?" Cherish asked.

"Yes. I'll cheers you to that." Favor picked up her milkshake and wanted Cherish to do the same.

"I don't do cheers. The glass might break."

"Suit yourself." Favor took a sip.

"Isn't it great to have a day away from the orchard?" Cherish asked.

"It is. I love it. If only *Dat* would let me work in a place like this." Bliss looked around.

"No. We're destined to only ever work in the orchard. Well, I would be except I've got the farm."

"And, you're also allowed to work at the café one day a week. I don't know why they won't let me." Bliss sat there looking glum.

"It's not *Mamm* not letting you, it's only Levi. Hey, wait. Since you're so upset lately, it's a perfect time to ask your father."

"Ask him if I can start work again at the café?" Bliss sat up straighter.

"Yes. They're looking for workers now too."

"Are they?"

Cherish nodded. "I think so."

Favor interrupted, "You don't seem certain, Cherish. Are they looking for staff or not?"

"I know they were a few weeks ago." Cherish turned her attention back to Bliss. "And anyway, they think you're a great worker."

"Thanks. I'll ask *Dat* tonight. It would really help take my mind off Adam. We're not so busy in the orchard this time of year. I know we've got other chores and we've got the quilt to sew, but it's still nice to get out and see other people. I've missed that."

"I like to see Krystal when I go anywhere. It was so good when she lived with us, don't you think?" Favor asked.

Cherish shook her head. "No, not really."

Favor huffed. "You wouldn't."

At that moment, their burgers arrived.

"What do you think, girls?" Favor stared at the large burgers.

Bliss said, "It looks difficult to eat."

"I like to eat things with a knife and fork," Cherish said.

"Then you both shouldn't have said you'd have a burger." Favor opened her mouth wide and munched into her burger with the works.

Cherish opened her burger and rearranged some items, closed it up again, cut it in half, and then picked up one half of the sandwich and started eating. "Mmm, it is tasty."

"Bliss, come on. Just try a little bit."

"I'll ask for it to go. I might feel hungry later."

"Then at least have some milkshake," Favor said.

Bliss picked up her shake and had a swallow.

"So are you going to marry Simon?" Favor asked Cherish.

"I'd like to get to know him better."

"He seems nice, but you can't get married before me. I'll have to find someone quickly," Favor said.

Since she wasn't eating, Bliss kept her fingers busy by playing with one of the tiny packets of sugar from the little bowl on the table.

"And how good is it that he lives close to the farm?"

"That is good," Bliss said. "Very convenient."

"You should really try to eat something," Favor said to Bliss. "It's delicious."

"I'll eat it later."

"You better or you'll waste away to nothingness."

"That's the least of my problems."

Favor and Cherish looked at each other. They weren't being very successful in cheering her up.

"What would you like to do when we leave here?" Cherish asked.

"I don't know. All my free time for the last two years was taken up by Adam, so I don't really know what I like to do anymore. Other people have hobbies, but my hobby was Adam."

"What you need is a new hobby."

"I know, but now we all have the quilt to sew. That will keep my mind busy."

"Maybe you should have something else. Something that is yours alone."

Bliss popped the packet of sugar in the bowl with the others as she looked up at Cherish. "I'm not against that idea. What do you suggest?"

"Um." Cherish had no idea so she looked at Favor, hoping she'd say something.

Favor just sat there, eating.

Cherish suggested, "What about basket making? I did some at the farm and I loved it."

"It doesn't interest me. I've always thought I'd like to draw. I used to do that when I was younger. My mother used to draw and she'd send people post cards that she drew herself. It's like a letter on one side with a picture on the other."

"That sounds like a great idea. What do you need to start off with?" Favor asked. "We could get some things before we go home."

"I'd like that. We'd need some thick drawing paper and some different hardnesses of lead pencils. I'll start off by sketching the orchard. Some of the trees have such interesting formations."

By the time they were ready to go, Bliss seemed more like her old self. The waitress put Bliss's burger in a small box to go, and as the girls were walking out the door, Favor said, "Last one to the buggy has to do the washing up and the drying tonight."

Favor ran off first, followed by Cherish. Normally Bliss wouldn't be bothered to join in, but today she did. She overtook the girls. "You're letting me win," she called over her shoulder.

Then as Bliss turned the corner, she ran smack into something hard. She'd run into a person. She looked up, straight into the eyes of Adam Wengerd, the man who'd broken her heart.

CHAPTER 7

*A*fter Bliss realized she'd run into Adam, she was frozen to the spot.

She didn't know where to look.

He stood there, scowling at the hamburger that had broken out of the box. Ketchup was everywhere, making it look like one of them had suffered a serious injury.

"Are you all right?" Adam's voice didn't sound as annoyed as he looked.

"I think so. Are you?"

He then looked down at his shirt and said nothing.

"I'm so sorry. Your shirt is ruined. I'll wash it for you. I'm sure I can get the stains out."

"No. It's fine. I've got plenty more shirts."

She picked up the flattened box that the burger had come in. She straightened it out so she could put all the mess on top of it.

He stepped back when she tried to get some ketchup and lettuce off his shirt. "It's okay."

She looked down and saw an onion ring clinging to the middle of her apron. She peeled it off and then knelt down and picked up the burger bun that was on the ground.

He got down on one knee and helped her put all the scraps back into the box. "Let me buy you another..."

"It was a burger, but no thanks. I'm not hungry anyway."

"Are you sure?"

"Quite sure."

Behind them, Cherish and Favor huddled together looking on.

Adam then took the box from her and stood up. "I'll get rid of it." He walked away and put the remains in a nearby trash can. Then instead of coming back to talk to her, he just called out goodbye and walked off as he dusted off his hands.

Bliss looked at Cherish and Favor and they looked back at her. Then Bliss ran to the buggy. Cherish and Favor hurried after her.

When Favor and Cherish reached the horse and buggy, Bliss was in the back seat, crying.

"What did he say?" Favor climbed in next to her.

"Nothing. And then he walked away. Why did I have to come here today? I didn't want to. Everyone forced me."

"Good news. You won the race to the buggy. Cherish and I will do the washing up."

"I don't care," Bliss said. "I just want to go home."

"I'll go back and get you something else to eat," Favor said.

"No! I'm not hungry."

"I'll get you something for later."

"No. Please, Favor, I just want to go home. Right now."

Cherish was in the driver's seat. "I do think you need to try to eat something. Get her a ham and cheese sandwich. I know she likes those," Cherish told Favor.

"Okay." Favor leaped out of the buggy before Bliss could stop her.

"Why are you doing this to me, Cherish? I just want to go home."

"You have to eat. We're worried about you."

"I'm fine. I will be fine when I get home. I wish I'd never left the house."

Cherish didn't know what to do. This whole thing had been a disaster. Where had Adam been going before the collision? And, why had he turned around and walked in the opposite direction afterwards? He was acting so mean and he had to know how kind and soft-hearted Bliss was.

"I'm sorry, Cherish. I know you and Favor are trying to help, but I don't want to be helped."

"There must be something we can do."

"There is. Leave me alone."

Cherish faced the front. Now everything was so much worse. Adam had smiled at Bliss, but he only spoke to her about the hamburger.

"What's taking her so long? Why are people trying to force me to eat?"

"You need to eat, Bliss, that's why."

"I don't have to eat every single day."

"Of course you do. You need three meals every day."

"Or what? I won't die."

Cherish didn't know what to say. She'd never seen Bliss so

disagreeable like this, and Bliss was normally someone who enjoyed her food.

A few silent minutes later, Favor was back with the take-out sandwich.

"Now we can find an art supplies shop."

"No. I don't want to do that anymore. I don't want to do anything. Let me drive, Cherish."

"No. You're too upset to drive."

"Are you going to take me home now, Cherish? Because if you don't, I'm getting out of the buggy right now."

Cherish exhaled deeply. "Relax, we're going home." Cherish moved the horse forward.

The drive home was spent in silence.

CHAPTER 8

*W*hen they pulled up at home, Bliss jumped out of the buggy and ran into the house.

"I'll go after her," Favor said.

"No. Just leave her alone for a while."

"I don't take orders from you!" Favor got out of the buggy and headed to the house, leaving Cherish to unhitch the buggy and tend to the horse. It was typical.

When Cherish walked into the house, the first person she saw was Levi. He looked up from the newspaper he was reading. "Bliss just told me she's going into her room and never coming out. What happened today? Wilma said she let you and Favor go out today to cheer her up."

Cherish shook her head. "She's not doing well. She literally bumped into Adam and then he was so short with her. A hamburger got squashed between them and he said a few words, helped her pick up the hamburger and then he left."

He gave a nod. "Favor told me as much. She's up there now

trying to comfort her. I'm not sure how to fix this." Levi folded his paper, leaned forward and placed it on the table beside him.

"Are you thinking of talking to Adam?"

"No. I'm wondering if Bliss should go somewhere. I could send her to a relative for a vacation."

"She wouldn't like that. She'd want to stay here in case Adam changes his mind."

He picked up his large black Bible from underneath the newspaper. "We can pray about it, but if he's not the right man for her, it'll not work out the way she wants—not right now. She'll see later that it's the right thing."

"But couldn't Adam be the right man if we pray that he is?"

Levi stroked his graying beard. "I don't think it works like that. We pray that His will be done. We should go back to having our nightly Bible readings."

"Yes, I think that'll help."

Wilma walked into the room. "Don't be sarcastic, Cherish."

Cherish swung around to face her mother. "I'm not. I think it'll help her. I'm being honest."

"So do I, but I didn't think you would."

Cherish didn't know what to say. Her mother must've been thinking she was a dreadful person.

"That's settled. We'll start our readings again tonight," Levi said.

"Good," Wilma nodded. "I don't know why we ever stopped."

"It was my heart attack. We never—"

"Ah, that's right. That changed our routine a lot."

Cherish slumped into the couch. Levi said he wanted to do something, but was doing a Bible reading going to help matters? Didn't faith need action as well? The Bible said faith needs works, that was one thing Cherish knew. After what her mother had just said to her, she didn't feel like saying that to Levi.

If Levi wasn't going to act, Cherish knew it was up to her.

She had to find out more about Adam and his past. There was one person in the community who probably knew everything about Adam and that was his good friend and business partner, Andrew Weeks. Now she just had to figure out how to get Andrew to talk with her about Adam.

But her plans would have to wait. Tomorrow, John's parents were coming to see Debbie. Everyone was going to stay home to support her.

"There's one thing that might help, Levi." He kept reading and didn't even look at her.

"What about allowing her to do a day a week at the café? She loved it when she worked there before and then she'd be meeting different people and it would take her mind off Adam."

"That's something to think about." And that was all that Levi said about the matter. Cherish knew not to push him, but at least she'd planted a seed.

CHAPTER 9

he next morning, Levi opened the door to John's
parents, Nehemiah and Rebekah Bontrager. They
introduced themselves and Levi brought them into the house.
Everyone was gathered in the living room. Wilma sent Favor,
Cherish and Bliss into the kitchen to make tea and coffee.

Nehemiah moved in front of everyone and sat in Levi's chair.
Debbie stared at him and wondered if she should say some-
thing. Then she looked at Levi, who appeared slightly disturbed.
No one sat in Levi's chair—ever.

Rebekah sat in the smaller chair next to Levi's, which was
Wilma's new chair.

Wilma, Levi and Debbie went across and sat down on the
couch. What was she supposed to say to her late husband's
parents? They had known nothing of the secret marriage and it
would've stayed a secret if she hadn't gotten pregnant. Even at
John's funeral, before she knew she was pregnant, Debbie felt

she should keep the marriage a secret. That was what John had wanted, but she never wanted a stupid secret marriage.

As Debbie sat across from the Bontragers, she wondered why John had been so reluctant to tell them about the marriage. He had to have been embarrassed about being married to her. That, and he knew his parents wanted him to marry Mary Smith. They were her parents-in-law, but without John here and with him having kept their marriage hidden from them, she had no such feelings toward them. None at all.

"Thank you for allowing us to speak with Debbie," Nehemiah said to Levi. "We trust you knew we were coming?"

"We did," Levi replied.

"Could we speak with Debbie alone?" Rebekah asked.

"No," Wilma said. "We'll stay."

The Bontragers looked at each other, then Nehemiah started, "We're here, Debbie, because we are offering for you to come back with us."

"Tell her the other thing, Nehemiah," Rebekah whispered to him.

"We bought you a house, Debbie. It's not far from us, and we thought you'd like your privacy rather than coming to live with us and John's younger brothers."

"You bought me a house?"

"We did," said Rebekah. "We had a talk about it and decided that would be best. We wanted to make sure you'd be comfortable. This is the way for us to show you how serious we are about being close to both you and Jared. After all, you're the only reminders we have of John. And why wouldn't we want our grandson close to us?"

Nehemiah said, "You never have to worry about another thing. It's a five minute walk to our house."

Rebekah started saying, "It's three bedrooms and—"

Nehemiah cut her off. "We don't need to go into all the details now, Rebekah. You'll like it, Debbie. It's a good house."

"I'm... stunned. You bought me a house?" Debbie repeated, trying to let it sink in.

"Yes. We thought you'd like to have your own place rather than live with other people." He gave Levi and Wilma a sidelong glance.

Debbie didn't know what to say. She never thought she'd have a house—ever—unless she married again.

Wilma interrupted, "Debbie is starting her own business."

"Oh, Debbie, you won't need to work if you come back with us." Rebekah shook her head as though having her own business was a dreadful idea.

Nehemiah was quick to agree. "That's right. Your house is waiting and all you need to worry about is raising little Jared. We'll look after everything else for you."

"We're not making her work." Wilma sounded more than a little annoyed.

Levi touched Wilma's arm lightly, and then said, "Debbie has an interest in tea and that's why she's pursuing that line of work."

"Bah, work!" Rebekah swiped a hand through the air. "Work is for men. You're a woman, Debbie. As soon as you come back with us your life will be easy."

Levi cleared his throat. "We told Debbie she's welcome to stay with us for as long as she likes. She's part of our family."

"That's right, she's our niece," Wilma said.

Nehemiah looked at Wilma. "She's Levi's niece. She's not *your* niece, is she, Wilma? She's only *your* niece because you married Levi. We're Jared's grandparents."

Wilma narrowed her eyes at him, but before she could respond, Rebekah spoke. "We bought the house for you because we knew that's what John would've wanted."

From the kitchen, Favor whispered to Cherish, "Oh, that was mean."

Cherish agreed, "They're manipulating Debbie. I hope she doesn't fall for it. I hope they don't keep talking about John. I wish they'd just get up and leave."

Back in the living room, Debbie put her hand to her head which was now aching. She had been prepared to tell them she wouldn't live with them. She wasn't prepared for them to have bought her a house. This was a real shock. As much as *Onkel* Levi and Aunt Wilma had made her welcome, she'd always feel like a guest in their home. She never saw herself living in her own house with just her and Jared. "There's a lot to consider."

"Consider? What is there to *consider?*" Nehemiah asked, clearly not used to anyone resisting his plans.

"Nothing," Rebekah said. "We've done everything for you. Debbie, your new house is waiting for you and Jared. Your parents are also looking forward to you living near them. They knew we bought you a house but we wanted to be the ones to surprise you with the news. They didn't let anything slip, did they?"

Debbie shook her head.

Cherish and Favor looked at each other. "She's not going to go with them, is she?"

Favor shrugged her shoulders. "I don't know. They've

bought her a house. I'd go with them. Maybe they'll adopt me. I wouldn't have to work or do anything. They're going to provide for her forever, it seems."

"I know. I heard." Cherish bit her lip and kept listening. Without Debbie, the house would be way too quiet. "Surely she'll choose us. This is so unfair. Why did they have to come here?"

"Shush. I'm listening."

"Move over so I can see what's going on."

"I can't. I'm right against the wall. You move over. You're squashing me."

Bliss sat at the kitchen table. "You two shouldn't be listening."

"How else will we hear what they're saying?" Cherish stepped to the side and now she was in the middle of the doorway. Wilma turned her head and saw Cherish and frowned at her. Cherish moved back so she'd be out of sight.

Nehemiah said, "We're staying in the area for a couple of days, Debbie. That should give you enough time to pack and get your things together."

Rebekah said, "We'll leave early on Friday morning."

"I'll still want to do my tea."

Wilma stared at Debbie. "You're not seriously considering it, are you?" she blurted.

Back in the kitchen, Bliss gasped at what Wilma had said in front of the Bontragers. Cherish and Favor were shocked, too.

CHAPTER 10

John's mother stared at Wilma. "She's not just considering it, she's coming back with us. I'm sorry, Wilma. I know you probably got used to her being here, but I hope you didn't think it was going to be permanent. After all, Jared has two sets of grandparents in Willow Valley."

"Are you leaving us, Debbie?" Levi asked.

"No. I mean, I just want to do my tea." Debbie looked down at her hands in her lap.

"You can make your tea here. Thank you for your kind offer, Rebekah and Nehemiah, but Debbie has already said she'd be staying here with us," Levi told the Bontragers.

"But, we bought her a house," Rebekah said. "It's just sitting there empty waiting for her."

"It's okay," Nehemiah told his wife. "Debbie didn't know about this. It's a big change. She'll just have to get used to the idea. Just like we had to get used to the idea that John is no longer with us."

Debbie jumped to her feet. "Excuse me. I think I hear Jared."

Rebekah brightened up. "Oh good. Bring him down so we can meet him. We've been dying to see him."

Without a word, Debbie hurried up the stairs.

Favor left the kitchen and followed her, leaving Cherish in the kitchen with Bliss.

Without knocking, Favor burst into Debbie's room. Debbie was just sitting on the bed and Jared was nowhere to be seen. "You can't go with them, you just can't."

Debbie looked up at her. Favor rushed to her side when she saw tears streaming down Debbie's cheeks. "Don't cry, Debbie. It's going to be okay."

Debbie shook her head and then gasped for air. "I... I'm confused."

"About what?"

"I want to stay here but I feel so bad for them. They lost John, their oldest son, and they bought me a house."

"I know I heard that from the kitchen."

"If I say no, then that would be like throwing it in their faces. It would've cost them a lot."

"You said they're rich."

"They are."

"Did you ever think that they did that just to make sure you went back with them?"

Debbie sniffed. "Do you think so?"

Favor nodded. "Well, John had a certain way about him. He wasn't exactly straightforward with..."

"You mean he wasn't totally honest?"

"That's right, and, from what you said, he was scared of his parents. That's why he didn't tell them about your marriage."

"What are you saying, Favor?"

"You've got to stand up to them. Don't go along with them like you said everyone else does. Be strong or you'll end up being just like your parents."

"Nehemiah and Rebekah are Jared's grandparents. What do you expect me to do?"

Favor bolted to her feet. "You disappoint me. You said you wouldn't go with them. I don't care that they bought you a house or whatever else they say they're going to do." Favor planted her hands on her hips. "How do you know they won't let you stay in that house for a year and then sell it out from underneath you? Then where will you go?"

"I'd have to move in with them or my parents."

"Exactly."

"I see what you mean."

"They didn't even say they were going to put the house in your name, did they? No, because they've already bought it. So if the house isn't in your name, is it really your house when you don't have a say with what happens to it in the future? They could sell it from underneath you whenever they wanted. It could be their way of controlling you and Jared for years to come."

Debbie's mouth fell open. "Favor, you're so smart. Did you just think of all this now?"

"Yes. I'm just putting two and two together and coming up with 22."

Debbie frowned. "You mean four."

"No. Twenty two because you'd expect the answer to be four, but not when you can't trust the people."

"Even if they give me the house as my own, I still don't want to go there."

"Don't do it then."

"I want to stay here with all of you."

"Good. Then go down and tell them that."

Debbie put her hand over her forehead and massaged her temples. "It's so hard. They must feel so bad about what happened with John. Do you think *Onkel* Levi will tell them for me?"

"*Nee.* They wouldn't believe it. It's got to come from you. Of course they'll be upset, but someone's going to be upset and I don't want it to be us."

The bedroom door opened and Cherish slipped into the room. "What's going on?"

"I told you to stay in the kitchen," Favor said.

"I don't take orders from you." Cherish sat on the other side of Debbie. "Tell them you're staying here."

"She doesn't want to hurt their feelings, but I told her it's the only way. They have to hear it."

"What do you want to do, Debbie?" Cherish asked. "Stay with us or go with them?"

"I was just telling Favor I want to be here, but after all John's parents have been through, I know it'll upset them." Debbie swallowed hard. "I told them I heard Jared, but he's still asleep. I just needed to get away from them and think for a while. I lied to them just now."

Cherish said, "*Gott* will forgive you. You're under so much pressure. Just tell them what you honestly want. They wouldn't want you to move there if they knew you want to stay here."

"Maybe they're not thinking of Debbie," Favor said.

"They are thinking of me, they bought me a house."

Favor shrugged her shoulders. *"Jah,* but like I said, is it really yours? And for how long?"

Cherish stared at Favor. "I never thought of that." Favor was a lot smarter than she seemed.

"I guess there's no other way around it. I'll have to tell them."

Favor put her arm around Debbie. "What's the worst thing that can happen if you tell them you're staying put?"

"They'll be upset."

"That's right, so take Jared down with you and they'll be so pleased to see him that they'll get over it."

Debbie bit her lip. "Do you think so?"

"Of course."

At that moment, they heard Jared making noises from his bedroom next door.

"He's awake. I'll have to feed him and then I'll bring him down. Can you tell them I'll be down soon?"

"Okay," Favor said. Then she and Cherish left the room and started walking downstairs.

Cherish whispered to her, "How did you think of that about the house just now?"

"Because John couldn't be trusted. Where did he learn that?"

Cherish opened her mouth in shock. "His parents?" Favor didn't answer except to quirk an eyebrow at her sister, because they were now at the bottom of the stairs.

SAMANTHA PRICE

Everyone looked at them and Favor said, "She'll be down soon."

Cherish and Favor rejoined Bliss in the kitchen. *Mamm* followed them in and asked them what was happening with the tea and coffee they were supposed to be making.

"Are they staying that long?" Cherish asked. "We were waiting to see if they might leave right away."

"Of course they are staying for a good while. They need to see their grandson. Why? What did Debbie say? Is she thinking of leaving us?" *Mamm* set her beady, brown eyes on Favor and then Cherish.

Favor told her, "She says no, but she's also feeling sorry for them."

Mamm shook her head. "They're doing everything they can to make her go with them. How can we keep her? We can't buy her a house. Is that what we need to do?"

"She doesn't want that, *Mamm*. She just wants to stay with us."

"I hope that's enough for her. Wanting to stay with us will have to be stronger than her feeling sorry for them," Bliss said.

"I better get back to them. Levi isn't much of a talker."

Meanwhile, Debbie was upstairs feeding Jared, trying to find the right words to tell the Bontragers she wouldn't be leaving with them. Neither would she be moving into that house they'd bought for her. Pangs of guilt gnawed at her stomach. It would be one of the hardest conversations she'd ever have.

They'd bought her a house! That was a huge thing to do.

How ungrateful would she sound to turn her back on that? Favor's words echoed through her mind and that led her to wonder, what if it was just some carrot they were dangling?

Then her mind drifted back to before she and John got married. John's parents never saw her as a suitable match for him. Not only that, they wanted him to marry Mary Smith. They never wanted her as a daughter-in-law. That was clear because they never showed her family much respect at all. Her father was just someone who worked for them.

But then again, if she moved to Willow Valley, Jared would grow up near both sets of grandparents.

If she stayed at the Baker Apple Orchard, her son would grow up with Joy's child and Christina's twins, and soon Hope would have children too. There would be loads of children for him to play with, and many adults who loved him. Wilma and Levi would be substitute grandparents along with Ada and Samuel.

Her mind was made up. She'd be strong, follow her heart. People would be disappointed and there might even be tears.

CHAPTER 11

Twenty minutes later, Debbie came downstairs with Jared. She allowed his grandparents to hold him. Jared vomited a little on Rebekah's shoulder, but Rebekah didn't mind. She laughed about it while Wilma and Debbie raced to the kitchen to get something to clean it off.

After a while, Jared started crying so Debbie took him from Rebekah and sat back down. Once the baby was back in his mother's arms, he settled.

After a quick and silent prayer, Debbie began, "I want to thank you both for coming here. It was nice of you to want me to come back with you, but I've decided to stay here."

Rebekah looked at her husband, but he just stared at Debbie and ignored his wife. "Debbie, I can't believe that's best. We have everything there that you could ever need. We have a house there that we bought just for you. Why don't you come back with us for a visit? You can see it and the type of life you could have there."

"Thank you, but I'd rather stay here. I don't like traveling and it would be too difficult with the baby."

Rebekah started crying, and Debbie sat there, not knowing what to do.

Nehemiah patted Rebekah's shoulder, and then looked up and said, "She's upset. We've lost John, and now… it looks like you're denying us our grandchild."

"She's not doing that at all. You're welcome to see Jared anytime you'd like, and see Debbie too," Wilma said.

Rebekah took out a handkerchief and dried her eyes. "We have another idea. Why don't you give the child to us to raise, Debbie? We—"

"She won't be doing that," Levi said firmly.

Debbie held Jared a little bit tighter. No one was taking her child from her.

Wilma stared up at her husband. He normally was so quiet and softly spoken.

Nehemiah grunted. "Levi, with all respect, I think Debbie should be the one making that decision."

Everyone then looked at Debbie.

Debbie looked down at her baby and muttered, "Oh, I don't like to upset anyone."

"Just say what you want," Wilma said. "You must think of what you believe is right for yourself and Jared."

"You didn't let me finish, Levi," Rebekah said. "Can everyone let me say what I have come to say? We came here with two ideas, Debbie. We have bought a house for you and Jared, but then on our way here, we thought about some different ideas. We could raise Jared and then you'd be free to have the life you choose. Everyone would respect that you've put your child first. We can offer the child so much more."

While Rebekah was drawing a breath, Nehemiah jumped in. "You're young enough to marry again and have more babies. If we take Jared off your hands, we'd be setting you free."

Rebekah continued, "Or if you don't like that idea, we'd love for you to leave with us tomorrow and we'll go back to Willow Valley and we'll help you get settled back in."

Debbie took a deep breath. "I'm staying here with Jared. I don't need or want to be *set free* from the child who is a gift from *Gott* to me. That's what I want and I believe that would be best for Jared too."

The Bontragers looked at each other, then Nehemiah said, "I don't think you've thought this through properly, Debbie."

"You've heard her answer, Nehemiah," Levi said. "She's staying here with family."

Nehemiah frowned and then faced Debbie. "Just take a while to think about it, Debbie. Don't let anyone influence you."

"I won't and I haven't. I appreciate you coming here, I do, but my mind's made up."

Rebekah opened her mouth in shock. "You're not leaving with us?"

Debbie shook her head.

"But we bought you a house," Rebekah whimpered.

"I'm sorry, but I wish you would've talked to me before you did that."

"It's done now." Nehemiah leaned over and once again he patted his wife on her shoulder, then he said to Debbie. "We were fully confident that you'd have the common sense to do the right thing. It seems common sense is not so common anymore. We're offering you everything we can."

"Thank you. I do appreciate it, but staying here is the right thing for me and for Jared."

"We should go now, Rebekah. I'm sure we've given Debbie a lot to think about. We'll be back tomorrow. Just think it over, Debbie. Will you at least agree to think about it some more?"

Debbie wanted to tell them no, and that there was nothing to think about. She couldn't say that, because she felt so sorry for Rebekah what with the way she was looking at Jared. "Okay. I'll do that, but I'm sure my decision will remain the same."

"Thank you," Nehemiah said.

When Rebekah moved to stand up, Levi and Wilma stood too.

Nehemiah turned to face Debbie. "One thing I've been meaning to tell you."

"What's that?"

"We have a few Jareds in the family. Going way back in the family tree."

"I didn't know that. That's a nice coincidence."

"My father's brother was a Jared. Sadly, he died some years ago. Now we have another Jared Bontrager in the family."

Debbie's breath caught in her throat. She swallowed hard looking at both of Jared's grandparents. "Didn't my mother and father tell you?"

Nehemiah stared at her. "Tell us what?"

"Jared's last name is Bruner, same as mine. His name is Jared Bruner."

"No, I mean, you and John were married so the baby takes his name," Rebekah said angrily. "And, so should you."

Debbie shook her head. "I know, but it doesn't have to be like that."

Nehemiah narrowed his eyes at her and then shot Levi an unkind look while Rebekah grabbed hold of his arm as though she was going to faint. "What nonsense is this?" he asked. "Children always take the name of their father. It's tradition."

Debbie regretted telling them face-to-face. They would've found out eventually and then wondered why they were never told. "It was my decision, and mine alone, to change that tradition for myself and for Jared. After all, the marriage was hardly traditional."

"Do you mean to shut us out of your life?" Nehemiah asked.

"Not at all. I think it's important that Jared know about his father's side of the family. The name is something I've done for my own personal reasons."

Nehemiah looked down at his wife. "I think we've stayed too long, Rebekah. It's time to leave." Then he said to Levi, "We'll be back late tomorrow afternoon."

After they said a frosty goodbye, Levi walked them to the door.

Then everyone sat back down. When Debbie heard the hoofbeats of the horse and buggy they'd borrowed from the bishop, she was able to relax a little. They were gone, at least for now.

"How are you feeling, Debbie?" Wilma asked as the girls came out from the kitchen to join them.

"I feel pretty awful. They bought a house for me without even asking me."

"They didn't ask you because they knew you would've said no," Favor said.

"Now they're coming back tomorrow. I feel so sad for them.

I know they want to be a part of Jared's life and I can't blame them for that."

"It's not about them, Debbie. It's what's best for you. You're the one raising the child," Wilma said. "And I don't like that they offered to take him away from you and raise him. You're quite capable of doing that yourself."

Debbie slowly nodded, pleased that everyone wanted her there. "I felt so bad for telling them about the last name. I thought my parents would've told them that for sure."

"Well, they know now. There was no easy way of telling them and it's only natural they'd be upset about it," Bliss said.

Cherish laughed. "I loved the way you said the marriage wasn't traditional so you're changing the tradition with the name."

Mamm scowled at her. "Don't take humor in someone else's pain."

"I wasn't. I didn't mean to do that anyway." Cherish bit her lip. She should've just kept quiet.

"They'll get over it in time," Levi said.

"Will they?" Favor asked. "A name is a big thing. It'll be something they'll always think about."

"You're not helping," said Levi.

"It's okay. Don't be mad at anyone. The name's done. It's official and I wouldn't want to change it anyway."

"Let's do something enjoyable with what's left of the day," Wilma said as she took the baby from Debbie.

"I like the sound of that. What should we do?" Bliss asked.

"We can start working on the quilt." Wilma rocked Jared to and fro.

Debbie nodded. "Good idea. That's just what I need to keep my mind off everything."

"Cherish and Favor, you can clear the kitchen table so we can cut the fabric."

Levi stood up. "I'll be out with the horses if anyone needs me."

"Thanks for being here when they came, *Onkel* Levi. It helped."

"We want you here, Debbie. Since that's what you want too, we'll all do everything to have you stay."

Everyone agreed.

CHAPTER 12

The next day, everyone in the Baker/Bruner household, except Levi, was working on the quilt when they heard noises coming from outside. Looking out the window, Bliss yelped, "It's a wagon. Oh no, it's Adam."

Cherish raced to the window and nudged her out of the way. "It's Adam and Andrew. That means they have my aviary ready."

"You didn't tell me he was bringing it today," Wilma whined. "Where will we put it?"

"It can go outside somewhere but not until the warmer weather."

"Why? Birds live outside in the winter."

"Not these birds. They're not used to it."

"They can get used to it."

Bliss recoiled in horror. "I can't let Adam see me. This is awful."

"You can't hide away from him," *Mamm* said. "He'll always be in this community."

"Unless he moves," Favor commented.

"It's not likely with his business doing so well," Bliss added. "I'll be in my room. He's only come to bring the birdcage. He hasn't come to see me."

"Don't be silly, go out and say hello. Go with Cherish," *Mamm* told Bliss.

"No, *Mamm!* The last time we spoke, it didn't go so good. I'll be up in my room." Bliss walked out of the kitchen.

Mamm then stared at Cherish. "Well, go on then. Show him where you want the cage. No good trying to talk to you about where it will go. You've always got your mind made up and you won't listen to sense."

"It's an aviary. I'll have him put it in the barn for now," Cherish said.

"Please yourself. Are you paying for this or do we have to?"

"I'm paying for it."

"That's one blessing."

Cherish walked outside. As soon as she saw Adam, she thought he looked just as uncomfortable as Bliss had looked just now. "You've finished it already?"

He smiled. "I did. Andrew has come along to help me install it."

She looked over at Andrew Weeks, and said hello. Then she wondered how she could get him alone to ask him questions about Adam. "It'll have to go in the barn for now."

"Really?"

"Yes."

"I guess there's no point in us assembling it then. It'll take up less room if we leave it in pieces."

"Great idea. Then you can come back when I'm ready for it? Will that be okay? I wouldn't know how to do it and I'd get it wrong."

"Sure. I was just going to suggest that."

Cherish looked at Andrew. He was much quieter than normal. It was clear he knew what was going on between Adam and Bliss. Probably everyone in the community knew about it by now. "I'll get the money. It's in the house."

"Okay. Shall we just put it anywhere in the barn?"

"Just at the side where it'll be out of the way." Cherish left them and went into the house. When she was up in her bedroom, counting out the money, Bliss walked in. "What did he say?"

"Not much at all. Andrew's with him and they're just putting it in the barn for now."

"Did he say anything about me?"

"No. Don't be upset. He's only here to deliver the aviary, and he wouldn't ask about you in front of Andrew."

Bliss put her hand to her head. "Oh, I hope *Mamm* doesn't invite them in for something to eat."

"Don't worry, I'll tell her not to."

"Thanks."

Cherish finished counting out the money and then left the room with a fistful of notes. Before she walked out of the house, she told her mother to stay put and not to come out of the house. Wilma agreed without asking questions—for once.

By the time Cherish got back outside, the two men had already left the unassembled aviary in the barn and were climbing back into the wagon. "Here's the money," Cherish said when she reached Adam.

"Thank you."

"It's all there. Count it if you want."

"I trust you."

Cherish smiled. "I hope so."

"Say hello to everyone. We can't stay. We've got another delivery to make."

Cherish was still figuring out how to get Andrew on his own to find out more about Adam. Today wasn't going to be the day. "Sure. Well, I guess we'll see you on Sunday. Thanks for making it for me. I can't wait for the birds to be able to use it. I'm sure they'll love it."

"I hope so. Bye, Cherish."

Andrew nodded goodbye, and then Adam wasted no time in turning the wagon around and heading back down the driveway.

When Cherish looked up at the house, she saw everyone appeared in the doorway. They just stood there, looking out. Even Debbie was there with Jared in her arms. They were all waiting to hear what Adam had said.

It was a weird moment. For an instant, Cherish just stood there. This moment would never have happened if she hadn't found those letters in Bliss's room. If she'd known things would be so awful, she would've left things well and truly alone.

Cherish swallowed hard and walked toward her family, wishing she had something better to tell them. She stepped up onto the porch with her footsteps echoing through the air, breaking the silence. "They said they couldn't stay."

Mamm frowned. "You asked me not to come out. Did you invite them in at least?"

"No. When they said they couldn't stay, there was no point inviting them in."

Bliss asked, "Who said they couldn't stay? Was it Andrew or Adam?"

"Adam. He said they had another delivery to make."

"That's reasonable. I'm guessing they're busy. What else did he say?" Debbie asked.

"Just stuff about the aviary, and then he said to say hello to everyone."

Favor gasped. "Oh, Bliss, do you think that was his way of saying hello to you?"

"I don't know. Do you think so?"

Favor looked at Cherish. "What do you think? You were there."

"I don't know." She didn't want to get Bliss's hope's up. "Maybe he was being polite. He didn't say anything about Bliss. Sorry, Bliss."

"Don't be sorry. I don't want you or anyone to lie to me. He hates me now and it might stay that way forever. I could see that when he looked into my eyes."

Mamm clicked her tongue. "He doesn't hate you, Bliss. You shouldn't even think that. He's just a bit upset. You two got along so well. It can't be over. He'll come around given enough time."

"How much time?"

"I don't know. Everyone is different." They all turned and looked when a horse and buggy approached the house. "It's Ada and Samuel. They're staying for the evening meal. They're bringing Levi back," *Mamm* said.

"Where has Levi been?" Favor asked.

"He was giving a friend a helping hand."

Bliss said, "Normally, Adam would've come back to eat with us. Now he's not here. Hope and Fairfax are away too and it'll be just us." Bliss's eyes filled with tears and then she moved into the kitchen.

Everyone looked at each other helplessly as Bliss walked away. No one knew what to do to make her feel better.

Cherish whispered, "I couldn't say he said something he didn't say. He might never want to even be friends with her. He's so upset."

"Just don't tell her that," *Mamm* said.

"I didn't, and I won't."

Mamm sighed. "Maybe Ada can make her feel better."

"Ada?" Favor and Cherish chorused.

"Yes. On the quiet, I'll tell her that Bliss is upset. All of you go inside and start peeling the vegetables. I'll talk to Ada."

While *Mamm* went to talk with Ada, the girls all moved into the kitchen. Cherish looked back at Samuel's buggy and saw Matthew getting out. He'd been working part time at Mark's saddlery store and they hadn't seen much of him. Everything was livelier and a little more fun when Matthew was about.

CHAPTER 13

At dinner that night, everyone knew about what had happened with Bliss and Adam. Wilma had told them all not to mention Adam's name.

"So what happened with your tea tasting, Debbie? Weren't you going to try it out on suspects?" Matthew asked.

Cherish giggled. "You mean prospects."

He grinned. "Depends how good the tea is."

Before Debbie could answer, Cherish spoke for her. "We were all set to try the tea out and get opinions. It's called a focus group, isn't it, Debbie?"

"That's right. We were going to do it and then Jared had a slight cold. He's over it now. Cherish is helping me with it. Who else wants to help me?" Debbie asked.

"We all will," Bliss said. "When do you want to do it?"

"Wilma and I will look after Jared. You just name the day," Ada said.

"How about the day after tomorrow? The Bontragers would've left by then. I'll have a day to prepare everything."

"That'll work for me," Cherish said. "I work at the café on Friday this week."

"Any day's okay with me," Favor said.

"Thanks, everyone. I really want to start this and see how far I can go with it." Debbie looked at each one of them.

"You can go as far as you want," Samuel said. "There's no stopping people who are excited about what they're doing. Your excitement transfers to others and pretty soon, you reach your goals."

Ada frowned at Samuel and didn't say anything. Samuel saw Ada looking at him and went back to eating.

"I'm so excited. I just hope the people like my tea."

"Of course they will," Wilma said. "Have faith. The only problem they'll have is choosing what flavor they like best."

Debbie was happy with Wilma's comment and hoped that everyone liked her tea as much as her family did.

WHEN DINNER WAS OVER, Cherish pulled Matthew aside and whispered to him in the corner the living room. "Matthew, I have a plan to get Adam and Bliss back together."

He frowned. "Since you're telling me, I'm guessing it involves me."

"It could."

"What is it?"

"I need to know if Adam's ever made a mistake."

"What for?"

Cherish took an exasperated deep breath. "You've got to

follow me with this. I'm trying to get Adam and Bliss back together. They're made for each other. He's not forgiving her for writing back to John, so I thought if I can find a mistake of his, I can go to him with it. I can make him see that he should forgive Bliss because everyone makes mistakes."

He pushed his hat back on his head slightly. "That's a crazy idea."

"It's not. Well, it might be, but I can't think of anything else. Maybe you could talk to Andrew Weeks and he might tell you something about Adam."

"I doubt it. Men don't gossip like women do."

Cherish hit his arm. "Don't be rude. It's not gossiping."

"Sounds like it to me."

"Will you help or not?"

"I'm willing if you've got a different idea, one that might work."

"I can't think of anything else. It took me long enough to think of this plan. I thought it was a good one."

Matthew shook his head. "It's not. If a man says it's over, that usually means it's over. The trust has been broken and that's a pretty big thing."

"I know, but you don't know Bliss like I do. She's so trustworthy."

"Why did she write to John then?"

Cherish didn't like the question. "It was a lapse in good judgement."

"And how many letters did she write? I heard it was a few so it's not just one mistake. It's the same mistake repeated all while she was dating Adam. I wouldn't like it."

"Well no one's dating you so you don't have to worry about it."

Matthew chuckled. "No one's dating me yet, but our time will come."

Cherish recoiled from his comment. "Our time? Separately maybe, but not together."

"If you say so."

"I do."

Matthew wasn't offended. "Let me think about it for a while. I'll come up with something better than your idea."

"Thanks. I can't keep seeing her so upset. It's awful feeling so helpless."

"Leave it with me."

Cherish didn't like things being out of her control. "Okay, but don't take too long. It needs to be done quickly."

Ada looked up at them. "What are you two whispering about?"

Matthew left Cherish and headed over to the couch. "Nothing."

"It can't be nothing," Ada said. "It must be something. Care to share? You must know it's rude to whisper in a room full of people."

Cherish said, "I was just trying to get Matthew to help me with something."

Mamm laughed. "It'd be the dishes."

"How did you guess?" Matthew asked.

Cherish went into the kitchen. Favor had already started the dishes and it was her turn to dry. Cherish picked up a tea towel.

Favor looked over at her. "It sure has been depressing

around here lately. I wish Krystal still lived here, that would brighten things up."

Cherish scowled. She couldn't think of anything worse. "I agree about it being awful around here with John's parents visiting. That's got to make Bliss feel worse as well."

"Yeah." Favor plunged a stack of dishes beneath the soapy water. "Our house is like this and it's all because of John. We never even met John but look how he's affecting all of our lives."

Cherish was quiet for a while as she thought about what Favor said. She was right. How could a complete stranger affect the lives of so many of them? "A secret marriage, and before that secret letters. That John guy sure had a lot happening. I wonder if there's more secrets that we haven't found out about yet."

Favor snorted. "I hope not."

CHAPTER 14

*L*ate in the afternoon the next day, John's parents returned. Debbie was nervous, but she was ready. Wilma told the girls to stay in the kitchen and Levi opened the door for the Bontragers. He then led them through to the living room where Debbie and Wilma waited.

They sat down, once again taking Wilma and Levi's chairs. Wilma sat on the couch with Debbie and baby Jared. Levi sat on the other side of them.

Nehemiah broke the awkward silence. "When we came here yesterday, Debbie, we thought you'd be delighted about the house and you'd be coming home with us. We didn't expect we'd be waiting for a decision from you. We thought you'd be only too happy with our generous offer. We've left you alone for a day to think it through."

"What have you decided to do, Debbie?" Rebekah asked.

Debbie took a deep breath. "I'm going to stay here."

Rebekah and Nehemiah stared at each other. Then Rebekah asked, "For how long?"

"They said I can stay here forever if I want."

Nehemiah said, "I don't know what to say."

Debbie lowered her head. "I'm sorry to upset you."

"We thought we'd be taking John's baby home with us," Rebekah whined.

Debbie said, "I'm not keeping him from you. You can see him whenever you want."

Nehemiah moved to the edge of the chair. "It's not easy for us to come here. I have a business to run. It would've been more convenient for us if you'd come with us so we could all be one big happy family."

"We'll try to visit," Debbie said in a small voice.

"Try?" Nehemiah asked.

"That's the best I can do. I have a life here now."

"What life do you have here, Debbie? How can you say you have a life here when you've only been here for a few months?" Rebekah fixed her gaze upon Debbie.

"Exactly," Nehemiah agreed. "You haven't been here long enough to have a life."

Debbie wanted to ask them why they thought she wasn't good enough for John, and why they wanted John to marry Mary. It didn't matter now, she reminded herself. "I feel at home here and this is the only place Jared knows."

"He's too young to even know where he is. Is someone trying to keep you away from us?"

Debbie tilted her head, wondering what he was getting at. "No, not at all."

"That's what it sounds like to us." Rebekah leaned forward

and whispered, "Do they have some kind of hold over you? It's all right, you can tell us."

Wilma's mouth fell open. "I hope you're not talking about us."

"We asked yesterday to speak in private and you refused us," Nehemiah said. "If today's rules are different we'd gladly talk to Debbie alone. Otherwise, we must speak freely."

"No one's keeping me here," Debbie said. "They've always been good to me from the start and I get along with every one of them. They've all been good."

"And why wouldn't they be good?"

"I don't know. You just said, do they have a hold over me. It sounds like you think they're forcing me to stay or something."

"We can't think of any other reason you wouldn't come with us. We even bought you a very nice house. We thought you'd be delighted." Rebekah pulled out a white handkerchief and dabbed at her tears.

"I'm very grateful—"

"It's there waiting for you. Your very own house," Rebekah said.

"How else would you ever get a house, unless you marry a widower like your parents are suggesting. Did they mention that to you?" Nehemiah asked.

"Yes. They gave me all their suggestions and that was one of them. I won't be making a marriage of convenience." Debbie shook her head.

"And you don't have to. You see? We think alike. We'll be your family." Rebekah lowered her handkerchief and sniffed a couple of times.

"She is already our family, Rebekah."

"Yes, that's what I meant."

Debbie didn't know what to say. She'd already told them she wasn't going with them and they just wouldn't stop. "I do appreciate you buying the house, but it might've been better to talk to me about it first."

"Then it wouldn't have been a surprise. John loved surprises and being his wife, we thought you would've too. You have to have something in common or he wouldn't have chosen you."

"That's right. Chosen you above the other women who would've liked for him to choose them," Rebekah spat out.

Debbie shook her head. "We must've had other things in common because I don't like surprises. I like to have things planned out and I have planned for my life to be here."

"So you've met another man, have you?" Rebekah fastened her beady eyes upon her.

Debbie nearly choked. "I've met someone I get along with, but we're very far away from anything becoming serious."

A single tear trickled down Rebekah's cheek. "I knew it. Didn't I say that was the reason, Nehemiah? Have you forgotten John so easily?"

"No. I'll never be able to forget him and the secret marriage we had." Now Debbie was starting to get upset. "I didn't want it to be a secret. Maybe he wanted to surprise everyone with it since he liked surprises so much. Seems he liked secrets too as well as surprises."

"That wasn't necessary, Debbie." Nehemiah put his arm around his wife as she sobbed. "We should go. Debbie has made up her mind."

Through her tears Rebekah asked, "Can we see the baby again, Debbie?"

"Of course you can, but he's asleep." She didn't want them to come into his room. "I'll bring him down."

They saw Jared, who remained asleep while they were saying goodbye to him, before they finally left.

"How are you feeling, Debbie?" Wilma asked.

"Pretty drained." She looked down at her sleeping baby. "I didn't want them in his room. I'm not sure why."

"I'll take him upstairs for you," Favor said.

Debbie handed him over to Favor, and he stayed sleeping.

Levi sat down after having walked the Bontragers to the door. "I thought I should keep out of things today. I didn't want to inflame the situation by having my say."

"That was best," Wilma told him.

"What did they say?" Bliss sat next to Debbie.

"Weren't you listening?"

"We heard most of it."

"They made me feel so bad."

"They meant to," Bliss told her. "Don't be concerned about them. I mean it's sad for them, but you have to do what you want to do."

"There is no easy answer in this situation. You did what you had to do. You told them what you wanted and what you thought was best for Jared," Levi told Debbie.

Wilma agreed with him. "And that's all you can do, Debbie."

Debbie nodded and she was pleased she wouldn't have to see John's parents for a very long time. It would take her a while to get over their visit.

CHAPTER 15

That night, Cherish went up to bed thinking she would drop right off to sleep, but she couldn't. She tossed and turned. After a while, she got up and wrote a letter to Malachi. When she finished that, she wrote a letter to Fenella, her best friend that she met at Miriam and Earl's wedding.

Then, she sneaked into Favor's room and retrieved the women's magazine Favor had hidden under her bed and took it back to bed to read. It was mostly advertisements, so Cherish was soon bored with that.

When she heard talking coming from downstairs, she crept up the hallway. It was *Mamm* and Levi and they were by themselves in the living room.

Cherish lowered herself onto her tummy and moved to the head of the stairs so she could see them and hear them better.

"What did you think about the Bontragers, Levi?" Wilma asked.

"I was upset for them about Jared not carrying on the Bontrager name."

"But you were very happy about it when Debbie told you."

"Of course I was because he is a Bruner now."

"I see." *Mamm* went back to her sewing.

"Names mean a lot." Levi continued reading his Bible.

"I'm finding that out. Ada can talk about nothing else—insisting babies have middle names and such."

"I don't think middle names are as important as she does. Last names are important to a man. Jared is the first grandchild and the first male, and he won't be a Bontrager. Naturally, they're upset by that."

"Oh. I see what you mean. I thought they were getting a bit angry there for a moment. I liked the way you said your piece to them yesterday."

"I didn't come across too strong, did I?" Levi asked.

"No, just perfect."

"That's why I thought I should keep quiet today. It allowed Debbie to have her say and that's how it should've been."

"Good idea. Everything worked out well. Mind you, I was a little shocked that they thought we might be forcing Debbie to stay."

Cherish grimaced when she saw how sweetly her mother smiled at Levi.

Wilma then continued, "I'm just thinking that it's so hard for Debbie. She is such a gentle soul and doesn't want to upset anybody. I'm glad she stayed strong. I do believe that staying here will be the best thing for her."

"Of course it will," said Levi.

"Well there's not much we can do about the name. Debbie is

not going to go back on that. I was a little surprised that she said what she said."

Levi looked up from his reading. "What did she say?"

"She said something about the marriage being unconventional so she did something unconventional with the name."

Levi chuckled. "I do remember that, but when Cherish said something about that, you growled at her."

"I had to. I didn't want her to be pleased that the Bontragers were upset."

"I don't think she was. She was just pleased that Debbie was starting to stand up for herself."

Cherish was delighted that Levi saw things the same way as she did.

Mamm continued, "If she wasn't pleased at their misfortune then what I said wouldn't upset her much. Not that it probably upset her at all. You know how thin-skinned she is."

"Do you mean thick-skinned?"

"That's right, thick-skinned. Nothing bothers that girl."

"It's going to be quiet around here when you're at the farm. How long will you be gone?"

"Just a few days. A week at the most. I don't like to be gone too long. Debbie needs me. Bliss also needs me with this dreadful ordeal happening with Adam. I do hope that's resolved soon. The girl's at the breaking point."

"Maybe Adam isn't the right one for her," Levi said.

"Of course he is. Do you know anyone better suited? Because I don't."

"No, but she's only young. She'll find someone eventually. It's no shame for a woman to get married later in life, you know. We married each other and we weren't exactly young."

Wilma grumbled. "Only a man would say that. Anyway, this is our second marriage for both of us."

"I mean it, Wilma, these things shouldn't be rushed. You said so yourself when you came back from visiting Mercy and Honor."

"I know, but we're talking about Adam and Bliss. I wasn't worried about Bliss rushing into something, I was worried about Cherish and Favor. I don't mind if they take their time. And Bliss can rush if she's rushing with Adam."

Levi raised his eyebrows and continued reading.

Cherish got up when nothing more was said, and headed back to bed. Once she was in bed, she moved her dog over to one side so she had room to stretch out. Her heavy eyelids closed thinking about what Favor had said about John. None of the Bakers had even met him and yet he was affecting all their lives. She knew that was profound in some way, but before she could think it through, her eyelids grew heavy and sleep overtook her.

CHAPTER 16

*O*n the day of the tea testing, Matthew met Debbie, Favor, Bliss and Cherish at the farmers market. He was bringing a trestle table. Cherish walked over to help him lift the table out of the back of the buggy.

"I've been waiting to see you again," Cherish told him.

His face lit up. "I've been waiting to see you, too."

"Good. So you've thought of a plan to get Adam and Bliss back together?"

"No. I forgot all about it. I thought you meant you were just pleased to see me."

Cherish made a face. "Seriously?"

He nodded.

"Matthew, I was relying on you."

"I'm sorry. I've been thinking about my future here. That's what I've been thinking about. Forgive me for being selfish. I'll come up with something."

Cherish grunted, "That's what you said a couple of days ago."

"Just trust me." He took the blanket off the table. They carried it to the entrance and placed it where Debbie directed them. Then they started setting up the tea.

A man walked past, but not before having a good look at them and what they were doing. Then he walked back to them. "Do you have a permit?" he asked Matthew.

Matthew stared at him. "I'm sorry, but who are you?"

"I'm a stallholder. I have a market stall that I pay for. No one's allowed to sell out here."

Matthew looked over at Debbie who was arranging her tea. "Hey, Debbie, do we have a permit?"

Debbie looked up. "For what?"

"To be here," the stallholder replied.

"No. Do we need one?"

"Of course you do. You just can't come here and start selling your goods. We all need to pay."

Cherish stepped up. "We're not selling anything. We're just testing samples for public opinions. We'll only be here for a couple of hours. Or maybe just one hour."

He frowned and then murmured that they'd still probably need a permit, and then he walked inside the building.

"Are we in trouble?" Debbie asked.

"Just ignore him. I think we only need a permit if we're selling things," Favor said.

Debbie looked around. "I hope you're right."

"We won't be here long, will we?" Matthew asked. "How many people do we need to taste the tea?"

Debbie bit her lip. That was something she couldn't answer.

She didn't recall how many she might need or whether her unofficial tea-making-mentor had even mentioned a number. "I don't know."

Matthew tipped his hat back on his head. "Ten, thirty, one hundred?"

"I think it only needs to be small. The main thing is that the people don't know us. We've only got enough hot water for fifty."

"Okay. People are starting to arrive now. Have we got the tea ready yet, Debbie?"

"It'll be set up in a minute." They had a portable gas burner to heat the water.

As Cherish helped out, she thought about the first time they were supposed to do this, when Simon said he'd come to meet her. She was a little surprised that so many of her thoughts were taken up by Simon.

Being at the farmers market reminded Bliss of Adam. But then again, everything reminded her of Adam. How would she go on without him? Her life was ruined.

Favor was pleased to be out of the house, away from the orchard. She was getting out of chores and for that, she was grateful.

When the samples were mostly all gone, Debbie became more withdrawn. It had been hard to get people to stop a moment and try out the tea. They did, once they were told it was free. The feedback wasn't great.

People weren't enthusiastic about the tea.

Cherish's heart was breaking for Debbie. Why were people being so mean?

Just when she was going to give up and go home, someone

arrived that Debbie knew. It was Fredrick Lomas, the man who owned the tea packaging and sales business.

"Fredrick, what are you doing here?" Debbie was embarrassed that people weren't raving about her tea. Now Fredrick would find out.

"I heard a whisper you'd be here. Mind if I try your tea?"

"I'd be honored if you would." Debbie took a sample cup and gave him the rose and pomegranate. He swallowed and moved his lips around as he tasted it. "What do you think?" Debbie asked.

He looked at her, then looked back down at the samples. "I'll try the lemon and hibiscus." She passed it to him and he took a sip. "What are people saying about this one?" he asked.

"I'm not sure yet. We haven't looked at what they've written down. I was going to do that when I got home. What do you think?"

"I think the flavor isn't coming through enough."

"Oh. What can I do?"

"Have a look at your feedback and if you're not happy, bring all the comments and your tea to me, and I'll see if I can help you adjust your formulas."

"You'd do that?" Debbie asked.

"Sure. I'd like to see you succeed."

"Thank you."

"You've got my number."

"I do."

"Call me and we'll make a time." He looked at the pages and said, "Is that how many people have sampled the tea?"

"Yes."

He picked up the pages, and flipped through them. "This is enough."

"Is it?" Debbie asked.

"Yes."

"Great. Thank you. I'll be in touch."

He nodded and then moved away.

"Was that your tea man?" Favor asked.

"Yes. Let's pack up. I won't look at what people said until I get home. I don't think people liked the tea as much as I hoped they would."

"Don't worry until you see what all the people said."

Debbie didn't say anything, but she had seen from the looks on their faces that most of them weren't impressed.

Matthew whispered to Cherish, "She's upset."

The manager of the farmers market walked up as they were packing up. "Who's in charge here?"

Cherish recognized him and stepped forward. She knew him from a few years ago when she and her sisters had a stall. "Hello, Mr. Pettigrew. I'm Cherish Baker. "

He looked at her with no recognition in his eyes.

Cherish continued, "My family had a stall here for a couple of years."

"Then you should know that what you're doing is not allowed." He pointed at the table.

"We're just leaving and besides, we weren't selling anything."

His eyebrows drew together. "What were you doing?"

Debbie stepped forward. "I'm sorry. This was my fault. We were taste-testing my tea. We needed a cross-section of people who didn't know us to use as a focus group."

His face got softer as he smiled at Debbie. "Still, it's questionable with my insurance and whether they'd cover any one of you who were illegally operating here."

"I'm sorry. We didn't know we were doing anything wrong."

Matthew said, "It was my fault. I suggested we come here because of all the people who'd be here. What do we owe you, moneywise, for setting up here?"

Cherish was pleased Matthew was taking control. He was acting like a real man and not the boy he acted like most of the time.

Mr. Pettigrew shook his head. "Just don't do it again unless you ask. I could've found some space for you inside, Mrs. ...?"

"Mrs. ... Ms. Bruner."

He nodded and then looked up at the sky. "Seems it's going to rain. The forecast is for a thunderstorm."

Cherish was quick to say, "We better get out of here before we get caught in the downpour."

Mr. Pettigrew gave a nod before he left them and walked into the building.

"That was a close call," Matthew said.

"Thanks, Matthew, but I think this was my idea. You didn't need to take the blame."

"I thought it would be better if he talked to another man. Men can talk reasonably to each other."

Favor sniggered. "Yeah, you did a great job, Matthew."

"You sure did," Debbie agreed. "I thought we might have to pay for a moment."

"Do you even have any money?" Cherish asked him.

"No. Not on me. Let's pack this up before we get caught in the rain."

Debbie was grateful to have so many helpers, but she knew she wouldn't feel as good when she looked at the results of the survey.

CHAPTER 17

*D*ebbie had been right. She sat down in the living room with Ada on one side and Wilma on the other as she read aloud what people had written about her tea.

Debbie read out the last two of the comments. "Not enough flavor. Here's another one. It tasted like dishwater. The only one that was popular was the lemon tea. I thought that was the boring one. Anyone can make lemon tea."

"Maybe these people weren't telling the truth," Ada suggested.

"They had no reason to lie. They don't know me and I don't know them."

"That is unusual. We like all your tea. Just sell the lemon tea, then," Wilma suggested.

"If I'm to make a real go of this, I'll need more than one flavor. Fredrick said he'd help me with the recipes."

"That's *wunderbaar*. And he's an expert, you say?" Wilma asked.

"He is. He knows so much about tea. I think he knows everything."

Ada patted Debbie's arm. *"Gott* has sent him to guide you."

"I agree. I need some guidance. I just feel so disappointed with these results."

"Don't be upset," Ada told her. "Everyone has to start somewhere. And if these opinions are true, it would've been wrong for you to put so much effort into something when you could've had better tea."

"I know. You're right. That's what Fredrick said. I have to sort out my flavors first."

"And that's what you're doing. I'm proud of you, Debbie."

Debbie turned to look at Wilma. "You are?"

"I am. You've had so many problems and mountains to climb and then you bounce back and start thinking about something other than your own problems. I'm sure you'll do well out of this."

"I hope so. I thought about giving up, but I'll keep going. I'm really enjoying it."

"What does Peter White think about you making tea?" Ada asked.

"He's so supportive. He's the one that took me to the tea factory in the first place."

"Ah, that's right. I did forget that."

Debbie straightened up all her pieces of paper. "Before I started today, I thought everyone would love my tea."

"We do."

"I know, but most people don't."

Wilma put her hand on Debbie's arm. "This is the first rung

on the ladder. Get that right and then you climb onto the next rung. Pretty soon you'll be up at the top."

"Thanks for all your encouragement, Aunt Wilma. It means a lot. You too, Ada."

Ada smiled, and said, "You'll always have our support."

CHAPTER 18

The next morning, it was Cherish's turn to take some meals over to Christina. She pushed Christina's front door open. "Hello."

"I'm in the bedroom."

Cherish left the casserole dish on the kitchen counter and then walked into the bedroom. One twin was on the bed, making small crying noises while Christina was changing the other twin's diaper.

Christina looked like she'd had a bit more sleep. She was fully dressed and the bed was even made. "Hi, Cherish, thanks for coming over."

"I left a meal in the kitchen."

"Great. The food has been such a big help."

"Good."

"Do you want to change a diaper?"

Cherish made a face. "No. I don't know how. I've never had much to do with babies."

Christina laughed. "I don't think that's entirely true. What about Faith and also Iris?"

Cherish smiled. "Well, I haven't changed Iris's diaper."

"So you do know how?" Christina asked.

"A little bit. Okay, I'll change her." Cherish found a diaper and set about changing the other baby.

Once the babies were changed, Christina put them into their shared crib for a nap.

Cherish looked over at the second crib. "I rushed out and got that second crib. Do you think you'll ever use it?"

"Of course. When they're bigger." Christina closed the door on them.

"Should I go? Do you want to get some sleep?"

"No, I'll be fine. Let's sit on the couch. I haven't had anyone to talk to for a while. As soon as Mark comes home, I'll get some sleep."

"Okay. I've got plenty of time." They both sat on the couch.

Christina said, "I had a good night last night. They both slept for five hours. I think I'll be able to go to the meeting next Sunday."

"That's great. Everyone will be so excited to see the babies."

"How's Bliss doing?"

"Just the same. Nothing has changed at all. I tried to get her to come with me, but she said she'd come next time. She's just so depressed. Things didn't go well the last time Bliss went somewhere with me." Cherish told Christina how cold Adam had acted when Bliss literally ran into him.

"It's hard for her, but everything will work out."

"How do you know?" Cherish asked.

"It always does. Everything works out for the best. Just look at my two babies. I had pain and heartache for many years and now I have two miracles."

Cherish couldn't deny that. Christina's babies were a true miracle. And that gave Cherish more faith to believe in miracles and to believe that God is a God who answers prayers. "It's true, but it's hard for Bliss because she's going through it now. It was hard for you before your babies arrived, before you got pregnant."

"Oh yes, I know what you mean. I was destroyed every day. Half the time I doubted that *Gott* was even there. Doubted that He was even listening to my pleas and my cries. He did, and He won't be any different with Bliss or anyone else."

"I can see that that's true. Maybe Bliss should talk to you."

"Of course. She was over here the other day, but she didn't say much."

"I think she's trying to put on a brave face in front of other people. She probably wouldn't want to tell you how she really feels. But if you ask her questions, she might open up to you."

"I'll do that."

"Thank you. Are the twins identical?"

"I believe so, but I can tell them apart."

"How?"

"There's a slight difference in the width of the forehead and their temperaments are different too. One is far more relaxed and the other is a little more uptight."

"It's interesting that they can have personalities right from the start."

"Everyone is born with their own personalities. I believe that."

"I wonder how many more babies you'll have."

Christina smiled widely. "As many as *Gott* gives us. We didn't start off young, but these twins have given us a good head start."

"I think having twins is a good idea. Only one pregnancy and one birth and then you have the two-in-one package. Two for the price of one." Cherish giggled.

"There's more work involved with twins, but I think it will be easier once they get older."

They heard scratching sounds at the door. "What's that?" Christina asked.

"That will be Caramel. He's got out of the buggy. I told him to stay there. He's a naughty dog sometimes. I should go now anyway." Cherish jumped up and Christina walked her to the door.

"Tell Wilma thanks for the food. It has been convenient having the food ready. We are very appreciative of all the help your mother has given us, and Ada, too, of course."

"Yeah, they're not bad for a couple of old ducks."

"Oh, Cherish." Christina laughed. "Whatever you do, don't let them hear you say that."

"I'm not *that* silly."

"Say goodbye to the twins for me. "

"I will."

"Do you have any names yet? Everyone's anxiously waiting for the names."

Christina shook her head. "We've got a short list. We'll most likely decide later today."

"I can't wait to hear what they are." Cherish walked out the door and Caramel jumped up on her, putting his muddy paws all over her white apron. "Get down. And get back into the buggy. See what you've done, Caramel?"

"That's why we don't have a dog." Christina laughed.

"You don't have a dog yet, but I'm sure the twins would like a puppy when they're older."

"Hmm, we'll see."

"That was a mother's response. You're learning already. *Mamm* always says 'we'll see' when she means no." Cherish gave Christina a sideways hug goodbye, careful not to get any dirt on her.

On the drive home, Cherish slowed down when she got to Eddie, the beekeeper's property, as she always did. She couldn't believe it when she saw Gertie's buggy there again. That meant Krystal was visiting. Again. She didn't have a buggy of her own and she used Gertie's.

"What's really going on between those two?" Cherish said out loud.

It wasn't right for a newly Amish woman, for that matter *any* Amish woman to keep visiting an *Englisher*.

Cherish slowed the buggy even more.

Should she confront them again? She'd done that last time and it seemed that Krystal didn't give two hoots about being caught alone with Eddie.

Then Cherish had a thought. If Krystal kept herself busy by visiting Eddie, she'd leave Adam alone.

Cherish moved the buggy forward, hoping that might be true.

CHAPTER 19

The day before Fairfax and Hope were due to arrive home from visiting relatives, Wilma had an idea. "Hope will be back tomorrow. It would be nice if you girls clean the cottage so it's ready for their return."

Cherish was chewing on a chocolate cookie and she stopped as soon as she heard her mother's suggestion. "I'm busy doing things."

"Me too," Favor said. "Besides, Hope said they're moving into the big house. It'd be a complete waste to clean up the cottage."

Ada butted in as she so often did, "What your mother meant to say was one, two, three of you," she pointed at Bliss, Favor, and Cherish in turn, "will stop what you're doing and go over there right now to clean the house and make it look nice for their return. Perhaps you could add some flowers to the kitchen table."

"We have no flowers in the garden at this time of year," Favor said.

"Well, just clean the place and make it look nice." Ada gave a nod at her suggestion.

The girls all stood up. "You want us to go now, *Mamm?*" Favor asked.

"Yes I do."

The girls walked out of the kitchen to get their coats.

"See, Wilma? That's how it's done." Ada and Wilma put their heads together and chuckled.

"This is a crazy idea." Favor stomped through the orchard on her way to Fairfax and Hope's cottage.

Bliss said, "It will be nice for them to come home to a clean place. They left so soon after the wedding so they might not have had much time to concentrate on their place."

Favor glared at Bliss. "You're always agreeing with *Mamm.*"

Cherish poked Favor in her side so Bliss wouldn't see. Any little comment was likely to set Bliss off in tears again.

Favor glanced at Cherish, and caught on to what Cherish was thinking. "I'm sorry, both of you," Favor said. "I'm just grumpy today, that's all."

"There's a lot of that going around," said Cherish. "But with the three of us, we'll get this done in no time. It's probably not even dirty. You know what Hope's like, she's forever cleaning things."

"That's true," Favor said.

When they got to the front door of the cottage, Favor retrieved the key from under the mat. As soon as they let themselves in, they noticed the brand new furniture.

"Wow, this is all so nice," Bliss ran her hands along the bleached wooden dining table.

Favor turned around in a circle. "And the place looks clean enough to me."

The girls then moved to the small kitchen. On the floor in the corner were wedding presents. Some were opened and some unopened.

Cherish picked up a wrapped gift and shook it. "Perhaps we can open some wedding presents."

Bliss giggled. "I think they'd be pretty mad if we did that."

"I guess so."

Favor said, "I can't wait till I get married. I can get some awesome presents."

Cherish rolled her eyes at Favor's comment. Anything could set Bliss off crying again, especially any talk of weddings or anything to do with weddings or marriage. "You get presents all the time for Christmas and birthdays."

"I know, but for weddings people give you better presents."

Bliss moved away. "I'll look in the other rooms to see where to start first."

Cherish moved closer to Favor, and hissed, "Will you stop talking about wedding stuff?"

Favor placed her hands on her hips. "It's a bit hard at the moment. That's why we're here. Hope's just gotten married so it's hard not to talk about it."

Bliss walked back into the room, looking like she was about to burst into tears. "I heard what you both said. "I'll never get any wedding presents now that I'm never going to marry."

Cherish was fumingly mad. "Good work, Favor," she blurted out.

"It's your fault. You wanted to open the presents, not me. You started it."

"No *you* started it." Cherish jabbed a finger through the air, pointing at Favor.

"So I should just continue my life having to watch what I say?" Favor's voice rose, which made it even more high-pitched sounding than normal. Cherish covered her ears.

Bliss sighed. "Stop it both of you. You're both making me feel worse."

Favor took a step closer to Bliss. "You'll forget about Adam soon. Don't worry."

"Thanks, but I doubt it. Well, where should we start? We're here for a reason. I don't want to think about Adam right now." Bliss looked around.

Cherish poked one of the wrapped wedding gifts. Favor slapped her hand away.

"Ouch."

"We're here to clean," Favor groused at Cherish.

"I don't see why. It looks clean to me."

Bliss said, "The kitchen needs a wipe over."

"We'll start in the kitchen then," Cherish said. "And, we'll wipe it over."

"That won't need three of us. I'll sweep the floor," Favor volunteered.

Bliss suggested Cherish should clean the windows.

Then all three went their separate ways.

An hour later when they were ready to go, Favor said, "I really don't know how Hope had the time to have the place so nice before she left. The place was already clean."

Cherish said, "Don't you remember, she wasn't at our place

much the day before she left. She came back here to clean. She should've been at home, cleaning up. It was her wedding after all."

Bliss agreed. "That's true, but it doesn't matter. We've done all we can. Now we can leave."

Cherish took a last look at the presents. "Can't I just have a little peek? It wouldn't hurt if I just lifted up a little of the paper and had a look inside. I can stick it back down again."

"No," Bliss and Favor said at the same time.

"What about just one of them?" Cherish asked.

"No," came the resounding reply from Favor.

"Unfair." Cherish pouted as she looked at the gifts. She had an overwhelming urge to know what was inside and didn't know why Bliss and Favor didn't feel the same.

Bliss took one last look around. "I do wish we could've had some nice flowers like Ada suggested. It would be a nice surprise when they come home."

"Where are we going to get flowers from at this late notice?" Favor asked. "Nowhere, that's where."

Bliss sat down on the couch. "I don't mean to depress everybody, but it's a bit sad for me being here." Bliss's bottom lip wobbled. "Hope has her husband. I thought I would be next in line to marry out of all of us."

"And you still might," Cherish said, quite forgetting she wasn't going to give her any false hope.

Favor sat down next to Bliss. "That's right, you might. He's got to realize how silly he is sooner or later. You're the most perfect woman for him. I mean, no one is as nice or as kind as you are, Bliss."

Bliss wiped a tear from her eye. "I'm sorry. I don't mean to be like this, but I can't stop feeling so sad. It's like there is no color in my world now. Everything is just blah without Adam. I loved spending time with him. And when I wasn't with him, I was thinking about him."

Favor looked up at Cherish, wanting her to say something to make Bliss feel better, but there was nothing she could say. She'd run out of encouragement and so, it seemed, had Favor.

Bliss wiped away some tears and stood up. "I'll get past this."

"Of course you will," said Favor.

"I agree," said Cherish.

"Let's go."

They locked up and replaced the key, and the three of them walked back through the orchard. All the way back home, Cherish prayed that Matthew would come up with a good plan or at least have had a good conversation with Andrew about Adam. Surely there would be something lurking in Adam's past to make him see that he wasn't perfect. That was the only thing Cherish could think of to get them back together.

CHAPTER 20

*A*fter dinner that night, Cherish pulled Matthew aside in the corner of the living room. There was nowhere else to have a private talk since it was too cold outside on the porch.

"I've been trusting you, Matthew. What have you come up with?"

"I decided I will talk with Andrew."

"I thought we'd already decided that you would."

Matthew opened his mouth to speak, but Cherish kept talking.

"And what will you say?"

"I'll just start a conversation about Adam and Bliss and see what he says."

"Don't make it obvious."

"I won't. I'll just try and lead the conversation in that direction."

Cherish nodded. "Okay, that sounds good."

"Trust me, I'm good at talking."

"I really think it would be a good idea to find out about Adam's history, but I have no idea how to do that because he's not from this community. And I don't know any way I can find anyone who knows him without Bliss or Adam finding out what we're up to."

"Leave it with me. I know what I'm doing."

Cherish smiled. "Thanks, Matthew. I knew I could rely on you."

He smiled back at her. "Always."

"But don't let me down."

"I won't."

"I really hope something works or Bliss will be sad forever. Everyone says she'll get over it, but what if she doesn't?"

"She'll get over it as soon as she finds someone else. That is, if they don't get back together."

"That won't be easy if she has to find someone else because Adam is pretty amazing."

Matthew cleared his throat. "I know, you keep reminding me. Looks aren't everything."

"I didn't say they were."

"I didn't say you did, but I do think you think that to a degree."

Cherish scrunched up her face. "What are you talking about? I never said anything of the kind."

"Maybe not, but you did list that as one of Adam's attributes."

"It doesn't hurt that he looks nice, but Bliss is in love with him not for the way he looks, he's got other things about him. He started his own business and it's going really, really well.

That means he'll be able to provide Bliss with a house and everything she'll ever need. And they won't have money worries when they have children to feed. That is, if your plan works."

Matthew rubbed his forehead. "So their future depends on me?"

"It does."

"Thanks a lot."

"Well I can't do anything, because I'm going to the farm soon."

"I'll do my best. That's all I can do."

"That's all I'm asking. When will you do it?"

"When the time's right." Matthew moved away and joined the others.

Cherish stood there, staring after him. 'When the time's right?' That didn't sit well with Cherish. To her, everything should be done immediately, especially with how much Bliss was suffering.

The right time was right now! Well, at least tomorrow.

CHAPTER 21

he next day, Hope burst into the house through the back door. "We're back!" Fairfax walked in after her. The whole family was sitting down eating lunch. Ada and Samuel were there too, along with Matthew.

"Has it been two and a half weeks already?" *Mamm* asked as though she wasn't expecting them.

"Yes, it has." Hope hugged her mother. "Was someone at the cottage while we were away?"

Ada said, "Your sisters were kind enough to make sure it was nice for you."

"Thanks so much. It was lovely to get home and for everything to be so clean. We left in such a hurry."

"I hope you're all ready to get going with work." Fairfax rubbed his hands together, looking at all the girls.

"It's winter. There's not much to do." Favor then looked at him. "Since we're the owners of the orchard, you work for us, don't you, Fairfax?"

Cherish was surprised she'd say such a thing, but it was true.

"If you want to get technical, I work for Florence. Since you've all agreed to work under Florence, that would mean you've agreed to work under me, which means I'm your boss."

Favor looked down, while Ada chuckled.

Fairfax continued, "There are always things to do in the orchard. We can check the fences, check the trees and then we can keep the equipment in good order. Even though the trees seem to be asleep, they're not asleep and neither should we sleep."

"Aren't you also looking after your parents' old orchard and Florence's orchard, too?" Wilma asked.

"That's right."

"That'll keep you busy."

Fairfax chuckled. "I don't mind being busy."

"How was everyone back at home?" Matthew asked.

"I was just about to tell everyone that, Matthew. You got in before me." Hope said, "They're fine. The boys are adorable and the babies are growing so fast."

"I wish I could've gone with you," Favor moaned. "It's not fair."

"There will be other times," *Mamm* said.

"No there won't. It'll be other people going and not me. I never get to go anywhere."

"It's a long way away. Perhaps they'll come for a visit," Cherish suggested.

"No they won't. They didn't come for Hope's wedding."

"That's only because their children are too young."

"Yeah, and next time their excuse will be something else.

They'll probably have more babies by then and they'll be too young."

"Hush, Favor. I haven't finished telling everyone my news."

Everyone made room at the table for Hope and Fairfax. While Hope told them everything they did while they were away, Bliss sat there thinking about Adam. She had thought she'd be the next one married after Hope—and thought she'd be married to Adam. Now she wouldn't have the next wedding in the family. That thought wouldn't stop playing over and over in her mind.

It was hard for Bliss to focus on anything other than her problems with Adam and all the what ifs. What if Krystal planned to take advantage of the situation? If Adam and Krystal started dating, it would be the most awful thing ever. Everyone knew Krystal had always had her eyes on Adam. And if he did date Krystal, it wouldn't be fair. He wasn't forgiving her for a past mistake, but what about all the mistakes Krystal had made in her life?

"Anyway, what's been happening here? What have we missed?" Hope asked.

"Nothing much," *Mamm* said.

"I'll have to see Mark and Christina's babies. I can't wait."

"I can take you there tomorrow if you want," Bliss said.

"Okay. I'd love that."

Cherish added, "We had people test Debbie's teas to see if they liked them. That was such fun."

Debbie looked down. "It didn't go so well."

"Why? What happened?" Hope asked.

"They liked the lemon tea, but hardly anyone liked the others. I'm having someone help me with the recipes. I'm going to play around with them tonight to see what I can come up with."

Matthew laughed. "While we were there, we got into trouble with the manager of the markets."

Ada gasped. "No one told me that."

"I wasn't told either," Wilma said. "It's nothing to laugh about, Matthew. We can't get a bad name around town."

"It was no problem. It wasn't a big deal. He was nice. He said if he'd known we were coming, he would've found us a place inside."

"Yeah, it was no problem," Favor said.

"I hope not. The last thing we want is for us to get a bad name just like Wilma said," Ada told Matthew.

Mamm continued, "We're well respected around town and I don't want anything to change that."

"It won't change, Wilma. It was really okay. Everything was fine."

Wilma stared at Matthew. "I'll have to take your word on that. But you should've asked if you could've set up there, in the parking lot."

"It was my fault. I'm sorry, Aunt Wilma, I just wasn't thinking." Debbie shook her head.

"It's okay. You've had a lot on your mind. You can't be expected to think of everything when you're concentrating on your tea."

Samuel said, "I'm sure Hope and Fairfax want to tell us more about their time away."

Then Hope took over the conversation and told them about every place they'd visited.

~

THAT NIGHT, Bliss burst into Cherish's room. Cherish was just settling into bed. Bliss hurried to sit on her bedside. "I need to talk to you about something."

Cherish hoped she hadn't found out that Matthew was going to talk with Andrew. "What is it?" Cherish sat up.

"I need you to find out how close Krystal and Adam are."

"Me?"

"Yes. I know we broke up but he doesn't have to ignore me completely. We are in the same community. I'm wondering if he's acting so distant because he's guilty. That's why I need you to find out if there's something going on. You and I both know that Krystal has always liked him."

"How will I do that?" Cherish gulped.

"Ask her."

Cherish rubbed her head. She didn't want to be anywhere near Krystal. "You want me to go to the quilt shop?"

"Great idea."

Cherish rolled her eyes.

Bliss's mouth turned down at the corners. "Well, you don't have to do it."

Cherish knew she had to do it. "I'll go if that's what you want. What will I say I'm there for?"

"Just make up something."

Cherish yawned and then covered her mouth. "I could say I'm looking at the patterns again."

"You could take *Mamm* with you."

"Are you crazy? Why would I do that?"

"She might like to spend time with you and she'd be more willing for you to leave the house."

"Or I could go there after I finish work. You pick me up tomorrow when I finish and drive me there. My shift finishes at three and her shop will still be open. You can park up the road so she doesn't see you."

Bliss thought about that for a while and then slowly nodded. "Okay."

"Why are you worried about Krystal? Have you heard something?" Cherish asked.

"Only that he's doing some work in the quilt shop."

"I told you that."

Bliss shrugged her shoulders. "That's the only thing I've heard. I need more information and I don't know how else to get it."

Cherish knew this wouldn't help toward getting Bliss and Adam back together, but she couldn't say no to Bliss. "I'll do what I can."

Bliss threw her arms around her neck. "Thanks, Cherish."

Cherish giggled. "Don't thank me now. I don't even know if I'll find anything out."

"I know, but I feel I have to do something. I can't sit around and do nothing."

How could Cherish tell Bliss not to get her hopes up? Cherish felt she had no reason to bring her down. Maybe Levi was right and in time, Bliss would forget about Adam.

CHAPTER 22

*A*s arranged, Bliss picked up Cherish from the café after she'd finished for the day.

"So what's the plan?" Cherish asked as she climbed into the buggy.

"Same as we agreed on last night. Just go to the quilt store and look around then get talking to Krystal. If something's going on, she won't be able to keep quiet about it."

"It's far too early for anything to be going on."

"No it's not. She'd swoop in on him. She'll see the opportunity and she'll go for it. You know what she's like."

Cherish faced the front. Yes, she knew what Krystal was like in regards to men. Like a hawk who sees a young chick who strayed too far from it's mother.

"How was your day?" Bliss asked.

"Good. I wish I could work there every day."

Bliss grunted. "No point even thinking about that. I can't believe they let you and they won't let me work there."

SAMANTHA PRICE

"It's *Mamm*, I think. Levi has the final say over you. *Mamm* must want me out of the house." Cherish giggled. "She might need a break from me. Weren't you going to ask Levi again if you can work at the café?"

"I was, but I haven't yet. Do you really think he'll let me?"

"If you say it'll make you feel better he might."

"I'll ask him. I'll wait until he's in the right mood. Now when you get to the quilt shop, don't be obvious about why you're there. If Krystal thinks you're there for information she'll clam up and won't tell you anything."

"I doubt there's anything to tell." Cherish felt sorry for Bliss. She was going to get upset when Adam started dating. It wouldn't matter if it was with Krystal or anyone else. There was no point to this, but Bliss was acting like an obsessed crazy person.

Bliss drove the long way so she wouldn't drive past the quilt store, then she parked up the road.

"Park closer. This is such a long way to walk."

"I can't. There are no closer parking spots, and if I'm closer, Krystal might see me. Don't be lazy. Walking is good for you."

Cherish got out, crossed the road and started toward the quilt store. She didn't like Bliss's comment just now about being lazy. She wasn't lazy so why did everyone call her that? It was annoying. Was Bliss becoming like the rest of them? What if she spent more time with Ada and *Mamm* and became just like them? Even more reason to get her and Adam back together.

Looking in the shop window, Cherish saw there were no customers. Krystal was sitting at the back, behind the computer. Cherish took a deep breath and walked up the front step and into the store.

126

Krystal looked up, seeming surprised. "Cherish. Are you here alone?"

"Yes. I just finished my shift at the café."

"Ah, you could've brought me a coffee. I was just thinking I could do with one right now. I can make one myself in the back, but it's not the same as from a café."

"I didn't think of it, sorry. If I'd known I was coming here I would've."

Krystal looked her up and down. "Why are you here? Have you changed your mind about buying one of the quilts?"

Cherish looked around. "Just checking on the quilt patterns again. It's the best way to see them all in one place."

"Didn't your mother already decide on a pattern?"

"Yes, but you know what she's like—always thinking ahead to the next project." Cherish kept looking around.

"How many do you guys plan to make?"

"Quite a few. It'll be an ongoing thing. This next one's for Hope and then it'll be Joy and then… I don't know."

"Bliss? Or are you doing them for when your sisters get married. Bliss won't be the next one like everyone thought. Isn't that the truth?"

The last thing Cherish wanted was to agree with her. "Who knows? They just have to work out their differences. I think they're getting there."

Krystal's eyes grew wide. "Really?"

"Absolutely."

"That's not the impression I got when Adam was here recently."

"What did he say?"

127

Krystal smirked, like she had a secret. "I don't like to repeat things told to me in confidence."

"He told you something in confidence?" Cherish asked.

"That's right."

"I don't believe you. He wouldn't have said anything to you."

"Believe what you want." Krystal straightened a price tag on one of the quilts. "He's doing some work here soon so we will be able to display the quilts better."

"Anyway, I didn't come here to talk about Bliss and Adam. How are things with you?"

"Great. I sold two quilts yesterday and one this morning. Also, one over the internet."

"That's great. You're doing really well."

"I know. And I love it. I'm helping two other businesses get their things on the internet. I told Adam I could help his business too."

"What did he say about that?"

"He said he's busy enough and if he got busier he'd have to employ more people. He's not ready to do that right now. How's Bliss doing? I suppose she's very upset over Adam breaking up with her."

Cherish's mouth turned down at the corners. "Why do you assume he was the one who ended it?"

Krystal cackled. "Who would break up with Adam? Any girl would be mad to do that. Besides, everyone knows what happened."

"What does everyone know?" Cherish hoped no one knew about Bliss writing to John. Ada knew and obviously Matthew had found out somehow, but they were the only ones outside the family who knew.

"I don't know the nitty gritty details if that's what you mean. So is Bliss upset?" Krystal asked.

"No. She's not upset at all. She's perfectly fine."

"But they've broken up for sure, haven't they?" Krystal took a step closer to Cherish.

Cherish was pleased that she didn't know what was going on. That told her nothing was happening between Krystal and Adam.

"I'm not sure. I don't like to ask too many questions. I don't like being nosy." Cherish did a full circle and looked at each of the quilts again. Then she spun around. "Thanks for letting me look around."

"I can't charge you for looking. If I could, I would."

Cherish laughed. "Have you seen Eddie lately?"

The smile left Krystal's face. "No. Why would I?"

"Just asking the question."

"I know what you think you saw a few weeks ago, but there's nothing between us. His family was good to me, and that's all. Don't start rumors. I don't want to have problems with the bishop. He's been really good to me about allowing me to leave the Millers' dairy farm."

Cherish wasn't ready to let it go. "So you were so close to Eddie in his shed because you were thanking him about something? Or... what was the reason?"

Krystal opened her mouth in shock. "I'm not sure what you think you saw, but you're wrong."

Cherish shrugged her shoulders. "Okay."

"You are wrong, Cherish. It's not what you think... or thought."

"I said okay. I don't really care anyway."

"Then why did you bring it up?"

"I was only being polite. Look, there's no reason that we shouldn't get along," Cherish said.

Krystal stared at her for a moment. "There is a reason why we've never gotten along. You don't like me and you never have. You've never been nice to me from the start."

"I can't believe you're saying that right now. It's you who hasn't liked me from the start. All I wanted to say is that we should try to get along."

"We should, but will we?" Krystal asked.

"We could try," Cherish said. "I'm willing."

Krystal nodded. "Okay. If you try, I'll try, but it doesn't help when you keep saying things to upset me."

"What, like ask if you've seen Eddie?"

Krystal nodded.

"Okay. I will never ask about Eddie again," Cherish said.

"Good." Krystal smiled.

"I should go. Next time I'll bring you a take-out coffee."

"Thank you. That would be nice. I'm here most days."

"Noted. Bye, Krystal."

After Krystal said goodbye, Cherish walked out of the shop, feeling stirred up. It was never nice to talk with Krystal, but hopefully they'd just made some kind of truce. As she walked toward the buggy, she turned back around and saw Krystal staring after her.

Krystal was looking past her, up the street at the horse and buggy.

Cherish knew she would've been able to see Bliss in the driver's seat.

"Oh no, She saw me," Bliss said, when Cherish got back into the buggy.

"I know."

Bliss stared at Cherish. "Did you tell her I was here?"

"Of course not. But she doesn't know you weren't taking care of something else and meeting me here. Right?"

"That's true." Bliss moved the buggy onward. Now, it didn't matter if they drove past the store. "What did she say?"

"She didn't really know the situation between you and Adam. That tells me they can't be close. I wouldn't worry about her if I were you. He is going to do some work in the quilt store. I'm not sure when, but you can't let yourself worry about all that. He could date anyone, not only her."

Bliss stared at her, taking her eyes off the road for a moment. "Thanks. That makes me feel a whole lot better," she said sarcastically. "Now I'm having visions of a line of women waiting to date him."

"That's not what I meant at all. There's no line of women. I just don't want you to worry about Krystal. He's clearly not interested in her and she didn't even try to make out there was something going on, even to annoy me."

Bliss sighed. "I can't do anything about anyone he dates. You're right. I don't know what to do. I wish I could travel back in time. I would've avoided John Bontrager and never written back to him. I didn't even know Adam when I first wrote to John."

"John's had a huge impact on Debbie and now you. Debbie probably wishes she had avoided him too, but then she never would've had Jared and I'm sure she wouldn't want that. I wouldn't want that either. He's part of our family now."

"I feel so helpless and hopeless. Have you ever felt like that?"

Cherish nodded. "Most days."

A glimmer of a smile hinted around Bliss's lips. "Don't make me laugh. I don't want to be happy. I'm too sad to be happy."

Cherish sat there in silence because she didn't know what to say. She couldn't comfort her and tell her that Adam would change his mind in case he never did. Normally, Cherish could talk people into things, but nothing she had said to Adam had helped. Maybe this really was the end for Bliss and Adam, as much as that was hard to believe.

As they drove along, listening to nothing but the clip-clopping of the horse's hooves, Bliss tried her best to put Adam Wengerd out of her mind. It seemed the more she tried not to think about him, though, the more she did think about him. At this point, she was sure she'd ruined her life. She and Adam would've had a good future and she was the one who'd messed it up. "You know something?"

"What?" Cherish asked.

"What hurts the most is I only have myself to blame. What hurts the second most is that there's not one single solitary thing I can do about it."

"That's not quite true," Cherish said.

Bliss looked over at her. "What can I do?"

"You can pray. Leave it in God's hands."

Bliss nodded. "I have been praying." It seemed a simple thing to say, but leaving something in God's hands and not worrying about it, that part was very hard.

"I've been praying too."

"Thank you." Bliss didn't say any more. There was such a hole in her heart without Adam. She didn't know how she'd ever get over it. "Cherish, just make sure you make the right decisions because some bad decisions can ruin your life. Just one bad one can."

"Okay. I'll do my best." Now Cherish knew she had to take her time getting to know someone before she rushed into a relationship. Adam had seemed so lovely. She never realized he could be so hard-hearted and unforgiving. "Have you been to the bishop?" Cherish asked.

"About Adam?"

"Yes. Maybe he could talk to him about forgiveness."

Bliss shook her head. "I don't want him back if he only forgives me because he's been told to. Thanks for thinking of that anyway. The other thing is, he might tell the bishop that I wrote to John. I'd feel awful if anyone else found out about that. It's embarrassing enough for both me and Debbie. I think I can trust Adam enough to keep quiet about it."

"Let me know if you think of anything I can do that might help."

"Thanks, Cherish, I will."

CHAPTER 23

The next day, Hope had planned to visit Christina with Debbie, but she'd come down with a cold so Debbie went alone while the girls and Wilma looked after Jared.

"Thanks for coming over," Christina said when she opened the door. "You'll have to bring Jared with you next time to see the babies."

"I will. They'll be good friends growing up."

"I know it."

"Do you have names yet? Ada made me promise I'd ask you."

"We do. Their names are Anna and Olivia. Anna is the oldest one."

"Nice names. I like them. Oh, and Ada wanted me to also ask if they have middle names, of course."

"No. I'm going to be like you and give my babies one name only. No middle names."

Debbie laughed. "Ada will be disappointed."

"I know. I got the speech about needing the middle name, but the only people I have to please are myself and Mark."

"That's true. Can I tell everyone the names tonight? Ada, Samuel and Matthew will be there for the evening meal."

"Yes, I don't mind if you tell them. How are things going with you and Peter?"

"He's very supportive and I haven't had a lot of that in the past."

"How's he supportive?"

"He wants to be involved with Jared, and he's supportive of me making tea. He's doing everything he can to help."

"You need someone like that. Do you think you'll marry him?"

Debbie shrugged her shoulders. "I don't know. With everything that's happened to me, I've gone off the idea of marriage."

"Have you told Peter that?"

"No."

"But didn't you tell him not to move away when he had that job opportunity?"

"That was just to work with his uncle. I don't think it was a big opportunity."

"Aren't you wasting his time if you're not going to marry him?" asked Christina.

"No. He likes to spend time with me and we're getting to know each other. I told him how I felt."

"You did?"

"Yes. I'm pretty sure he knows how I feel. I told him I want to take things slow."

"That's good. Sorry. I didn't mean to pry. It's none of my business."

"I'm glad you asked. We're friends, almost family, so it's normal to ask."

When the babies woke, it was feeding time. Debbie helped Christina arrange pillows under the babies so she could feed them both at once.

While the babies were being fed, Debbie cleaned the kitchen and then swept and mopped the floors. By the time that was finished, Christina was yawning. Debbie changed the babies' diapers to give Christina a break and then the babies went down for another nap.

Debbie left Christina to have a rest while the babies were sleeping.

On the way home, Debbie thought about what Christina had said about Peter. Was she wasting his time?

She didn't have overwhelming feelings of love for him like she'd had for John, but just look how *that* had turned out. The only good thing to come from her marriage with John was Jared.

There was no one she could talk things over with right now. Wilma and Ada would just tell her that feelings for Peter would grow. Wilma's daughters didn't have enough experience with love. Hope and Joy had only ever loved one man and the younger daughters had never loved anyone, apart from Bliss. But she couldn't talk to Bliss about love—not after what happened with Adam.

Was she being selfish holding onto Peter? She hadn't thought much about stopping him from moving away until Christina had brought it up.

After dealing with her own parents and then John's parents, it was almost too much to think about. Peter wasn't putting any pressure on her, so maybe he was happy with the way things were too. She hoped so because she enjoyed having someone look after her and make a fuss over her.

CHAPTER 24

*A*da, Samuel, and Matthew were at the Baker/Bruner household for the evening meal again. Debbie had held onto the information about the names until everyone was there. It had been difficult, as she was excited and couldn't wait to tell them.

"What have you decided to do, Matthew? Everyone's here and I think it's about time they knew," Ada said.

Matthew cleared his throat. "Okay, everyone. I've been working part time at the saddlery store for Mark as you all know. Fairfax has offered me a job at the orchard. Not your orchard, just his orchard."

"It's not his orchard," Ada corrected. "It belongs to Florence."

"I know that."

"Then why call it Fairfax's orchard just because his parents once owned it?"

"Yes, that's so, but it's the easiest way for everyone to know which orchard I'm talking about."

"We're not simpletons, Matthew," Wilma said with a laugh. "So you're staying on?"

"I am, if everyone doesn't mind." He looked round at everyone.

"We're all happy about that," Samuel said.

Favor agreed. "I'm glad."

"Good."

Wilma asked, "So you're staying permanently with Ada?"

"No. I've arranged to stay at Fairfax's old cottage. I'll be housemates with someone else. I haven't met him yet."

"An *Englisher?*" Levi asked.

"Yes, I think so. And don't worry there won't be parties and wild nights and drinking. This man is older and he's a quiet-living man, so Fairfax said."

"If it doesn't work out, you can always move back in with us," Ada told him.

"Thank you. I think it will be all right. I'll just be there to eat and sleep. I'm not there to become best buddies with my housemate."

"Not if he's an *Englisher,*" Wilma commented. "I'm surprised that Fairfax arranged such a thing."

"Don't fuss, *Mamm,*" Favor said. "It'll be okay. Just go with it and everything will work out."

Wilma rolled her eyes. "All the adults at the table are just trying to prevent you younger ones from making mistakes."

Cherish said, "I'm the youngest and that means we're all adults at the table. I think we should be free to make our own mistakes."

"Cherish has a point," Samuel said, earning a glare from Ada.

"How do you figure that out?" Ada asked him.

Samuel put his fork down and finished his mouthful. "People learn from mistakes. It's not believable to expect no one makes any errors during their life. We're all human."

"That's true, Samuel, but errors are painful sometimes. We're trying to stop them from having to go through that pain," Wilma said, siding with Ada.

Debbie got up and excused herself and hurried out of the room. She was closely followed by Bliss.

"Is it something I said?" Wilma asked.

Favor picked up a chicken leg and munched on it. She chewed and swallowed before saying, "They both think they've made terrible mistakes. Hey, wait. Both their mistakes involved John." Favor laughed.

"Don't laugh at the misfortunes of others," Wilma told her.

"I'm not. I'm laughing at John."

"That's worse," Wilma said.

Cherish whispered to Favor, "He's dead."

"I'm not laughing because he's dead. I just realized that they're both upset about John. That's why I laughed. I wasn't really laughing at him. You people are so judgmental."

"Don't be rude, Favor. Bliss is upset about Adam. I don't think she's upset about John," Ada said.

Wilma set her knife and fork down. "Will we ever be able to just have a happy family dinner with everyone staying at the table? It seems someone is always running off."

Samuel said, "There do seem to be a lot of arguments here. More than what we had when our children were younger."

Ada smiled. "That's right. We had happy times around our table, didn't we, Samuel?"

He nodded.

Wilma pressed her lips together and then said, "That's because girls are harder to raise than boys."

"And how would you know that, Wilma, since you only had girls?"

Cherish held her breath and looked at her mother. Was Ada forgetting about Wilma's first born—the child Wilma's sister raised?

Mamm didn't seem to notice. "That's what you told me, Ada. You said your sons were easier than your daughters."

"Did I say that?" Ada asked.

"You did."

"Oh, well it must be true. I can't recall saying it, though."

"Cherish, why don't you run upstairs and check on Debbie and Bliss?" Levi suggested.

Cherish didn't want to. She had no idea what to say to either of them to make them feel better. "Maybe they both need someone older to talk with them."

Ada laughed. "You're an adult when it suits you, it seems."

Cherish nodded. "That's true and I think both of them could use your wisdom, Ada. The wisdom that's come from all your years of life experience."

"That's true. Never send a girl to do a woman's job. Come on, Wilma. While the girls fix dessert, let's see if we can coax them downstairs to finish their meals."

Wilma and Ada left the table.

"Ada brought chocolate cake for dessert," Samuel announced.

"Wunderbaar. She's such a good cook," Matthew said.

Cherish finished off her chicken, thinking about nothing in particular.

"Are you pleased I'm staying on, Cherish?" Matthew opened his mouth and guided in his last forkful of chicken.

Cherish looked up, surprised he'd say such a thing in front of everyone. "Of course I am. Your three good deeds a day might come in handy when I need a favor."

Everyone laughed.

"I'm pleased too," said Favor. "It's someone else around here that's our age."

Matthew finished his mouthful. "Well, I am a little older than both of you."

"Are you?" Favor asked.

"I am. I'm just a late bloomer. I'll be well over six feet tall when I finish growing."

"How do you figure that?" Cherish asked. "Your brothers aren't even that tall, are they?"

"I'm not sure, but I'm taller than they were at my age. I figure... I just figured it out."

Favor's face scrunched. "When does someone finish growing?"

"Men can grow even after they're twenty," Matthew said.

"I didn't know."

"Now you do."

Cherish noticed Samuel and Levi exchange looks.

"There's nothing wrong with being short," Samuel told Matthew.

"Who's short?" Matthew asked.

"No one. I just said there's nothing wrong with it."

SAMANTHA PRICE

Matthew sat there looking a little upset. "I think we're ready for the cake now."

Cherish and Favor cleared the table of dishes and then placed the clean dessert bowls and plates on the table. Just as they were carrying the cake and the fruit salad to the table, Ada and Wilma came back into the room followed by Bliss and Debbie.

"Let's just, everyone, be happy," Wilma said. "Unwise things were said, Bliss and Debbie, and I'm sorry about that. Let's all move forward."

Ada said, "Debbie, you went to visit the twins today, didn't you?"

Debbie smiled, thinking about the babies. "I did."

"Well, have they come up with names?"

"Oh my, they're taking a long time about it," *Mamm* said.

"They have names now." Debbie got ready to address the issue about no middle names.

Wilma and Ada leaned forward and all eyes were on Debbie.

"Shall we try to guess?" Favor asked.

"No. Hush, Favor." *Mamm* glared at Favor.

Debbie took a deep breath. "Their names are Anna and Olivia."

Levi nodded. "Nice names."

"Delightful," Wilma agreed.

"I think so too. What about their middle names?" Ada asked.

Debbie shook her head. "They decided not to give them middle names."

Ada's eyes opened wide. "I'm not going to say anything about that. I already told Christina my thoughts on the matter."

144

Matthew kept eating and didn't say a word.

"What do you think, Matthew?" Samuel asked.

Matthew looked up. "About what?"

"About a middle name," Samuel said.

"Oh that. I'm not bothered."

Ada narrowed her eyes at Matthew. "You of all people should have an opinion on this."

"If they don't have a middle name then it's okay. At least they each have a name," Matthew said.

"And if they grow up and don't like their name, it's too bad. Is that right?" Ada asked. "Because they can't use their middle name like you did."

"Why does it bother you so much, Ada?" Levi asked.

"It's something that niggles me. It's not so much the name, but when I give my time to tell someone my opinion and they don't listen, it's annoying."

"Are you annoyed at me, Ada?" Debbie asked.

"I wasn't thinking about you just now, but you're right, you didn't listen to me either."

"But I did, and so did Christina. I thought about it and decided I didn't want to give Jared a middle name. Your comments made me think more about it."

"And that's her baby so it's her choice," Favor said.

Mamm glared at Favor. "You don't talk to adults like that. I've told you before. If you do that again, I won't take you to the farm with us."

"I'm Favor, *Mamm,* I'm not Cherish. Cherish is the one going to the farm."

"I know that, but I was thinking of taking you too. If you'll behave."

Favor jumped up and leaped into the air. "Really? I'd love to go somewhere—anywhere, even the farm. Do you mean it? Are you serious, Mamm?"

Mamm nodded. "If I see some decent behavior."

Favor looked over at Ada. "I'm sorry for what I said."

"I would hope so. I'm only trying to help. That's all I ever do."

"I know." Favor nodded. Then she clapped her hands before sitting back down. "I can't believe I get to go somewhere. This is so exciting."

"Can I take Caramel?" Cherish asked.

"No," *Mamm* said. "I think he'll be happier staying here. He'll take up too much room in the house."

"I'll look after him," Debbie said.

"So will I," said Samuel.

"I thought you didn't like dogs," Bliss said to Debbie.

Debbie giggled. "I know, but Caramel and I have been getting along. I'm starting to like him a little."

Cherish was pleased she had two volunteers to look after her dog. "Okay thanks. He needs a lot of attention."

"I'll look after Tommy and Timmy," Bliss said.

"Thanks, Bliss."

"We won't be gone that long. We're aiming to leave January second," Wilma said.

CHAPTER 25

*C*herish was delighted when she got a real letter from Simon, through the postal service. After she read it, she wanted someone's opinion. Her mother would only have negative things to say. Ada thought Simon was wonderful because she was friends with his parents. What she needed was to talk with someone who didn't know him. Then Cherish realized she needed to talk with Florence.

She made an excuse to leave the house and headed through the orchard to see her older half-sister.

Florence was enjoying her easier life. Fairfax, her newly appointed orchard manager was back, and it was also winter, so things were slow. That gave her time to recover from the hectic schedule. And, moving forward, things would be even better. The steel frame of the house was up and for the first time, Florence could see an end to the building work that had gone on for more than a year.

Carter had finally stopped making changes to the new house,

thanks to the architect saying he was locking in the plans and the frame had gone up, so no further changes would be accepted.

Having become used to living in the small two bedroom cottage, Florence didn't know how she'd get used to living in a six bedroom three bathroom home. It seemed such a waste to have so many bedrooms since they didn't want a lot of children. Their ideal number was two since Florence felt she'd already raised her six younger half-sisters.

Florence heard a noise outside and thought it was Carter back from his meeting in town. When Spot jumped off the couch and started barking, she knew it wasn't him.

She looked outside and there was Cherish. Florence opened the door and saw her sister had an envelope in her hand.

"Hi, Florence. What are you doing?" At that moment, Carter's car pulled up alongside the house.

"I'm waiting for Carter to come home, and here he is."

"Oh, I brought you a letter from Simon. I just want you to tell me if you think he likes me."

"Come in. Do you mind if Carter sees it?"

Cherish shrugged. "I guess not. Two opinions are better than one."

Several minutes later, Cherish, Carter and Florence were sitting down with coffee while Iris sat on a cushion watching TV.

Cherish read out her letter from Simon. After that, she looked up at them. "Well, what do you think?"

Carter frowned. "I think it's strange that he wants his parents to go to the farm with him."

"He said they're like friends more than parents."

Carter laughed. "There's a red flag right there."

"Oh, Carter." Florence shook her head.

"What do you mean?" Cherish asked.

"I got along well with my folks too, but I wouldn't have taken them somewhere with me if I was interested in a girl. I wouldn't take my friends either. Sounds like he might be too attached to them, if you know what I mean."

"I don't think it's like that."

"Neither do I. Just ignore him," Florence said.

Carter leaned back on the couch. "Ignore me at your own peril."

Cherish laughed. "So are you going to give me a lecture about old people, knowing better?"

"What old people?" Carter asked.

"She means you," Florence told him.

Carter chuckled. "No, I'm not going to give you a lecture. You can find out for yourself. You might even like a man like that. They say when you marry someone you marry their family as well. You might as well get to know them too."

"Let's not get ahead of things. I'm not marrying anyone. I do like him. I'll admit to that."

"What's so special about him?" Florence asked.

"I don't know. There's just something about him."

"I think that's called chemistry."

"And all this mushy stuff is my cue to leave. I've got work waiting for me in the kitchen." Carter stood up.

When he walked out, Cherish asked Florence, "He's cooking?"

"Not tonight. His office is also the kitchen. We're so

cramped in this house. We're going to go from having too little space to having way too much."

Cherish wasn't really listening, she was too involved with thinking about Simon. "This is the first time I've met someone that I can see a future with. I mean, I have liked some men before but they haven't been very good for one reason or another."

"You don't have to rush in. Take your time."

"I am taking my time. I don't want to make a mistake like Debbie made. I don't mean to be rude, but John wasn't very nice. I'm also shocked by Adam's attitude toward Bliss so all these things are concerning."

"I heard about Adam and Bliss. I thought they would've been back together by now."

Cherish shook her head. "I don't think it's going to happen."

"I can't believe that. I think he'll come around."

"I hope so. Anyway, what do you think of my letter?"

Florence looked down at it. "It sounds hopeful. He really likes you too so that's great."

"Don't forget what I said," Carter called out from the kitchen.

Florence whispered to Cherish, "And that's another reason we need a bigger house."

Cherish giggled. She looked at Iris, who was sitting and watching the TV. "I can't get used to it. I'd probably watch it all day too if I could. If we had one, which we never will."

"Carter and I do like watching shows at night—documentaries, nature shows, and such. Sadly, watching the TV is all that Iris seems to want. She cries until we turn it on. We never should've allowed her to watch it to start with."

"What will you do about that?"

"We've been limiting her to just an hour. We're trying to distract her with other things, but it hasn't been easy to entertain her with the weather being so cold. She loves being outside, but the weather isn't being agreeable."

"What did we do when we were that young?"

"You and your sisters played with each other, or played with simple wooden toys. You just seemed to entertain yourselves."

Cherish looked down at the letter. "I'm glad you think he likes me."

"I'm sure he does, but it's what you think of him that counts. Don't like him just because he likes you."

"I won't."

"Do you want me to make you a new dress?" Florence offered.

"You mean it?"

"Yes."

"Oh, I'd love that."

"I've got a new electric machine. I still use the treadle sometimes. It'll only take me two days to finish it."

"I can't wait. What color would be good for me?"

"How about I get the fabric, choose the color and I'll surprise you with it."

Cherish wasn't so sure about that, but Florence seemed to be so excited that she didn't want to ruin the moment. "I'd love that. I haven't had a new dress for a while. All mine are hand-me-downs. We're leaving on the second. You know what colors I like, don't you?"

"I do." Florence sighed. "I can't help but be concerned about Bliss."

Cherish leaned closer. "Did you hear why they broke up?"

"Yes. Favor told me all about it."

Cherish gritted her teeth. "It figures. She can't keep her mouth shut. She's the one who told everyone. If it weren't for her, Bliss and Adam would still be together."

"She says it was your fault for finding the letters."

Cherish shrugged her shoulders. "I can't help that. I didn't know what I would find. I was just trying to discover why Bliss and Debbie didn't get along. And, I found out."

"That's for sure."

"At least Debbie and Bliss have cleared the air now, once Debbie got over the shock of the letters."

Florence nodded. "It would've been hard for her to hear."

"It was. Thanks for letting me share my letter with you."

"Anytime and don't listen to Carter. I think it's nice that Simon wants his parents to go with him."

"Good. I'll write back and tell him his folks are very welcome. I should get back home. I just needed a quick opinion on this." She got down on the floor and said goodbye to Iris. She managed to get a smile from her.

Carter stuck his head around the corner. "Remember what I said, Cherish. You don't want someone who lets his parents lead him around by the nose. You need a man who'll stand up for you."

"I'll remember. Bye, Carter."

After Carter said goodbye, Florence walked her to the door. Then she whispered, "Don't worry about what he said. He's being overly dramatic."

"I think so too. Simon is nothing like that. Maybe he thinks his parents need a break from their farm."

"What?" Carter yelled out. "They need a break from their farm to go to another farm?"

Cherish's mouth fell open. "The sound sure does travel in this place. You do need a bigger house."

Florence laughed and then she hugged Cherish goodbye.

Cherish walked back through the orchard, concerned about what Carter had said. Then she dismissed it, reasoning that Carter was an *Englisher*. Besides, Florence agreed with her.

CHAPTER 26

When Cherish's house came into view, she was delighted to see Joy's horse and buggy by the barn. She picked up her pace, hurrying toward the house.

After she greeted Joy and Faith, Joy's daughter, *Mamm* had Cherish start peeling the vegetables for dinner. Cherish sat and peeled at one end of the table, while everyone gathered around the other end.

Joy said, "Isaac and I are looking forward to Christmas. Will Christina and Mark be coming here for the Christmas family dinner too?"

Mamm answered, "I haven't asked them yet, but I hope so. I'd love to have the new twins here to celebrate with us for our Christmas dinner."

"Christina won't be leaving the house until they're a lot older," Cherish said. "It's a lot harder with twins."

Ada suggested, "Wilma, we should get the ladies together

and visit Christina once a week. Since she can't go out, we'll come to her."

"Does that include me?" Joy asked.

"Of course it does."

"I like that idea, Ada. We'll get it organized immediately. I think Christina will appreciate it."

"I think she will too," Wilma said.

Joy raised her eyebrows. "It's a shame no one thought of that when I had Faith. I was often so lonely."

"But you were going out a couple of days after you gave birth," *Mamm* said.

"I wouldn't have had to if anyone offered to visit. No one visited me for months."

"I don't think that's true, Joy. We all visited you."

"Early on you did, but now I hardly see anyone. Anyway, what does that matter now? That was a long time ago. It's a great idea for Christina."

"Yeah, sounds like loads of fun," Cherish said.

Everyone stared at Cherish. "We don't need your sarcasm," Ada said. "It might not seem much to you, but you're spoiled. You've never been by yourself because you've always had people around you."

"I never asked for it. I can't help it."

Joy appeared to agree with Ada. "Just try to be a little more understanding of people, Cherish. It's very isolating for me when Isaac goes to work and I'm home alone all day with Faith. I can't talk with her. She's too young, so it's not the same as having an adult around."

"Sorry I said anything."

"Make us some tea, would you?" Ada asked. "And you know I like mine extra hot."

"So, do I peel the vegetables or make the tea?" Cherish asked.

"Make the tea," Ada told her. "Then you can go back to the vegetables."

Joy continued talking, "I'd love people to visit me more. I can't really get out unless I wake up super early and wake Faith too and take Isaac to work so I can have the buggy for the day."

Cherish got up to make the tea. "You sure complain a lot, Joy." Cherish hadn't meant to voice her thought. It just slipped out of her mouth.

Mamm pressed her lips together, then she said, "It's not complaining when she's just saying how she feels."

"Okay. Sorry, Joy. I didn't mean to say something wrong."

Joy looked at her mother and then Ada. "Does everyone else think I complain a lot?"

"Of course we don't." Ada patted Joy's hand. "Don't listen to Cherish. She's too young to know what she's talking about."

"I might be young, but that doesn't mean I'm unaware of things. I'm young and smart," Cherish said.

Mamm laughed. "I don't know about that. Young and loud might be more fitting."

Cherish filled up the teakettle.

"I can't believe you're taking her back to the farm, *Mamm*. You said yourself she doesn't even need to go," Joy whined. "I'll even feel more alone with you gone."

Cherish lit the gas flame and placed the teakettle on top, hoping her mother would tell Joy that she did need to go back to the farm.

"I've said I'll take her. That was before I knew about that young man that's coming there too."

"Who's that?" Joy asked.

Ada answered, "He's a delightful young man, Simon. He's a good family friend. Samuel and I have known his family for years. We just found out he doesn't live far from Cherish's farm. He's going to visit her when she's there."

"So you're helping her find a man before Favor? And what about Bliss?" Joy asked. "Surely Bliss needs more attention."

"No, Joy, you're wrong. It's nothing like that. Simon just happens to live close. I met him at Hope's wedding and after that I found out who he was and where he lives. There's nothing in it," Cherish said. "We're not dating. That's just ridiculous. He's just a friend."

"I know it is. You're far too young in the head to get married. Some say that I married young, but I think I was mature for my age." Joy looked over at Favor and Bliss who had just walked into the kitchen.

"We were just talking about you, Bliss. Come sit beside me," Ada said.

"How have you been, Bliss?" Joy asked.

"Fine."

Joy said, "I think you need to find a nice man so you can stop being upset about Adam."

"You shouldn't remind her of him," Favor told Joy.

"It's okay. Everything reminds me of Adam." Bliss let out a loud sigh.

Matthew walked into the kitchen and looked around. "Why's everyone so quiet? Were you all talking about me? Is that why you stopped talking just now?"

Ada laughed and everyone else smiled. "No. We're just having our usual disagreements over one thing or another."

Matthew looked at Cherish. "Ah, making coffee, are you?"

"I can make you a cup. Why aren't you at the saddlery store?"

"I've finished for the day. Mark is working the last two hours."

"I do worry about Christina by herself with the twins," Ada said.

"Don't worry. She's not by herself. Mark said Krystal was there, helping her this afternoon."

"Krystal?" Favor asked.

"Yes."

"She didn't tell me she was helping Christina. She's supposed to be working in the quilt store," Favor said.

"I don't know where she's supposed to be, but right now she's with Christina. That's what Mark said and he'd know."

Ada clasped her hands and set them on the table. "I'm glad the girl is making herself useful. Yes, she made mistakes with the lying and whatnot, but she's turned a corner as far as I'm concerned. Gertie is happy with her and she's a hard woman to please."

Cherish knew there was only one reason that Krystal was helping anyone. She wanted all the single men to think she was a good Christian woman, who worked tirelessly to help others. It couldn't be further from the truth as Cherish perceived it. Krystal was working tirelessly to help one person and one person alone. That person was Krystal.

CHAPTER 27

Three days after Florence had agreed to make her a dress, Cherish went back to check on the progress. She took Bliss with her to get her out of the house and keep her mind occupied.

With Bliss on one side and Caramel on her other side, Cherish nearly skipped through the orchard. "I haven't had a new dress in years. A good one, I mean. Florence is an excellent seamstress. When she was still living at home, she used to make all the clothes for the family. We still wear many of those dresses."

"Sounds like they were made to last, handed from older sister to the younger sisters."

"You've got that right. Sadly, I was the youngest and many of the clothes got all worn out by the time they came down to me."

"I never had that problem with two older brothers."

"That's right, you're the only girl."

"I was until I joined your family."

"I hope I look good in the new dress. Simon might appreciate me looking pretty."

They walked through the orchard and then she slipped through the fence that divided the two properties, helped Bliss get through without her clothes catching, and they walked up to the door and knocked on it.

Carter answered the door and stared at Cherish. "You're back, and you've brought Bliss."

"I sure am back. I believe Florence has been sewing a dress for me."

"Yes I think so."

Iris came running toward her, reaching her chubby arms towards her. Cherish leaned down and scooped the little girl into her arms. "Good morning, Iris. Can you say Aunt Cherish? Aunt Cherish is my favorite?"

"Hey unfair," Bliss said. "What about me?"

Carter laughed. "I'll just get her for you. She's upstairs."

"Cherish is my favorite. Say it."

Iris made an attempt at saying it.

"Pretty good. We can work on it."

"Come to me," Bliss said, clapping her hands.

Iris looked over and reached out her hands to Bliss.

"Oh, you're leaving me," Cherish said, "You're my favorite too, but don't tell anybody."

Florence came downstairs and Cherish looked up to see a dark pinkish-red, almost magenta, dress in her half-sister's hands.

"Wow. It's bright," Bliss blurted out.

"Oh no, I was worried about that. Is it too bright?" Florence asked.

"No. I think I'll be able to get away with it," Cherish said.

Iris struggled, so Bliss put her on the floor just as Florence handed the dress to Cherish.

"Do you want to try it on?"

Cherish held it against herself. "I think this looks about right." Then Cherish had a closer look at the dress. "I wish I was as good at sewing as this."

"You could be. All you need to do is practice. I've shown you how to sew many a time."

"I know that."

"All you have to do is put your mind to something and practice it. If you keep doing it over and over again, you'll get good at it," Bliss said.

"That's right. That's all I did," Florence agreed.

"Yes, but I don't like putting effort into anything."

Florence laughed. "Are you serious?"

"Kind of."

"What you need to do is find something that you enjoy doing and then you'll be happy to put the effort into it until you become good at it."

Cherish shrugged her shoulders. "I know, that's what everybody says."

"Really? I don't like to be the same as everybody else. Who says that?"

"Mostly Ada, I think."

"Are you sure you don't want to try it on, Cherish?" Bliss asked.

"No, that's okay. I'll put it on when I get home. I'm sure it will fit."

"I think it will too. Are you sure the color's all right? I can make you another one before you go to the farm."

"It's perfect."

"I thought it suited your personality. When I saw it in the fabric store, I couldn't resist it."

Cherish leaned forward and gave her a hug. "It's simply perfect."

"Good. I hope it does the job."

"What job?" Bliss asked.

"You know, what we were talking about on the way here."

"Oh that." Bliss giggled. "I hope it does the job too, then."

Cherish gave a nervous laugh. "We'll see. Anyway, it doesn't hurt to have another friend, does it? Simon will be a good friend at the very least."

"Yes, at your age, that's all you need to be worried about. There will be plenty of time for boyfriends." Florence smiled at her, raising her eyebrows. It was something *Mamm* did when she was trying to assure her of something. It was the first time Florence had reminded her of *Mamm*.

Cherish nodded. "That's what everyone says. *Mamm* says it the most."

"Oh no, again? Seems I'm becoming boring and predictable."

Cherish stared at her, not knowing what to say. Florence had always been boring and predictable, as far back as she could remember. "That's what comes from being the older sister," she said.

"Yes well, I suppose it does. When are you leaving?" Florence asked.

"Not until after Christmas. On the second of January, *Mamm* says. Unless she can't get a car for that day."

"That's right. You told me the date when you were here the other day. Have a good time there."

"I always do."

"Say hello to Malachi for me," Florence said.

Cherish rolled her eyes.

"Why did you do that?" Bliss asked.

Cherish shrugged her shoulders. "I forgot about Malachi."

Florence folded her arms. "How could you forget about your farm manager?"

"I've been too busy thinking about Simon, I guess. Oh and then I'll probably have to put up with Annie Whiley as well."

"Don't you get along with her?" Florence asked.

"She's okay I guess. But Malachi and she are way too friendly. I think they're dating, but he denies it. I still think they are."

Florence laughed. "Did you ask him?"

"Of course I did. Like I said, he denied it. Thanks for the dress. Now I'll have to go somewhere nice while I'm at the farm so I get a chance to wear it."

"What about the Sunday meeting while you're away?" Bliss suggested.

"I will wear it if we're going to be there for it. *Mamm* doesn't want to go for a whole week, so we might miss out. They have fortnightly meetings there, same as here."

Florence looked at Bliss. "I'm sorry to hear about you and Adam."

"Thanks. It's okay. I'm getting used to it now."

"You don't think there's—"

"No chance at all. We should go, Cherish."

"Yes, we should. We've got a lot to do. Thanks again, Florence. I love the dress. It's amazing."

"You're welcome."

Carter came out from the kitchen. "Do come and tell us all about your trip when you get back."

"I will."

CHAPTER 28

*W*ith her dress over her arm, Cherish walked into the utility room to get a hanger.

Mamm looked up from the kitchen table where she was drinking tea with Ada. "What's that you've got there, Cherish?"

"A new dress. Florence made it for me to wear if we go anywhere special while we're at the farm."

"We've got Christmas to get through first." Wilma stared at Cherish. "Why did you want a new dress?"

"She offered to make me one."

Wilma pursed her lips. "As a Christmas gift?"

Cherish slipped the dress onto the hanger. "I'm not sure. She didn't say so. She just asked if I wanted her to make me one, and I said yes. I haven't had anything new for so long."

"No point in you having anything new when your sisters' old clothes fit you just as well."

"By the time they come down to me, they're all worn out."

"I know that happens sometimes, that's why you've had new

clothes in the past. We just can't give you new things all the time," *Mamm* said.

"I understand that, *Mamm,* and I'm not complaining."

Ada's lips turned down at the corners. "You're certainly doing a lot of talking about it though."

"*Mamm* started it so I was just explaining what happened. Should I be silent next time?"

"Ah, silence. What I'd give for a whole day of silence. That would be golden." Ada put her teacup up to her lips and took a sip.

Cherish was tempted to tell her to go home if she wanted silence, but she was too scared of Ada to say that.

"We'll never have silence, Ada. I'm fine with that. I'm determined to enjoy as much of Favor and Cherish as I can before they leave us," *Mamm* said.

Ada huffed. "You can't keep them here."

Cherish said, "I will be moving to the farm. You'll have to get used to the idea of that, *Mamm.*"

"When?" Ada asked.

"In a year. I'll be way over eighteen by then."

Mamm frowned. "Way over? Hardly. Only by a few months."

"Still. You can enjoy me for a year, *Mamm.*" Cherish put the dress on the table and sat down with them.

"You might change your mind. What is there at the farm for you? Just keep Malachi there and he can run the farm for you," *Mamm* suggested.

"*Nee.* That ruins the whole point of having the farm."

"Let her try it out, Wilma. She'll be home in no time once she realizes how hard it is."

"No I won't. I know what it's like there—I lived there,

remember? Helping Aunt Dagmar with all of the work. I know I might get lonely, but Favor or Bliss might want to move there."

"I don't think so. Bliss will be back with Adam before long. I just know it," Ada said. "And I don't think Favor will leave this community or her family and her friends to live at your farm."

Cherish shrugged. "I'll go by myself then."

"I think you'll have to. And then I think you won't be there for long before you decide to come back."

"It's not that isolated. Simon doesn't live that far."

"Too far to go there and back in one day."

"He can stay overnight. He's bringing his parents. I got a letter from him and he said when he visits, he's bringing them. So they'll be staying at the farm too."

"I'll be pleased to meet them. And there are enough bedrooms in the house, aren't there, Cherish?" Ada asked.

"There are five bedrooms. One for Malachi, one for Simon, one for Simon's parents, Favor and I can share, and that still leaves one for you, *Mamm.*"

Ada counted them up on her fingers. "That's five."

"I know."

"How long will they be staying?" *Mamm* asked.

"I'm not sure. I didn't ask. It doesn't matter, does it?"

"No. We'll take enough supplies from here to feed everyone."

Cherish shrugged. "Okay, if you want, but there will be enough food on the farm."

"Still, I like to be sure. I can't have anyone going hungry."

"It is lovely and peaceful on your farm, Cherish. I have enjoyed my visits there," Ada said.

"Good."

Ada stared at the dress. "That's very bright."

"But not too bright, is it?"

Ada smiled. "I like it. What do you say, Wilma?"

"Well, since Cherish didn't ask my opinion, it hardly matters."

Cherish had to ask, "What do you think, *Mamm?*"

"I like it. It's a happy color, for a girl who's becoming a lady, but not too quickly." *Mamm* stared at Cherish, as though she was trying to make a point.

"What will Malachi do when you move back there?" Ada asked, still talking about the farm.

"I'm not sure. We haven't discussed it. He knows I'm coming back. Perhaps this time, I'll tell him exactly when I'm coming back so he can start making plans."

"Good idea," Ada said. "Just don't leave yourself without a manager."

Cherish had it all figured out. "It won't matter. If he leaves earlier, I'll have to move there. I'm old enough to move there now, but I'm staying on here for you, *Mamm.*"

"Aren't you lucky, Wilma?" Ada said. "*Gott* is blessing you with your loving daughter for an extra year."

"I know." Wilma laughed as she got up and topped up the water in the teakettle. Then she lit the stove and placed the kettle on top.

"Will you take your birds with you, Cherish?" Ada asked just as *Mamm* sat down with them.

"Of course I will. I'll be taking everything with me. Timmy, Tommy, and Caramel."

Ada grunted. "It'll certainly be quiet without you. That's all I'm saying on the matter. But, as I said before, you might go there and find you don't like it and then you'll move back here. Then the best thing you could do is sell the farm."

Cherish sat there looking at Ada. "I'm never selling the farm. It was Aunt Dagmar's."

"Yes, but she wouldn't expect you to have a tough life away from your family. She'd be happy if you're happy."

"And I will be happy at the farm. I've always said I'm moving there. I think that everybody has to get used to that idea." There was a silent moment where Cherish stared at each woman in turn. She had thought they'd get used to the idea by now. She'd been telling them what she was going to do for the past few years.

Ada took a deep breath. "We hear you, but the reality of it all will be very different from the story you're telling yourself about it. Yes you were there with Dagmar, but I'm sure you didn't see everything she was doing every day. It'll take a lot of hard work. And like I said before, there are always house repairs and barn repairs."

"I'm figuring that out. It can't be that hard. It's just a matter of learning what to do." Cherish offered a bright smile to show them that they weren't discouraging her in the slightest.

"Don't bother, Ada. She's someone who can't be told anything. She'll have to find out for herself."

"That's right. I'll find out for myself, so what's all the fuss?" Cherish asked.

Ada shrugged her shoulders. "I'm just trying to save you some pain."

"Thanks for the thought."

The kettle whistled. "Who's making the tea?" Ada asked. "I need another cup before Wilma and I start sewing the quilt.

This one has gone cold. Cherish, you can make the tea because you made me talk so much that I neglected to drink this cup."

"I'll get it." Cherish got up and turned toward the pot that had just boiled. She took the kettle off the stove and poured the water into the teapot.

"Did you put tea leaves in the pot?" Wilma asked.

"No. I didn't. You were talking too much."

"So it's my fault?" Wilma complained.

"Kind of."

"Why don't we try some of Debbie's tea, Wilma?"

"That's right. I must have been thinking you might want to try some of Debbie's tea and that's why I didn't put your usual tea leaves in right away."

Ada and Wilma laughed at her, and she soon joined in.

Cherish picked up a jar from Debbie's selection of teas. "The lemon tea was the most popular when we did the tasting."

"Have we tried the lemon, Wilma?"

"No. I haven't, anyway."

"Lemon it is then." Cherish shook in some tea leaves.

"Use a spoon," Ada ordered.

"Too late. Now, I'll let that sit for a while."

Ada shook her head. "You know I like it hot."

"It'll be hot." Cherish went to the shelf for a clean towel and wrapped it tightly around the teapot.

"I hope so. That's a good idea—wrapping it up, I mean."

CHAPTER 29

*A*fter she made Ada and Wilma another pot of tea, Cherish took her new dress upstairs to her bedroom. While she was hanging it up, Favor walked in the door.

"Was this your idea about me going to the farm, Cherish?" She sat on the bed.

"No, because I didn't think *Mamm* would let you. You know how she's always going on about us doing work and all that."

"I know. We'll have such fun."

"I know it. I'm so excited. I'm glad you're coming." Cherish was in such a good mood, almost nothing could ruin it.

"You're always talking about the farm and I've never seen it. I might even move there with you when I'm older."

"I'd love that. You can tell me what you think about Malachi. I guess you'll meet Annie Whiley too. She'll probably be hanging around talking about her gingerbread houses. Oh, I shouldn't be mean. She really is a nice girl. I'll make more of an effort to get to know her this time."

"I already met Annie at Hope's wedding."

Cherish sat on the bed next to Favor. "Oh that's right. It's weird that she was there at the wedding, don't you think?"

"Not really."

"I thought it was odd. She only knew me and Samuel and Ada. It was just an excuse to get Malachi to go somewhere with her, but it backfired because he didn't show up at all."

"He couldn't, could he? Who would've looked after the farm?"

"I don't know. One of his friends perhaps. He could've arranged something just for a few days."

"Why do you keep talking about Malachi when you like Simon?"

Cherish lifted her chin. "I do like Simon. I don't like Malachi at all. I don't know why you said that."

"Then what does my opinion on him matter?"

"It doesn't."

Favor sniggered. "Yeah right."

"Don't be annoying like that or I'll tell *Mamm* not to take you to the farm."

"Too late. She already said I could go. I wonder if she'll let Krystal go too. There would be enough room in the car."

"No. I don't want Krystal to go because you'll spend all your time with her and leave me out of everything."

"We wouldn't do that."

"Yes you would. You've done that ever since Krystal arrived."

"I suppose she has to stay here and work in the quilt store anyway. All right. We'll have fun together like we used to."

"That's right. She does." Cherish pointed to her dress. "What do you think about that?"

Favor stared at the dress. "It's beautiful. How did you get that?"

"Florence made it for me."

Favor's mouth fell open. "Where's mine?"

"Is she making you one too?"

"I don't know. If she made you one she should make me one."

"She offered to make it because she knew I was going to the farm and I'd see Simon."

"Unfair." Favor pouted. "I'm going to the farm too. I might meet some nice man."

"She would've made you one if she had known. I'm sure…"

"It doesn't matter, I'll just borrow yours."

"No you won't! That's my special dress. It's my new Sunday best."

"Such a pretty color. I want one just like that."

"I'd love that and then we'd be matching. Ask Florence to make you one when we get back."

"I sure will."

CHAPTER 30

*A*t daybreak on Christmas morning, Wilma sat by herself watching the winter sun rise over the tops of the apple trees. Over her first cup of coffee for the day, she pondered the events of the past year.

So much had happened.

Debbie had come to live with them and they had the added surprise of baby Jared, being a product of a secret marriage. That had been a tumultuous ride for poor Debbie, having to keep quiet about the marriage to her late husband so she wouldn't offend his parents.

Then there was the pleasant addition of Fairfax to their family after marrying Hope. A big surprise and a double blessing was Mark and Christina's twins.

There was also the *wunderbaar* news that Earl and Miriam would be parents of twins at some stage next year. Wilma smiled as she looked forward to the day she'd meet Earl's twins. She felt bad about cautioning both Earl and Miriam that Miriam would be too old to have babies. Miriam had proved her wrong and, for once, Wilma was pleased to be wrong.

The year had brought some disappointment though, with Adam Wengerd turning away from Bliss. Hopefully, they'd reconcile soon and their rocky time would just be like a pothole in the journey of their relationship.

For now, Wilma was determined to enjoy the remaining girls left at home. She wasn't in a hurry for them to marry. The house would be way too quiet once they were all gone. She feared being left alone, and with Levi's heart problems, she knew being alone in the future was a real possibility for her.

When Wilma heard noises coming from upstairs, her mind started ticking over about traveling to Cherish's farm. She had to know how serious Cherish was about Simon. If he wasn't right for her, she wanted to be there to prevent Cherish from making an impulsive decision. That was the real reason she agreed to go to the farm this time. That and, she'd have extra time to spend with both Cherish and Favor. It would be a good time for her to reconnect with her youngest daughters.

Wilma poured herself a second coffee and stayed by the stove to warm herself. It had been a mild winter so far and she hoped the weather would remain that way for their drive to the farm. There was nothing worse than traveling in a blizzard.

Today, Christina had promised they would come with the twins, and Florence and Carter and Iris had been invited too, although Wilma wasn't sure that either couple would come. Anything with the twins might prevent Christina and Mark coming at the last minute. Florence and Carter's invitation had been late-notice. They'd never come to any other Christmas dinners, so Wilma held out little hope they'd come today.

An hour later, the girls were awake and in the kitchen helping to prepare the food. This year as well as the traditional turkey, she had decided on roasted chicken, stuffing, mashed potatoes and gravy, salads and a wide variety of desserts for the menu. Ada was cooking a pork roast with apple sauerkraut, and she was also bringing a couple of her specialty desserts. Hope was bringing salads and Joy was bringing her special apple custard dessert that everyone loved.

ADA, Matthew and Samuel arrived well before one in the afternoon, which was when the special meal was scheduled. Ada burst into the kitchen followed by Samuel and Matthew. "Whoopie pies and chocolate chip cookies. Put the boxes on the counter," Ada told the men. Then she greeted Wilma with a kiss. "I tried to do a gingerbread house but it fell flat again. I can't work out what I'm doing wrong. I need another lesson from Annie and her mother. Looks like I'll have to take you to the farm sometime next year, Cherish, so I can do just that."

"That would be great."

Favor whined, "She's already getting to go there in a few days. If you take her, that'll be twice in one year. Will I be able to go with her?"

"We'll see," *Mamm* said.

Bliss told Favor, "Just be pleased you're going this time."

Favor pouted at her, but Bliss kept setting the table without noticing.

Closer to one o'clock, Christina arrived bringing two store-bought cakes. Wilma was delighted to share Christmas with her stepson and his wife, and especially with their newborn twins.

Hope and Fairfax arrived at almost the same time, along with Joy, Isaac, and Faith. Their food offerings were brought into the kitchen amidst a flurry of greetings and hugs and hanging of coats.

Just before the meal was due to start, Wilma stepped out of the house and looked up the road. There was no sign of Florence and Florence was never late. That meant she wasn't coming.

Cherish stuck her head outside. "They only said they might come, *Mamm.*"

"I know."

"Carter said they're not that big on Christmas."

Wilma nodded. "I understand." Wilma headed back to the kitchen, thinking about her two eldest daughters, who lived too far away to come to family events.

Debbie sensed what was going on and put her arm around Wilma. "Just be happy with who is here rather than who isn't."

Tears filled Wilma's eyes. "Thank you, Debbie. You're right. I'm happy to share this day with everyone here."

Ada sighed as she looked at the table. "A gingerbread house would've made a delightful decoration for the center. Perhaps next year."

Cherish grinned. "There's always next year."

"Next year," Timmy said.

"Oh, did you hear that, everyone? Who heard that? Timmy clearly said next year." Cherish ran over to Timmy. "Oh, good boy, Timmy. Who's a pretty boy?"

Ada laughed. "I did hear something similar but it wasn't that clear."

"I heard it," Debbie said. "I thought it was clear."

Once Christina had fed the twins and they were both asleep, Wilma then called everyone to the table. "I hope everyone's hungry."

"We sure are," Matthew rubbed his tummy. "I've been saving up. I didn't eat breakfast."

Once seated, Mark looked over at Faith who sat by herself at a small children's table. "Next year, we'll have a few more children sitting at that table."

Ada gasped. "Oh, Christina, you're not having another baby, are you?"

Mark laughed and answered for her, "No. I meant our two might be sitting there. They should be sitting up by then."

"Give us a chance, Ada." Christina laughed.

When everyone settled, they closed their eyes and said their silent prayer of thanks.

AFTER EVERYONE HAD their fill of the main course and the desserts, Levi announced,

"Ladies, I'd have to say this is the best meal I've ever tasted. Thank you. And, the company's not been bad either."

"I agree," said Samuel.

"Me too," added Matthew, patting his tummy.

"Thanks for inviting us," Mark said.

"You're always welcome. You don't have to be invited, just show up," Wilma told him.

"For once, I feel this family cares about me. I know you all did before the twins came, but I had... I was too upset in my own grief to open my eyes to what was really going on," Christina said. "I don't know how Mark and I would've coped with the twins without the help and support from everyone at this table. I know other women have babies and can do all kinds of things and get back to normal fast, but it's taken me a long time."

"That's what happens with twins," Ada said. "It's not as easy as one. We've moved passed all our disagreements now, Christina. We're heading into a new year with new possibilities."

"Agreed," Wilma said. "We're grateful for both of you and the twins."

Mark smiled. *"Denke,* Wilma. I can't believe we have two babies. I'm still getting used to the idea I'm a *vadder* to two girls."

"The Lord has blessed each one of us," Samuel said.

"He has," Levi agreed.

While they all sat there, too full to move away from the table, Matthew had a suggestion.

"I know a game we could all play."

"What kind of game is that?" Ada asked.

"We will each be given a name of somebody sitting at this table. And without saying who we are, we have to talk and act like that person and then everybody else has to guess. The first person to guess gets a point. The person with the most points is the winner."

"That'll be easy," said Hope. "What's the prize?"

"Um, I hadn't thought of a prize. I don't have one."

"I might have an extra box of candies hidden away some-where," Ada said.

"Excellent!" Samuel grinned. "The winner can have a box of candy."

Favor clapped her hands loudly until Cherish poked her side to make her stop.

"Okay. I'll need a piece of paper and a pen," Matthew said.

Wilma had Cherish fetch the paper and a pencil from the kitchen drawer.

Matthew wrote everybody's names down and then ripped the paper into sections. He mixed up the pieces in a bowl and took it around to everybody so they could select a name.

"When you get the name, don't show anyone." He sat back down.

"Who'll start first?" asked Wilma.

"Why don't you go first, Wilma?" Matthew said.

"Okay. What do I do? Can I stand up and walk around?"

"Yes, you can do whatever you want," Matthew told her. "Just act like the person whose name's on the bit of paper."

Wilma stood, pulled her shoulders back and lifted up her chin. "What are we going to do today? I am so bored. Nothing ever happens around here. *Mamm,* stop being mean to Timmy and Tommy."

Everyone yelled out, "Cherish."

Wilma smiled and showed everyone the paper that said Cherish.

Matthew laughed. "Good guess. I think Favor was the first one to say Cherish's name. One point to Favor." He wrote that down on his notepad.

Favor clapped her hands. "Yes, I was first."

"Do you think I really act like that, *Mamm?*" Cherish pouted.

Ada leaned forward. "It's not only your mother who thinks that. Everyone else does too."

"Okay who's next? It's you, Samuel."

Samuel looked at his bit of paper. Then he stood up, adjusted his imaginary prayer *kapp,* frowned at everyone, and then gave an exaggerated giggle and clapped his hands loudly.

"Favor," Cherish shouted out.

"Ow, my ear, Cherish," Favor complained.

Cherish loved this game. Now she had one point and Favor had one. "I got that first. Write a point down for me, Matthew."

"This is fun," said Hope.

"How did you know about this game?" Ada asked Matthew.

"We played it a couple of times at home."

Then it was Cherish's turn. She had Ada. She got up off the chair and walked to the door. Then she walked towards the table with her shoulders hunched. Speaking in a crotchety voice, she said, "Wilma, why aren't the girls doing any work? You're not hard enough on them. Cherish, make me a cup of tea and make sure it's hot. You know I like it hot."

Everyone laughed and Samuel was the first to say it was Ada, earning a glare from his wife. She was the only one who didn't think it was funny.

"I don't talk like that, Cherish, and I certainly don't walk like that. I'm short so I make sure I stand tall."

Cherish delighted in saying, "Everyone guessed you, so..."

Ada scoffed. "That's ridiculous."

Matthew looked at Favor. "Your turn."

Favor let out a big yawn and covered her mouth and then said in a deep voice, "No, Bliss, you can't work at the café. I don't care that Cherish works there. Where's my paper? Has anyone seen it?"

"Levi!" everyone shouted before they chuckled.

Matthew scratched his head. "That's a hard one. I can't tell who was first."

"I think Hope was first with that one," *Mamm* said.

"Okay, Hope it is."

"I was before Hope," said Favor.

Hope shook her head. "I was the first."

"It should've been you, Bliss," Cherish said. "You should've guessed that one."

Bliss nodded, and her lips turned upwards at the corners. Although she was smiling, she wasn't happy. Adam loved Christmas and he hadn't come to see her. She'd spent most of the day looking out the window, in the hope that he'd at least come there to say hello.

Bliss thought back to the last Christmas dinner she'd shared with Adam. They'd had such fun… but things were different now. It was hard to be happy and join in the fellowship and the laughter when her heart was broken into tiny pieces.

She looked at how happy Hope and Fairfax were. Then she saw Joy and Isaac with their young daughter, and Christina and Mark with their twins. Why had her happiness escaped from her?

Adam should've been there with her.

What plan did God have for her life that didn't include Adam? Bliss tried not to be bitter but she couldn't understand what God was doing.

When Jared cried upstairs, Bliss saw her chance to escape

the fake smiles she'd been offering all day. "I'll check on him, Debbie."

"Would you? He's been fed. He might need his diaper changed. Then he should go back to sleep. He always sleeps longer than this."

"Okay."

"Are you sure?" Debbie asked.

"Quite sure. You stay." Bliss headed out of the room. As she headed up the stairs, the laughter got farther and farther away. She didn't belong with happy people. She felt better when she was alone. If Adam had any thoughts in the back of his head about reconciliation, he would've come to say hello, today of all days.

AT THE END of the guessing game, it was Favor who won the box of candies. She squealed with delight as Ada handed the box over. Then she opened it and shared it with everyone, but not everyone had any room left after the huge meal and the sumptuous desserts.

It was late afternoon when Christina and Mark left, followed quickly by Isaac and Joy.

The men were too full to move, so they stayed in the kitchen while everyone else cleaned up around them. After that, Favor and Cherish headed upstairs to share some candies with Bliss. Everyone knew she was still upset over Adam and the girls were determined to take her mind off him.

CHAPTER 31

Christmas had come and gone and the New Year arrived quietly. Today, Cherish, Wilma and Favor were leaving for the farm. Samuel, Ada and Matthew had come to the house early to say goodbye.

Cherish was already packed and was upstairs making her bed. Everyone else was gathered around the fire in the living room, waiting for the car to arrive.

"We'll miss you, *Mamm,* but don't worry, everything will be fine. We're taking more meals to Christina and we'll look after *Dat,*" Bliss said.

"I'm not worried. I know you'll handle everything."

Favor said, "Thanks for letting me go too, *Mamm.*"

"Well, you haven't been anywhere for a while. None of us have been anywhere since Earl and Miriam's wedding."

"You've been up north to see Honor and Mercy, Wilma. Did you forget that?" Ada asked.

"I meant, I've been away, but the girls haven't."

Cherish was even more excited when she looked out her window and saw the car. The day had finally arrived and now the car was here, so for sure her mother wouldn't change her mind about going.

"Cherish, the car's here," Favor called out.

"I'm coming." Cherish hugged Caramel, who was asleep on her bed. "You be a good boy. Debbie is going to look after you and so will Bliss. And just between you and me, I've got Samuel checking up on them because he did such a good job of looking after you when I went to Earl and Miriam's wedding. I'll miss you."

He opened his eyes and gave her a lick up the side of her chin.

"Yuck." She wiped her cheek with the back of her hand.

"Cherish, we're paying the driver by the hour. Hurry up!" *Mamm* yelled out.

"Coming." Cherish grabbed her suitcase and headed out of the room. Debbie was at the bottom of the stairs, holding the baby. Cherish looked down at Jared. "Don't grow too fast while I'm gone."

Debbie laughed. "You'll be gone for less than a week."

"Unless I can talk *Mamm* into staying longer."

"Bye, Cherish. Have a good time."

"I will. Oh, you see your tea man today, don't you? I hope that goes well." Cherish hurried to the door. "Good luck with that, today, Debbie."

"She needs prayer, not luck." Levi held the front door open for Cherish.

"That's true. I'll pray about it as soon as I get into the car."

"Thanks, Cherish," Debbie said.

Then Cherish stepped out to the porch where Bliss and the others were waiting. The driver took the suitcase from Cherish and closed it into the trunk.

Before she got in the car, Cherish turned around and saw Bliss's face. She looked so sad. Cherish whispered to her mother, "Can't we take Bliss too?"

"Does she want to come?" *Mamm* asked.

"I guess so."

"There's enough room in the car," Favor said.

"Well, ask her," *Mamm* said to Cherish.

Cherish turned around. "Bliss, do you want to come with us?"

Bliss's mouth fell open. "Can I?"

Mamm called out, "You can if you can pack your things in two minutes."

"I'll do it." Bliss hurried into the house.

Cherish was delighted and ran behind her. "I'll help."

"It's okay, I can do it."

Cherish remembered she hadn't said goodbye to Tommy and Timmy. She stopped and changed direction and headed to the birds.

She had Bliss looking after them, but now she was coming with them. Matthew walked up beside her. "Matthew, you'll have to look after the birds. Samuel will show you what to do. You have to be here every day."

"Every single day?"

"Yes. Will you do that please? Bliss was going to do it, but now she's coming with us."

"Okay."

"Thank you. Bye, Timmy and Tommy. I'll miss you." She put

her hand in the cage and stroked each bird. Then she heard Bliss running back down the stairs.

"I'm ready," Bliss called out. "Oh, I can't go, Cherish."

"Why not?"

"The café. I'm taking your shift."

"It's only one shift. They'll be able to find someone else. Ask Levi to call them and tell them you won't be able to make it. They've got three days to find someone else. That's plenty of time."

"Okay." Bliss hurried out to talk with her father, then Cherish turned her attention to Matthew.

"Have you talked to Andrew yet?"

He rubbed his head. "Not yet."

Cherish huffed. "You've had ages to do it. It's been weeks since you agreed you'd do it."

"I will."

"When?"

"Um… very soon."

"Do it today." When he didn't say anything, she added, "Do you have anything else to do today?"

"No."

Samuel looked around the kitchen doorway. "Your mother's getting anxious."

"I'm coming right now. Matthew has agreed to look after the birds. Will you show him what to do?"

"Of course."

"I'll do it today, Cherish," Matthew whispered.

"Good." Cherish walked out, hoping she hadn't forgotten anything. Everyone was gathered on the porch and Cherish saw Bliss was already in the car, in the front seat.

"Be sure to look after Bliss. Don't ignore her," Levi said quietly as Cherish walked past him.

"I won't. I'm surprised she agreed to go. I thought she'd want to stay here in case Adam changes his mind."

"It's good that she's going," Ada whispered. "Try to keep her busy."

"Okay." After Cherish said a second goodbye to everyone and even said goodbye to the house, the horses, and the apple trees, she opened the back door to sit next to Wilma.

"I'm not sitting in the middle," Wilma said. "You go in the middle."

Wilma got out of the car so Cherish could get in. Cherish ended up being sandwiched between her mother and Favor. Now there was nowhere to put her head. Normally, on a long drive, she'd snuggle down and go to sleep. But, she couldn't complain too much because at least she was finally going back to the farm.

"I never thought so many of us would be going. We've left the house in the hands of Debbie and Levi."

"Ada will be around to help out. Matthew said he'd look after the birds and Samuel said the other day that he'd check on Caramel," Cherish said.

Bliss turned around. "Don't worry, *Mamm*. I'm sure everyone will be fine. Hope will be close by too if anyone needs a hand with anything."

An hour into the journey, Wilma told them, "I got a letter from Simon's parents the other day. They asked us to stop at their farm on the way. Since we drive through their town I said that we would."

Cherish grabbed hold of her mother's arm. "Wait. You got a letter from Simon's parents?"

"I did. I was leaving it for a surprise. Don't you like surprises?"

"No," Favor and Cherish said at the same time.

"How do they even know you?" asked Bliss.

"I've never met them, but when Ada found out I was going back to the farm, she called them and they reached out to me by letter. They have a phone in their barn like we do, so I called them and spoke to Harriet."

"You could've told me." Cherish looked down at the old clothes she was wearing. If she'd known she was going to meet Simon's parents today, she would've made more of an effort with her appearance. She might've even worn her new Sunday best that Florence had made.

"Oh, that'll be so boring. We'll have to sit in their stuffy house and be bored while you all talk nonsense about nothing in particular. We'll eat stale cake and drink lukewarm tea instead of hot tea. We don't even know these people," Favor said.

"We will know them after today. Besides, we know Simon, and his parents are good friends of Ada and Samuel."

Favor groaned. "Can't they just visit us at the farm like Cherish had already arranged? Why do we need to meet them before that? It's just a waste of time and it'll be dark when we get to the farm. I want to see all the animals."

"Hush," *Mamm* said. "It's all been arranged. So, you can be happy about it or suffer in silence. I don't care which."

Favor wasn't finished talking about it. "I'll just say this, I thought we were paying the driver by the hour. Visiting them will add to the time."

"We are, but we won't be there for long."

Cherish thought about it a little more. "I'm excited to meet Simon's parents. He keeps telling me how close he is with them."

Mamm said, "I guess that's what happens when you're an only child."

"I would like to have been an only child," Favor said.

"Thanks very much. What would happen to me then?" Cherish asked.

"You never would've been born. Aunt Dagmar would've left the farm to me, so your farm would be my farm."

"Or perhaps Florence's farm," Wilma said with a laugh. "Or was Florence not born either in your imaginings?"

"That's right. Just me. No siblings and no half siblings."

"Just lots of weird pen pals," Cherish added.

Favor opened her mouth in shock. "You're so mean."

"So are you. You're sad that I was born, and what about Bliss? Do you even want a stepsister at all?" Cherish asked.

Mamm raised her hand. "Stop this nonsense at once, girls. Is this what's going to happen at the farm? If it is, I'll bang both of your heads together to knock some sense into you."

Bliss sat in the front, saying nothing at all.

CHAPTER 32

*B*ack in Lancaster County, Matthew tried to sneak out of his aunt's house. He was nervous about speaking to Adam's business partner, but he was more nervous thinking what Cherish would do if she found out he hadn't done what he'd promised.

He was halfway out the door, when he heard Aunt Ada's voice.

"What are you doing today, Matthew?"

He stopped and moved back inside and saw his aunt sitting by the fire, knitting. "I've got a free day. I'm not working at the saddlery store and I'm not starting at the orchard for several weeks."

She looked him up and down. "I heard you ask Samuel if you could borrow the buggy. Mind telling me where you're going?"

He looked down. "I can't really say."

"Sit!" Ada ordered, patting the chair next to her.

Reluctantly, he walked over and sat down.

"Now, tell me why you don't want to tell me anything. Does it involve a young lady, hmm?"

"Yes. Well, maybe, but not a young lady for me. A young lady for someone else."

Ada looked up at the ceiling. "So you're going to visit a young lady on behalf of someone else?"

"Not exactly."

Her head snapped around and her eyes bore through his. "Then what?"

"I'd rather not say." He had thought he could slip away unnoticed. She'd never been this interested in where he was going before today.

"What's the secrecy? I'm your aunt. You're nearly like my own son. If something's wrong. I should know about it."

Matthew shrugged his shoulders. If she kept going on like this, he'd have no choice but to tell her. "It's nothing that's wrong. It's just that I'm trying to do something to help some people."

"Some people, eh? Why would you involve yourself when it has nothing to do with you?"

"Because these are nice people and I feel someone has to do something to help." He was going to hold out, hoping she'd give up and let him go.

"Just tell me what it is, would you? Or would you rather sit here all day answering questions?"

Matthew swallowed hard. His aunt was never going to give up. "I was going over to Adam's workshop to see if—"

"You're trying to get them back together?" Ada grinned from ear-to-ear.

"If I can."

"What do you plan on saying to him?"

Matthew grunted. "All right. I might as well tell you the whole plan."

"You might as well and don't leave anything out." Ada put her knitting in her lap and leaned in close.

He told Ada of Cherish's plan for him to talk with Andrew to find out if Adam had ever made a mistake.

Ada rubbed her chin after she'd heard everything. "So what will you do if you arrive there and Andrew isn't alone?"

"My plan was to wait up the road and when I see Adam leaving, I'd go in and find some excuse to be there and I'd talk with Andrew."

"Cherish thought this up, did she?"

"Well, not me waiting up the road. The plan was to talk with Andrew. I thought about the waiting up the road bit. I know Adam is doing some work on jobs where he has to go and measure up. Like in Gertie's quilt store."

"That's interesting. I didn't know that. I'd say that would have to be Krystal's idea." Ada tapped on her chin.

"Exactly. That's what Cherish said. So if I find out Adam has made a mistake, Cherish wants me to tell her. Then she'll go to—"

Ada held up her hand. "I can see where this is going."

"Do you think it's a good idea?"

"It's a terrible idea. What Adam needs is to talk with his mother. All men need their mother's advice no matter how old they are. And, since his mother isn't around, I'll talk with him."

"You?"

"Exactly. Everyone says I remind them of their mother. I'm a motherly kind of woman—concerned and caring. You can drive me there. I don't like driving by myself anymore."

"Sure." The only thing Matthew could think about was how disappointed Cherish would be that he didn't follow her plan. And worse, that Ada had gotten the truth out of him. She'd never let him forget it. "Do you think talking with him would work? If I broke up with a girl, I wouldn't want to talk with my mother about it. I'd talk with a friend, or someone who's been through the same thing."

Ada stared at him. "You'd have to get a girl to agree to date you first before you talk to your mother about anything. Let's go. There's no time to waste."

Matthew was shocked at her comment. His aunt thought he had no hope of getting a girl to like him. Up until that moment, he had thought he was a pretty good catch.

Half an hour later, Ada and Matthew arrived at Adam's workshop. "You wait here in the buggy," Ada said as she stepped down.

Ada was focused on one thing only and that was to get Adam and Bliss back together. She walked into the workshop and saw Adam immediately and she called out to him and he turned around. Then he put down his tools and walked toward her.

"Morning, Ada. How are you?"

"I'm fine. I'm here to have a serious talk with you."

He raised his eyebrows. "About what?"

"You and Bliss."

Adam looked down. "Did Bliss send you?"

"No. That would be the last thing she'd do, but she is very upset."

"She's not the only one. There are things you probably don't know."

"I know everything. That is, if you're talking about the letters. Wilma tells me everything."

Adam looked over his shoulder. "Let's talk outside." He walked with her through the workshop and out a side door. Ada pulled her coat further around herself to keep out the cold.

Ada looked down at his bare arms. "Do you want to put on a coat?"

"No. I'm fine." He unrolled his long sleeves.

"What are you doing, Adam? You let Christmas go by and Bliss didn't hear a word from you."

"I thought about her. Of course I did. We were together for so long. Are you sure you know what happened, Ada?"

"I do."

He shook his head. "I'm not okay with it. I can't believe she'd deceive me like she did."

"But her mistake is not who she is. We all know that Bliss is a wonderful young woman. She's sweet and she's kind. She told me she kept writing to that man out of fear. Out of fear of losing you. That's how much she loves you, she feared losing you. And maybe this fear of hers led her to do that stupid thing."

"With respect, Ada, this has to be my decision. I've thought it through and I'm happy with my decision."

"And what is your decision?"

"To end things, which I have done."

"Would you reconsider? I mean, the girl's distraught. We're all so worried about her. Can't you just forget about the past and move on? You would still be with her if you didn't find out about it."

"She's not the Bliss I knew. She's not the woman I thought she was."

"We've all failed in one way or another. Who is without sin? Not one of us." Ada shook her head so much that her cheeks wobbled.

"That's a mistake that is not okay. Not with me. Some other man might be fine with it, but I'm not."

Ada didn't like how stubborn he was being. "I came here today because I thought you needed someone motherly to talk with. If you were my son, I'd tell you not to let Bliss get away. She loves you more than anyone else will. You two get along just fine. You're the perfect couple."

He nodded. "I can see how someone would think that. I thought that too, until I found out we weren't the perfect couple."

"But there is no perfect couple and there is no perfect woman. Can't you see that?"

"Thanks for coming to see me. I appreciate it, but my mind is made up."

Ada was shocked that her advice was falling on deaf ears. "Why are you being so hard-hearted?"

"Because I know myself. I know that what she did will always eat away at me. It's not only what she did, but the fact that she kept it from me. She only stopped writing to him because he stopped writing to her."

"Do you know that for certain?" Ada asked.

"That's what she told me."

"See? She was being honest with you. She's not a dishonest person."

"Too little too late. I do appreciate you coming out and pitching Bliss's case to me."

"We miss having you at the house too. Everyone does. It was like you were already part of the family."

"I know. I miss you all too, but that's just how things have to be for the moment."

Ada stepped closer to him. "For the moment? So there'll be a chance for you two in the future?"

"I didn't mean to imply that. Thanks for coming, Ada." He moved toward the door.

Ada stayed where she was. "Have you ever made a big mistake, Adam?"

"I'm sure I have. We all make mistakes."

"I want you to think about that." Ada gave a sharp nod and walked back through the building and then out to the waiting buggy.

"How did it go?" Matthew asked.

Ada shook her head. "It didn't go well."

"What did he say?"

"His mind is made up. Just take me back home, would you, Matthew?"

"Sure."

Ada was disappointed. She hadn't expected Adam to be so determined. Now she was concerned that she might have made things worse.

CHAPTER 33

*A*fter the third stop on the side of the road due to Favor being carsick, Wilma ordered Bliss to yield the front seat to Favor. The rest of the trip went smoothly, and Wilma and the girls finally arrived at Simon's parents' farm.

Wilma was the first one out of the car. She turned around and told the driver they'd be half an hour at the most. Cherish was still upset about her clothes, but she tried to put it out of her mind.

A short woman wearing a pale-green dress, that was longer than typical, came hurrying out with outstretched arms to meet them. She was smiling from ear to ear. "Wilma, I can't believe we've never met. Ada talks about you and your family all the time in her letters." She embraced Wilma. "I'm Harriet."

"I'm so pleased to meet you, Harriet. These are two of my girls, Cherish and Favor. This is Levi's daughter, Bliss."

"Pleased to meet you all. Come inside. Melvin and Simon

would've seen your car from the fields, so they'll be here shortly. I've been waiting anxiously."

They walked from the warm car, through the freezing cold, into the warm house. Cherish hurried to stand near the fire at the end of the room to keep warm.

Simon walked in through the back door, grinning. He took his hat off, smiled at Cherish and greeted everyone. Then his father followed. Simon introduced his father to everyone.

Cherish couldn't help noticing that Simon looked very much like his father.

When the adults were speaking among themselves, Simon spoke to Cherish, "I'm so pleased to see you."

"Thank you. I was surprised you left so suddenly."

"I make up my mind and then I have to do whatever it is. You know?"

"Not really. I think about how my actions will affect others." Cherish wasn't letting him off that easily for leaving without saying goodbye in person. A quick note in the mailbox wasn't good enough.

"We can't stay long," Wilma announced after Harriet invited them to stay for afternoon tea. "We have the driver waiting for us."

"It won't take long. Everything's ready in the kitchen."

They all moved to the kitchen and sat around the table.

Melvin said, "It's not often we get visitors. We haven't had many at all since we moved here. It's a nice change."

"Did you know we're going to the farm, Wilma?"

"Yes. Cherish mentioned that. We're only staying for six days. We'll be going home on Tuesday."

"We'll be there tomorrow, with Simon."

"Okay. That'll be fun."

"Simon and I will find some jobs to do on the farm."

Wilma laughed. "I think Simon and Cherish... well, the young folk might want to have some time alone."

"There'll be plenty of time for that, but I do like to keep busy." As Harriet cut the cake, she said, "I think the cake is still okay. I baked it last week."

Favor leaned forward and whispered to her mother. "I told you."

Wilma frowned at Favor.

"Simon tells me the farm is Cherish's," Melvin said.

"That's right," Wilma replied.

He scratched his head. "I've never heard of a woman owning a farm. Not someone so young either."

"Her aunt left it to her," Bliss said, speaking for the first time since they arrived.

Favor said, "And our aunt was a woman."

Melvin slowly nodded, "I guessed that."

Wilma frowned at Favor.

"When she marries, I guess she'll pass the farm over to her husband."

Wilma told him. "It's too far off to think about such things."

"It's nice that when Cherish moves to her farm that she and Simon will be so much closer," Harriet said, while Simon sat there in silence.

"Yes." Wilma was getting a little worried that Simon and his parents thought Simon was in some kind of relationship with Cherish. Had Cherish given Simon that impression? Was she in a relationship—a secret one? It would be just the kind of thing Cherish might do.

Harriet smiled at Cherish as she handed her a plate with a slice of cake. "I've always wanted a daughter, but a daughter-in-law might be just as good."

Cherish took the plate and then tried to cut the piece with a knife. Either the knife was very blunt or Simon's mother was a terrible baker.

"Could we take something out to the driver?" Bliss asked.

"He's welcome to join us," Melvin said.

"He will prefer to stay in the car. We've had the same driver before," Wilma said.

"Yes. Take something out to him. I'll pour him a cup of tea and you can put some of the cake onto a plate."

"Thank you."

When Bliss took the cake and tea out to the driver, he moved the window down and looked at it. "Is this the stale cake your sister was talking about?"

Bliss laughed. "Possibly."

"Nice of you to offer, but I brought my own food and a flask of coffee."

He nodded to a cup in the cupholder.

"You don't want it?" Bliss asked.

He shook his head. "Thanks anyway."

Bliss didn't know what to do. She didn't want to take it back to the house untouched. Just before she got back to the house, she tipped the tea into one of the bushes and buried the cake under some leaves. When she got back into the kitchen, she put the dishes into the sink.

"That was fast. He drank the tea and ate the cake already?"

Bliss froze. She wasn't thinking straight with the lack of sleep. "He was hungry. And thirsty."

Harriet raised her eyebrows. "Sit back down with us, Bliss."

Bliss sat down, hoping Simon's mother wouldn't find the cake in the garden later.

"Cherish, what do you think of Simon?" Harriet asked. A hush of silence fell over the room, except for Favor, who suddenly choked on her tea.

Cherish didn't know what to say. She looked at Simon, hoping he'd tell his mother to hush, but he just sat there. "He's lovely. Very nice."

"We think so. I'm glad you're so honest."

"There's no point in being any other way."

"My thoughts exactly. We'll get along just fine. Melvin and I are very close with Simon. You'll all find that out soon enough. We're more like friends than mother and son, and Melvin and he are more like friends too."

"Yes. He told me that," Cherish said.

"So, when he marries, that girl will be in a group of four with us. Instead, for now, it's a group of three friends," Melvin said.

Cherish couldn't work out what Simon's father was talking about. "Pardon me?"

"My wife and I are hoping Simon will marry a woman that can come into our group as a friend."

"What group?" Wilma asked.

"The friendship group that my husband and I have with Simon."

Cherish got it. "Oh."

"Do you like the sound of that?" Harriet stared at Cherish.

Cherish didn't like the sound of that at all and now she was starting to worry about Simon's parents coming to the farm. It would totally ruin everything. "I've got a great idea. We've got room in the car. Why don't we take Simon with us now and you can come when you arranged?"

"We don't have room," Bliss said. "There's already five of us in the car."

Harriet shook her head. "No. Simon wouldn't like that anyway. We like to go places together. When Simon went to your sister's wedding, it was the first time he'd been away from us since he was born."

"Really?" *Mamm* asked.

"That's right."

Cherish noticed her mother staring at the clock.

They left twenty minutes later when the driver knocked on the door reminding them of the time.

Once they were all back in the car, Cherish was relieved.

"Can you believe the things they were saying?" Favor asked.

"Shoosh. They'll hear you," *Mamm* waved politely as the car moved away.

"The only problem with Simon is his parents," Favor said. "They're acting like you're for sure going to marry Simon."

"Cherish," *Mamm* began, "have you been totally honest with me about your relationship with Simon?"

"I think so. I'm not sure what you mean. We're only friends."

"Hmm." *Mamm* didn't sound convinced.

"Will we only have one day on the farm before they arrive?" Favor asked.

"It seems like it," *Mamm* said.

"I wish I knew about this before I agreed to come." Favor folded her arms and glared at Cherish.

"I only invited Simon. Or did I? I'm not sure, but I can tell you for sure that I didn't invite his parents. They invited themselves. Maybe I did. I can't remember. I should've met them first before I did such a thing. If I did."

"It's all right," *Mamm* said, "we'll make the best of it."

"I thought they were lovely," said Bliss. "Simon has such lovely caring parents. He'll be a good father. He's had a good example of how to be loving."

"Loving or smothering?" Favor asked. "I was uncomfortable with what they were saying."

"They were only being honest," Bliss replied. "Bad things happen when people hide things. I learned that the hard way. I liked that they said what they had to say in front of everyone."

Cherish changed the subject so Bliss wouldn't dwell on her recent break-up. "I am looking forward to showing you the farm, Favor and Bliss. I think you'll both love it."

"I know I will just from what you've told me about it," Favor said.

Bliss added, "I'm looking forward to just getting away. Thanks for letting me come, *Mamm*. I know there's less people at home now."

"It'll all work out. Don't you worry, Bliss. Just enjoy yourself," *Mamm* said. "Ada is sure to help out. She always does."

Bliss nodded.

Cherish looked out the window thinking about how Simon just sat there while his parents said all those strange things—all in the space of several minutes.

What would their stay at her farm be like with Simon's parents?

Would Malachi mind that she was bringing so many people? All Malachi knew was that she was coming with her mother.

WHEN THE CAR stopped at Cherish's farm, Cherish jumped out first. She looked at the house and was pleased when the door opened and Malachi appeared. Her heart fluttered a little even though he was the same as always— totally disheveled. His hair was all over the place and the closer he got, she could see his clothes were all tattered and he was dreadfully untidy, and where was his hat?

Then she noticed a goose waddling behind him. Cherish opened her mouth in shock. "What's that, Malachi?" she shouted out.

He turned around and glanced at the goose. "That's Wally. He's the surprise I was telling you about."

"But... you don't like birds."

"He's not really a bird. He's a goose."

"Yes, but he's got wings and that makes him a bird."

Malachi shrugged his shoulders. "He's my new best friend. He follows me everywhere. He was caught in one of the fences a few months back and I untangled him. He won't leave me."

Mamm got out of the car. "I hope you don't have the bird inside."

"I do. It's a goose," Malachi said.

"Leave him alone, *Mamm*. It's Malachi's house, at least for a while." Cherish grinned at him. Then she saw the smile fade from his face as he noticed the other two girls getting out of the car. "Oh, I forgot to tell you. This is Bliss and Favor. They've come too."

He smiled. "That's great. The more the merrier, I suppose."

Cherish knew she had to break the news about Simon and his parents coming tomorrow. "I also have something else to tell you." Malachi had walked over to help the driver get the bags out of the car.

"Malachi, we've heard so much about you," Favor said.

"I've heard about all of you too," he said, while he took two bags to the porch, with the goose waddling behind him.

Cherish pulled the two remaining bags out of the trunk and hurried to Malachi so she'd be the one to break the news.

He came toward her and took the bags from her. "I would've had the other rooms ready if I'd known."

"We can do that. I need to tell you something."

"What?" He kept walking.

"Stop and listen."

He stopped and put the suitcases on the ground and looked down at her. "I'm listening."

"We have some other people coming tomorrow."

Malachi folded his arms. "What people?"

"Simon Koppel and his parents."

Deep furrows appeared in his forehead. "Simon Koppel?"

"You know him?"

"I do." Malachi huffed and then looked down at the ground. "Do I have to stay here?"

This was worse than Cherish had imagined. Simon and Malachi didn't get along. "Of course. It's your house while you're living here."

"Not for the next week it seems. It's not surprising he's

coming with his parents. They never let him out of their sight. And he doesn't seem too bothered by that, which is even stranger."

Cherish had to wonder once again, was Florence's husband right about Simon being a mama's boy? Surely that would change when Simon married, wouldn't it? Or, would he always do what his mother told him? "You're wrong about his parents. Simon came to Hope's wedding. He was the one I was telling you about that I thought was you from behind."

"Yeah, well you didn't tell me it was Simon Koppel. Are you and Simon..."

"No." Cherish shook her head vigorously as though that was the very last thing on her mind.

"So why's he coming here?"

"Well, he's just a friend. Like you and Annie are just friends."

He glanced over his shoulder at the barn. "You do what you want. I'll bunk in the barn with Wally."

"No, you can't do that."

"It's okay. I really don't mind."

"No. You'll freeze to death and *Mamm* won't allow it. The girls and I will sleep in one room and then there'll be plenty of room for everyone."

He shook his head. "I have to tell you I'm disappointed. I was looking forward to you coming. I wanted to have some time alone with you. Now that seems impossible."

"You wanted to have time with me?"

Malachi nodded. "I enjoy our talks."

"We can still talk."

"Come on, you two," *Mamm* yelled from the front door.

"You'll catch your death of cold if you stay out there without coats."

Malachi picked up the suitcases and then they continued walking to the house with Wally close behind. Cherish hoped things wouldn't get out of hand this week with all the large personalities in one house. Add to that the fact it was winter and it could even snow, forcing everyone to be mostly confined indoors.

"Oh boy," Cherish said under her breath. "This could be the longest week of my life."

Thank you for reading A Season for Change.

AMISH FARM MAYHEM

BOOK #26 THE AMISH BONNET SISTERS

CHAPTER 1

Cherish finally arrived at her farm and a weight lifted off her shoulders as she breathed in the air. It was so different from the air in Lancaster County. She was home.

She, along with her mother, Bliss and Favor, had stopped along the way to visit Simon Koppel, Cherish's potential boyfriend, whom she'd met at Hope's wedding. He lived with his parents and they were there too. The Koppel threesome were arriving at the farm tomorrow and were planning to stay a few days. The way their brief visit with them had played out, Cherish had left wondering how they'd all survive in the same house for days.

Malachi, Cherish's farm manager, had come out of the house to meet Cherish and her family members with his new friend. The friend was a goose—a real one. Cherish wasn't really surprised, not after Malachi explained he didn't consider a goose the same as the chickens about which he had a lifelong phobia. Nothing about Malachi surprised her anymore.

The goose, whose name was Wally, followed him everywhere and much to Wilma's disapproval, the goose even followed him into the house.

"So what is this with the bird in the house, Malachi?" Wilma asked.

"It's a goose," Bliss and Favor said at the same time.

A giggle escaped Cherish's lips.

Wilma lifted her chin. "I'm always corrected, even when I'm not wrong. Do you know what the girls have done to me, Malachi? At home, we have two birds, a dog, and a rabbit in my house when I don't want any animals in the house at all—not one. They know this and they don't care."

"Don't worry, Wilma. Wally's housetrained." Malachi leaned down and rubbed Wally's neck.

Then *Mamm* crouched down and studied the goose. "How can a wild animal be house trained? Oh dear, help me up, Cherish." Wilma held up her arm and Cherish pulled her to her feet.

"Stop worrying, *Mamm*," Cherish told her. "Malachi wouldn't say he was housetrained if he wasn't."

Malachi smiled as he explained, "Wally isn't really wild anymore. He's tame. He goes to the door if he wants to go out. He does what he needs to do and then he comes back in."

Wilma's lips turned down at the corners. "I'll see it when I believe it."

The girls laughed at her.

"What's funny?" Wilma looked at each one of them.

"You said it the wrong way around," Favor told her. "You mean, you'll believe it when you see it."

"That's what I said."

"No, you didn't." Bliss tried to stifle her giggles.

Wilma sighed. "I'm tired from the long car ride and from you girls constantly belittling me."

The smile left Bliss's face. "I'm sorry, *Mamm*. We don't mean to do that."

"We won't do it again," Favor added. "I agree with Bliss. We didn't mean to do that."

"Good because it's tiring. The food smells good, Malachi. What do you have on the stove?" *Mamm* asked.

"I made us a beef stew for dinner and I'll be cookin' mashed potatoes and beans to go with it."

"It does smell delicious," Bliss said.

"Thanks."

An hour later, *Mamm* and the girls were peeling the potatoes and stringing the beans. They wouldn't let Malachi do anything, telling him he'd done enough in making the stew. Malachi sat down at the kitchen table with them, drinking coffee while they worked.

"I wonder how Debbie made out today with her tea," Bliss said.

Mamm looked up at the ceiling. "That's right. She was going to the tea expert."

Cherish couldn't stop worrying about her birds and her dog. "I hope Matthew remembered to feed Tommy and Timmy."

"What's Timmy's friend like?" Malachi asked.

"Tommy? He's pretty much like Timmy, but he doesn't talk yet. Timmy's getting so good at talking."

"What does he say?" Malachi asked.

"Nearly everything. Whatever you want him to say."

"That's not so, Cherish." Favor went on to tell Malachi

exactly what few words Timmy could say, including the words he tried to say, but weren't too clear.

Cherish sat there, wondering if she should've left Favor at home. Her sister had embarrassed her just now. What if she did that when Simon and his parents were here? The only thing to do was to have a talk with her. Hopefully next time, she'd close her mouth.

Cherish's opportunity came when Malachi went outside to fetch some more firewood. "Favor, please don't say I'm wrong in front of people. It sounded like I was lying or exaggerating."

"What do you mean?" Favor asked. Cherish didn't waste time telling her exactly what she was upset about.

"Oh that. I'm sorry. I didn't know it would make you upset, and you really were exaggerating. Everyone knows Timmy can't talk that well."

"If I do anything like that again…"

"Yes?"

"Keep your mouth closed."

"I agree," Wilma said. "If it's not your conversation, Favor, keep out of it."

Favor sighed. "Okay. I am sorry, Cherish."

Cherish breathed out the air she'd been holding on to and then nodded to acknowledge Favor's apology. That had gone a whole lot easier than she'd expected it would.

"It's nice that you girls are getting along so well, and you're able to sort out your differences in a mature way. I think we're going to have a lovely time here at the farm."

"We will, *Mamm*," Bliss assured her.

Favor got up and looked out the window. "It's funny how that goose follows him everywhere. It makes Malachi look intriguing, don't you think? If I didn't know him and I just saw him walking down the street with Wally, I'd want to get to know him."

Everyone stared at Favor and no one said anything.

Favor kept talking. "Well, that's what I think. No one has to agree with me. I'm used to being the odd one out. I was probably adopted."

"No, you certainly were not! I gave birth to you, suffered in agonizing pain for several hours. You didn't want to come out."

"Sorry, I didn't mean it. It's not my fault. I couldn't help it. I don't even remember it."

Mamm made a face. "I'm just saying you aren't adopted."

"Favor knows that. She looks too much like the rest of us," Cherish said.

Bliss finally joined in the conversation. "I know what Favor means, saying a man being followed by a goose would look interesting and intriguing. For me, no man looks interesting. There's only one man in my heart. Well, there was."

Mamm leaned over and put her arm around Bliss, who was sitting beside her. "You're here to forget about Adam. Don't go thinking about him for at least three days. Can you do that?"

"I'll really try. It'll be hard because he's always on my mind, and in my heart. I will try to forget, that's all I can do."

"Good." *Mamm* rose to her feet and then headed over to the stove and stirred the stew. "It smells delicious. I can't wait to taste it."

"Thanks for allowing us all to come, *Mamm*," Cherish said.

"I know how you love it and I do try to let you come here once a year. Just don't get too used to it. I'll be happy if you wait a few years before you move here permanently if that's what you decide to do."

"I know. I'll think about it."

"Do you mean, 'we'll see?' That's what *Mamm* always says when she means that she won't think about what we asked her and the answer is most likely no." Favor giggled.

Cherish laughed at what Favor said and even Bliss managed to curve her lips upward.

Mamm lifted her chin. "I hardly ever say 'we'll see.' I don't know what you're talking about, Favor. First you say you're adopted and then you go putting words into my mouth. What's gotten into you?"

"Yes, you do say 'we'll see,'" Favor said.

"You do, *Mamm*," Cherish told her.

"I see what's going to happen here. Everyone is going to make fun of me and tell the Koppels unkind stories about me."

"Not everyone will do that," Favor said. "I'm sure Bliss won't and Malachi won't."

Cherish laughed, pleased that Favor was in such a fun and playful mood. She used to be like this before Krystal came to stay with them. Then she turned moody and sullen when Krystal left.

"The Koppels won't think much of you if you make fun of me," *Mamm* warned.

"They're joking," Bliss told *Mamm*.

"I hope so."

"They are, don't worry. They're only teasing you. Aren't you? Tell her." Bliss looked at Favor and then looked over at Cherish.

Cherish huffed. "I like the way I'm dragged into this when I haven't said anything at all. It's all been Favor."

"You laughed with me." Favor poked her shoulder.

"I might have been laughing *at* you." Cherish pouted.

"You were laughing with me. Stop it," Favor said. "You're always making excuses as well as exaggerating and telling half-truths."

"Both of you make up with each other," Bliss told the pair of them. "We all need to have this time away to clear our heads."

Favor and Cherish looked at each other. "I'm glad you're finally here at the farm, Favor." Cherish hugged Favor, and Favor hugged her back.

"I'm pleased too. Let's not argue. Let's just agree that I'm always right because I always am." Favor giggled again and Cherish laughed along with her.

"Okay. You're always right. Just don't embarrass me and we'll get along fine."

"Good. Now let's get on with it," *Mamm* said just before she sneaked a taste of the stew.

CHAPTER 2

Back at the orchard…

*A*da had looked after baby Jared for the afternoon while Peter took Debbie to see Fredrick Lomas, the tea expert.

Peter wanted Debbie to bring Jared. He insisted he'd look after him while Debbie talked with Fredrick. But Debbie didn't want Peter getting too attached to Jared just in case things didn't work out between herself and him. She enjoyed his company, but he'd come into her life too soon after John.

"I'll come in, but you do all the talking. Or, would you rather have me stay in the buggy?" Peter asked.

"No. I want you to come in. You can help me remember everything he says."

"Okay." Peter pulled up the buggy outside the factory, and then they walked in with a box of Debbie's new and improved tea samples.

A half hour into their meeting, Debbie was a little concerned when Fredrick said her tea blends still needed work. Thankfully, he advised Debbie how to fix them, encouraging her by saying they just needed a little tweak.

"Have you thought about the packaging yet?" Fredrick asked, as they sat across the table from him.

Debbie swallowed hard. The thought of taking those next steps filled her with fear. "I haven't. I want to work on the recipes first. I thought I'd just make small quantities and sell them at my family's little shop that they have in front of their house. They open in the apple growing season and through the harvest."

"You'll still have to package it somehow," Fredrick said.

"I know. I thought it would only be plain." Debbie bit her lip, feeling way out of her league.

"Plain is good. Like I said before, I like the idea of black and white." He picked up a sample box. "This would hold twenty tea bags. Then of course you'd have to choose a name."

"I've been thinking about that, and I haven't come up with anything."

"Nothing at all?" Fredrick asked.

"No, but I do like the idea of the black and white boxes that you mentioned. I was thinking a lot smaller than you are. I was just thinking I'd sell tea with no labels and nothing on the boxes."

"No. You can't do that." Fredrick pursed his lips. "There needs to be something to identify it as your product line.

"Maybe you should think a bit bigger," Peter suggested.

Debbie looked at Peter. He had said he'd keep quiet. "Maybe."

Fredrick leaned back in his chair. "What's holding you back, Debbie?"

"I don't know. I just thought of starting off small, and now I don't know if this… the tea… my tea is good enough, or ever will be good enough."

"They all just need simple adjustments. You can do this, but you've got to start off right and then you won't have mistakes to fix when you get bigger."

Debbie nodded. Talking to Fredrick gave her more confidence. "That makes sense."

"Grow at your own pace, in your own comfort zone."

"I could handle that."

"Do what I said, make those changes and you'll be ready to go."

"Really? It''ll be good enough to start selling?"

He nodded. "Absolutely. I can arrange the bags for you if you want to fill them yourself. When you get bigger, our factory can fill them for you." He chuckled. "You make money and I make money. Everyone needs someone to give them a hand up the ladder."

"That would be great. I'll fill them myself to start with. And I'll need some small boxes too."

"I can arrange that. We've got some unbranded sample boxes."

"Perfect."

"But you'll really have to think up a name soon."

"I will."

After they discussed the prices of the bags, Fredrick insisted on giving her a few dozen of the 20 teabag boxes for free.

"Are you sure?" Debbie asked.

"Yes. Just come back when you're a big tea mogul and use us for the packaging."

"I definitely will come back sooner than that. You've been so helpful."

"Yes, you have. Thank you," Peter said.

Fredrick looked at Peter. "And are you involved with this?"

Peter smiled. "I'm just the driver, and I can do anything she wants. I could be the delivery man."

Debbie laughed. "I don't think there'll be much to deliver for a while."

"Don't be surprised if it takes off. What you need to do is get yourself a website and sell online. A whole new world will open up to you. Are you allowed to do that with your religion?"

"Oh yes. I know someone that can help me with that. She's recently joined our community and she's helped other people. I'm sure she'll do the same for me."

"Okay. Of course, you'll need your name and branding before that."

"I know."

"Then there'll be nothing to hold you back."

Debbie liked the sound of that. What she wanted was to make enough money so she and Jared wouldn't be a financial burden on Wilma and Levi. If she achieved that, she'd be more than happy.

When they left, Debbie suggested that Peter drive her to see Krystal. Krystal could possibly help her with the website.

WHEN DEBBIE and Peter walked into the quilt store where Krystal worked, they saw her behind the counter looking at the computer monitor. She jumped up when she saw them.

"Debbie, and Peter. How are you both? Are you looking for a quilt? It just so happens that I can offer you a good deal today even though we're selling like hot cakes."

"No. I'm looking at getting a website. I was wondering if you'd be able and willing to help me?"

"Of course I can." Krystal moved away from behind the counter. "What is the website for?"

"I'm making tea blends. I want to get a website that will allow me to sell the tea. People can make the order, pay for it and then I will mail it to them."

"Oh. That sounds like a good idea. I should've thought of that. Too bad. Yeah, I can help you."

"Can you give me a rough idea how much it will cost?"

Krystal said, "I won't charge you for the work I do on it, but there will be some costs. There'll be ongoing hosting costs."

"Oh, I will be able to pay you. I have some savings to work with before the tea money comes in."

Krystal shook her head. "It's the least I can do. Your family took me in when I had nowhere to go. It's the very least I can do."

"Thank you."

"Are you ready? Have you got stock ready?" Krystal asked.

"Not yet, but I will have soon."

Peter said, "She hasn't got a brand name for the tea."

"I know that I want the packaging, black and white, but that's all I know so far."

Krystal made a face. "That sounds a bit plain."

"I like things plain."

"Why don't you call it Plain Tea?"

Debbie drew her eyebrows together. "I don't know."

Krystal said, "Amish are plain people, you're Amish so Plain Tea. Do you get it?"

"It's as good a name as any," Peter said.

"Or do you think the name is *too* plain?" Krystal asked.

"Kind of."

"What about Bruners Plain Tea? Or Debbie's Plain Tea?" Krystal suggested.

"Oh, I love Debbie's Plain Tea." Debbie looked at Peter. "What do you think?"

"I love it too. It's perfect."

"Great. Now you have a name." Krystal smiled.

"Thanks so much for helping me, Krystal."

"I do this a lot. I'm great at marketing. Why don't you come back tomorrow about this time. I'll work on some looks for your webpage and we can go from there."

Debbie hugged Krystal. "Thank you."

"You're welcome. Maybe you could bring me some tea next time."

"Tomorrow I'll bring you some of my new recipe. You'll be the first to try it."

"I love being the first."

"I do have one sample that I've been told is ready. I'll get that for you," Debbie said.

"I'll get it." Peter turned and headed out the door.

"So... what's going on between you and Peter?"

Debbie laughed. "I'm not really sure. I like him, but I don't know if it's more than that."

"I think it's great what you're doing. You've inspired me. I need a way to make some extra cash. I'm doing a lot of things, but I need more if I'm ever going to move out of Gertie's house."

"How is it living with her?"

"We get along great. She's like the grandmother I never had."

"And do you have a boyfriend yet?"

Krystal sighed. "I'm starting to realize that the single men don't see me as a proper choice for a girlfriend. I'm Amish now, but not really because everyone sees me as the new girl. The girl who told lies and then joined the community. I'm feeling kind of… I don't know… unwanted."

Debbie rubbed Krystal's arm. "Don't worry. I felt kind of lost and then everything turned around. It will for you too. All you need is one man who will see you for the person you are. He'll fall in love with you."

Debbie's words brought a smile to Krystal's face and then they couldn't say any more because Peter was back.

Peter handed a small bag to Krystal. "Here you are."

"Thank you so much. I can't wait to try it."

"We'll be back tomorrow," Peter said.

"Okay. I'll be waiting."

Once Debbie and Peter were back on the road, Debbie looked over at Peter. "Thank you for driving me to see Krystal. I feel like things are finally working out."

"They are."

"It was all just an idea I had and now things are taking shape. I couldn't have done it without your help. You even found Fredrick Lomas for me."

"Ah, that wasn't hard. I like doing things for you. How about we bring Jared with us tomorrow when you come back to see Krystal?"

"Are you sure you can spare the time? Someone else would be able to take me or I could borrow a buggy."

"I can move my work around, so yes, it'll be fine."

"I am able to drive myself. I'll just borrow a buggy and leave Jared with Ada."

He looked over at her and smiled. "No need. I like doing it, and I'd love it if you brought Jared. I can't get enough of that little guy."

"Okay." He made it hard to say no. But with each thing he did for her, she felt more indebted.

CHAPTER 3

That first night at the farm, Cherish and Malachi stayed up late, talking. Everyone else had gone to bed.

"Why are they coming here?" Malachi asked her, meaning Simon and his folks.

"I just… because I thought…"

Malachi shook his head. "I thought as much."

"Don't be like that."

"He's not right for you. He's so wrong. He's as far from right for you as he could be. He's so wrong. He's so far from right, he's left."

"You said he's wrong twice."

"I know, because I wasn't sure you heard me the first time." Malachi raised his eyebrows.

Cherish was interested to learn all she could about Simon, and Malachi had already met Simon and his parents. "What do you know about him?"

"He moved to the area not long ago with his parents. They were in our community for a while before the bishop decided our people covered too large an area for one meeting. It was too hard for people to get together, so we split into two smaller groups."

"Why's he wrong for me?"

Malachi stared at her. "So he is a potential boyfriend and that's why he's coming here? And bringing his folks?"

Cherish didn't want to admit it. "No."

Malachi folded his arms. "Your words say no, but your face is saying yes."

"He's a friend. Just like Annie Whylie is your friend."

"Only thing is, Annie is just a friend and she'll only ever be that."

Cherish sniggered as though she didn't believe him, but he spoke so definitely that part of her did think it might be true. "If that's so, does Annie know?"

Malachi rubbed the back of his neck. "We've never had that conversation. It never came up and there's a reason for that. Neither of us feels that way."

"Well, you better watch out. She might already think you're dating her."

Malachi laughed. "No, it's not like that. People who are dating talk about the future and that kind of thing. We've never talked about anything like that."

"What do the two of you talk about?"

"Just stuff."

Cherish looked down at the goose. "What does Annie think about Wally?"

"She thinks he's amazing and intelligent. And he is."

"I never thought of having a goose as a pet."

"Your mother will never let you. I've seen the way she looks at Wally."

Cherish laughed. "I know. I should be grateful I've got the birds and Caramel. I wonder how Caramel will be with Wally. I nearly brought him, but *Mamm* said we wouldn't have enough room in the car."

"Is Caramel good with cats?"

Cherish nodded. "He doesn't chase them or anything. He's not so good with Bliss's rabbit. He looks like he wants to eat her."

"Before you bring him here, you should check to see how he is with another goose, to see how he reacts."

"I'll do that. There are geese at one of the parks. We wouldn't want anything to happen with Wally."

"That's right."

Cherish took a sip of her hot chocolate. It was so nice just sitting and talking to Malachi. It felt like they were the only two people in the world as they warmed themselves in front of the crackling fire. There was also nothing like the smell of a fire in the wintertime. "I'm sorry I didn't tell you so many people were coming."

"You've already said you're sorry. It's fine." He shrugged his shoulders. "If it gets too much for me, I'll bunk in the barn. Please don't try to stop me if I wanna do that." He stared at her waiting for a response.

"I won't. My mother might though. Now tell me the truth about something. Why don't you like Simon?"

"First, I always tell the truth. Second, I never said I didn't like him. I just said he's not for you. How do ya get that I don't

235

like him outa that? Anyway, I should keep me mouth shut. You'll find out for yourself soon enough."

Cherish rolled her eyes. She didn't like people telling her what to do or who to like. He was trying to turn her off Simon. "His parents are a little different."

"You noticed?" He laughed. "They sure are different. Yes indeed."

Cherish nodded. "I just hope they will all like this place."

"Of course they'll like it. What's not to like?"

"You've done a great job with it. I can't wait to see all of it tomorrow morning."

Malachi's eyebrows rose. "Hey, that's the first time you've told me I've done a great job."

"I should tell you more often. I do appreciate you."

Was it just the reflection of the fire, or was he blushing?

He swallowed hard. "I'm glad. Wake up early and we can feed the animals together. You can have a good look around before the visitors get here. We mightn't have much alone time after that."

"Okay." Cherish stared into the fire trying to figure out how much of what she loved about being at the farm was because of Malachi's friendly nature. He always welcomed her and whoever she had with her.

When Malachi and she decided it was time to get some sleep, Cherish crept into her room trying not to wake her sisters.

Favor sat up in bed. "I can't sleep."

"Shh. You'll wake everyone else and then no one will be able to sleep. Just close your eyes." Cherish hadn't even unpacked.

She retrieved her nightgown from her suitcase and changed into it.

"Are you excited about Simon coming?" Favor whispered.

"I sure am." Cherish slipped between the sheets. The bed was nice and warm. That was one benefit to sharing her bed.

"Bliss thinks it's nice how close he is with his parents."

"It is nice." Cherish pulled the quilt over herself. It was crowded in the double bed with the three of them.

Favor moved even closer to her and whispered, "When will you know how much you like him or do you know already?"

"I'm not sure. We'll just have to wait and see how things work out. Move over. I've got no room."

Favor moved back a couple of inches. "It sounds like you're not sure. Either you like him or you don't."

"I do."

"How much?" Favor wouldn't let up.

"Enough to want him to come to the farm."

"Let me know if you decide you don't like him." Favor turned over the other way and faced Bliss, who was fast asleep.

Cherish didn't like the sound of that. Favor must've liked Simon. "Why?" Cherish asked.

Favor turned back around. "Because I might like him if you don't, but I'll let you see how you feel first. I won't even talk to him until you tell me you don't like him."

"Thanks a bunch."

"You're welcome." Favor turned away.

That confirmed to Cherish that she should've left Favor at home. She was going to be nothing but trouble.

Cherish grabbed the clock on the nightstand and set an alarm for five. She wanted to be up early to help Malachi.

CHAPTER 4

*C*herish and Malachi were up early doing chores.

"How long will your visitors be staying?" Malachi asked.

"I'm not sure. Probably a day or two. They'd have to get back to their sheep."

"I thought a shepherd never left his flock."

Cherish laughed. "Well, they must've found someone to look after the sheep."

Malachi scratched his cheek and kept walking.

"It'll be okay. You seem really tense. Just relax." Cherish leaned over and gave him a playful shove.

He looked at her and smiled. "I will."

"Anyway, it's because of you that I met Simon."

He stopped walking. "Me? How so?"

"I told you already. You said you might be coming to Hope's wedding with Annie and her folks. I saw Annie there and I looked around for you. I saw someone walking and he looked like you."

"Okay, okay. I didn't know that was him, when you told me that story. We look nothin' alike. There must be somethin' wrong with ya eyesight."

Cherish gasped. "There's nothing wrong with it. How could you say such a thing?"

Malachi laughed. "I'm telling ya we look nothing alike."

"You do from behind."

Malachi shook his head. "Nah, I don't think so."

"Don't be jealous."

Malachi gasped. "Jealous of what?"

Cherish realized what she said didn't make sense so she thought fast for something that he could be jealous about. "Simon's close relationship with his parents."

"I'm not jealous. I just can't understand it. I mean, would you want your mother speaking for ya and fixing up your hair?"

Cherish frowned at him. "What are you talking about?"

"His mother brushes his hair off his face all the time. Haven't you seen it."

"Oh, well, it saves him doing it." Cherish figured Malachi was exaggerating.

"I can see you're gonna make excuses for 'im. I'll just keep quiet. I won't say another thing. You make up ya own mind about 'im."

"I will."

Malachi walked off. Wally was digging in the ground with his beak. "Come on, Wally. You don't want to be left behind." Both Wally and Cherish walked behind Malachi, trying to catch up.

Suddenly, Malachi turned around. "What time are they comin'?"

"They might've left early, and it'll be however long it'll take the horse and buggy to get here."

"It'll take a long time. Are ya sure they're not going to hire a car?"

"They didn't mention it."

Malachi tipped his hat forward and rubbed the back of his neck. "If they hire a car, they could be here early."

After Cherish and Malachi fed the animals, Cherish joined the women in the house while Malachi did more outside work. Wilma and the girls had gotten started early, preparing the house for their visitors.

They'd cleaned the living room and the bathroom and now they'd moved into the kitchen. "I'm quite surprised how clean the house is," Wilma said, looking around.

"Malachi said he did a special cleaning when he heard we were coming." Cherish leaned on the broom.

Wilma looked around. "I think he has risen in his cleaning capabilities since last time I was here."

Bliss wiped down the kitchen countertops. "It is very clean. You do have a high standard when it comes to cleaning, *Mamm.*"

"There's no other way to be. I'll tell him when he comes inside. It might encourage him to keep along the cleanliness path."

"Tell him what?" Cherish asked.

"I'll say what a good job he's done. He must work from the minute he gets up to the minute he goes to bed."

"I guess he does when he's not having visitors like Annie Whylie." Cherish stopped herself from rolling her eyes.

"Will we see Annie again?" Bliss asked.

"I guess so. Supposedly, she and Malachi are good friends. She's been here the last few times I've been visiting. It's nice for him to have friends who live close by."

"It is. Now, are all the beds made?" *Mamm* asked.

"I've just got one more bed to do," Bliss said.

"Hurry because we don't want them to arrive and see us in all this mess."

There was no mess, but to Wilma, everything had to be just perfect.

"We'll get it all done in time, *Mamm*, don't worry." Bliss rinsed out the cleaning rag and then hurried away to make the bed.

Mamm wasn't through with complaining. "They are so looking forward to coming here that I don't want them to be disappointed. I'll be letting them down."

"We'll get it all done. There's really not much to do."

"Why didn't you find out the time they were coming?" *Mamm* glared at Cherish.

"I didn't want to be rude."

"That wouldn't have been rude. It would've been sensible."

"Sorry." Cherish shrugged her shoulders. "I'll do it next time."

"I guess if you learn from all the errors you make, then that'll be something," *Mamm* said.

When they heard a car, Favor was the first to the window. "It's them. They're here."

"They came in a car? They didn't say they were doing that when we saw them yesterday," *Mamm* said.

"No, it's a truck," Favor told her.

CHAPTER 5

*C*herish leaned the broom against the counter and *Mamm* said, "No. Put the broom away."

"But I want to be first out there."

"Put it away. If you girls learn to put things away after you've used them, you won't have such a mess."

Cherish put the broom away. Then she ran to the window in time to see Simon's mother open the truck's door and get out. "Yes. It is them." She wiped her hands on a tea towel, straightened her *kapp* and her clothes and walked out to greet them.

She wasn't first, she was third to greet them. Bliss was already there, helping them with their luggage. Cherish frowned at the number of bags being pulled out of the truck. It looked like they were moving in.

Simon looked up at her and waved. "Hello, Cherish."

She walked toward him. "Hi, hi to everyone."

Wilma said, "Welcome. I've got all the sleeping arrangements figured out."

"It looks like a large house, Cherish. A large house for just you if you ever decide to move here," Harriet said.

"Large enough so all my family can visit me." Cherish saw Malachi near the barn and called him over. He walked over, with Wally waddling behind him. "This is Malachi, my farm manager."

The visitors said hello, but they couldn't stop looking at Wally. "Is he your pet?" Simon asked.

"I dunno. I think it's more that I'm his pet. He just follows me."

"I've never seen that before. Did you train him to do that?" Harriet asked.

"No. I think they have an instinct to follow. He is misguided if he's followin' me." Malachi laughed.

A gusty wind started to blow. "Everyone into the house," urged Wilma. "We weren't sure when you'd be coming, but I'll make us some soup to warm us. Malachi, we'll need more wood brought in for the fire."

"Sure. I've got some already chopped, but I should probably help with the bags first."

Everyone else got out, including the man who'd been driving the truck. Melvin introduced their friend, Wayne. "Wayne offered to drive us and we couldn't say no."

"That's nice," Wilma said as the men got the bags out.

Malachi offered to help, but the men said they could manage. Everyone was still amazed by Wally.

"He's sorta my pet, but more like my shadow," Malachi told them. "I should fetch that wood now." When he walked off, everyone watched Wally, waddling behind him.

Wilma said, "He follows him everywhere but don't worry,

he's housetrained. I didn't believe it until I saw it with my own eyes."

Then everyone stopped looking at the goose and looked over at the house. Cherish had no idea what they were staring at. She turned too and saw Favor. Cherish blinked hard because she couldn't believe her eyes.

Favor was walking toward them and wearing Cherish's brand new deep-pink dress that Florence had specially made for her.

Cherish was furious!

"My, that's a bright dress," Harriet said.

Favor put up her hand and waved at everyone. "So nice to see you all."

Cherish was so angry she didn't know what to do. She put her head down and stomped into the house. When she passed Favor, she couldn't even look at her.

Cherish walked through the house and sat in the living room, wondering how to handle what had just happened. That dress was supposed to help her impress Simon, and if she wore it now he'd think she was borrowing Favor's dress.

Malachi sat next to her and Wally sat at his feet. "Hey, what's wrong?"

"That's my dress," Cherish hissed. "Favor is wearing my new dress without even asking me."

"The red one?"

"It's pink!" Not only was Malachi the most untidy person she'd ever seen, he couldn't speak properly and he was color blind.

"So your sister is wearing your dress. Is that why you're upset?"

Cherish bit her lip. "Don't worry. You wouldn't understand." She knew she had to pull herself together fast because soon, they'd all be in the house. She'd have to impress Simon's parents and act like a gracious hostess.

Cherish got to her feet, and wore a bright smile while she held the door open for everyone. Then after they said goodbye to their driver, she showed everyone to their rooms and told them to come to the kitchen once they were ready and lunch would be served.

Cherish headed to the kitchen, bypassing Favor without even looking at her. Needing a moment to breathe, she stepped outside. It didn't matter that it was bitterly cold, she didn't want to lose her temper and have a row with Favor in front of her possible future in-laws.

Mamm came up beside Cherish and whispered, "Why's Favor wearing your dress?"

"I don't know. Why don't you ask her?"

"You didn't know?"

"No. She just took it without asking. That was my special dress. I was going to wear it... on a special occasion."

"You still can. I'll have her take it off and we'll wash it. It'll be as good as new."

"No, don't worry about it. Thanks anyway."

Mamm patted her shoulder. "I'll have a word with her."

"Thanks, but can you wait until the visitors go? You know how Favor can be sometimes."

"I will."

Cherish knew she'd have to sit through lunch watching her sister wearing *her* new dress all the while.

Bliss then walked up to Cherish and whispered, "Shall I ask her to take it off and ask her to wear something else?"

"No, it's okay. I don't want to make a big fuss about it. I won't even say anything while the guests are here."

"Good idea. I'm sorry I didn't know or I would've stopped her."

"Thanks, Bliss. I know you would've."

Favor was keeping right out of Cherish's way. She was the first to sit down at the table. Then she was joined by Simon and his parents.

Cherish turned around and saw them sitting at the table. "I'll just find Malachi, and then we can all eat."

"Cherish, can he leave the goose outside while we eat?" *Mamm* asked.

"I'm not sure. I'll ask Malachi."

"It's your house, I thought, Cherish," Simon said with a grin.

"It is, but it's kind of his place too while he's here. Right now, it's more his place."

Mamm sighed. "Just ask him to leave it outside."

"I'll serve up while you're gone," Bliss said.

"Thanks. I won't be long." Cherish grabbed her coat and stepped outside. She ran to the barn and opened the door. There he sat on a bale of straw with Wally beside him. "What are you doing in here?"

"Just getting some space. I'm not used to so many people."

"It's lunchtime. We're all waiting for you."

He jumped to his feet. "I won't say no to food."

They walked back to the house. When Cherish reached the

front door, she remembered what her mother said about Wally. She turned to Malachi. "Can Wally stay outside while we eat?"

Malachi looked down at Wally. "If he can't come in, I won't come in. It's okay, we can eat in the barn. It's nice and warm in there."

"It's not. It's freezing in the barn. Don't worry. I'm sure *Mamm* will get used to him."

When they walked into the kitchen, Cherish saw everyone sitting there, waiting. All the food was spread out on the table.

"Thanks, Bliss," Cherish said as she took her place at the table.

"I helped too," said Favor.

Cherish ignored Favor. Then Malachi sat down and Wally waddled over and settled on a mat in the corner of the room. Everyone closed their eyes for their silent prayer of thanks for the food. When all eyes were open, Harriet leaned over her husband and pushed Simon's hair out of his eyes. "There, that's better."

Simon smiled at his mother. "Thank you."

Cherish could feel Malachi looking at her. It's exactly what Malachi said Simon's mother did. It was painful to see it. Simon was a grown man. Funny thing was, Simon didn't even seem embarrassed by his mother. Cherish kept her head down, wondering what everyone else thought of what had just taken place.

CHAPTER 6

Wilma then started handing the food around for everyone to help themselves from the bowls.

They had the soup Wilma had promised, along with fried chicken, and Favor and Bliss had helped with the mashed potato, beans, and baked vegetables.

"This all looks wonderful. I didn't expect such good food," Melvin said.

"We want your stay here to be comfortable. I brought a lot of food from home."

"You didn't need to do that, Wilma. I have plenty here. It's all from the farm," Malachi said.

Cherish was quick to say, "I told her that, but she wanted to bring food as well."

"We won't be a burden on you, Malachi. You keep that food in store for yourself."

"Malachi, will you show us around the farm after we eat?" Melvin asked.

"I'd love to do that."

"We have sheep back home."

"I know. Cherish told me you do. And you used to have a dairy farm?" Malachi asked.

"That's right. Sheep are so much easier. We also had sheep at our former place, as well as the cows. The land we have now is more suited to sheep."

"Why did you move?" Malachi asked.

"We got a good price for the farm. We couldn't refuse it."

Simon was quick to explain, "They're developing the land, but they're developing it into what they call hobby farms. It'll still be green. We wouldn't have sold out for a mall or something like that, no matter what the price."

Mamm said, "I thought you knew the Koppels, Malachi. You've all met before, haven't you?"

Malachi nodded. "We've met, but we never really had the chance to have a decent talk."

Harriet leaned over her husband and took another piece of crispy fried chicken. "Cherish, can you cook like your mother?"

Cherish opened her mouth to speak, but Favor answered before her. "*Mamm* taught all of us to cook. We can all cook really well."

Mamm laughed. "I hope so. I tried to do a good job with all my girls. It wasn't easy sometimes."

"That's right, your first husband died. Was that the father of Cherish and Favor?"

Wilma nodded. "That's right. Then I married Levi, who's Bliss's father."

"Isn't it great that you all get along?" Harriet said.

Cherish glanced over at Favor. "That's right. We're all just one big happy family." Now Cherish was growing even more annoyed. Favor could drop food on her new dress! She looked away, swallowing her anger the best she could. It was vital she make a good impression.

"I'd like a big family one day. Being an only child has made me want loads of offspring." Simon smiled at Cherish as he spoke.

Harriet laughed at her son. "You make them sound like sheep when you say offspring."

Cherish grabbed her glass of water and took a mouthful. All the while, she was thinking about the births she'd seen. She wasn't ready to go through that. Besides, most of the time she still felt like a kid herself. Maybe she'd responded too quickly when Simon invited himself to her farm. She should've made up some excuse, but she did really like him. The whole thing was so confusing.

"Sadly, we couldn't have any more children after we had Simon," Harriet told everyone.

"I keep telling people you got it right the first time so you didn't need any more." Simon laughed at his own joke and everyone at the table chuckled. Cherish had heard him say that before, so she could only manage a smile. Now she knew how her older sister, Mercy, felt when her husband told the same jokes over and over.

Harriet looked around at the girls. "Any of you girls courting yet?"

"No," Favor said quickly. "I'm not."

"If that's so then there can't be many men in your community. We don't have girls your age here," Harriet said.

"There's Annie Whylie," Cherish said. "She's a friend of Malachi's."

"That's right. We've met Annie, but I meant in our community after we made the split."

Mamm said, "Annie makes the most amazing gingerbread houses."

"I know. Ada told me about them."

Wally made a noise and everyone turned around to look at him.

"What did he do that for, Malachi?" Wilma asked.

"I'm not sure. He just does that when he feels like it."

"Does he want to go outside?"

Cherish laughed at her mother's suggestion. "You'd like that, wouldn't you, *Mamm?*"

Wilma nodded. "I certainly would. What do they eat, Malachi?"

"Grain, and he likes seeds, nuts and grass. He's poking his beak in the ground and tasting all the plants about the place. He eats some of the food as I go around feeding the animals. He also likes to taste the vegetables I cook."

"Raw or after they're cooked?" Favor asked.

"Raw. I give him bits while I'm cutting them."

Cherish noticed that Bliss had been very quiet. She was probably thinking about Adam, thanks to Harriet asking about courting.

"I'm so glad you were all able to come. We're going to have a lovely time here," Melvin said.

Harriet nodded in agreement. "Thank you for allowing us to stay. We do things as a family, just the three of us. It's always been that way. When Simon told us he wanted to visit Cherish on her farm, we thought it was a good time for us all to have a break from our farm."

Wilma smiled at Harriet. "It's lovely that your son is so close to you."

"We're more like friends than parents," Melvin said.

"I brought apple pie for dessert made from our own apple orchard." Wilma knew most people loved apple pies and she knew she made them well. She always got compliments about her pies.

"We love apple pie, don't we, Simon?" Melvin asked.

"Yes, we do."

Wally made some funny goose-sounds again. Everyone looked around to see him closing his eyes.

"What do you do with a goose? Do you bake them?" Harriet asked.

Everyone stopped looking at Wally and stared at Harriet.

Malachi said, "No one's eating Wally."

Harriet laughed. "Oh, I don't mean that, but I mean what purposes do geese serve? People don't regularly eat them like you'd eat a chicken or a turkey."

"Not in this country, but in the old country they'd regularly eat goose," Melvin told his wife.

"I didn't know. I never heard of it."

"Now you have," said Simon.

Harriet laughed at her son. "Oh you're cheeky, Simon. Isn't he cheeky?" Harriet looked at everyone.

Malachi said, "I'm told that goose eggs have a strong flavor and that's why they're not popular. I've never tried one meself."

Melvin looked at Malachi. "You mean myself."

"I don't know what you've tried. I'll have to take ya word on it."

"You mean, you'll have to take your word on it."

"That's right." Malachi frowned and kept eating. When he finished his mouthful, he said, "I hope y'all have a good time 'ere at the farm."

"You mean—"

Harriet nudged her husband to stop him talking.

Melvin whispered loudly to his wife, "He needs to learn."

"What do I need to learn? How to talk proper? I think I can speak how I want in me own house."

Cherish held her head. This wasn't good. She'd never seen Malachi be so rude to someone.

Bliss bounded to her feet and picked up a bowl from the center of the table. "More mashed potatoes, anyone?"

"Not for me. Excuse me, everyone. I forgot to do something outside." Malachi stood and walked out of the room and headed over to the sink. He left his plate there and headed outside. Wally was quick to follow and so too did Cherish.

"Why were you so rude just now?" Cherish whispered when he was nearly at the front door.

"Me rude? How rude is it to correct me? I can talk proper if I want. I know how to do it."

"I know it was a bit rude, but he probably thought he was helping you."

"I don't need help from any of 'em." He glanced at her. "Any of them. This is my home. They're my guests as much as they're your guests. They disrespected me and embarrassed me."

"Just do your best while they're here."

"About that. When are they leaving?" Malachi asked.

"I'm not sure yet." Cherish hoped it was soon. It would've been better if Simon had come by himself.

Harriet poked her head around the corner. "Need any help in here?"

The woman was everywhere! Cherish turned around and smiled at her. "Thanks, but we're fine."

"Cherish, why don't you come back in and talk to Simon? I'll take over from you."

"No!" Malachi blurted out. "Cherish has to help me outside. No one else."

"Oh. But surely—"

Malachi said, "Cherish and I have an agreement that she would help me in the kitchen tonight. We need to collect vegetables for that."

Mamm appeared out of nowhere. "That's right, Harriet. You come back and let them do their thing. They like to get the vegetables."

"Okay. If that's what you want."

When she walked out of the room, Malachi whispered, "I get the feeling that none of them take no for an answer. If they do, they don't take it well."

"I think you might be right. Well, I'll have to come outside with you now."

"Yeah, and I'll have to cook the dinner tonight."

Cherish laughed as Malachi took her coat off the hook by the door and handed it to her.

"I'm glad you came outside with me," he said, as they walked.

"It was better than staying there." Cherish wrapped her coat more securely around herself.

"I'm just pleased to get some time alone with you. Do something for me next time when you come, would ya?" Malachi asked.

"What's that?"

"Don't bring so many people, and don't invite anyone else that you're not related to."

"Sorry about that. I was only coming with *Mamm* and then it kind of got out of control. Then I realized how close Simon lived and so I thought…"

"They don't live that close. That's why the community had to split to make it easier on people. There was too much travelin.'"

"Yeah, but still, they're pretty close. You're right. Next time I'll come by myself. I just thought of something. Next time might be the time I'm moving here permanently."

Malachi grimaced. "Be sure to give me plenty of notice. I'll have to find another place to live."

"Don't worry. I won't leave you homeless."

"I might have to sleep in the barn."

Cherish laughed. "You really want to sleep in that barn, don't you."

He laughed along with her. "Not especially."

CHAPTER 7

$\mathcal{B}$ack at the apple orchard, Debbie had been up at the crack of dawn perfecting her tea recipes while baby Jared slept. She had done two hours work on the recipes when Ada, Samuel and Matthew arrived.

Debbie and Ada sat in the kitchen while the men busied themselves helping Levi with the outside chores.

"I need some advice about love, Debbie."

"Don't ask me, Ada. I failed at love, remember?"

"Oh, don't say that. You have Peter now and he adores you."

"We'll have to wait and see where that leads. Are you and Samuel having problems?"

Ada frowned. "No. I'm worried about young Bliss. I fear I could've made things worse for her."

"How so?"

"I went to see Adam the other day. I was trying to make him see sense. I told him how wonderful Bliss is. We all think she is.

She's sweet and she's kind. It stands out even more when she's with Wilma's daughters."

Debbie gasped. "Oh, Ada, you shouldn't say that."

Ada laughed. "I'm joking, but I know that you know what I mean. She deserves a good man like Adam."

"And what happened when you talked with him?"

"I went to his work and he seemed dreadfully uncomfortable to discuss it with me, but I was forced to do it. And you know why?"

Debbie shook her head.

"I had to because if I didn't talk to him, Matthew was going to do it. It would've been better coming from me."

Debbie took a sip of tea. "Go on. What did he say?"

"Just a whole lot of nonsense about her not being the kind of woman he thought she was. He can't get past her writing to John, and then still writing to John when they were dating."

"It is hard to get over it when someone disappoints you. I know how he feels."

"She made a mistake," Ada said.

Debbie shrugged her shoulders. "It wasn't a mistake, like an impulse. She deliberately wrote to him a few times."

"I thought you and Bliss were good now."

"We are, but I can see why Adam feels the way he does."

Ada nodded. "Then you should be the one to bring that up with Adam."

"Me? No, I can't."

"You should. The whole thing affected you as well. If he sees you of all people have forgiven Bliss, then he might too."

"He might already have forgiven her but he just doesn't

want her as his wife anymore. The two are very different things."

Ada looked down at the table. "You're probably right." Ada sighed as she looked up at the ceiling. "There's no hope for her now. No hope at all."

Now Debbie felt guilty for saying she wouldn't talk with Adam. She disliked disappointing anyone. "I'm sure Adam doesn't want all these people telling him he should get back to how things used to be."

"He obviously doesn't. Forget it. Just forget I said anything." Ada looked up at her. "I just thought that since she and you are cousins…"

"You're making me feel awful."

"Someone can't make you feel something. What you feel is what you feel and has nothing to do with me. Maybe you know in your heart there is some way you can help Bliss."

Debbie wanted to help if she could. "How?"

"I don't know. If I did, I'd tell you. All I can think of is that you could have a conversation with him."

"I just don't think that talking to him will do any good."

"What then?" Ada blinked hard.

"I don't know." Debbie shook her head.

They heard the front door open and the sound of heavy footsteps. They knew Samuel, Matthew and Levi were back.

They walked into the kitchen. "Cup of tea time, is it?" Levi asked.

"Make mine coffee," Samuel said.

Matthew sat down. "Me too, please."

Ada glared at Matthew and he sat up straight under her

intense glare. He cleared his throat. "I mean, could I please have a cup of coffee, Aunt Ada?"

Debbie stood up. "I'll make it. Coffee for everyone?"

"Yes, please," Samuel said as he sat down next to Ada.

"I'd prefer tea, please," Levi requested. He sat in his usual position at the end of the table, looking back and forth between Ada and Debbie. "I'm sensing something serious is going on. Has something happened?"

"Something has happened and that something is Bliss and Adam." Ada hung her head and her shoulders seemed to collapse. "The poor things."

"What happened to them?" Samuel asked.

"She means they're no longer dating," Matthew told them.

Samuel frowned. "Is that all? I thought there'd been an accident."

"No, Samuel." Ada sounded as though she was close to tears. "Adam won't listen to sense."

"You can't talk a man out of something when he's made up his mind. If anything, it'll make him even more determined to stick to what he's decided," Levi said.

"Don't make me even sadder. It can't possibly end like this. You've all seen them together. They just make sense."

Levi continued, "Nothing can be done. You can't force him to accept things. Just leave things be and if they're meant to be together, it'll happen."

Ada wasn't giving up. "Maybe if he can just look at things from Bliss's side."

Samuel patted his wife's hand. "Bliss is young. She'll get over Adam in time."

"I just think we as a family should try something." Ada's voice quavered as though she was holding back tears.

Levi said, "You already tried, Ada. It didn't work out. You can't force a man to do something against his will."

"Levi, you don't understand. He will want to patch things up with Bliss."

Levi shook his head. "All right. You're not going to listen to me."

"No, not if you're saying things along those lines." Ada pulled out a handkerchief from her sleeve and dabbed at each eye.

Debbie placed several mugs and the coffee pot in front of the men. Then she put a jug of cream and a bowl of sugar in the center of the table before turning around to get Levi his tea.

"What do you think about what Ada's saying, Debbie?" Samuel asked.

"I'm not sure. I'm just upset for Bliss. If Ada's talk didn't change his mind, I don't know what will."

"Perhaps he needs the opinion of an older man," Matthew said.

Samuel and Levi looked at him. "Not me," Samuel said.

"I wouldn't. I can't do it because I'm Bliss's father. I wouldn't want to interfere. These things should sort themselves out."

Matthew had other things on his mind. "Aunt Ada, do we have any of your chocolate cookies left?"

"Maybe, if Cherish didn't eat them all."

"I'll have a look." Debbie got up and brought the cookie jar to the table and placed it in front of Matthew.

He wasted no time prying off the lid. "Five left. One for each of us."

Ada sighed loudly. "I thought one of you might've been bothered to have a discussion with Adam and see how you could help."

"I was going to do it," Matthew said.

"I'm not talking about you, Matthew." Ada shook her head. "I'm asking the men."

"You want me to do it?" Samuel asked.

"Oh, thank you. I knew I could rely on you."

"No, I mean… I was asking you if you expect me to do it. I wasn't volunteering. I agree with Levi."

Ada's lips turned down at the corners. She picked up her tea cup and saucer. "Come along, Debbie. We'll leave the men to themselves and we'll drink our tea by the fire in the other room."

Debbie got up and followed Ada out of the room. They sat down on the couch and placed their cups down on the low table in front of them. "Don't be too hard on Samuel. He wouldn't know what to say."

"I know, but he could try." Ada pursed her lips.

"Why don't we think of something else? You've tried talking to him and that didn't work."

"What else is there?" Ada asked.

"I don't know yet, but it wouldn't do any good me talking to him. He'll probably just shut down."

"The girls fear that he'll date someone else and forget all about Bliss. What will become of her? What if he marries hastily to forget her, and then he realizes he's made a big mistake? He'll ruin both their lives."

"He's not dating anyone, Ada."

"Not yet, but I have heard a whisper that Krystal likes him."

"I've heard the same." Debbie sipped her coffee.

"I've even heard she's getting him to do work in the quilt store just so she can be closer to him."

"Time without Bliss might make him miss her."

"What if we make him think she's found someone else?" Ada asked, with a glint in her eyes.

Debbie shook her head. "That would be deceptive."

"Not if we don't say it. We'll just let him think it. He doesn't know she's away, does he?"

"I doubt it. It was a last minute thing."

"I have an idea. See what you think about this. I'll have him come here to put up the aviary that's in pieces in the barn. While he's doing that, we'll say something about Bliss that will leave him wondering. You can't tell me he doesn't still have feelings for her."

"That's right. You can't turn your feelings off and on like a tap." Debbie was a little nervous about this, but as long as they didn't have to tell a lie, it might work.

"I'll have Matthew call him and tell him we want the aviary put up as a surprise for Cherish for when she gets back."

"And tell him not to say anything about Bliss. We'll say something when he gets here."

"Okay. I'll have him call Adam now. Matthew!" Ada yelled out.

Ada's voice was so loud that Debbie had to block her ears.

CHAPTER 8

*E*veryone was surprised that Adam said he'd be there within the hour. That had to mean he thought Bliss would be there, didn't it? Why else would he rush over there? He was always telling everyone how much work they had to do.

When Adam arrived, Debbie handed her baby to Levi and went outside with Ada to greet Adam.

"Thanks for coming straight out, Adam. We want the thing up before Cherish gets back from the farm."

"I thought Cherish didn't want it up until the warmer weather."

Ada waved a hand in the air. "That girl doesn't know what she wants. She and Wilma are at her farm, and Favor and Bliss have gone with them. They've only gone for a few days. Thank you again for coming out at short notice."

He tipped his hat back on his head. "Matthew made it sound like an emergency."

Ada gave a nervous laugh. "That young man is always over

exaggerating everything. He takes after his father. He doesn't take after my side of the family."

Debbie tried to get the conversation back to the aviary. "We did want it up for when she comes back."

"Okay, not a problem. Where do you want it?"

Ada replied, "Out the back beside the kitchen window. The roof overhangs a little which will offer the birds protection against the weather."

"I'll do that now." He walked toward the barn.

Ada and Debbie looked at each other, both thinking the same thing. Adam hadn't taken the bait and asked why Bliss had gone to the farm. And they didn't want to be too obvious.

"What will we do now?" Ada whispered.

"I'm not sure. We'll have to say something else or he would've come out here for nothing. Let's help him carry it."

"Matthew!" Ada yelled loudly once again, causing Debbie to grimace.

Matthew ran out of the house toward them. "Yeah?"

"Don't just stand there. Adam's here and he needs help."

"Okay."

Then Ada stepped closer to Matthew. "Have him come inside before he leaves. Do NOT take no for an answer."

"I'll try."

"Don't try, just do it."

"Yes, Aunt Ada."

Matthew walked into the barn just in time to pick up one end of one of the aviary walls.

As they carried it out, Adam asked Matthew, "Why has Bliss gone to the farm?"

Ada overheard it and was relieved. He cared. Otherwise, why would he have asked?

An air-splitting cry rang through the air. "Sorry, Ada. I really should take him from Levi."

"Do what you have to do. I can handle this." Ada hurried over and spoke to Adam before Matthew could draw a breath. "It was a last-minute decision. There will be a lot of people staying there." Ada followed them while she talked. "There was a lovely young man we all met at the wedding. He'll be at the farm too and he's bringing his parents along."

"Favor's gone too," Matthew added.

Ada glared at Matthew and then he kept quiet. "There'll be quite a crowd there," Ada added.

"Sounds like they'll have a good time," Adam said.

Ada studied Adam's face. He didn't seem at all bothered by the news that Bliss would be in close proximity with an unknown male. Now Ada was bothered. They couldn't say anything more or it would be far too obvious.

After Ada showed Adam where to erect the aviary, Adam said, "Why don't you go inside, Ada? Matthew and I can handle this. It's too cold out here."

"Okay. When you're done, come in for a nice hot drink. Or I could heat you up a bowl of soup."

He smiled. "I'd like some soup, thanks, Ada."

"We might as well all have some and we'll call it lunch." Ada walked through the back door and into the kitchen. As she was turning on the gas stove under the soup pot, she realized Samuel and Levi were still in the kitchen.

"Did your plan work?" Samuel asked.

"Shh. He'll hear you. They're only just outside. Yes, I

mentioned Bliss was away and he didn't seem upset. He's coming inside for soup when he finishes outside, so I want you two to be on your best behavior."

Samuel and Levi looked at each other. "When are we anything but well-behaved?" Samuel asked.

Ada turned away from the stove and placed her hands on her hips. "Just don't say anything silly to him. If we leave out some information, he might think Bliss could be interested in Simon."

Levi shook his head. "I don't like that idea."

"And why not? Something's got to pull at Adam's heart. And if he feels he could lose her forever, he might snap out of whatever it is that he's in."

"You could make things worse."

Ada walked over and sat down with the two men. "How could that make anything worse?"

"He could think that he never meant much to Bliss if she could forget about him so fast. Nothing could be further from the truth."

Ada pushed out her lips while she thought about Levi's comment. "Well, at least I'm doing something. The two of you aren't doing much."

Debbie walked into the room. "I've just put Jared down for a nap. I hope he'll sleep with all that banging."

"It can't be helped. I think our plan is working," Ada said.

"Oh. Good. Did you say anything?"

Ada nodded. "I did, but these two aren't happy with me."

Debbie sat down at the kitchen table. "It's hard to know what to do in a situation like this."

"Doing nothing won't get anyone into trouble," Levi said. "Let the two of them sort things out for themselves."

"I think Levi's right, Ada," Samuel said. "We all want the best for both of them, but they both have to want to be together."

Ada stood up and headed to the stove to stir the soup. "I just want everyone to be happy."

Debbie got up and sliced the bread that she'd made earlier that morning. Then she helped Ada set the table.

Half an hour later, Matthew came inside. "Aunt Ada, do you want to come outside and have a look?"

"Sure. Everyone will come."

Everyone went outside to look at the new aviary.

CHAPTER 9

*A*da smiled when she saw the aviary all set up. "Ah, Cherish will love this."

"So will the birds," Matthew said. "But when will we put them out here? She said she didn't want to put them out in the cold."

"She can make that decision when she gets back. For now, we've got soup on."

"Um… I might give that a miss, thanks all the same."

Ada wasn't taking no for an answer. "Nonsense, Adam. You need to keep your strength up. Besides, we've all been waiting for you to finish so we could eat."

Adam grinned. "Well, in that case, I'd love to."

"That's the way." Samuel patted him on his back. "You both did a great job."

"I just held onto the bolts," Matthew said.

"You were more help than that," Adam told him.

They all moved into the house and sat around the table

while Ada ladled soup into bowls. Debbie came back into the room and helped Ada take the bowls of soup to the table. Then after they sat down, they all said a silent prayer of thanks for the food.

Ada smiled at Adam. "Ah, it's just like old times having you at the table with us, Adam."

"Yes. I can't count the amount of times I've had a meal here." He went a little red in the cheeks and picked up his spoon.

"Who cooks for you, Adam?" Samuel asked.

He laughed. "Andrew and I take turns. Sometimes we have take-out if we've had a long day at work."

"How's your business doing?" asked Levi.

"We've got steady work. It's been like that since we started. I just hope it stays that way." Adam took a mouthful of soup. "This is lovely."

"I hope so." Ada gave a nod.

While Adam then buttered a slice of bread, he said, "It's so quiet here today."

"It is quiet without Favor and Cherish. They're the noisy ones."

"What is this soup?"

"It's chicken and corn soup. I'm glad you like it. I made it yesterday. It always tastes better on the second day. I'll make some for you boys and I'll bring it to you. It keeps well."

"Oh no. I don't want you to go to any trouble." Adam shook his head.

"It's no trouble. Since Wilma's been gone, I have a lot more time on my hands. That reminds me. Matthew, you have been feeding Cherish's birds, haven't you?"

"I sure have. Every day. Changing their water and cleaning their cage."

"Good boy."

"Who's a good boy?" Timmy said.

Everyone laughed.

Adam's eyes grew wide. "Was that the bird speaking just now?"

"It was. Cherish taught Timmy how to speak. Haven't you heard him before?"

"I've heard him say one or two words, but never that much."

"That's because you haven't been around lately," Samuel blurted out. Then he looked up. "Oh, I'm sorry."

"It's okay," Adam said. "I haven't been around much, it's true." Then there was a tension-filled moment of silence. "I hope you don't mind if I leave as soon as I finish the soup. I've got to get back to help Andrew with something we've got to finish up today."

"You do that." Ada got to her feet. "I'll put soup in a container for you to take to Andrew. Can't have one of you go hungry."

"That's nice of you. Thanks, Ada. He'll appreciate that. We usually work through and don't have time to eat during the day."

"You must have food in your bellies to help you carry on."

"We always try to, but some days it doesn't work out that way."

"What do we owe you for today, Adam?" Levi asked.

"Nothing. Cherish already paid for it and I said I'd come back and put it up when she was ready."

Once everyone had finished eating, Ada put some soup into

a container and some buttered bread in a brown paper bag. Then everyone walked to the door to see Adam off.

They waved as his horse and wagon headed down the driveway.

"He's a nice young man," Levi said. "It would've been nice to have him as a son-in-law, but it doesn't look like it's *Gott's* will."

"That was a bit awkward," Debbie said. "Did anyone else think so?"

"I did," Matthew agreed. "He asked me about Bliss when we were outside."

Ada gasped. "What?"

"It's true."

"What did he ask?"

"How she's been. He also thought it was funny that she went to the farm when she's never gone before, and stuff like that."

Ada grabbed Matthew by the sleeve and dragged him into the living room. "Sit," she said, pointing at the couch.

He sat down. "Did I do something wrong?"

"No, but I must know everything he said about Bliss from start to finish. Go!"

Samuel interrupted, "Excuse me, Ada, Levi and I have something to do in the barn."

Ada waved her arm at them, without even looking in their direction.

Debbie sat on the other side of Matthew. "Start at the beginning," Debbie said.

"Let's see now." Matthew drew a deep breath. "It's just what I've already told you."

"Well, did he ask about the farm first?"

"I think so. Then he asked how she'd been."

"And what did you say?" asked Debbie.

Matthew nervously rubbed his hands together. "I had to tell him the truth. I told him that she was very upset about the breakup."

Ada held her head. "Oh, Matthew. That wasn't our plan. We wanted him to think she was slipping away from him. If he thinks she'll always be here for him, there's no urgency."

Matthew raised his eyebrows. "I can't think quick enough. I'm sorry."

"But you knew the plan. No good being sorry. Why would you go off thinking for yourself?"

Matthew frowned. "I didn't go off."

"Ada means, why would you go away from the plan that Ada told you?"

"I don't know." He hung his head.

"You knew."

Matthew nodded. "I guess I did, but when faced with telling a lie, I couldn't."

Ada sat back in her chair. "It's not a lie. She's gone to the farm and she will enjoy herself. And she'll enjoy the company of Simon and his parents because they are wonderful people. So, where's the lie in all that I just said?"

"He asked me how she was doing. Every time I see her she's crying or about to cry or she's just finished crying. Did you want me to say she was overjoyed? If she's overjoyed, why are her eyes red all the time?"

Ada shook her head.

"Don't worry, Ada. It was a good plan." Debbie saw Matthew looking upset. "At least you tried."

Ada ground her teeth and stood up. "What is the point of trying when people around you don't follow through? There's no follow through."

"I'm sorry, Aunt Ada. It's hard for me. I don't do well with this kind of stuff."

"We know that now, but it's too late."

Debbie said, "Adam's thinking about her, Ada, so that's a good sign."

"Yeah, Aunt Ada. It's a good sign, so maybe what I said was good." Matthew's face brightened up. "Did you think about that?"

Ada tapped her finger on her chin and then sat back down. "It is possible *Gott* used you like he used Balaam's donkey to speak through."

"Hey, are you calling me a donkey?"

"No, because I'm pretty sure it was a mule, wasn't it, Debbie?"

"I believe so. It was a mule, but are mules and donkeys the same?"

Matthew stood up. "Mules and donkeys aren't the same. I don't want to be either. Are you really calling me a mule, Aunt Ada? Is that what you think of me?"

"Don't be offended. If *Gott* was able to speak through the mule, He can talk through you as well. If we apply faith, we can believe that Bliss and Adam will be back together in no time. I do miss Adam."

Debbie agreed. "Me too. He's so nice."

Matthew shook his head. "I'll be outside with Levi and *Onkel* Samuel." He stomped out of the house.

"I wonder why he's so upset. I didn't say he was a mule, did I? That's not what I meant."

"I know. I can't figure out why he suddenly got offended. I thought you were giving him a compliment. Don't worry about him. He's turning into a man and you know how strange they can be sometimes."

"Ah, that's the problem with him."

Debbie laughed. "I'll make you a cup of tea."

"Thanks, Debbie. I was just thinking I could do with one right about now."

CHAPTER 10

*A*dam left the Baker Apple Orchard with one thing on his mind—Bliss. He missed her more than anything. She was the whole reason he'd come back to live in her community. He started the business so he'd have the money to support himself and, eventually, her and their children.

She'd hurt him more than anyone had ever hurt him. Didn't she feel the same way as he did?

If he'd been writing to a woman, Bliss would've done the same thing as he did. She would've ended their relationship and everyone would've said how dreadful he was. But no one seemed to think Bliss had done anything wrong. Her family was supporting her and couldn't see why he had a problem with the deception.

He couldn't forgive and forget as though nothing happened. She'd kept that from him and only told him when she'd been caught out. He could've married her and then he might've found out when it was too late.

At least he found out now.

Adam realized he was going in the wrong direction. His mind was all over the place right now.

He got back to his workshop, parked his buggy and got out the food that Ada had packed for his business partner.

Andrew looked up when he walked in. "How did it go?"

"Just like I thought. They were trying to make me reconsider my decision about Bliss."

"Why else would they get you out there? Cherish said she didn't even want that aviary up until the warmer weather."

"I know that, but I could hardly say no. Here's some soup and buttered bread from Ada."

"Oh great! I'm starving. Did you eat with them?"

"I did."

Andrew took the food from him, opened the soup and held up a spoon. "Hey, she even put in a spoon."

Adam chuckled.

Then and there, Andrew started eating the soup. "Well, have they talked you into making amends with Bliss?"

"No. I found out she's gone to Cherish's farm along with Favor and Wilma."

"She's never gone there before."

"I know. There's some man going there too. I'm not sure what that's all about. Matthew didn't say much and I didn't want to ask too much."

"Are you willing to lose her?"

Adam nibbled on his fingernail. "It's not as simple as that."

"I don't think she thought what she was doing was that bad."

Adam took off his hat and ran a hand through his hair. Why

didn't anyone understand what he'd been through? The only person he'd confided to about what Bliss had done was Andrew. He had needed to talk to someone. "I wasn't writing to another girl. Or even talking to another young woman. Bliss was the only woman I thought about."

Andrew suggested, "Why don't you ask to see the letters if they bother you so much?"

"She offered and I declined."

Andrew shook his head. "If she offered, those letters won't be as bad as you're thinking."

"It's the fact that she wrote them at all and thought nothing of it."

"You're gonna have to do something, Adam. You've been moping about for weeks. Your work has slowed up ever since this upset with Bliss."

"I know. I'll do better. I can't leave everything to you."

"Thanks for the soup."

"Thank Ada. She was the one who forced me to bring it to you. She said she's making us a whole pot of soup."

"I'd love that. I thought you were gone for longer than you should've been."

"Well, I better get back to work."

"I'll just finish this. Nearly done."

"Take your time. Don't rush. Don't want you to get indigestion." Adam walked off to the job he'd been working on before he got Matthew's frantic call. Then Adam did what he'd been doing for weeks, he pushed Bliss out of his mind as best he could, and carried on.

CHAPTER 11

*O*ver dinner at Cherish's farm, everyone was on their best behaviour. Malachi had cooked a roast and Melvin complimented Malachi on his cooking skills.

Then everyone stayed up late playing the card game Dutch Blitz, except for Malachi who said he needed an early night.

When the girls finally went to bed and closed the bedroom door, Cherish had to say something to Favor about her special dress. "Why were you wearing my new dress today?"

"Because I didn't pack enough clothes." Favor pulled the dress over her head and hung it on a hanger, then she slipped into her nightgown. "Relax. It's not even dirty."

"Yeah, no thanks to you. You could've borrowed any number of my dresses. I've even got spares hanging in the closet from last time I was here. Did you have to take my brand new one that I haven't even worn?"

"You weren't wearing it, so I thought you wouldn't mind."

"I wasn't wearing it because I was saving it for a special occasion."

"You can wear it for something special whenever you want."

Cherish was outraged. She did her best to keep her voice down. "Everyone's seen it now. Everyone's given you the compliments that they would've given me."

Bliss intervened, "Cherish wanted a special dress so she'd look even better for Simon."

Favor snapped back, "He should like you for you, not for what you're wearing."

"I know that. Will you just say you're sorry? You're unbelievable, that you think it's okay to wear my new dress—my new and special dress that Florence made me specially."

Favor wasn't bothered over Cherish being so upset. She just climbed into bed. "How about I keep it and you can have Florence make you another one? Will that shut you up?"

"Cherish just wants you to say you're sorry. And she probably wants a reason why you wore it without asking when you knew it was a special dress."

"So you're on her side now, Bliss?"

"No. I'm not on anyone's side. I'm just telling you what you need to say. You've done something wrong now you've got to make it right."

Cherish was glad Bliss was telling Favor how it was.

"You're both picking on me." Favor whipped the bed coverings off and jumped out of bed. "I'm going to tell *Mamm.*"

Cherish tried to grab hold of Favor before she left the room, but Favor ducked out of her way.

"Oh no. I hope she doesn't make a big fuss. How embarrassing."

"I couldn't believe it when I saw her in your dress." Bliss shook her head.

"Thanks for helping out just now."

"Well, there's right and wrong. Favor was wrong and she won't even apologize."

Cherish sighed as she got into bed. "I know what's going to happen now. I'll fall asleep and Favor will come back and wake me up. I hate getting woken up out of a deep sleep."

"Yeah, I don't like that either." Bliss climbed in the bed from the other side.

"Favor will sleep in, but I can't. I've got to get up early in the morning to help with the farm work."

"Do you want me to find Favor and tell her to get back to bed?"

"Would you?"

"Yes." Bliss got out of bed and moved down the hallway. She pushed open Wilma's door. *"Mamm,"* she whispered. Wilma rolled over.

"What is it?" *Mamm* asked.

"Where's Favor?"

"Isn't she with you?"

"No. She said she was coming to talk with you."

"She's not here," *Mamm* said.

"Okay. Sorry to wake you."

"It's fine. I wasn't asleep yet."

Bliss quietly closed Wilma's door and made her way through the dark house. She saw a light coming from the kitchen, and moved closer, being careful not to trip over anything that might be in her way.

285

When she stepped into the kitchen, she saw Simon and Favor talking. "There you are, Favor."

Favor looked around, seeming annoyed to see her. "I was just getting a drink of water."

"Me too," Simon said.

"That's a good idea. Can you get one for me as well?"

"Sure. I'll bring it into the bedroom for you."

Favor was acting as though everything was fine. Bliss turned and walked away, but something told her she should listen in to what was going on with those two. They'd been close all day. Simon was supposed to like Cherish, and Favor knew that.

"I'll see you tomorrow then," Favor said to Simon.

"Yes. I'm so glad we came. It was good of Cherish to invite us. My folks like getting away from the farm. It's rare that they can get a day off."

"I hope we can do something fun tomorrow," Favor said.

"I'm sure we will, but I will have to make time for Cherish tomorrow."

"She won't mind. She likes being around Malachi anyway. That's all she talks about at home."

"Wait a minute. Cherish talks about Malachi?" Simon asked.

"That's right."

"I thought Malachi and Annie were dating."

"No." Favor laughed. "What made you think that?"

"I'm pretty sure Cherish told me."

Then someone turned on the tap and the running water drowned out what they said so Bliss couldn't hear them. Then the tap turned off.

"So, we'll be able to do something fun tomorrow?" Favor asked once again.

"I guess. We'll see what everyone's plans are."

"Okay. Goodnight, Simon. I had fun today."

Bliss hurried back to her room, not so worried this time about bumping into anything as she ran through the dark house. She got back to their shared room and dove under the covers.

"What's wrong?" Cherish asked.

"Nothing. Why would anything be wrong?" Bliss couldn't tell Cherish right now. There'd be a huge scene in front of their guests and no one would get any sleep. She'd tell Cherish about what Favor had said, but she wouldn't do it until the time was right.

"Where's Favor?"

"In the kitchen getting water. She didn't go to Mamm's room."

"Okay. Thanks for backing me up about the dress."

"That's fine."

Favor walked into the room with a glass of water for Bliss. "Here you are."

"Thank you." Bliss sat up and took a mouthful and then put the glass on the nightstand.

Favor climbed over Cherish and got under the covers between Bliss and Cherish. "Good night."

"Is that all you're going to say to me, Favor?"

"I'm sorry for wearing your stupid dress. Good night."

Cherish grunted. "You're so rude."

"I'm trying to sleep," Favor said.

Bliss leaned over and turned off the small gas lamp beside her.

CHAPTER 12

The next thing Cherish knew, she heard someone hissing her name from outside the bedroom door. It was Malachi and that meant it had to be morning. She got out of bed and moved to the door. Without opening it, she said, "Yes?"

"You helpin' with chores, or what?"

"Yes. Give me two minutes. I've just got to change."

"I'll be in the kitchen. You want coffee?"

"Yes please." Cherish quickly changed out of her nightgown and pulled on her warmest clothes. She even pulled on two pairs of her warmest black stockings and her thickest undergarments. Then she found Malachi standing at the kitchen sink with Wally beside him. They both turned and looked at her.

"I love being up this time of the mornin.'" Malachi passed her a cup of coffee.

"Thanks. Me too." She sat down at the table and looked out the window. "The farm sure is pretty."

"It is." Malachi gulped down half his coffee and poured the rest down the sink. "Let's go."

"Give me a minute."

"I've already given you a minute."

"I know, but I have to drink my coffee."

He sat down beside her. "I can always make you another one when we get back."

Cherish took a mouthful and then another. "Okay, I'm ready."

They moved outside, careful to keep quiet so they wouldn't wake anyone.

"We'll feed the pigs first."

"Okay."

As they mixed up the feed, Malachi said, "Whoever marries Simon, she will be marrying his parents too."

Cherish was taken aback. That comment had come out of nowhere. "Don't be silly."

"It's true. He's never going to leave 'em. I reckon he'll marry and expect the girl to live on the farm with him. No... with them."

"There's nothing wrong with that, is there?"

"Not if you're okay with it. Not if you want to marry his parents as well as him. Your children will have four parents."

Cherish hit his arm. "Don't say it like I'll be marrying him and having a million babies."

Malachi laughed. "Maybe not a million, but it sounds like he'd be happy with ten, twelve, or fourteen. Especially if he's got his folks living in the same house to lend a helping hand."

"If I ever get married, the man will have to come here and live with me. What would be the use in me going to live on

someone else's farm when I have a perfectly good farm
here?"

Malachi smiled. "Exactly."

"You agree with me?"

"I do."

"Where will you go when that day comes?"

He swiped a hand through the air. "I'm not worried about
that. That'll be years away, won't it?"

"Yes. So many years away. Years and years before I get
married. But, I told you before I'm going to live here in about a
year, so where will you go?"

"Dunno yet." He passed her a bucket and they made their
way to the pig pen. "The more you try to convince me, the more
I'm not convinced. You must like Simon. Why would he be here
if you didn't?"

"Think what you like." She knew she couldn't keep denying
it. She wasn't fooling anyone. "And what if I do like him?"

"I knew it." Malachi shook the contents of his bucket into
the pigs' trough. "Well, it's good for me then if you marry him."

"Why's that?"

"Because I can stay here while you're helping them on their
farm." He took the bucket of feed from Cherish and poured that
in too.

"Humph. If that happened, their farm would be part my
farm too."

"No it wouldn't. You'd be just working there. They're not
going to give you a share of their farm just for marrying Simon."

"I know that, and I wouldn't expect that, but… it would be
like mine. I'm not saying that'd ever happen. I'm just saying if it
did happen, then it would be okay."

Malachi looked back at the house. "They sure are sleeping a long time for farmers."

"They're probably just enjoying the break away from their farm."

"Yeah. That must be it."

They took their time feeding the animals, and when they were through, the sun was well and truly over the horizon.

WHEN CHERISH WENT INSIDE, she saw Favor talking to Simon. They were all cozied up in front of the fire. So her temper wouldn't boil over, she headed into the kitchen. There she saw everyone else at the kitchen table drinking hot chocolate, apart from Bliss and Harriet who were having a good time baking bread.

Cherish turned on her heel and went into her bedroom and closed her door. It was like she didn't matter at all. No one even looked up when she walked in.

A minute later, someone was knocking on her door. Cherish had been slumped over her bed. She quickly sat up. "Come in."

It was *Mamm*. She looked at Cherish sympathetically and hurried to sit next to her. "Are you okay?"

"I don't know. This is the first time I've felt out of place in this house. I should be the one cooking with Harriet and getting to know her. And I should be the one wearing the pink dress and talking to Simon."

"Maybe it would've been better if both of them stayed at home. Anyway, she's not wearing the pink dress today. That's something at least."

Cherish's mouth fell open. "So it is awful? This is what I thought."

"No. It's not awful and keep your voice down unless you want everyone to hear you. Go out now and join in. It's no good moping about in your room and it's a little rude."

Cherish knew her mother was right. "Do I talk to Simon? I'd have to join their conversation and that would seem a bit weird."

"It's not weird at all. He's here to see you. He's not here to see Favor or anyone else." *Mamm* moved closer and put her arm around her. "Just act normal and smile."

"I'm trying. I can't decide whether to help them bake or whether I join in Favor's conversation."

"Do whichever one you feel like. These are your guests."

"They didn't even look up at me when I walked into the room. I'm still so upset by Favor wearing my dress."

"I know, but it's just a dress. Forget the dress."

Cherish looked down at her hands in her lap. It wasn't just a dress, it was her new Sunday best that Florence had sewed for her. It represented a new hope and possibly a new direction in her life if things with Simon went well. "She might as well keep it."

"Cheer up."

"I will when there's something to cheer up about."

"You're here at the farm. That should make you happy. You know it's not easy for any of us to get away from the orchard."

"You're right. Favor should've been left at home."

Wilma shook her head. "You two used to get along so well."

"I know, before Krystal came along. Now everything has changed. She's not the sister I grew up with. The old Favor

293

would never have worn my dress without even asking. She would've known to ask."

"What's done is done. She's still your sister. And Bliss is loving being with Harriet because she has no mother of her own. She enjoys the company of other people's mothers."

Cherish sighed. "I know. I'm not mad with her."

"You shouldn't be mad with anyone. Forgive and forget. She'll come to you and apologize and you can tell her how much it upset you."

"I will, don't worry."

Wilma stood. "Now come out and entertain your guests. They're all here to see you." Wilma grabbed Cherish's arm and pulled her to her feet.

"Okay."

"And smile. We want the guests to feel welcome, not be scared away."

Cherish flashed her mother an exaggerated smile.

"That's better."

Cherish couldn't allow Favor to steal away her first possible boyfriend. She had to do something. It was time to act.

CHAPTER 13

$\mathcal{C}$herish went out into the living room and sat down between Favor and Simon. "What are we talking about?" she asked.

"Favor was just telling me about life on the orchard."

"Oh, nothing bad I hope."

Favor smirked. "Why would it be bad?"

Cherish shrugged her shoulders. "I'm not sure."

"You like living on the orchard, don't you, Cherish?" Simon asked.

"I do most of the time. It's fun at harvest time. It's exciting when we have the first cookout of the season and everyone gathers there. I do like it here better though. This is my true home."

"Can we do something together today, Cherish?" Simon asked, turning away from Favor.

"Sure. What would you like to do?"

"Excuse me." Favor bounded to her feet and walked off into the kitchen.

Cherish said, "There's not really any place we could go. How about I make us a picnic lunch and we can find a quiet place to eat?"

"It's a bit cold for a picnic, isn't it?"

"That's true. We could take the horse and buggy somewhere. Then we can park the buggy and have a picnic together. At least we'd be alone."

"I like it. I can't wait. I really want to be alone with you just to have a conversation without anyone else around. It doesn't seem like too much to ask, but it never seems to happen."

"It will today. I'll start making some goodies for the basket."

"Want some help?"

"Sure." Together they walked into the kitchen.

When Simon announced that Cherish and he were going on a picnic, Bliss said she'd make them some fancy dinner rolls to take with them.

"What a great idea. Let's join them on their picnic, Melvin."

Cherish opened her mouth in shock. Then she waited for Simon to say that it was just for the two of them.

"We haven't been on a picnic for years have we, Harriet?" Melvin said, smiling.

"It's not exactly a picnic. Simon and I were just going to drive until we found a quiet and sheltered spot somewhere. Then we were just going to have lunch in the buggy so it's not really a picnic." Cherish stared at Simon, hoping he'd jump in and say something. All he did was... nothing. His face was expressionless.

Melvin laughed. "Sounds like a picnic to me. Don't worry, we'll make it fun. I know some good games we could play."

Cherish's bottom lip curled. "Games?"

"Yes. Charades, I Spy, and the like."

Then Cherish stared at Simon a little more deliberately so he'd get the hint. He didn't notice, he was still expressionless. Cherish couldn't work it out. He said he wanted to be alone with her. It didn't make sense he'd want his parents to come with them.

"Why don't I come too?" Malachi suggested. "I love games."

Cherish frowned when she saw Malachi smirking.

Melvin said, "No, Malachi, I don't think there'd be room in the buggy for five of us to have lunch. Besides, I'm sure you have a lot to do around here. I saw some panels on the back of the barn need replacing."

"I know that, but no point doing it now when it could snow at any time."

Melvin shook a finger at him. "When you get to my age, you'll learn that you should never put off until tomorrow what you can do today."

"I'm sure Malachi knows what he's doing. He's doing a great job with the farm," Wilma said.

Cherish was a little shocked that her mother spoke up.

"Don't get me wrong, Wilma. I wasn't saying anything like that. I'm just saying that the young can learn a thing or two from their elders. We've been through many things they haven't been through yet. I'm trying to help guide him."

"I'm fine thanks," Malachi said. "Excuse me. I've got some things I need to see about in the barn." Before he walked out, he said, "And it's not those loose panels."

Melvin raised his eyebrows and when they heard the front door close, Melvin said to Cherish, "How well do you know that man?"

"He's Bishop Zachariah's nephew and he came highly recommended."

"I didn't know that."

"Yes," Wilma said, "he's been doing a great job here for years."

"Great job, eh? If you want, I can look around and make an assessment on his work."

"No, that won't be necessary. Cherish is quite happy with him."

Favor said, "Yes. Cherish is very happy with Malachi."

Cherish frowned at Favor, wondering why she was butting in.

"Forgive me for saying this, but Malachi might not work as hard for a woman boss as he would for a man. I'm not saying he's dishonest, but—"

Harriet said, "Melvin and I think men work harder for men. Simon agrees too, don't you?"

"I'm not sure, Ma."

Harriet turned toward Melvin. "Why don't you go and talk with Malachi? He seemed a little upset just now."

"I don't think that's necessary," Wilma said. "I've always found that men need some time to think things through if they're upset."

"I'll go talk with him."

Wilma stood up. "No. I will."

"Sit down, Wilma. What good would it do for you to have a conversation with him? You're a woman. This is the problem."

Cherish couldn't stop herself from blurting out, "It's a problem that my mother is a woman?"

"Yes. Women can't deal with workers."

Wilma's mouth fell open. Cherish was shocked and Favor and Bliss kept quiet and looked on.

"Simon." Cherish hoped he'd tell his father to stop.

"Yes, Cherish?" Simon asked.

"Nothing." Cherish just shook her head as Melvin headed out of the house to talk with Malachi.

"I'll just finish making your bread for the picnic." Bliss fussed around the kitchen, talking trying to take the attention off what just happened.

"This is your farm, Cherish," Wilma told her.

Cherish fiddled with her prayer kapp strings. "I know." Cherish didn't want to offend Simon's parents in any way. They were only trying to help.

"Well, go out there and be an owner." Wilma pointed at the door.

"What are you saying, Wilma?" Harriet asked.

"Now it's time to put the dough in the oven. Oh, this bread is going to be so tasty," Bliss was still doing her best to defuse the tenseness in the room.

"I'm saying that your husband shouldn't be saying anything to Malachi about how he manages this farm. It's Cherish's farm. She hasn't asked for help, or have you, Cherish?"

"I don't think so, no."

"Sometimes people don't know they need help. They are the people who need the most help," Harriet said.

Mamm folded her arms. "Well, Cherish?"

Cherish took a deep breath, not knowing what to do. She

looked at Simon, and realized he was no help at all. "I'm going." Cherish headed to the barn, not knowing what she'd find. She found Malachi showing Melvin how he'd organized all his tools in the barn. They both turned and looked at her.

Melvin smiled at her. "Seems this young man is very organized."

"Is he?" That was news to Cherish.

"Yes. He's given me some ideas for my place."

"And, after looking closer at the boards, Melvin agrees that we should leave them for now."

"Oh good. I'm glad."

"I think this young man is doing a good job for you, Cherish."

"Thanks. I do too. I never doubted him for a moment."

"Shall we go back inside? It's a little chilly out here."

"You go back in. Malachi is showing me around. Seems we might be able to learn a thing or two from each other."

"Okay." Cherish was pleased with what she'd found. It could've been a disaster if they weren't getting along. Malachi had managed to turn things around somehow. Sometimes Malachi was surprising.

She was met at the front door by Simon. "Simon, why didn't you say something to your parents?"

"It never works with them. It's no use. They never listen."

"They might if you actually stood up to them."

He looked at her blankly. "Trust me. It never works. It's a waste of energy."

"I thought you wanted time alone with me."

"I do, and we'll get some time alone, just not today."

"I don't know when. I was really looking forward to it. Now we have to have a picnic with your parents hovering over us." Cherish folded her arms.

He shrugged his shoulders. "That's just the way it is."

CHAPTER 14

*B*ack at the orchard...

"Things haven't changed much with Wilma and the others gone," Ada commented. "We're still over here nearly every day."

"I know, but we have to help out. We can't leave everything to Debbie and Levi."

Levi smiled at Samuel. "I'm sure Debbie and I could manage everything."

Matthew said, "No. Cherish made me promise to look after her birds."

Ada looked down her nose at him. "Made you promise? Wasn't your word good enough?"

Matthew grimaced. "She might not have made me promise but she was very worried that I do what she said. I'm not going to let her down."

"No one's suggesting you don't help. I was just saying we're still here nearly every single day. I thought with Wilma gone, we wouldn't be."

"How was your day, Debbie?"

"I've been busy with my tea every spare moment. Oh no. I forgot to see Krystal. She was going to help me with the website. Wait, Peter was supposed to take me and he didn't come here."

"If you ask me, the teas were already good," Samuel said.

Ada grinned. "Now they'll be even better, won't they, Debbie?"

"I sure hope so."

"Of course they will. I have confidence that you'll make the best tea in the whole country and you'll end up selling your tea everywhere."

A giggle escaped Debbie's lips. "Oh, Ada, you have more faith in me than I have in myself."

"We all believe in your ability. You've been through a lot in your young life and that has made you strong minded."

Debbie didn't know if that was true. She didn't feel that way. Most of the time she felt like she was floating along with a river's current, tossed to and fro by the wind. Making the tea was the first thing she'd done with a purpose and the first thing that she'd done for herself and for Jared's future. "I'd love it to be successful."

"We're all behind you," Levi said.

"Thank you. It means a lot that you're all taking this as something that's serious. My parents couldn't understand what I was doing and why I was doing it." What they'd wanted was for her to marry a widower, but Debbie couldn't even say that aloud. She was not going to make a marriage of convenience. Neither was she going to marry for anything other than love.

Ada pushed her lips out. "Speaking of your parents, have you heard from them since you refused John's parents' invitation to live with them?"

Debbie shook her head. "I haven't heard anything from them. I know they'll be so disappointed."

"In time, I'm sure they'll understand," Samuel said.

Debbie noticed Levi's beard twitching. Levi knew his brother wouldn't ever understand. He was too narrow minded and Debbie realized her mother was no better. "Maybe I'll write to them and tell them what happened. I should keep in contact."

"Yes, you should," Ada said. "You might be very different people but it doesn't mean you shouldn't write to them, and visit when you can. They're still your parents."

"I know."

"If it weren't for them, you wouldn't exist." Ada laughed.

"I know it." Debbie bit her lip. "I just don't know why Peter didn't come here. We arranged it for the morning. I think it was the morning. He said he'd be here."

"I'll take you," Levi offered.

"Would you? Krystal will still be at the quilt shop. That's where we arranged to meet."

"I'm ready any time you are."

"Thanks, Onkel Levi. Ada, would you—"

"Of course I'll look after Jared."

"Thanks. Hopefully, we shouldn't be away too long."

CHAPTER 15

Krystal had contacted Adam and told him how urgent it was that he get on with the job he'd quoted at the quilt shop. He put other jobs aside, and concentrated on getting that job done. His other clients weren't in such a hurry with it being the middle of winter.

Before he arrived, Debbie and Levi Bruner came to her store. She spent half an hour with Debbie going over how Debbie wanted the new website to look. It didn't take long to lock in some design concepts. Then they didn't waste time chatting because Debbie had to get back to her baby and Krystal, who was expecting Adam any minute, didn't want Debbie to see him.

"BEFORE YOU START, Adam, will you have something to eat? I don't want you working on an empty stomach. I've brought some sandwiches and some coffee."

"Thank you. I don't mind if I do."

Krystal smiled. She knew the way to a single man's heart was through his stomach. She grabbed another chair from the back room and pushed it up to the serving counter so they could both eat there. Then she opened the take-out sandwiches. "They're all toasted ham and cheese. I hope that's all right."

"Very good. Thanks for this."

"And the coffee's black, just how you like it."

He raised his eyebrows. "You remember how I like my coffee?"

"I do. I have a very good memory for things that are important."

He opened the lid of the drink container and took a mouthful.

"So, how are things with you, Adam?" Krystal pulled her sandwich out of its wrapper.

"Things are going well. Andrew and I are still busy at work. We have orders coming in continually. It's slowed up over Christmas but that's given us a chance to catch up with everything."

"I wish I could say the same. We were doing great sales up until Christmas, but now it's fallen off. I guess that's why there are such things as after-Christmas sales, but quilts aren't some-thing that we can discount. It takes too long to make them and there's not a lot of profit in them."

"Sounds like you'll just have to wait out the quiet times."

"That's why I asked you to come now so we could close the store and not lose too much business."

"You won't have to close the store. We make what you need off site and it won't take long to put it up."

"If you don't mind me asking, how are things between you and Bliss?"

He looked away and pushed his hair behind his ears. "You know we broke up?"

"I heard that."

"Well, nothing's changed since then."

"Oh, that's awful."

He scrunched his shoulders. "These things happen."

"I know, but I really thought you'd both last the distance. I guess it wasn't meant to be. Have you seen her lately?"

He shook his head. "She's gone to Cherish's farm."

"What? Instead of Favor?"

"No. With Favor. Wilma went too."

"That's something I didn't know. I really hate to be out of the loop. Favor told me she was going and she didn't tell me about Bliss."

"I heard it was a last minute thing."

"Heard from who?"

"I think it was Ada. She told me when I was putting up Cherish's aviary yesterday."

"That explains a lot." Krystal put down her sandwich and stared into space.

Adam finished chewing his mouthful. "What do you mean?"

"I heard that there was a man going to Cherish's place too. I thought the man was interested in Cherish, but now..."

"Wait. Do you think Bliss is moving on from me that quickly?"

"Things between the two of you are over, aren't they?"

"Yes, I guess so."

"Sometimes the best way to get over a break up is to find

someone else, don't you think? Don't worry, Adam, it just shows that she can't have thought that highly of you in the first place."

"You think so?"

Krystal covered her mouth. "Forgive me. I shouldn't be saying such things. I'm always getting myself into trouble for speaking my mind. Some people don't appreciate it."

"I'm glad to hear your thoughts, but I'd rather not talk about Bliss if that's okay. That's all people want to talk about."

As he ate his sandwich, he wondered how he'd feel to see Bliss with another man. He wouldn't like it one bit.

"Adam, I just want you to know that I'm not the kind of person a lot of people think I am. Sure, I've made mistakes but now I feel like a totally different person. Looking back, it feels like it was someone else who did those dreadful things. Do you know what I mean?"

He looked over at her. "You mean pretending you were Caroline?"

"That's exactly what I mean. There are so many things I feel deeply shameful about. That's just one of them. Will anyone ever truly forgive me? Everyone in the community knows what I did. How do you think I feel about that? I'm not even the same person who did those things. I wouldn't do them now."

"I think everyone's okay with it now that you're one of us."

"Yes, but that's another thing. Will I ever truly be one of you since I wasn't born into the community? I'm starting to think I'll always feel like an outsider."

"No one wants you to feel like that."

"Will you be honest with me if I ask you an important question?" She ran her fingertip around the rim of the coffee cup.

"Sure."

"I think we know each other well enough to ask." She looked up at him. "Will the single men in the community always see me as an outsider? Have my lies marked me as someone to stay away from even though *Gott* has forgiven me?"

He looked away, scratching his cheek. "I can't really speak for others."

"What about you?"

His eyebrows pinched together. "What do you mean?"

"Just pretend that you and I were in love. Could you forgive my mistakes?"

He squirmed in his chair. "Are you saying this because you know why Bliss and I are no longer together?"

"No. No one told me anything. Not even Favor told me."

"Oh."

"Don't worry. You don't have to answer. I just thought…"

"If I knew the mistakes at the start of the relationship I'd be fine with that. There's nothing worse than something that's been hidden from you. I can't speak for anyone else, but that's how I would feel."

"Thank you for being honest with me."

He popped the last piece of sandwich in his mouth. "I hope that was of some help."

"It was. More than you'll ever know."

He stood. "Thanks for the sandwich and the coffee. I better get back to work. I'll drink the rest of the coffee while I'm working."

"Sure."

He looked down at her. "I can lock up for you if you don't

want to stay. Do I just twist the knob on the door or something?"

"It's okay. Gertie would want me to stay until you finish. I don't have anything else to do with my time. I'm happy to watch you do whatever."

"Okay." He wondered if Krystal liked him. Was that why she was asking all those questions? He hoped he hadn't given Krystal too much of a hint of his reason for the breakup with Bliss. Too many people knew already. He went about his work, making sure he'd cut the metal to the correct length before bolting the metal rods to the ceiling.

"I can help if you want. I can pass you up tools."

From the top of the ladder, he looked down at Krystal. "It's fine. Thanks anyway, but I'm used to working by myself."

Krystal walked back to the computer and was quiet for a while. In the end, he did need Krystal's help to loop the quilts over the fixtures once he'd finished.

CHAPTER 16

Krystal and Adam stood back and looked at the finished work. Krystal said, "You've done a great job. Gertie's going to love it. I told her this was the way to go. The quilts look much better displayed like that and we can keep more in the store."

"I'm glad you're happy with it."

"I am and your price was so reasonable. Gertie thought so too. Are you going home now?"

"No. I have to go back to the workshop and see what's happened since I left. We always prepare what we need the night before."

"After that, why don't I take you out for a quick meal to say thanks?" Krystal asked.

"Ah. Thanks, but I've got to get back to Andrew and the workshop."

"Bring him too if you're worried about him being alone."

Adam chuckled. "I'm sure Andrew can be alone for a few hours."

"Great. I'll take you to that new Chinese restaurant down on the corner. It'll just be a quick meal to say I'm grateful for you fitting us in at such short notice."

"It's really not necessary."

"I know, but it would make me happy to do something different tonight." Krystal sighed. "I'm always doing the same thing, just going home. You'd be doing me a favor. We could just make it an early dinner. I don't want to take up too much of your time."

"Thank you, Krystal. I'll do that. I'll meet you there at six. I don't know if Andrew will be able to make it, but I'll ask."

"Err… okay. I'll see you at six."

Adam packed up the last of his tools.

"It looks great. Thanks again."

He glanced up at his handiwork. Those quilts did look good, hanging from the ceiling. "It was a good idea."

"It was my idea. It just makes sense." Krystal looked down at his tool boxes. "Do you want me to help you out with those?"

"No, it's fine. I'll make two trips. They're quite heavy."

When Adam drove away, he started to second guess his decision about Bliss. He'd thought about her so much over the last few days that his head felt like it would explode.

He was still thinking about Bliss when he got back to his workshop.

"How did it go?" Andrew asked.

"Good. It took longer than I thought. I had a bite to eat with her."

314

Andrew laughed. "You always get the best jobs where people want to feed you."

"Not only me. She wants us to have a quick meal with her to say thanks. An early dinner."

Andrew's mouth drooped at the corners. "We need money for that job. She's not paying us in food, is she?"

Adam chuckled. "Relax. We're getting paid."

"All right then. Where and when are we going?"

"She wants to go to a Chinese restaurant near her shop."

"Okay. I don't mind. As long as I don't have to eat your cooking again, or mine."

"I'm with you there."

"Anything wrong?" Andrew asked, studying him closely.

"No why?"

"You seem quiet."

Adam took a deep breath. "I'm just thinking."

"Bliss again?"

Adam shrugged his shoulders. "Did I do the right thing?"

"What is the right thing? Who knows what's right and what's wrong? If you love her, don't let her go. We've all made mistakes. By the sounds of it, she really upset you somehow. I don't think she would've done anything deliberately to hurt you."

"Now you say that."

"I said that at the start. You just didn't want to hear it."

"You said that?"

Andrew nodded. "I did."

"I'm sorry."

"You haven't been yourself since the two of you parted."

"She was a big part of my life. I thought we'd be married and have children together. I thought we'd raise them, and grow old together."

"You still can. It's not too late. I don't want to know what she did to upset you because it's none of my business, but I don't like seeing you like this."

"I've been that bad?" Adam asked.

"Yes. You've been a total pain in the neck."

"I'm sorry if I haven't been—"

"Don't be sorry, just figure out if you love her enough to overlook that she's only human and has failings. She's not perfect, none of us are."

"I know, but she's Bliss. I thought she was perfect."

"She's not. Don't you want to be the kind of man who'd stand by her no matter what?"

"You have no idea."

"Is it worth this torture you've been putting yourself through and probably putting her through?"

Adam said, "I only hope I'm not too late. What if she's already moved on and found someone else?"

"No. That wouldn't happen. I've seen the way she looks at you. Her whole face brightens up whenever you're around."

"That was in the past. Oh, Andrew, what have I done?" Adam put his head in his hands.

"Hello."

They both turned around to see Matthew walking toward them, carrying something covered with a blue and white checked dish towel. "I've got the pot of soup Ada promised you."

"Thank you," Adam and Andrew said at the same time.

"Hey, Adam, I offered to bring this over for Ada because I'm sorry for what happened back at the orchard. You had to have known they were trying to get you back together with Bliss."

"I know. I figured that out at the start. Cherish didn't want that aviary up just yet. Matthew, how would you like to accompany Andrew for a Chinese meal?"

"I love Chinese food. I only had it once before and it was great."

"I was going to go with him, but I just remembered I have something else to do."

"Krystal will be there too," Andrew told Matthew.

"Krystal, eh? Count me in. When are we doing this?"

Andrew said, "We'll have to leave in ten minutes. I'll meet you at the new Chinese restaurant just down the road from the quilt shop where Krystal works."

"Great! I'll head there now and wait outside. Thanks for the invite." Matthew turned around and headed back to his horse and buggy.

Andrew looked at Adam. "Where are you going?"

"Home. I just want to be alone for a while. I need to think things through. Give my apologies to Krystal. I hope she won't mind too much."

"She probably will. She has a secret crush on you. I've told you that before. Just be careful."

"I don't know about that." Adam shook his head.

Andrew folded his arms. "Are you going to think about Bliss? Is that why you want to be alone? You've never wanted to be alone before."

"I've got a lot to think about."

"Hey, you're not going home and running out on me and the business, are you?"

"No way. My home is here now. We built this together and that's how it'll stay. I just wish my personal life was going as well."

"It used to be."

"I know. That's what I've got to think about while I'm eating this soup." He picked up the soup Ada had made them and headed out the door.

CHAPTER 17

*B*ack at the farm, Cherish was trying to enjoy her picnic with Simon, but she couldn't do so. They were having the so-called picnic in the buggy due to the weather, and Simon's parents were in the front seat.

"This isn't really much like a picnic," Cherish blurted out as Harriet passed her a piece of chicken from the picnic basket Wilma and Bliss had prepared.

"In this weather, a picnic outside's not practical," Melvin said.

"This is okay, isn't it?" Simon asked her.

Cherish stared into his eyes, and chose to change her attitude. "Yes. It is."

Simon laughed. "It's a buggy picnic, a different kind of 'buggy' than in the summer when ants or flies bug picnickers."

"I guess that's what it is." Cherish smiled, but she couldn't relax with Simon's parents listening to every word. How could she get to know Simon better?

319

"It's lovely, all four of us being together like this." Harriet passed Cherish and Simon napkins. "I'm so glad we could all come."

Cherish took the napkin. "Thanks." Now Harriet was mothering her too. She didn't want to be treated as a child. Why was Simon okay with it? This could be something that she wouldn't get used to. Carter, Florence's husband, had seen it just from hearing about Simon. She didn't want Carter to be right about Simon being a mamma's boy.

"We've got fried chicken and cold cuts, coleslaw and beets. Leftovers from last night," Harriet said, looking down at her plate.

"That's right. And there's also the buttered rolls that Bliss baked for us."

"I'll have one of those," Melvin said.

Cherish passed one over. Then she arranged a plate for Simon and one for herself.

"This is a real treat. Thanks for thinking of this, Cherish."

"I thought it would be a good way for Simon and myself to have some alone time."

"Just pretend we're not here. You two can talk about whatever you like. Melvin and I will stay quiet."

Cherish looked over at Simon, but he was more interested in his food. His parents didn't even know she was more or less saying she wished they hadn't come. They didn't take the hint, but it was too late now anyway.

Cherish chewed on some chicken and when she had swallowed, she said, "How do you like the farm, Simon?"

"It's great."

"It's a lot smaller than our farm," Melvin said.

Harriet touched her husband's shoulder. "We're supposed to be quiet, remember?"

"Oh." He turned around to look at Cherish. "I'm sorry."

"That's okay."

"Tell us something about yourself, Cherish," Melvin said.

"There's not much to tell. You've met my mother and my sister, also my stepsister."

"Do you have a hobby?" Harriet asked.

"I like quilting and basket weaving."

"Oh, those are useful things. Very practical for when you're running your own home."

Then there was a strained silence. This was dreadful! Cherish just wanted to run. She should never have agreed to this. "What about you, Harriet? Do you have a hobby?" Cherish took a mouthful of chicken while she waited for Harriet to answer.

"I do like my needlework. I like to knit, too, but I'm saving up knitting for when I start having grandchildren."

Simon sniggered and Melvin smiled, and both parents looked lovingly at Simon. Cherish had always longed for her mother to be more affectionate and loving, but now she was glad that *Mamm* was exactly like she was.

"I don't have time for hobbies," Melvin said. "There's always so much work on the farm."

"That's true," Harriet added. "So much work. We had a hard time keeping up with it all when Simon went to your sister's wedding, Cherish."

"I'm surprised you didn't go with him."

"We couldn't. We thought about it but the people who are

looking after our farm right now were away. Simon said he'd go by himself."

"I'm sure he missed you both very much."

Simon nodded. "I did."

Cherish looked down at her plate of food. That was maybe why Simon left so quickly. He had wanted to get back to his parents.

BACK IN LANCASTER COUNTY, Matthew was excited to be having a meal with Krystal. Of course it would've been better if Andrew wasn't going to be there as well, but this could be the start of something.

He parked his horse and buggy and walked down the road to the restaurant. He passed an alley and glanced down it. Then he took a couple of steps back. Krystal was there. She was leaning against the brick building, and she was smoking.

He was a little shocked to see it. He knew a couple of the men in the community smoked, he'd seen them at horse auctions, but it didn't look good for Krystal to be doing it.

She looked up and saw him and he walked toward her.

"Matthew, what are you doing here?"

"Adam invited me to eat with you all. I hope you don't mind."

"That's okay. Why would I mind? I wasn't going to be alone with Adam anyway because he was going to ask Andrew. I figure he'd come too."

Did she clearly just admit to preferring to be alone with

Adam? Everyone was right about her. He coughed slightly because the smoke was aggravating his throat.

She put the cigarette to her lips and inhaled. Then she tipped her head back and blew smoke rings into the air. "I'm sorry. It's a dreadful habit. I've tried giving it up so many times. Now I've given up on giving up. Want one?" She held the cigarette pack toward him.

"No thanks."

"Suit yourself." She tucked the pack back into her apron.

"How have you been, Krystal?"

"About the same. Selling quilts, and doing stuff with websites for some Amish businesses. I heard nearly everyone in Favor's family went to the farm."

"I was just at the orchard today. I'm looking after Cherish's birds. Favor went, so did Bliss and naturally Cherish went and Wilma too."

"Have you heard from them since they've been there?"

He shook his head. "Not a word."

"So, do you think there's a chance that Bliss and Adam will get back together?"

"I don't know. She's been very upset about it. I think that's why they took her to the farm."

"Cherish likes Simon, that's not a secret. Not to me anyway because Favor told me."

Matthew was a little shocked to hear her say that, and Krystal noticed.

"Oh, you poor thing. Don't tell me you like Cherish?"

"Of course not."

"Good then I'll tell you a secret and I'm the only one who knows it. Favor likes Simon too."

His eyes grew round like saucers. He had no idea. "That's not going to end well. They both like Simon?"

"They do."

"Hmm. What's Simon got that I don't?"

Krystal looked him up and down and then laughed. "Oh, you're serious."

"Yes."

"You're just a boy. That's how everyone sees you. Simon is more of a proper man. He's bigger and taller."

Matthew looked down at himself. "I'm a late bloomer. I'm just waiting to go through my growth spurt."

Krystal laughed. "And what if that never happens?"

Matthew's mouth fell open. He'd never even considered that. There was nothing wrong with being short, but he wanted to be tall. He'd always imagined himself being at the height of six feet tall or even more. He would look down at his wife when he admired how pretty she was. It wouldn't feel right if his future wife was taller and she was the one doing the looking down.

"And Favor reckons it's only fair that she gets a proper boyfriend before Cherish does because she's older."

It took Matthew a moment to realize that Krystal was still talking about Simon and Favor. "That makes sense."

"I thought so too. I told her to go for it."

"What does that mean?"

"She has to do whatever she can to make Simon like her more than he likes Cherish." She glanced up the alley. "Oh, there's Andrew. Adam can't be far behind. Let's go." She threw the cigarette down on the ground and just left it there.

Matthew couldn't leave it there, alight. He stomped on it and then hurried to keep up with her.

"Wait up, Andrew." Krystal called out.

Andrew turned around and smiled. "Hi, Krystal. Did Matthew tell you Adam couldn't make it?"

Krystal's mouth fell open. "No! I was just talking to Adam. He never once said he couldn't come." She turned to look at Matthew. "Why didn't you tell me Adam wasn't coming?"

CHAPTER 18

*H*e shrugged his shoulders. "I clean forgot to mention it."

"I'm out here in the freezing cold, waiting, shivering, and he's not even coming?" Krystal put her hand on her forehead. "I can't believe this."

"I'm sorry," Andrew said, "but Mathew and I are here."

"There's no point in this anymore. I wanted to thank Adam for doing the job, not feed a dozen people."

"There's only three of us. I can pay for the meal." Matthew put up his hand. "No need to worry about that."

Krystal rolled her eyes at Matthew. "Don't raise your hand. You're not in school anymore."

Matthew lowered his hand just as Andrew said, "Adam and I are business partners, so you can thank me if you want, otherwise if you don't want to join us, Matthew and I will—"

"Great idea. Matthew and you can eat yourselves silly. Have

a nice meal." Krystal turned and left. Before she walked two steps, she yelled out, "Unbelievable!" and kept going.

"Wow. She was really upset." Matthew stared after her, admiring the way she walked with the sides of her coat flapping in the breeze.

"Yep. Looks like it."

Matthew grinned and looked back at Andrew. "Are you ready to eat?"

"I'm always ready to eat." Together they walked to the restaurant.

While they were in the middle of eating their dumplings and spring rolls, Matthew decided to learn more about Adam so he could help Bliss. "I'll just come right out and say this. Everyone I know wants Bliss and Adam to get back together."

"Same here. Me too, I mean. I thought they were great together."

"So, do you know what's stopping Adam from telling Bliss he made a dreadful mistake?"

Andrew looked up from his food. "I got the impression she did something wrong, but he's keeping that to himself."

The way Andrew's gaze was darting about the place, Matthew figured he might've known more than he was letting on. "It doesn't matter who did the thing. What I meant was that he made the mistake of letting her go."

"I can agree with you there." Andrew nodded.

"Good. Someone had this idea that we should find out if Adam had ever made a mistake. Then we could confront him with it. He'll see that everyone makes mistakes and he'll forgive Bliss."

Andrew pulled his mouth to one side as he picked up

another spring roll in his fingers. "It depends."

"On what?"

"Exactly how big a mistake did she make?"

Matthew held up his hand and then placed his thumb and forefinger an inch apart. "About this size. No this size." He moved his thumb and finger closer together. "It was hardly anything. That's why he should see that he's made a dreadful mistake. Where will he be able to find anyone better than Bliss? She's so nice. She's so nice that she makes everyone else look horrible."

"Yep. I'd agree with you on that. I can let you into a secret. I think he's realizing that he's made a mistake."

"Yeah?"

Andrew nodded. "He said he's got a lot of thinking to do. I think Krystal helped. He's been different since he came back from doing her job. I wouldn't be surprised if she had a good talk with him."

"For real?"

"I'm just guessing, but it makes sense. He came back from there looking worried. He also said he thinks Bliss has found someone else."

"It must be what everyone said when he was at the orchard. I didn't agree with doing that, but my opinions don't matter much."

"Well, don't tell Adam that's what happened. If that helps him get back with her, it'll be worth him thinking it. I told him just today that he hasn't been the same since she left."

"I agree. We won't tell him." Matthew took a mouthful of soda. He couldn't wait to get home and tell Aunt Ada what he'd found out.

CHAPTER 19

*B*ack at the buggy picnic, they'd finished their food, all but the dessert.

"I've never had a picnic in a buggy before," said Harriet.

Melvin agreed, "Me either. It's a little cramped."

Simon joined in, "But it is warm in here compared to outside."

Harriet turned around to face them. "Yes it is. Are you going to be the one to serve us the dessert, Cherish?"

"Yes, of course." Cherish leaned over behind the backseat and pulled the basket next to her. The basket held the cheesecake. There was nowhere else to put it except between herself and Simon. She couldn't even sit close to him. This picnic was a disaster and it was all because of Harriet and Melvin.

Simon helped by pulling out the bottle of cider and the glasses. He poured everyone drinks while Cherish got the cheesecake out and arranged it onto four plates. She passed two plates over to the front.

Harriet took the two plates and gave one to her husband and kept one for herself. "Your farm's great. It's actually bigger than I thought it would be. I thought it would be more of a hobby farm," Harriet said.

Melvin was quiet as he ate a spoonful of cheesecake.

"No, it's a real farm." Then there was another awkward silence. Why wasn't Simon saying anything? "How long are you able to stay?" Cherish finally asked.

"I don't know. It depends on my folks."

There were sniggers from the front seat, and then Simon smiled and kept eating. He had a better connection with his parents than he had with her. Cherish knew that if she wanted to be Simon's girlfriend, she had some competition and it wasn't from Favor.

Simon then looked over at her. "You look nice today."

Cherish was delighted he'd say such a thing in front of his parents. "Thank you. You look nice too."

Again there was stifled laughter coming from the front seat.

"I try," Simon said. "Not too hard though. That would be prideful, but I do try to keep my clothes nice when I'm not on the farm. I see that Malachi's clothes are always dirty. I don't want to end up like that, not caring."

"Yes, he likes it that way. He's always doing things outside, and it'd be hard for him to keep changing his clothes to keep clean."

"I understand. Farm-life is like that sometimes." Simon smiled at her. "Your clothes are never dirty even when you've been out with the animals."

"That's because Malachi has done most of the work for me. I guess things will be different when I'm alone on the farm."

"Maybe you won't be alone." Simon gave her a wink.

Cherish appreciated what he said, but she didn't appreciate him saying that in front of his parents. Well, in reality he'd said it *behind* them. All they were doing was listening. It just wasn't normal. Not even Levi and Wilma would do such a thing. No parents she knew would do it. "How come you're so close with your parents?" She knew she was taking a risk in asking that in their hearing. They had said they'd be quiet, so that was a test. A test they were failing.

Simon answered, "It's always been that way. I'm an only child. I guess that's why."

Cherish tried to think of people she knew who had no siblings. "I've never seen any parents this close to a grown man."

"It's great, isn't it? We've got a special bond." Simon glanced at his parents and then she saw his parents smiled at one another. It looked like they were now holding hands. Simon continued, "We're always together. We're a threesome. When I meet the right woman, we'll become a foursome. Ma can't wait for that day to come. She's always said my wife will be her special friend."

"That's good to know. Very good." Cherish looked in the basket for a clean napkin to wipe her hands. She was done with eating. All this talk was making her nauseous.

"I can tell you're close with your mother," Simon said.

"Just normal, I'd say. She is my mother, so..."

"The difference is I genuinely like my folks."

Cherish's mouth fell open in shock. "I like my mother and I liked my father." She always got sad when she thought about her father. She didn't have enough memories of him. "I just wish I had gotten more time with my father, you know?"

"What was he like?"

"He loved his trees. He was always outside with them. He mainly spent time with Florence teaching her about the trees because she was the one who was going to take over one day."

"Wait, doesn't Florence have older brothers?"

"That's right, but they weren't interested in the orchard, only Florence was. The rest of us were too young to show a real interest. *Dat* tried to teach all of us, but we were too young to take it all in. He was a calm and quiet man."

"Like Levi?"

"Same, but different. They were happy days when I look back on them. Everything in life was good when he was around. He always fixed everything. *Mamm* was much happier. That's how I remember it anyway."

"Don't say that in front of Levi." Simon grinned.

"He'd understand. His wife died too."

"Ah, yes of course. Bliss is from his first marriage."

While Cherish had been talking about her father, for a moment she'd forgotten about Simon's parents in the front seat. "Anyway, I'll get too sad if I talk about my father any more."

"I didn't mean to make you sad. I just want to know all about you, everything."

Cherish laughed. "There's not that much to know. You know all about me already."

"So far, I like what I see."

"What about my family?" Cherish asked.

"They're all nice, and Ma said before she even met your

mother that she must be a nice woman to be such good friends with Ada."

Cherish had to get away from the parents. "It would be nice if we could go outside for a walk."

"Let's do that."

"By ourselves?" Cherish asked.

"Sure. It doesn't seem quite as cold now."

"Make sure you both have your coats on," Harriet said before they got out of the buggy.

"Ma, you're supposed to keep quiet."

"I know, but I do worry about you both getting cold in this weather."

Once they were out of the buggy and away from listening ears, Cherish said, "I didn't think they'd come on our picnic with us. It's way too much family togetherness."

"It's okay, isn't it?"

"No, it's not. I told you that. Why didn't you say something when they said they'd come with us?"

Simon shrugged his shoulders. "What could I have said without hurting their feelings?"

"Tell them that we need time alone. They'd understand."

"You don't know what they're like. They won't listen to me."

"You should make them listen. You're a grown man now. You're not their little boy anymore. Your mother doesn't need to fuss with your hair like you're a three-year-old."

"That's just her. She always does that. I told you from the get go that we were close."

"But I just wanted a quiet time alone with you today."

"We're alone now."

Cherish glanced back at the buggy. "What if your future wife wants to live away from them and away from their farm?"

"Then that'll be our way of knowing whether she's the right woman or not."

She couldn't believe what he just said. "Our?"

"Yes. Me and my folks. Anyway, I'm not ready for marriage. Not yet. I plan on having a very long courtship. I think that's the way to go to be sure you're with the right one."

Cherish kept quiet and kept walking. A long courtship was fine with her.

"I have fun with my parents. I wouldn't want—"

Cherish interrupted, "Why did you go to Hope's wedding by yourself?"

"My parents couldn't leave the farm. They thought I should go."

"So it wasn't your decision? I'm just trying to work everything out."

"Sure. I don't mind telling you. Ma thought I should go to try and meet some new people. And I did, I met you."

"And if she hadn't suggested it, you wouldn't have gone?"

"That's right. I wouldn't have even thought of going without them unless they were okay with it."

"It's convenient that they have someone to look after the farm now for these few days."

"I know. The Kerslakes next door were away when the wedding was on. They're back now and they're the ones looking after our place until we get back."

"That's good of them."

"They're a retired *Englisher* couple. They don't have a lot of land, so they've got a lot of time on their hands. We arranged everything before we left so they don't have a lot to do. They just have to feed the animals and make sure the water's topped up."

"I wonder if it will snow soon." Cherish looked up at the sky.

"It's been warmer than normal. Maybe that'll end soon and we'll have snow for days. We might have so much that we'll all be trapped in your house together."

"I don't think that'll happen."

He laughed.

Cherish had something else on her mind that had been bothering her. She had to clear it up. She was nervous to ask, but she held her breath and then asked, "Simon, why have you been talking to Favor so much?"

He stared at her, and then looked away. "She's talking to me. I can't be rude. What do you want me to do?"

Cherish shrugged her shoulders. "Nothing."

He smiled. "Wait, are you jealous?"

"No. Not at all. I've never been jealous of anyone."

"Then why did you ask?"

Cherish laughed as though she didn't care. The last thing she wanted was to be called jealous. "I just thought you might like her, that's all."

"Not any more than I like anyone else, and not near as much as I like you." He took hold of her hand. "Don't go thinking any silly stuff."

Cherish was relieved to hear it.

"We better get back. We'll find some alone time later, okay?"

"Sure."

They both walked back to the buggy.

CHAPTER 20

The next day for Cherish had started out bad. She'd woken up late and then saw that Malachi had fed all the animals without her. He was acting awfully strange over breakfast. Simon's parents were getting on her nerves as usual, and that was why Cherish was so pleased when Annie Whylie arrived.

Cherish rushed out to meet her. "Annie, how lovely to see you again."

Annie gave her a big smile as she stepped out of the buggy. "Thanks. I hear you have visitors."

"Yes. Come in and I'll introduce you."

After Cherish had introduced her to everyone, they all sat in the living room with hot chocolate and sugar cookies.

Harriet said to Annie, "Ada can't stop talking about the wonderful cakes you and your mother make."

"Oh, you must mean the gingerbread houses."

"That's right. Ada says try as she might, she just can't do it."

"I don't know why she's finding it so hard." Annie put her fingertips over her mouth and had a little giggle.

Harriet then said, "I would love to learn while I'm here, if you wouldn't mind teaching me."

Cherish gulped. While she was here? How long was she planning on staying?

Annie said, "Why don't you come to my place tomorrow? My mother is making a house for the first show of the year."

"I don't know. Cherish might have something planned for us."

Cherish shook her head. "No, it's fine. I have nothing planned at all." Cherish tried not to smile at the thought of finally having some peace. Hopefully if Harriet went, Melvin would go too.

"In that case, we'd love to go."

"Who would be coming with you?" Annie looked around at everyone.

"My husband and my son," Harriet said.

Cherish gulped. She had not expected that.

Annie giggled. "Why don't we go today? I can take you there now. It won't matter whether we start on the house today or tomorrow. *Mamm* was just waiting so I could be there to help."

Harriet looked over at Cherish. "Would that be okay?"

"Sure." Cherish didn't know what else to say.

"We might as well go now," Annie said.

Favor bounded to her feet. "Can I come?"

"Sure. I've got five seats in the buggy."

Cherish glared at her sister. That meant she'd have a whole day without Simon and Favor would be with him. The worst thing was, Simon was just sitting there in silence.

Melvin stood up. "Let's go. I'll drive if you don't mind, Annie."

Annie opened her mouth in shock, and then she stammered, "Okay."

Before Cherish knew it, they were gone.

Cherish stared at Annie's buggy as it left the property. "What just happened?"

Bliss stepped forward. "That was quite unbelievable of Favor. She should've let you go."

Cherish's lips turned down at the corners. "I didn't want to go, but why did he go without asking me? I mean, Simon could've stayed here and let them all go."

Mamm put her arm around Cherish. "You heard what Harriet said, they go everywhere together."

"But they're visiting us and now they just go off. They'll be gone for ages. Simon just left without asking me if I minded."

Bliss said, "They thought you'd have something planned for the day, but they knew they were coming here. There's nothing really to do except farm work."

Cherish sighed. "I know."

"We shouldn't talk like this behind their backs. I'm going inside to put my feet up and have a rest. I haven't cooked breakfast for so many people in ages."

"It's about the same number when we have Ada and Samuel there for breakfast," Bliss said.

Mamm sighed. "Is it? It seems like much more. Let's get inside. It's chilly out."

"You two go in. I'll find Malachi."

Malachi had said hello to Annie and then left soon after.

Cherish wrapped her coat tighter around herself and headed

341

up the hill. From there, she could see the whole farm. With every step she took, she grew more and more annoyed with Favor, how she volunteered to go with them without a second thought. Simon was here as her potential boyfriend and Favor was acting like he was hers. She looked up at the gray sky. It was as dark as her mood was right now.

"Hey, Cherish."

She turned around and saw Malachi near the barn.

He walked toward her and they met in the middle. "What are you doing?"

"Looking for you. Did you know Annie has gone?"

"Where's she gone?"

Cherish grunted. "She took all the visitors, plus Favor, back to her place to watch her mother make a gingerbread house."

"And you're not happy about that, right?"

Cherish shrugged her shoulders. "It's just the way it happened."

He tipped his hat back on his head. "How did it happen?"

"Don't worry."

"I'm not worried. I'm just askin' ya."

"I'm the one that invited them and then Favor jumped in and said she'd go with them. First it was only Harriet and then she made her husband and son go with her."

"Didn't they want to go?"

"Who would?" Cherish snapped.

"It seems Favor wanted to go, and Harriet. You seem upset. Just enjoy them being gone."

"That won't be hard. Anyway, what have you been doing?"

"Same thing as I do every day, feeding the animals."

"Sorry I didn't wake up early enough to help you today."

"Don't worry about it. I'm sure that when you take over the farm, you'll wake up."

"I will. It's just that I didn't have enough sleep last night, and you didn't wake me."

"Were you up late talking with Simon?"

Cherish sensed he was jealous and couldn't help smiling. "No. It wasn't that. I'm sleeping with three in the bed, don't forget. Favor's in the middle and she keeps tossing and turning. I'm wondering if it wouldn't be easier to sleep on the floor. I nearly fell out of bed a couple of times."

"Sleep on the couch."

"I might do that."

"Or take my room and I'll bunk in the barn."

Cherish shook her head and grinned at him. "No. You're still trying to get away from the house, aren't you."

"Well..."

CHAPTER 21

"It's not going to happen. Forget it." Cherish looked down at the bucket in Malachi's hand. "Have you finished?"

"Nearly. I just have to feed the pigs. Want to help me?"

"Sure."

He seemed to be back to his normal self now. In the barn, they mixed the feed for the pigs. Cherish carried two buckets and Malachi took two.

Together they walked to the covered pig pen.

"It does kind of feel better with them gone."

Malachi laughed. "Why did you invite them?"

"It seemed like a good idea at the time. I should've left Favor at home. Did you know that pink dress she was wearing was actually mine? It was my best dress. I hadn't even worn it yet."

"Is that the one she had on yesterday?"

"Yes."

"Don't sisters share clothes?"

"No. Not if we can help it. I don't anyway. I like to keep my things nice. I'm just going to give it to Favor now. She's probably wrecked it."

Malachi looked at her. "You get uptight about small things. It's just a dress."

"You wouldn't understand." Cherish huffed in frustration just as they reached the pen. The pigs came out and started snorting at them, which made her laugh.

"Just pour it into the tray."

"I know what to do," Cherish snapped, the laughter snuffed out.

When they'd poured out all the food and all the pigs were eating, Cherish found herself smiling at them. This was what she needed. She needed to be around animals rather than people.

"I'm sorry for being mean just now."

"I didn't notice."

Cherish giggled. "I was taking my bad mood out on you and I didn't mean to."

"It's okay."

"*Mamm's* saved some bacon and eggs for you."

Malachi grabbed Cherish's arm and pulled her away from the pigs. "Shh. Don't let them hear you say that."

Cherish's mouth fell open and she realized what he meant. "Oh no. Sorry."

"It's nice having your mother here. I get a break from cooking. One less thing I have to do." They put the containers back inside the barn and headed to the house.

"Did Bliss go too?"

"No. She stayed and *Mamm* stayed as well."

"They don't like gingerbread houses?"

Cherish covered her ears. "I'm over hearing that name."

"What, ginger—"

Cherish covered his mouth so he wouldn't say it again. "Don't say it." She took her hand away.

"Gee. I'll try not to. I didn't know they made you this upset. You're so uptight."

"I have reason to be."

"Not really."

She stopped and stared at him and he stopped too. Just at that moment, soft snowflakes fell from the sky. They both looked up.

He put out his arms. "You need to be out here, away from the people who upset you."

"You're right, I do. I need to be away from sisters who take my clothes without asking. It sure is beautiful here on the farm."

"Come in out of the cold, you two." Wilma stood in the doorway, beckoning for them to come inside.

"You'll catch your death," Cherish murmured under her breath.

"You'll catch your death of cold," Wilma called out.

Malachi laughed. "How did you do that?" he asked Cherish.

"It's what she always says. We better go inside. She won't let up until we do."

While Malachi ate his breakfast, Cherish sat at the kitchen table, keeping him company while drinking a cup of coffee.

Bliss and *Mamm* were settled in the living room, sewing.

"I really thought Bliss would've been the one to go with them," said Cherish. "She likes Harriet. Why didn't she go, you ask? She didn't get a chance because Favor jumped in and volunteered herself to go with them."

"I didn't ask."

"I knew you would've if you didn't have a mouthful of food."

"Forget about them."

Cherish slumped in her chair. "I'm trying." Then she leaned forward. "I should've left Favor at home. It was Mamm's idea to bring her."

"Have you always not gotten along with her?"

"We were close when we were younger. Things are different now. We do get along sometimes."

"That's what it's like with siblings. You don't get along with them all the time. Are you going to see Ruth while you're here?"

"Definitely. We should go soon. Do you want to come with me?"

"Do I have to?"

"Yes."

"Can I finish my coffee first?"

"Okay."

CHAPTER 22

They found Ruth wasn't home, so they left a note on her door that they'd be back tomorrow.

Late that afternoon, Cherish was even more annoyed when Annie's buggy pulled up and they all got out, laughing.

"How was it?" Cherish asked, walking toward them.

"Great!" Harriet said.

"Annie's mother sent a cake with us to have for dessert," Favor said.

"Please thank your mother, Annie." Cherish smiled at Annie. If that was a ploy or a hint to stay for the evening meal, Cherish wasn't asking her. There were already more than enough people in the house.

Cherish noticed Annie was looking around. Was she looking for Malachi?

"Want to go for a walk, Cherish? I've hardly seen you," Simon said.

Cherish couldn't keep the smile from her face. "I'd like

that." As the others headed to the house, Cherish walked away with Simon. "You were gone a long time."

"I'm sorry. I wanted you to come too, but then Favor said she was going."

"You could've stayed here."

"But my folks were going. They would've wanted me to go with them."

"It's not always about what they want. What about what you want?"

"I've got to consider them. They've done so much for me."

"What, more than any other parent? Every parent does things for their child. You don't have to repay them."

"I'm not doing it because I have to. I love my parents. I love being around them."

"I noticed. I've spent all day today alone, and that's because you wanted to be with your parents? You see them every single day. How often do you see me?"

"There's no need to raise your voice, Cherish."

"I think there is."

He put a hand on her arm and she immediately calmed down.

"I'm sorry, but I've been bored all day. You'll be gone soon and we could've spent more time together."

"My folks really wanted to go to see the gingerbread houses. They work so hard. I don't even remember when they had a day that they didn't have to work. When I saw the excitement on my mother's face, how could I say no?"

Cherish frowned. "You didn't have to go with them."

"I told you, we go everywhere together."

"Not everywhere."

He rolled his eyes. "You don't understand."

"I think I do. I know your mother wanted to go, but couldn't she have given you a day off from hanging around with them?"

"I want to spend time with them. I know it's hard for you to understand. Not many people understand what our relationship is. It's special."

"I can think of a few other words for it."

He moved closer to her. "Don't be mad."

"I'm not exactly mad, I'm just upset that the day's been wasted. I don't get to the farm much and I thought we'd have more time together—alone."

"We're alone now."

Cherish kept walking.

"Favor said she loves how me and my parents are so close. She has no one close with her. She told us about the friend she had living with her for a while. It seems to have really upset her when she left."

"What else did she tell you about Krystal?"

"That's all. Why, is there more?" Cherish shook her head. It would've taken too long to explain the whole Krystal situation. "Favor is a little dramatic sometimes. I hope she wasn't complaining too much."

He laughed. "She was a little bit. She really gets along with my mother. You should spend some more time with her."

"Who, Favor?"

"No, my mother."

"Oh. I thought I was."

"Not as much as Favor or Bliss."

"I'd rather spend time with you. Wouldn't that make more sense?"

He shrugged his shoulders. "Maybe Ma thinks you don't like her that much."

"I like her just fine. Did she say that?"

"Something like that. Don't say I said anything."

Now Cherish was growing agitated. "I won't change what I'm doing. I like your parents, but you're the one I want to spend time with. I thought they'd entertain themselves while they're here so you and I can be together."

"I know and that's what I want too, but they've done so much for me that I just want to make them happy. The whole reason they're working so hard is so they can leave me their farm."

Cherish didn't say anything. What could she say without him thinking she was a horrible person?

"What would it hurt to get to know them a bit better?" Simon asked.

CHAPTER 23

Cherish knew she wouldn't get far with Simon if she didn't get to know his parents, but she was never one to follow anyone's expectations. She had to do what she felt was right. It bothered her to compromise, but she decided she'd try it just this once. "I will, after I get to know you better, Simon."

He stopped walking so she stopped too. "Maybe they think that you..."

"That I what? Go on, say it."

"That you aren't interested in them until something develops between the two of us."

Cherish thought about that for a moment. "That's right. I'll get to know them later. Don't you think it's only natural? I like them, of course I do. Who wouldn't? They're lovely people."

"You don't seem to get it."

"What?" Cherish was growing frustrated with the whole situation. Why was this love business so hard? No one told her it would be like this. She thought you met someone and everything fell into place. She'd never given one thought to her potential husband having weird relatives.

"Just say you and I get serious and start dating, we'll be spending a lot of time with my parents."

Cherish shrugged. "A reasonable amount of time is okay. That's fine."

"But they've got to get to know you before that happens."

"Wait. You mean you need their approval before we get closer?" Cherish asked.

He breathed out heavily. "I wouldn't put it in those exact words, but kind of."

"Let's go over here." They walked toward the hill.

"What do you think about what I just said?" Simon asked, when Cherish didn't make a comment.

"I'm a bit shocked. I'm trying to take it in."

"There's nothing to be shocked about. I told you how I felt about my parents."

"How does that leave any room for anyone else in your life?"

He laughed. "It's not like that. I've got a lot of love to give."

"Have you ever had a girlfriend before?"

He shook his head. "I've never met anyone who interested me up until now." He reached out and took hold of her hand.

She'd often heard love was about compromise. Was this the compromise she had to make, to share Simon with his parents? She didn't have restrictions like that.

"What are you thinking, Cherish? Say something."

She shook her head. "The thing with your parents, I find it odd."

"I've heard that before from other people. I'm willing to change things though. I'll do it for you." He squeezed her hand.

Cherish was shocked at his response. "You will?"

"Yes, and if I'm willing to do that, you should be willing to get to know them better."

Cherish nodded, not sure what she was agreeing to. "Okay. I'll do my best but I still want to spend time with you. We're not here for very long and then I'll be heading back home."

"I can agree there. Why don't we go back to the house and you can start getting to know my parents?"

Cherish sat down on the freezing ground. "Or we could sit down and have some quiet time alone."

"Okay." He sat down next to her. "I suggested going back because it's so cold."

"I don't mind."

"If you don't mind, I'll try not to think about how numb my fingers and toes are."

"Good. How do you like my family?"

"They're great, all of them. Wilma reminds me a little of Ada."

"That's because they spend so much time together. They see each other every day. It's only natural they'd start to act like each other."

"It'd be great to have a friend like that."

"No. I don't think you should have a friend like that. You'd have no room in your life for them because of your parents." Cherish held her breath, thinking she'd gone too far.

"Perhaps we can be each other's close friend."

Phew! He didn't mind. "That would be nice, but we wouldn't be able to see each other every day."

"No. That's true, but you never know what the future might hold." He stared into her eyes.

Then something took Simon's attention. Cherish turned around to see what he was staring at. It was Malachi, walking toward them.

"There you are, Cherish. Why are you both on the ground?"

"We're just sitting. Is there something wrong?"

Malachi rubbed the side of his face. "Your mother was looking for you."

"Can you tell her I'm here?"

He placed his hands on his hips. "Then I'll have to tell her you're out here with no coat and sitting on the freezing ground."

"She wouldn't like that."

"No, she wouldn't."

"Tell her I'm coming soon."

Malachi shook his head. "I'm sorry. I can't do that."

"Why not?" Simon asked.

"Because she'd be cross with me for not getting you to come with me."

"We better go now, Cherish. We don't want your mother being upset with me again. I heard a whisper she was upset with me once."

"When?"

"When I asked if you and I could walk outside after dinner that evening when we were at the orchard."

"Did Favor tell you that?"

"I can't say."

Simon got to his feet and held out his hand for Cherish. She put her hand in his and he lifted her to her feet while Malachi stood there looking on.

"Sorry to interrupt the both of you," Malachi said.

"It's fine. I don't want anyone to be upset with me. It'll make the next few days pretty difficult."

"Few days?" Malachi asked. "How long are you able to stay?"

"We'll stay until Cherish leaves."

The three of them headed back down the hill together.

Cherish walked past Bliss and Favor in the living room and joined her mother in the kitchen where she was sitting talking to Harriet over a pot of tea. "I'm here, *Mamm.*"

"Won't you sit with us, Cherish?" Harriet asked. "Your mother was just telling me all about you."

CHAPTER 24

*C*herish wasted no time sitting down. What had her mother said about her? A whole host of things ran through Cherish's mind. Did she tell Harriet about the time Levi and *Mamm* went away for a few days and the girls held a party, causing a fire in the house? Was she complaining about her keeping Caramel in the house and Caramel sleeping on her bed? Or was she telling Harriet how lazy all her daughters were? Ada, no doubt, would've mentioned that to Harriet since they were such good friends. "What did my mother tell you?"

Harriet laughed. "Simon hardly tells me anything. I really know nothing about you. I found out from Wilma that you work in a café."

"Only one day a week. I'd do more if I could."

"That's wonderful. I do like my coffee. One day you'll have to make me a coffee, a proper one out of one of those big machines."

Cherish gulped. "I haven't done any barista training yet. That's what I'd like to do next."

"You have to do a course to make a coffee?"

"At my café you do. We take the coffee seriously."

Harriet laughed. "Serious coffee. Never heard of it."

"Cherish just takes the coffee and food to the table and then clears the tables."

Harriet stared at Cherish. "That's okay. Don't feel bad. Everyone's got to start somewhere."

"I'm happy just doing that. I get to meet so many people and the people I work with are so nice."

Wilma said, "She likes to have a change from being at the orchard every day."

"We'd all like a change, Cherish, but you said you want to live here on the farm."

"That's right."

"When you make that commitment to move here, every day will be the same. Are you sure the farming life is for you?"

"Quite sure. I know it."

"You can't tell Cherish anything. She knows it all."

Harriet chuckled. "I was a little like that when I was younger. It's only when I got older I realized that maybe I didn't know everything."

"Are you enjoying yourself here so far, Harriet?"

"I am. I'll have a lot to write to Ada about. It's so nice that we've finally all met. Ada told me so much about you and your family, Wilma. What did Ada tell you about my family?"

Cherish wasn't aware that Ada had said anything. From the way *Mamm* was stammering and fidgeting with her fingers, Cherish guessed Ada had never mentioned the Koppel family.

"I know that you have a sheep farm and that you used to have cattle. And I know that Simon is your only child."

"That's right."

Mamm had gotten out of that one fairly well.

"Your mother said you were very sick when you were younger, Cherish."

Mamm interrupted, "And they never found out why. She just grew out of it. That's why her sisters say she's spoiled, but she's not. We had to give her extra attention because she was ill, and that's all."

Cherish just sat there, realizing she couldn't even remember that far back. One thing was for sure, she was thoroughly sick of everyone saying she was spoiled. The last thing she wanted was Simon or his parents knowing she had that reputation. "I'm fine now. That was when I was really young."

"Do you have any serious illnesses running in the family, Wilma?"

"No. I don't know of any."

"Maybe Cherish has something that will rear its head later in life." Harriet turned to Cherish. "You really should get checked out. You wouldn't want to pass anything along to your children."

"I'm fine, truly."

"Yes, but you can't know that for sure. You should get tested."

"What, by a doctor? I haven't been to a doctor in years."

Harriet wasn't going to let it go. "They have new tests all the time. Maybe they didn't know what you had back then because they didn't have the proper testing and now they do."

"I'll think about it," Cherish said just to keep her quiet.

Harriet turned to Cherish's mother. "What do you think, Wilma?"

"I think she's fine and her children will be fine." Wilma sipped her tea.

That clearly made Harriet upset. She leaned forward, closer to Cherish, and whispered, "If you marry my son, I'd like to know if you're sick or not. I'm not saying he wouldn't still marry you if it turns out there's something wrong with you, but it would be good to know in case the illness strikes back."

A shiver ran through Cherish. She felt like she was close to the grave or something the way Harriet was carrying on.

"It was probably just a lingering virus or something," Wilma said. "I'm sure it's nothing to be concerned about. I shouldn't have mentioned it."

"I'm very glad you did, Wilma. I won't say any more about it, but I won't forget it either. You can do what you will with my advice, Cherish."

"Anyway, Cherish won't be someone who'll marry when she's too young. My four older daughters married before they were even twenty. I don't think Cherish will do that."

"That's interesting. So what do you think is a good age to marry, Wilma?"

"I think twenty two or twenty three would be fine, or even older. Cherish looks older, but she's not older up here." Wilma tapped on the side of her head.

"Hey, thanks a lot, *Mamm.*"

"It might be due to the illness," Harriet shot back.

Cherish had heard enough. "While you two plan my life for me, I'll see what they're doing in the living room." Cherish got up and left the room before either lady could say anything.

"Oh my, she's quite rude, Wilma. I'm a little shocked by her comment."

"She speaks her mind."

"You think it's okay that she talks like that?" Harriet asked.

"No, but she's tired. They're sleeping three to a bed. Cherish isn't a good sleeper at the best of times. It's only to be expected that she's not presenting her best self today."

"When I grew up, we were sleeping four to a bed. It was that way until I left home to marry Melvin."

"And it's cold. She's not good with the cold either."

"It'd be cold here most of the time. I've never heard of anyone being rude because they're tired or cold."

"That's Cherish for you. She's her own self." Wilma sipped her tea and said nothing more. She knew it wouldn't work between Cherish and Simon. His parents were far too involved in his life and that meant they'd get involved in Cherish's life. The whole thing would be a disaster.

Cherish walked out into the living room and sat down between Malachi and Simon.

"Did you talk with my mother?" Simon asked.

Cherish flashed him a smile. "Yes, we had a lovely talk."

His face beamed. "Good."

CHAPTER 25

*T*he next day, back in Lancaster County, Matthew staggered out to the kitchen. Aunt Ada was sitting at the kitchen table, sipping a cup of hot tea.

"Breakfast?" she asked.

"Yes please."

She got up and then placed a cup of coffee in front of him before she put two sausages into a frying pan and then cracked two eggs. "Where were you last night? You came home so late."

"Sorry, Ada, but I ended up having a Chinese meal."

She placed her hands on her hips. "You might've told me."

"It was a last-minute thing."

"And can I know the name of the young lady?"

Matthew laughed. "If only. No, it was Andrew, Adam's business partner. We were meant to have a meal with Krystal and when she found out Adam wasn't going to be there, she just left."

Ada pursed her lips. "Is that right?"

"I wouldn't say it if it wasn't so."

"I'm not surprised. She has a crush on him and what woman wouldn't?"

"What makes him so special?"

"I don't know where to start."

"Will a girl ever like me, Aunt Ada?"

"Of course, when you're older."

"I'm plenty old enough to date, but no one's interested in me."

"Perhaps you're trying too hard."

"But if I don't try at all, nothing will happen."

"Just forget about women for a while."

"It's hard because that's all I ever think about."

Ada laughed. "You'll be too busy soon when you start work in the orchard."

"That's what I'm hoping. I can't wait to move out on my own. There'll be someone else living with me, but I'll be responsible for myself."

"That'll help you to grow up and become more mature." Ada stared up at the ceiling. "I wonder how Wilma is getting along with Harriet. They'll be having such a great time."

"I do have some good news."

"Do you?"

"Yes, about Bliss and Adam."

Ada gasped and both hands covered her mouth. "You must tell me right now."

"Andrew told me that Adam is starting to soften towards Bliss. They weren't his exact words, but that's what he meant. He thought Krystal had a talk with him about Bliss. I didn't think that was right, but I didn't want to say anything bad about Krystal."

"Why did Andrew think Krystal had a talk with him?"

"Because it was right after he'd been at Krystal's quilt shop. And not only that, he seems to think Bliss might be interested in someone else."

"Oh, well this might change everything. Good work, Matthew."

"I didn't do anything."

"You did. You found some things out."

"Happy to do it. Will do it again if I can do it while eating Chinese food."

"I'd say that Krystal made him think Bliss was interested in someone else so he'd forget about her. It backfired on Krystal."

"Surely she wouldn't have done that."

Ada shook her finger at him. "Never underestimate a desperate woman."

"She's not desperate. She can have her choice of men."

"No, she can't. The ones she wants don't want her."

Matthew slumped further into his chair.

"I'm sorry, Matthew."

"Don't be. I guess I'll just have to get used to it until I go through my growth spurt."

Ada leaned over and patted his shoulder. "I'm sure that will happen one day. Now, I can't waste any time. Drive me over to talk with Adam. Samuel's not back yet. You'll have to take me."

"No. I don't think we should interfere. Adam told Andrew he needed time to think."

"But I want to do something."

Matthew shook his head. "You will be doing something by staying away and letting *Gott* work on Adam's heart."

Ada stared at Matthew and sat back down. "You're probably right."

"I know I am."

"You might be short, but you do have some wisdom."

"Thanks... I think."

CHAPTER 26

*H*aving had a sleepless night, Adam paced up and down the small living room of the house he shared with Andrew. He'd moved his whole life for Bliss. He'd left his family and started anew so they could eventually be married. Maybe he was to blame for not giving her enough assurance that they'd marry. He'd told her they were heading toward marriage, but maybe she had needed to hear more than that.

She told him she feared he might leave her and that was why she had kept the door in her mind open to someone else.

He rubbed his head. It was aching from doing so much thinking. Perhaps Bliss was more insecure than he had thought she was. She'd never complained about anything and never asked for anything, but that didn't mean she wasn't praying for their relationship to go to the next level.

Every girl wanted to marry and Bliss was no different. He'd

blamed her for writing to John in the early part of their relationship, but perhaps it was his fault she had done that.

He'd never been good at communicating his feelings, but he'd made the effort when Hope and Fairfax announced they were getting married. He knew Bliss might be feeling they needed to get married. That's when he told her they were heading in that direction.

The more he thought about it, the more he realized just how wishy washy that must have sounded to Bliss. He was caught up in his business, making it successful so he'd have enough money to keep a wife and a family, but what good was that now without Bliss?

He was still upset with her, but he missed her.

Now he was faced with the fear she'd be so upset about the break up that she might jump into another relationship. From what Krystal had said, it sounded like that was what was happening.

He half thought about hiring a car and going to Cherish's farm to see Bliss and sort out their differences. But he didn't want to rush into anything. He'd give it some more thought before he did something overly spontaneous.

He slumped into the couch and thought about what his future would be like without Bliss. "Bleak," he said aloud. That was the only word that came to his mind.

Instead of going to work that day, Adam was determined to sort things out between him and Bliss. Maybe there was a chance for them.

Krystal had helped him before and he wanted to talk things through with her. She was a woman, so she could have a good insight into Bliss. And she'd lived with the Baker family for over a year, so she would've gotten to know Bliss fairly well. He hitched his buggy and headed to Gertie's house where Krystal lived.

Krystal opened the front door when he knocked, a surprised look on her face as she adjusted her prayer kapp. "Adam, what are you doing here?"

"Do you mind if we talk?"

"Fine. Of course." She glanced behind her. "Gertie has fallen asleep in the living room. I'll wake her up soon for her breakfast."

"I hope I'm not too early."

"No, it's fine."

He followed her past Gertie and into the kitchen. When they sat down, he didn't want to blurt all his feelings out. He had to work up the courage to ask advice. "How did your meal go at the restaurant last night?"

"Oh that. I decided not to stay. I remembered I hadn't let Gertie know where I'd be and it was my turn to cook. Coffee?" Krystal asked.

"No. I'm fine."

"How did things go with... whatever it was that you were going to do last night?"

Adam licked his lips. "Well, I've been doing a lot of thinking. I was hoping you could help me."

"I will if I can."

"Thank you. If someone has made a huge mistake, how is someone able to forgive them?"

She hoped he was referring to her, but the way her life had been going lately, she was pretty sure he was asking because he was still in love with Bliss. "I think it's not fair if people aren't

371

forgiven. If someone makes a mistake, it's an error in judgement. When they know better, they do better. It's unfair not to be given a second chance."

"I'm trying to get my head around how someone could do—"

"I'm guessing you're talking about Bliss. What did she do that was so terrible?"

He shook his head. "I'd rather not say."

Krystal's eyebrows rose. "It must've been really bad."

"It was more of a shock. You think you know someone and then you don't."

"No one's made more mistakes than I have. I came here pretending to be Favor's pen pal. When I wasn't. Is what Bliss did worse than that?"

"No. I don't think so, but it was *Bliss*. I thought I knew the type of person she was, then I find out what she did and it makes me think that I don't know her at all."

"Did you ask her why she did what she did?"

He nodded. "It didn't make much sense to me. It was just her making an excuse. There was no reasoning behind it."

"I'm guessing that she told you from her heart and you didn't listen. Men don't really listen. I've found that out. Do you even remember what she told you?" Krystal asked.

"Every single word."

"Close your eyes and think about it now."

He closed his eyes.

Krystal continued, "Now, imagine her standing there telling you again, and this time you really believe her and understand. See things from her side."

He opened his eyes a moment later. "I think I've made a terrible mistake."

"It's not too late to fix things. Go to her and tell her how you feel."

"She's gone away."

"Oh that's right. Then why don't you hire a car and go see her?"

"Do you think I should?"

"Yes. Women love grand gestures like that. You'll win her over. And it'll make up for the break up. Hey, that rhymes."

He leaped to his feet. "Thanks, Krystal. You're a good friend."

She felt good to be able to help him, but she did feel a little bad that he never looked at her the way he looked at Bliss. "Let me know how it goes. I hope everything works out all right for you." She walked him to the door. Then she watched him get into his buggy and drive away. When she closed the door, she saw Gertie was awake. "Ready to eat?"

"That was a good thing you did just now."

"What?"

"I heard every word of it."

Krystal laughed. "And here I thought you were asleep."

"You're a peacemaker. Blessed are the peacemakers."

Krystal smiled. "I know many people who wouldn't agree with that. They think I'm a troublemaker." She walked over and sat beside Gertie. "He's such a nice man. I wanted him for myself, but it's no use. He's in love with Bliss."

Gertie patted her hand.

"Will I ever find anyone in the community who will love me and want to marry me? It's even worse for me than just being new here. Everyone knew me as Caroline so they know the complete truth about me and it's not a nice story. I'm not proud of what I did."

Gertie nodded. "It's never easy for the outsiders when they join us."

"I'm not an outsider anymore. That's what I'd like to think. I've been baptized and I've joined the community. God has forgiven all my sins."

"To some, you'll always be an outsider."

"That means I don't truly fit in anywhere."

"That's not so. You fit in here with me and all the other people you've helped. In time, everyone will accept you. The man you choose will be a blessed man."

"Thanks, Gertie."

"*Gott* loves peacemakers," Gertie mumbled to herself. Then she fastened her eyes on Krystal. "Is the meal ready?"

"Yes."

"Let's eat."

CHAPTER 27

$\mathcal{B}$ack at the farm, the girls had slept in the same bed again, despite Favor saying she was going to sleep on the couch if Cherish and Bliss didn't stop talking. They'd stopped their conversation then, and all three had gone to sleep.

When morning came, Cherish had stayed in bed a little longer than usual. It was way too cold to leave the cozy bed. She was glad Malachi hadn't knocked on the door to have her help with feeding the animals.

"I just want to say one more thing if I can, Favor," Bliss said. "Then I'll be quiet."

"Go on, if you have to."

Cherish kept her eyes closed and mumbled, "Okay, I'm listening."

"I've decided that I'm going to forget about Adam. I don't want a man who is so un-Christian-like. We're told to forgive, but did Adam forgive me?"

Favor gave her opinion. "Maybe he forgave you, but it's

changed how he thinks about you and then he thinks you're a different kind of person compared to what he thought you were."

"That's even worse. He knows me well, and he should know that I'm the same person. I told him my reasons for doing what I did."

Favor sat up. "I'm sorry, all right?"

"Sorry for what?" Cherish asked.

"I'm sorry that I told Adam about the letters from John."

Now Cherish felt bad too. "And I'm sorry, Bliss, for finding the letters."

Favor added, "And I'm sorry for overhearing Cherish when you discovered she'd found them."

"You've both apologized to me before and I have forgiven you both. It's okay. This isn't either of your faults. It's my problem."

Favor lay back down. "If I were you, I wouldn't forgive me. You must hate us both, we're not even your real sisters. You probably wish your father married someone else and you'd have different stepsisters."

"Don't be silly. We're family. It doesn't matter how we became family, we are all in this together."

Cherish didn't know how Bliss could be so forgiving and kind. They'd both played a part in her losing Adam and she'd been so quick to forgive them. "You're right, Bliss. If Adam doesn't realize what he's missing out on, he doesn't deserve you. He deserves to grow old alone and never have any children."

"Don't say that, Cherish." Bliss shook her head. "He'll meet someone. It probably won't even take him very long. He's got everything going for him."

"No he doesn't," Favor said. "He doesn't have you, and that's a big mistake for him to make. He'll know it one day and he'll be so sorry when he wakes up to himself."

"Thanks, both of you. You've made me feel so much better. I'm going to stop being upset about Adam. Something I didn't realize about him is that he's hard-hearted. I don't want a man like that."

"Good for you," Favor said. "I agree with you! Now just stick to it and don't go running back to him."

"I won't."

"Now can we all get out of bed?" Favor asked.

Bliss agreed and threw back the covers. "Yes. *Mamm* shouldn't have to make the breakfast all by herself."

LATE IN THE AFTERNOON, everyone on the farm got a surprise.

Favor looked out the window and shouted out, "It's Adam!"

"Who?" *Mamm* asked.

"Adam's here?" Bliss jumped up.

Cherish pulled the curtains in the living room aside. "It's Adam! It's true."

"Is it?" asked *Mamm*.

Favor bounded to her feet. "Shall I tell him you don't want anything to do with him anymore, Bliss?"

"No. I'll talk with him." Bliss rushed to the door, opened it and stepped outside.

Favor followed her to the door, saying, "Don't forget what you said to us this morning."

Bliss rushed down the porch steps while everyone watched from the window.

"What's going on?" Harriet asked.

Favor swung around to face everyone. "It's Adam. Bliss and Adam were dating and then they broke up. But we can't tell anyone why because it's a secret."

"Oh. Yes, I heard a little about that." Harriet looked at her husband.

"Sounds interesting," Simon said. "You can tell me later, Cherish." He gave her a wink.

"No! Cherish isn't allowed. The whole family is keeping this secret," Favor snapped.

Mamm sat there, speechless, shaking her head slightly at Favor. Finally, she said, "It's nothing. Just personal things they have to work out between them. It's nothing interesting."

"So it's nothing we need to worry about?" Harriet asked.

"No, nothing at all," Wilma said.

Harriet folded her hands in her lap. "Then you can tell us about it to stop us from worrying."

Wilma shook her head. "It's between Adam and Bliss."

Cherish looked out the window, wondering what Adam was saying to Bliss. He had to have missed her to come all this way.

Favor went to go out the door too, but *Mamm* told her to come back and let them speak privately.

Bliss rushed over to Adam. "Adam, what are you doing here?" She could tell by the way he looked at her that something within him had changed.

"Bliss, can you ever forgive me? I couldn't waste any

more time. I had to come here and see you and tell you how I feel. I love you, Bliss. I know I said I wasn't ready for marriage, not just yet, but will you marry me? We could marry about this time next year. That is, if you still want to marry me."

Bliss threw her arms around him with so much force she nearly knocked him over, and he felt tears welling up in his eyes.

He laughed and a tear escaped and trickled down his cheek. "I'm guessing that's a yes."

Tears streamed down Bliss's face. "Yes, and yes, and yes."

Malachi had walked into the house through the back door. He saw everyone looking out the window. "Who is it?" Malachi asked.

"It's Adam," Favor said.

"I keep hearing the name Adam, but no one's explaining exactly who he is," Malachi said.

"Adam is Bliss's boyfriend."

"Yes, that's right. I remember now."

"Why's he here?" Simon asked.

"Looks like they're back together." Favor huffed. "After everything she said this morning, I find it shocking."

"Hush," Cherish told her. "This is the best thing that could've happened."

"He could've waited until we got back home," Wilma said. "It's a long way to come for a reunion."

Then they watched as the hire car drove away, leaving Adam behind.

"Now we have another guest, it seems," said Malachi. "I'll sleep on the couch, he can have my room."

"That's nice of you, Malachi. Cherish can make up the bed with fresh sheets for him."

Cherish wasn't happy about Malachi having to give up his room because technically this was his home for however long he was living there as her manager. "That's nice of you, Malachi. Are you sure you want to do that? Adam will be fine on the couch. He wouldn't want you to be turned out of your room."

"It's fine. Or I could always go to the barn." He smiled at Cherish.

"Oh, don't be silly, Malachi. The barn is so cold," *Mamm* snapped.

"I told you she'd say that," Cherish told him.

"Look at them hugging like that for everyone to see," Harriet said, peering out the window.

Favor laughed. "Um, I'm pretty sure they don't know we're watching. Look at them. I reckon they'd feel like the only people in the world right now."

"So romantic," Malachi said, sarcastically.

Cherish hit him playfully on his arm. "It *is* romantic."

"Still, they're being far too familiar," Harriet whined.

"They had a fight and they're getting back together. Personally, I think it's great," Cherish said. "Finally. I knew it would happen."

"No you didn't." Favor made a face at Cherish, and Cherish ignored her. No one was going to ruin this moment.

"I guess I should go out and see what's going on," Wilma said.

"I think that would be a good idea, Wilma," Melvin told her.

Wilma opened the door and then the couple looked around.

"*Mamm*, it's Adam."

Wilma laughed. "I can see that. Welcome, Adam."

"I hope you don't mind me coming here unexpectedly."

"No, not at all. You're welcome to join us."

"I wasn't planning this. It was a last minute thing. I had to speak to Bliss." He looked down and smiled at her.

Wilma could see from their faces that all was forgiven and forgotten.

"I just learned from Bliss that the house is full. I could sleep in the barn. I don't want to inconvenience anyone. I've booked a car to drive me back tomorrow."

"That's fine, Adam. We'll squeeze you in somehow. Malachi has already offered up his room if you were staying."

"That's mighty kind of him, but I'll sleep on the floor somewhere. I'm one of those guys who can sleep anywhere. It really doesn't bother me."

"Cherish is already making up the bed for you. It's all organized. Welcome back to the family, Adam."

"Thank you. And, Wilma, if it's all right with you, Bliss would like to travel back in the car with me tomorrow."

Wilma looked at Bliss. "Is this what you want?"

"Yes. I've seen the farm and I've had a lovely time. I've met everyone Cherish has been talking about so I'm ready to go home."

"Very well. I'm glad you two have sorted out your differences. Come in and meet everyone, Adam."

Adam and Bliss followed Wilma into the house.

When Wilma opened the door, all eyes were on her. "Good news, everyone, we have an extra guest. It's Adam Wengerd." Wilma introduced everyone.

After a while, Favor pulled Bliss aside. "What about all that stuff you were saying this morning about him being hard-hearted?"

"Will you keep your voice down? Do you want to ruin everything?" Bliss hissed.

"Well, you were the one that said it."

"He's come all the way here to make up. That means a lot."

Favor pushed out her bottom lip. "Yeah, it means you're compromising."

"That's what relationships are about," Bliss shot back. "Don't you know that? You should, by now."

"Wow. You've never spoken to me like that before," Favor said.

"I'm sorry. I don't mean to be like that, but please keep quiet about what I said before. It doesn't apply anymore, because he's here, and he's apologized, and I've forgiven him. I was going to forget about him and now I don't have to."

"I'm happy for you. I truly am and this gets me off the hook for telling Adam about—"

"Shh. Yes, it gets you off the hook." Bliss left Favor and went back to sit down with Adam.

CHAPTER 28

That evening, Adam and Bliss had some time on the couch after everyone else had gone to bed. Adam had insisted on Malachi sleeping in his own bed, and he had blankets and a pillow to set up the couch for himself.

"Shall we tell everyone we're engaged?" Adam asked.

Bliss shook her head. "No, let's not. I just want a little time to get used to that first before I share it. Is that all right?"

"Whatever you want."

"What made you change your mind about me?" Bliss asked.

"I just realized what I'd be losing if you were out of my life. I did talk to a couple of people."

"I hope you didn't tell them anything about me."

Adam shook his head. "I'd never do anything to embarrass you. Krystal helped me see things for what they are."

"Krystal?"

"Yes."

"I thought she'd be the last person who'd want to help us. Or who'd want to help me."

"I think she's grown up a lot. She's had some bad experiences and it was good to hear her point of view about mistakes and forgiveness and the like."

"Are you sure she doesn't like you?" Like Cherish, Bliss had never entirely trusted Krystal.

He laughed. "I'm sure. You don't have to worry about anything like that."

"I know, but I do worry sometimes."

"Don't worry anymore. We're engaged. We'll be married before you know it. You've got a whole year to get used to the idea that we'll be husband and wife."

All Bliss's worries were over. "Where will we live?"

"I'm not sure. We'll sort that out when the time gets closer. I might have to kick out my roommate."

Bliss laughed. "I wouldn't want you to do that. We can find somewhere."

"Leave that up to me. I don't want you to worry about a thing. I've already put you through enough and I'm so sorry for that."

"I can't believe you came all this way."

"It was something I needed to do. Andrew's covering for me at work for a couple of days. We can have the whole rest of the day together after we get back."

"I'd love that. Are you sure you can spare the time?"

"I think we need time together after what happened."

"I agree."

He whispered, "Now, fill me in. Why are the Koppels staying here?"

Bliss told him about Simon and his parents.

BLISS ARRIVED BACK at the apple orchard the next afternoon. Everyone was surprised to see her, and even more surprised that she arrived with Adam. After a quick evening meal with Ada, Samuel, Matthew, and the Bruners, Adam went home. Ada stayed at the Baker/Bruner house so she could find out what had happened between the pair.

Ada ordered the three men into the living room so she and Debbie could talk with Bliss alone while they cleaned up from the meal.

"What happened between you and Adam?"

"We're back together."

"We know that, but how?" Debbie asked.

"He just arrived at Cherish's farm. He had some talk with Krystal and somehow she helped. I'll have to thank her."

"That is a huge surprise," Debbie said.

Ada nodded. "It's another example of *Gott's* wisdom if Krystal said something to help the situation. *Gott* using a mule to speak. Or was it a donkey?"

"It was a mule," Debbie said. "In fact, my bible says it was an ass that belonged to Balaam that did the talking, not a donkey or a mule."

Bliss knew there was a scripture story where a donkey spoke to a man, but rather than talk any further about that, she had news that was bursting to come out. "I've got something to tell you both. I meant to keep this quiet, but I don't think I can."

"Are you getting married?" Ada said.

Bliss's mouth fell open. "How did you know?"

"I can tell just from how your face is glowing."

"It's not until next year, but we're engaged. Do you know how good that feels?"

Debbie leaned over and hugged her. "I'm so happy for you. I do remember how that feels, but mine was a secret. Just don't keep yours a secret for too long."

"I didn't even think of that. No, Adam doesn't want to keep it a secret, I do."

"Same thing. If you keep it quiet for too long he might think you're ashamed of him. That's how I felt."

"I don't feel anything like that and Adam seemed fine with it, but I'll still take your advice. I just wanted a moment to think about it before I tell the world. I haven't even told *Mamm*. I couldn't because I didn't have a moment alone with her."

Ada leaned forward and hugged her. "This is so exciting. I'm so happy for you."

"Me too. You know how sad I was and now I'm the opposite. It's a miracle. Now everything is even more perfect than it was before Adam and I broke up." Bliss gave a satisfied sigh. "It's so good to be home."

"How is everything at the farm?" Ada asked.

"Fine, but it was pretty crowded."

"How's Cherish getting along with Simon?"

"Okay I think, but she's worried about his parents. The three of them seem way too close, which I thought was kind of nice at first, until I saw it for myself. They go everywhere together and his mother fusses over him."

"I was surprised that she likes Simon. What about Malachi?

The way she talks about him and waits for his letters made me think that she had a soft spot for him," Debbie said.

"No, I don't think so although they did go off for long walks. I thought they were just talking about the farm. Now you've got me thinking."

"Don't think about it too much. I might be wrong." Debbie said. "Is Favor having a good time?"

Bliss nodded. "Yes, I think so. She gets along well with the visitors. She really likes Simon."

"That's good. Wait, you mean Favor *likes* Simon too?"

Bliss sighed. "That's right."

Ada raised her eyebrows and looked over at Debbie, who seemed just as surprised.

CHAPTER 29

Back at the farm...

Wilma got her chance to talk with Harriet alone when everyone went outside to look at the patterns the ice had made on the roof of the barn. Wilma and Harriet preferred to stay and drink their coffee by the fire where it was warm.

"Exactly how many children do you have, Wilma?" Harriet asked.

"I have six with my first husband, none with my second, although he has one girl, Bliss, and two older boys, who we hardly ever see because they're married with their own families. My first husband was a widower. He already had two boys and a girl and I helped raise them."

"You've been blessed."

"I have, but I only have Cherish and Favor left and I'm going to enjoy the time I have left with them before they leave home."

"I won't say I'm envious, and jealousy is a sin, but then so is envy I suppose. But I would've loved to be surrounded by so many children. I'd like to see Simon marry while he's young so he can provide me with all the children I missed out on."

Wilma had visions of Simon's wife being pushed to the side while Harriet took over the raising of them. "And they'll all be living at your house?"

"I do hope so. We'll have to extend of course, but Melvin is a good builder. He's one of those men who's been good at everything he's put his hand to. How long did you have between husband one and two?"

Wilma was a little shocked that she asked a question like that, but perhaps she just wanted to know a little more about the family. "Many years. Cherish was only a young girl. She'd have memories of him, though. The girls were mostly all grown up when I married Levi. Florence, my oldest stepdaughter had already left the home. She married an *Englisher.*"

Harriet gasped. "I'm so sorry. I had no idea. You poor thing. You must have felt you failed your first husband when that happened."

"Not really. It was such a love match that nobody or nothing could've prevented it," Wilma said.

Harriet set her cup down on the table. "I don't believe that. Aren't you forgetting something?"

"What?"

"God, of course. He could've prevented it and he wouldn't have been happy with that match."

"Florence said she didn't leave God. She left the community."

Harriet laughed. "Haven't we all heard that before? She left because she wanted to leave."

Wilma stayed silent. Harriet knew nothing of their family

and she was very quick to judge. "All I know is that Florence and Carter, her husband, have been a blessing to us. She now manages our orchard. She's so knowledgable about everything. Her father taught her well, and she's been quick to learn the new methods also."

Harriet smiled and picked up her coffee cup again and took a sip.

It irritated Wilma even more that she wasn't saying anything —just silently jumping to assumptions and doing some more judging.

"Have any of your other children left the community?"

Wilma wasn't even going to mention Carter, and she was pleased that Ada had kept that knowledge a closed book. "No. They've all stayed. My oldest stepson has moved away to a community in another state. He married a lovely woman and they're having twins soon."

"More twins? Didn't someone in your family already have twins?"

"Yes. My second oldest stepson and his wife."

"Oh, that's delightful. You certainly have a lot to be happy about. I hope you thank the Lord every day for all that He's given you."

"I do." Wilma took a mouthful of coffee, hoping everyone would come back soon. And when were the Koppels leaving?

"I probably wouldn't mention to Melvin that your step-daughter, who's fallen from grace, is now in charge of your orchard."

Fallen from grace? Wilma was shocked at Harriet's choice of words. "I won't say anything unless he asks."

"Good because he would think that your husband would be in charge, as it should be."

"He tried running the orchard and then he admitted that he didn't have enough knowledge. Some might see that as failure, but I was happy with him that he was... that he saw his short-comings before it was too late. He's a humble man."

"He could've learned."

"He is learning, but he's not been well and Florence has a lifetime of knowledge."

"What's wrong with him?" Harriet asked.

"He had a heart attack not long back and he has to take things slow."

"That makes a whole lot more sense. You had no choice but to let her take over. I hope you're keeping a close watch on the finances if she's keeping the books."

Wilma laughed. "I don't need to worry about that. Florence's husband is a very wealthy man. They have more money than they'll ever need. He's the richest man I know. Anyway, even if that wasn't the case, Florence is not like that."

"But you don't know her, not really, now that she's left."

Wilma was a little shocked at Harriet's remark. She was almost saying that Florence would steal from her own orchard. "I do know her. She's still the same as she always was. She's reliable, honest, and hard working."

"The world can be a seductive place. And how did he get all this money? Are you sure it was from honest places?"

"Oh yes. He owns a whole company. They make games."

Harriet's nose wrinkled. "Games?"

"Yes, computer games and games on phones."

"I know nothing about that." Harriet shook her head.

Wilma stood up. "I might go out and see what they all find so interesting. Care to join me?"

"No. I don't see the sense in getting cold when I don't have to."

Wilma grabbed her coat from the hook behind the front door and headed out as she pulled it on. It mystified Wilma how Ada could be friends with Harriet, and now she'd decided she definitely had to put an end to Cherish liking Simon. It just wouldn't work. The two families wouldn't mesh. Both Harriet and Melvin had far too many opinions. They were like two Adas, only much worse.

CHAPTER 30

When Wilma got outside, she rushed over to where everyone was standing. Then she saw it. A whole nativity scene had been carved out of the ice on the roof of the barn. "Oh my! Who did that?" Wilma asked.

"Malachi," Favor said.

"It's so lovely. I didn't know you could do this, Malachi."

He laughed. "It's something I tried last winter. It'll melt as soon as the sun starts shining. It's not that good. It's very rough."

"It's good enough to know what it is. And it's lovely. If only Bliss was here to see it. She would've loved it."

"How did you do it, Malachi?" Simon asked.

"Just with ordinary tools."

"You must've been up early," Melvin said.

"I always get up before sunlight. I like to watch the sun rise."

"I'll get Harriet. She'd love to see this." Melvin started walking to the house.

"She's pretty settled in front of the fire," Wilma told him.

Melvin laughed. "She's enjoying the fire too much I'd say. I'll talk her into it."

"I'll come with you, pa."

Melvin and Simon walked off together.

Wilma couldn't help herself. She said a quick prayer that the Koppels would go home soon. Then Wilma noticed Cherish was looking around for Simon. "He's gone inside with his father."

"Okay, thanks."

"Isn't it wonderful what Malachi has done, Cherish?" Wilma asked.

Cherish stared up at his artwork. "It truly is. I had no idea he could do anything like that."

Malachi climbed off the roof. "It's a shame I can't sell it."

Wilma laughed. "Not everything is about money. Look how much pleasure you've brought everyone who's seen it." Wilma shivered. "Even though we're all probably going to die from frostbite."

"You go inside, *Mamm,*" Cherish said.

"No. I'm not done looking at it. Every time I look, I see something different. Look, there's Wally."

Malachi pointed to two small figures in the corner. "And that's me in front of Wally."

"Malachi said he often does this. We've never seen it because we've never been here when the roof was iced up like this."

Favor excused herself and headed to the house.

"What made you think of doing it?" *Mamm* asked.

He shrugged his shoulders. "Dunno. I just started doin' it and I enjoyed it. I didn't think anyone else would be this interested."

"It's so beautiful and it will all melt away."

"It's a bit like life," Malachi said. "We're all here and then one day we won't be here."

Wilma sighed. "Sad in a way, but true."

Cherish suddenly thought about Ruth, the neighbor. "I must go back to Ruth's and see her while I'm here. I left a note on her door that I'd be back and I haven't been there yet."

"You want me to drive you over?" Malachi asked.

"I can do that if you loan me your buggy, Malachi. I'm sure you've got work you could be doing."

"That's true. There's always something to do. Sure, take the buggy. Tell me when you're ready, Cherish and I'll hitch the buggy for you."

"Thanks, Malachi. If you're not busy maybe you could come too," suggested Cherish.

Malachi shook his head. "It's okay."

"We could invite her for a meal. I'll see if she can come for lunch today," Cherish said.

"She's an *Englisher*, right?" Melvin had just come back with Harriet.

"That's right. We do have *Englisher* friends, don't you?" Wilma asked, looking at Melvin and then glancing at Harriet. Harriet didn't look very pleased about being out here in the cold instead of beside the warm fire. She wasn't even impressed with Malachi's handiwork. She just stood there in grim silence.

"Not really. We know our *Englisher* neighbors, but we don't invite them into our home."

"Everyone's different," Wilma told them. Then she turned to Cherish. "Please see if Ruth can come for lunch. I'll make vegetable and noodle soup and Bliss can make... Oh, Bliss isn't here."

"I'll do it, *Mamm*. What did you want Bliss to make?" Favor asked, walking toward them from the house with Simon not far behind.

"I was going to say she could make some more bread. She makes it so light and tasty," Wilma said.

"I can do that. I'll try to do it as good." Favor gave a nod with a slight smirk hinting around her lips.

"I'm sure your bread will be great," Simon said, smiling at Favor.

"Thank you." Favor smiled up at him. "I'll let you be the first to taste it."

Cherish glared at Favor. Why was she being so nice to Simon? She was making it clear that she liked him. Wilma and Cherish were the first ones back at the house. "Did you hear Favor just now? She likes Simon."

"You mean she wants him for a boyfriend?" Wilma asked.

"Yes."

Wilma shook her head. "That won't do."

"I know it won't. Can you talk to her?"

"I will. I don't think Simon is suitable for either of you girls."

"*Mamm!* Don't say that. What's wrong with him?"

"It's not so much him, it's his parents."

"Oh, yeah well, I can agree with you there. They are a bit protective of him. They want the woman he marries to be close to them as well. I think he should be alone with his wife, don't you?"

"Yes, but you're saying you still like him, is that right?"

"I do and that's why you need to talk with Favor. Tell her to stay away from him. She knows I like him. What's she trying to do?"

"I'll talk with her. You go and see Ruth."

"Okay. Thanks, *Mamm.*" Cherish leaned over and hugged her mother and her mother patted her on her back.

Cherish walked out of the house, figuring the buggy should be hitched by now. She saw the horse and buggy waiting. Malachi was patting the horse's neck while talking to Simon who was sitting in the buggy.

Cherish hurried over, said goodbye to Malachi and climbed in next to Simon. She was surprised to see him in the buggy. There was no talk about him going with her. She hadn't asked him to go with he hadn't offered.

"Let's go." Simon moved the horse away.

Cherish looked over at him. "I'm surprised you got away alone, without your parents."

He glanced at her and then looked at the road ahead, seeming very serious. "They wanted to come. I told them I needed some time alone with you. They were a bit upset. I think Ma nearly cried."

Cherish burst out laughing and when he didn't laugh with her, she said, "Oh, you're serious?"

"Yes. When I said we go everywhere together, I meant it."

Cherish was delighted he had stood up to them. "I can see that. Turn left here and then keep going until you see another driveway."

"It's not a problem is it?" he asked.

"What?"

"My parents?"

"No. Not for me. I really like them."

"Sorry for asking what I'm about to ask, but I just need to know before we move ahead with anything between us. If you and I got married, would you be upset with my parents being so close?"

Yes, she wanted to scream, but she didn't want to lose the first possible boyfriend she might have. "Not if we get some private time and not if you and I get to make our own decisions."

"We would and we could."

Cherish smiled. "Then, it's not a problem."

"I was hoping you'd say that."

The only problem Cherish had now was Favor. She hoped her mother could talk sense into her sister.

CHAPTER 31

*B*ack at the house, Wilma caught up with Favor in the girls' bedroom. "Before we start, I need to have a talk with you."

"I need to make the dinner rolls now, *Mamm,* or they won't bake in time."

"A couple more minutes won't make any difference."

Favor sat on the bed. "Okay, what have I done now?"

"Cherish feels that you're being too friendly with Simon."

"What?" she shrieked. "That's just ridiculous. I'm only being myself. Tell her to mind her business."

Wilma sat on the bed next to her. "It's not just Cherish. I think it too. I've seen how you are with him. You like him."

"Yes, I do and what's wrong with that? They aren't even dating. He can choose who he likes best."

"The choice has been made. They are spending time with one another to perhaps progress in that direction and while I may not agree with her doing that, I do think you're stepping on her toes."

"How could you say that? I like him too. Are you choosing her over me?"

"No, but you must know they like each other so what are you trying to do?"

"I wish I'd never come here. I always thought you liked her better, but I hoped I was wrong. I don't feel like making bread now. I'm going outside for a minute. I should've gone home with Bliss. Even Aunt Dagmar chose her over me." Favor got up and stomped out of the room.

Wilma shook her head. She didn't want either girl to marry into the Koppel family, but she had needed to say something to Favor because she didn't like what she was doing to Cherish.

Just then Harriet came into the room. "Is Favor okay? I just passed her and she looked different."

"She's just upset about something. You know what teenage girls are like."

"No I don't. I wish I did."

"I can tell you what they're like. Everything is a problem for them." Wilma stood up.

"I hope we're not visiting at a bad time."

Wilma gave her a bright smile. "No, it's fine. We're all so happy to have you here."

"Thank you. Anything I can do to help?"

"Yes, you have a cup of hot tea with me. Ada and I always drink hot tea while we work in the kitchen and then we sit down together for a second cup."

"I do miss being around Ada. She's such fun," Harriet said.

"She is. She's like family."

"I was about to say she's like my sister. A sister that I don't see often enough." Harriet's mouth turned down at the corners.

They both walked out of the bedroom, heading to the kitchen. "You do write to her often, don't you?" Wilma asked.

"As soon as I get a letter from her, I write one back. It's been that way for years. Ada must talk about me all the time."

Wilma smiled. "That's very often."

"Wilma, I'm a little concerned that your daughters don't get along. I sense tension between them."

"They're a little upset with each other at the moment, but they're normally close. Don't be concerned."

"What's the problem with them?"

Wilma filled the kettle and talked over the top of the running water. "Who would know? Girls are like that sometimes. They can get niggly."

"Really?"

"Yes. You know how it is when you spend too much time with someone." Wilma put the kettle onto the stove then lit it.

"No, I don't."

Wilma looked up to see Harriet looking very serious. "It's nothing to worry about."

"You call them girls, but they're not girls. They are young ladies."

"I suppose they are, but they don't act like it." Wilma giggled.

"Would that be because you treat them like they are girls —children?"

The smile left Wilma's face. She wanted to scream at Harriet to get out of the kitchen. Harriet was making her feel that everything was her fault. But she couldn't help it if both girls liked Simon. Then Wilma remembered how Cherish once had a crush on Jonathon, who'd married Honor. That caused Wilma to smile. Cherish was getting a taste of her own medicine.

"Did I say something funny, Wilma?"

"No. I just thought of something."

"Do share. What was it?"

"I was just thinking about the little squabbles my girls have had over the years."

"I wouldn't know anything about squabbles since I wasn't blessed with more than one child. What's it like to have many children? I've asked a lot of people and they all say something different."

Wilma stopped and thought about it for a while. "It's like a juggling act. There's always someone with a problem that you have to help them with. While you're doing that, someone else will feel left out. Why are you giving this person extra attention? Why aren't you talking to me? Why did she get that? I didn't get one."

"I see that there could be a problem with jealousy."

Wilma got the cups and saucers out of the cupboard. "Why would there be a problem in my family? You asked me what it was like having a lot of children and I told you."

"Oh Wilma. Don't be upset with me. I thought you'd tell me happy warm stories of love and togetherness. I didn't expect what you said. I'm not used to those kinds of unkind emotions."

"Well, there are happy times too, but I didn't want to upset you with those since you only have one child."

"It's okay. I'd love to hear the happy stories."

Wilma thought for a minute. Those moments she mentioned were few and far between.

The best times for her were when all of them were in bed and she could have some peace, but she couldn't tell Harriet that or she'd face even more judgement. "The best times are when we all sit around the dinner table and talk about our day."

"That does sound nice."

"It is. Then the girls and I have started sewing quilts. That brings us all together. Ada helps too."

"That sounds delightful. You've always got someone to keep you company. I'm so lonely through the day while the men are working. It would be nice if I had a daughter-in-law to keep me company. That day will come and I'll be so grateful."

CHAPTER 32

*D*ebbie hadn't intended to talk with Ada, but she felt the need to discuss her feelings with someone. Bliss could have some good insights too. "I just don't know how I feel about Peter. He's dropping hints about the future. I just don't know what to say."

"How do you *think* you feel about him?" Bliss asked.

"I like being around him and I'm grateful he's done so much for me."

"So, you only like him as a good friend?" Ada asked.

Debbie thought about that for a moment. "I'm not sure. I think I like him a little more than that, but it's not the same."

Ada's eyebrows rose. "Same as what?"

Debbie didn't want to mention John's name, but now she had to. "It's not the same way that I felt about John. John was all I ever thought about. We were so in love, and the feeling was just different. There was more attraction."

"You don't think Peter's attractive?" Bliss asked.

"I guess he is, but I don't mean that exactly. John had something unseen that pulled us together. I can't quite explain it. It was like we had to be together. We couldn't keep away from each other. It's not like that with Peter."

"Just because it's different doesn't mean it's not real," Ada said.

"But what is it? Is it love, or is it gratitude that he was there at the right time?"

Ada shook her head. "I can't help you with that. That's something only you can answer."

"I hoped you would be able to help me. What if I tell him we have no future and then later I realize it was love, but just a different kind of love?"

"Hmm. The fact that you're doubting it so much makes me think it's not love, but love can grow." Ada gave her a big smile.

Debbie knew Ada would say exactly that—that love could grow. It sounded like a big risk to take because what if it didn't? "I know and he is a good man."

"That's true. It depends what you're looking for in a husband, I guess," Bliss said.

"I'll have to give that some thought."

"I never met John," said Ada, "but since he had a few women interested in him, I'm guessing he was a dynamic kind of a man with a great personality."

"He was that. That's exactly right."

Bliss nodded in agreement.

"Peel away that outer layer and what do you have? Did John treat you properly?" Ada asked.

Debbie shook her head. "He should've told his parents about our marriage."

"No!" Ada raised her voice. "You should *never* have had a secret marriage in the first place. He should never have suggested it and you should never have gone along with it. Don't you see that?"

"I do, but I just wanted him to be happy. And I thought that maybe if I said no, we wouldn't get married at all. Everyone would've found out eventually so at the time, I didn't see much harm in it."

"But didn't you want to have your family and friends be at your wedding?"

"Yes, but it wasn't as important as marrying John. That's all I ever thought about. I know it seems silly now to everyone else."

"No, it doesn't," Bliss said. "Love can cause people to do strange things."

"I remember what it was like to be young and impulsive," Ada said, smiling.

"I would've done anything for John and although I like Peter, it's not as intense."

"I see what you're saying, but I'm sorry I don't know the answer. You don't have to rush in." Ada patted Debbie's hand.

"I know that, but I feel I have to know because I don't want to waste his time. That's what I'll be doing if I decide in a year or so he's not for me."

"It's a hard decision to make. You'll need to spend time in prayer."

"That's what I've been doing and I still don't have an answer." Debbie shook her head.

"It'll come to you soon enough. Just relax and stop worrying."

Debbie took a deep breath. "It's hard not to worry about anything. Ever since I married John, my life has been full of worry about one thing or another. I'm counting my blessings. I know I've got a lot to be thankful for."

"You have and the number one blessing is Jared," Bliss said.

They all turned their heads when they heard footsteps. Joy walked in the door with a sleeping Faith in her arms.

"Joy! Put Faith on the couch and come sit with us."

"Will she stay asleep?" Ada asked.

"I think so. I'll try it."

A minute later, Joy was back in the kitchen. "Any news from the farm?"

"I was there. I came back with Adam. He came to see me and now we're back together."

Joy jumped up and down and then she hugged Bliss. "I'm so happy for you." Joy sat down with them.

"I can't wait to hear how Cherish is getting on with Simon. Maybe they'll fall in love. She might marry before Favor does," Bliss said.

Ada shook her head. "*Ach,* don't say that in front of Wilma. She's got her mind set on neither of them marrying until they're much older."

"That makes sense, but when you fall in love, you can't help how you feel," Joy said.

Debbie was tempted to ask Joy about love, but she didn't know her as well as the other Baker girls. "Can I get you some tea, Joy?"

"Oh, yes. I'd like some of your flavored tea please."

"Sure. How about the rose and vanilla?"

"That sounds lovely."

"And put some chocolate cookies on a plate while you're at it please, Debbie?" Ada asked.

"Sure."

Joy folded her hands together and placed them on the table. "Well, I have some news. Isaac and I have finally found a place to buy. We're moving out of Levi's house."

"Does he know?" Ada asked.

"No, not yet. I've come here to tell him. He's been so generous with us. We could never have saved the money we have if he hadn't made an arrangement with us about the rent."

"Where is the *haus* you bought?" Ada asked.

"It's only about a mile west from where we are now. A mile further away from here. The place is old and it's only two bedrooms, but Isaac said he'll be able to make it twice the size. There are two barns and they're in better condition than the *haus*. The fences are really good too."

"But the *haus* is where you'll be living. It's not falling down, is it?"

Joy laughed. "No. It's not. It's perfect for us. We both love it."

"Things are really working out for you, Joy. I'm happy for you."

"*Denke,* Debbie. Where is Levi?"

"He's gone out with Samuel to help someone with something. I think they're mending fences."

"Where is Isaac?" Bliss asked.

"He's at work."

"Oh, yes of course. Is he still liking it there?"

"*Jah,* he loves it. I was just with Christina, showing Faith the babies. She loved them and kept wanting to touch them. It will be wonderful when they're all old enough to play together. It's been lonely for Faith. She loves it when Iris comes to play, but it's not often enough."

"You'll have to have another baby for Faith to play with," Ada told her.

When she didn't respond, Debbie turned around to look at her. "Is there something you need to tell us, Joy?"

Joy put a hand up to her mouth and laughed. "Well, I was going to wait until *Mamm* came home so I can tell everyone together."

Debbie hurried to sit down next to her. "Yes?"

"Isaac and I are having another baby."

Both Debbie and Ada squealed. Bliss sat there with her mouth open.

"Shh. You'll wake Faith," Joy said, with a laugh.

Debbie put her arms around her and then Ada got up and moved around to the other side of the table to do the same. Then Bliss took her turn to hug her.

When they were all sitting down again, Joy said, "Please don't tell *Mamm* while she's away. I want to see her face when I tell her."

"This is perfect, and you'll be in your new *haus* when the baby comes," Debbie said.

"Yes. Isaac said he'll have another room added on by then."

"What do you want, a boy or a girl?" Bliss asked.

"I'm hoping for another girl. I want all girls like *Mamm* had."

"What's wrong with boys?" Ada asked.

"Nothing at all. If it's a boy, I won't be disappointed. I'll love him just as much." Joy put her hand over her tummy. "I already love my baby."

"Oh, to be young again," Ada said. "It's such an exciting time. I remember waiting for each baby to arrive, wondering what they'd be like. There's nothing like holding your newborn in your arms. It's *Gott's* greatest miracle."

"It sure is," Debbie agreed.

Faith toddled into the kitchen, rubbing her eyes. Then she saw her mother and ran to her and climbed on her lap.

"Hello, Faith," Debbie said.

Faith buried her face into her mother's shoulder.

"Aren't you talking to us today?" Ada asked Faith.

"She's gotten more shy lately. I'm not sure why."

"Oh, I forgot the tea." Debbie brought the teapot over and poured them all a cup.

CHAPTER 33

*B*ack at the farm...

On the way to Ruth's house, Cherish saw Ruth's car pulling out of her driveway. "There she is." Cherish put her head out the window and flagged her down. Ruth pulled her car over to the side, parked it, and got out. Cherish got out too and ran over. "Ruth, we were just coming to visit."

"I was just coming to see you. I hear your mother is with you this time."

"She is. She said to ask you for lunch. Do you have the time?"

Ruth grinned. "I have the time and the appetite." Ruth glanced over at Simon who remained in the driver's seat.

"This is Simon."

Simon then got out. "Hello, Ruth. I've heard a lot about you."

"You have?"

"Yes."

"I've heard nothing about you."

Cherish chuckled to break the awkward tension. Ruth was always so abrupt that she often sounded rude when she didn't mean to be. "Simon is staying with me for a few days. His parents are here too. You can meet them all."

"Oh, joy. There's nothing I like more than to get to know people I'll never see again." Ruth had no problem in speaking her mind. "You'll have to turn your buggy around and I'll drive up to your place."

"Okay."

Ruth got into her car and zoomed away, leaving them in a cloud of dust.

"She's your friend?"

"Yes. She's so lovely."

"She's hiding it well. I heard what she said."

"I'm sorry. You just have to get to know her."

"If she's your friend, I'll give it a try."

"Thank you."

They headed back home.

OVER LUNCH, Ruth slurped her soup. Then she looked up and stared at the Koppels. "Where do you all live?"

"We live a day's buggy ride away," Melvin answered.

"That doesn't tell me anything. How would I know what that is? I've never driven a buggy before and never wanted to drive one. The good Lord gave us the skills to invent things like cars, so I think we should use 'em. Not meaning to be rude, but… maybe I should keep my mouth shut. I don't want to start a debate."

Melvin laughed. "You won't get a debate from us. People have different opinions. We know we're in the minority and we're fine with that."

Cherish was pleased with Melvin's comment. Maybe Ruth coming over wasn't such a good idea, but at least Melvin hadn't gotten into an argument with her.

"We really don't have much to do with people who aren't in our community, Ruth. Do you know Cherish very well?" Harriet asked.

"I knew Cherish's aunt, Dagmar. We were good friends. I miss her every day. She died so suddenly. Cherish was with her when she died."

"Were you, Cherish?" Harriet asked.

"I was."

"Dagmar would've been happy about that. She wouldn't have wanted to die alone. No one wants to die alone."

"No, they don't," Favor agreed. "I certainly wouldn't."

"You're too young to think about that," *Mamm* told Favor.

"We're all young and then we wake up one day and we're old." Ruth put some buttered bread into her mouth. When she had swallowed, she said, "That reminds me. We've got a really bad storm coming."

"A storm?" Harriet clutched her husband's arm.

"What kind of storm?" Melvin asked.

Ruth glanced outside. "It's snowing now. Probably a snow storm."

Cherish knew the wood pile was low. They'd all freeze to

death if more wood wasn't cut and stacked in the dry wood shed. "We need more wood cut, Malachi."

"I'm onto it. If everyone will excuse me, I'll do that now."

"Yes, please do."

Simon jumped up. "I'll come with you."

"It's okay. I can do it."

Wilma said, "Take the help, Malachi. You need to hurry before the storm. When is the storm coming?" Wilma asked Ruth.

"Later today. That's why I was coming over here, to tell you. I heard it on the radio and I know you don't have one."

"Harriet doesn't like storms," Melvin said.

"No, I don't."

Simon and Malachi walked out the door together.

"How much wood do you have?" Simon asked.

"Plenty, but not much is cut."

"Why not? At home, we always cut the wood to have it ready and stored in the wood shed. You do have a wood shed?"

"Yep. It's that one there near the barn." Malachi pointed to it. "You head over there and I'll grab the axe from the barn." Malachi was going to take this opportunity to find out what was going on between Simon and Cherish. She said they were just friends, but it seemed to him there was obviously more going on.

He hoisted the axe over his shoulder and headed out to the chopping block, situated near the wood shed.

"So, what's the plan?" Simon asked. "Do you have two axes?"

"Nope. Just the one. We can take it in turns if you want."

"Okay. We might get through it faster that way."

Malachi hung onto the axe. "You can bring the wood to me."

"From that pile over there?"

"Yes."

Simon didn't seem impressed. "It's been out in the weather."

"It's fairly dry. I put it undercover a few days ago."

"It'll smoke the house up."

"No it won't. It's not that wet. You'll see."

Simon dragged a couple of logs over and Malachi started chopping. He'd planned to chop the wood but Cherish had distracted him. She always did that. He couldn't think properly when she was around. Mostly he was worried about what she thought about him. Apart from himself, he didn't have anything to offer her. Simon had loving parents and they had a farm. Maybe that was why Cherish liked him.

When he was tired and ready to have a break. He passed Simon the axe. "There you go."

"Thanks."

Before Simon could make his first chip, Malachi asked, "So what's goin' on with you and Cherish?"

Simon stopped, put his foot up on the chopping block and rested his elbow on his knee. "I was going to ask you the very same thing."

"I'm just her farm manager. Nuthin is goin' on between us."

"That's exactly what she said."

"And you didn't believe her?" Malachi asked.

"I was dubious."

Malachi nodded, making a mental note to find out what dubious meant. "So, I answered *your* question..."

A smile hinted around Simon's mouth. "I like Cherish and I

think she likes me. She wouldn't have invited me and my folks here if she didn't. I know she's young at the moment, but I'm willing to wait for a girl like that." Simon laughed.

"What's funny?"

"Cherish. She's entertaining and you never know what she'll say next. I think she's sensitive, creative and lively."

Malachi gulped. He didn't know what to say, so he didn't say anything else and then Simon went about taking his turn at chopping the wood.

CHAPTER 34

*a*part from Simon and Malachi, everyone else was in the living room, drinking coffee. Ruth stood up and looked out the window. "They're chopping wood. There's nothing like watching a man doing that. Sadly, I have to do my own without a man's help. Most of the time I don't mind, but it's nice when Malachi visits. I make him do it."

"I'm glad you're getting along better," Cherish said.

Ruth sat down. "I hated him when he first came here. Now, I can't think why." Ruth drained her coffee. "I must get home before this storm hits. It's said to be a bad one. Cherish, be sure to put food and water down in your shelter."

"What do you mean?"

"The underground tornado shelter."

"I have one?"

"Don't be silly."

Cherish stared at her. Was Ruth losing her mind?

Ruth continued, "Just outside the back door there's a door leading down to it."

"Oh, that door? I thought it was just a place to store extra firewood." Cherish leaped to her feet. "I must look at it. Maybe Favor can sleep down there so I can get a better night's sleep."

"Maybe *you* can sleep down there with the rats and the mice."

Cherish ignored her and hurried out the back door to get a better look.

"I'll get a flashlight," *Mamm* called out.

Cherish and Favor got there first. Cherish flipped the door open and saw steps. "You go down," Cherish told Favor.

"There's no way."

Ruth came up behind them. "It's just an empty room. There aren't any ghosts down there." Ruth chuckled.

Then *Mamm* switched on the flashlight and pointed it down the stairs.

"This is perfect," Favor said. "It would've made a perfect place to play if we were kids again."

"Thank you for showing us this, Ruth. I never knew it was here."

Ruth chuckled again. "You would've found it eventually."

Harriet and Melvin joined them in looking down in the shelter. "Are the stairs in good condition?" Melvin asked.

Mamm shone the light on the stairs. "They seem to be. I'll be coming here if the wind blows too strong."

"Just don't leave it too late, Wilma. The wind could lift you up and whisk you away. Anyway, I must go."

"It's been delightful getting to know you, Ruth," Harriet said.

"And you too. I must get home. I've got animals to feed before dark, as well as battening the hatches against the weather."

"I'll walk you out, Ruth." Cherish left them all there and walked away with Ruth. When they were a distance away, Cherish asked, "What do you think about Simon?"

Ruth stopped still. "What should I think about him?"

Cherish laughed. "I don't know. Whatever you want to think."

"Do you like him? Is that why they're here?"

"Maybe."

Ruth shook her head. "He's not for you."

Cherish frowned. "Why would you say that?"

"He's just not."

"I like him."

"Okay, but if you want my opinion, I just gave it." Ruth pressed her lips together.

"Thanks."

"Besides, I don't like him."

Cherish gasped.

"And I don't like his parents," Ruth added.

"Oh, Ruth, you can't say that."

"I can. I just did. I hid it from them so I didn't upset anyone. They think they're better than everyone."

"But if you remember, you didn't like Malachi at the start either."

"No I didn't. I was wrong about him."

"Then perhaps you're also wrong about Simon and his parents?" Cherish asked, hopefully.

"No. I'm not wrong about them."

Cherish was disappointed. She wanted everyone to like Simon.

"I don't think I ever said I didn't like Malachi. I just didn't trust him to look after your farm. Now I've seen that he is trustworthy. I'd even allow him to look after my farm. Not that I've got much of a farm anymore. He comes around once a week and I give him eggs. He gives me whatever he's got too much of from his garden. Our arrangement works out well."

"I'm glad you came over to meet them anyway."

"Me too. It's always good to see what you're up to. You've got a few more years to go before you start worrying about being left on the shelf." Ruth laughed. "That's what they called it in my day. If a girl wasn't married by twenty two, she'd worry that she'd never marry. From what I've heard, it's the same in your community."

"No. Well, maybe a little bit."

"Just don't look back years from now and see the man you're meant to be with was right in front of you the whole time. Bye, Cherish." Ruth got in the car.

"Bye, Ruth."

Ruth's window moved down and Ruth stuck her head out. "Be sure to come say goodbye before you go."

"I will." Then it dawned on Cherish. Was Ruth talking about Malachi? He was in front of her the whole time. Did Ruth think Malachi was right for her. "Wait, Ruth."

Ruth didn't hear as by now her window was back up. When Ruth drove off, Cherish looked up and saw Favor. She was walking toward the men who were still chopping the wood. Cherish cut her off by racing over to stand in her way. "What are you doing, Favor?"

"Just seeing who's the best with the axe."

"Leave them be. The storm will be coming soon and I don't want them to stop until we've got a good supply of wood."

Favor placed her hands on her hips. "Since when did you become the boss of me?"

"I'm the owner of this house and I'm just trying to keep us all safe and warm."

"Well, you wouldn't be the owner of this house if you didn't trick Aunt Dagmar into leaving it to you."

Just like that, Cherish had an overwhelming urge to slap Favor right across her face. It took every ounce of self-control to stop herself. "I never had one conversation with her about it. I had no idea she was going to do that."

"Why else would she do something like that? *Mamm* said it wasn't fair to any of us. You could've split it with us."

Cherish held back tears. "She wanted me to have it, so…"

"Oh don't cry. If anyone needs to cry it should be me."

"Since when did you become so hurtful and mean?"

"Since you always get everything you want. I'm thinking of sleeping in the storm shelter tonight just to get away from you. The spiders and whatever else is in there would be better company." Favor turned around and stomped back to the house.

"Cherish."

She turned around to see Malachi, and wiped a tear from her eye.

"What's wrong?"

"Nothing."

"It looked like the two of you were having an argument."

"She was having one with me. I'm all right." Cherish stared at Simon who was still chopping wood. "How's it going?"

"Good. I'll take another turn and chop some more and I think we'll be done." He looked around. "I see Ruth's gone."

"Yes. She just left. Do you need a hand stacking the wood?"

"You go inside and settle yourself down."

"I don't need to. I'm okay."

He offered a warm smile. "You go. Simon and I can handle this."

"Thanks." She walked into the house, trying to forget about her sister's cruel remarks. The house and the farm weren't about money to her. It probably wasn't even worth very much. It was the sentiment that meant everything to Cherish. Why couldn't Favor see that?

As soon as she was inside, Harriet looked up. "There you are, Cherish. You look cold. Come sit by the fire with us."

Cherish took off her coat, hung it on the hook behind the door and walked over to join Harriet and Melvin. *Mamm* and Favor were nowhere to be seen.

Cherish was worried about the approaching storm. "I guess we'll have to get food ready to take down to the shelter if we have to go. We probably won't have much warning."

"There's no sign of it yet. Just relax a little," Harriet said.

Cherish moved her chair a little closer to the fire and sat down.

"You have a lot of responsibilities for someone of your age," Melvin said.

Cherish shrugged her shoulders. "Not more than a lot of other people have. I have people to help."

"Have you ever thought of selling? Melvin knows a good realtor. He said things are selling quickly around here and for good prices."

Now Favor's conversation made sense. She must've overheard talk involving them saying she should sell the farm. "I'd never sell it. It has a lot of meaning for me."

"But is it practical? I'm sure your aunt wouldn't have wanted you to be disadvantaged by her farm."

"How would I be?"

"It could hold you back."

"From what?" Cherish knew her tone was revealing that she was annoyed, but after what she'd been through just now with Favor, she couldn't help it.

"From anything that might come up in the future."

"Then, I'll figure it out in the future, but right now, I'm very happy. Thanks for thinking of me." And trying to run my life, Cherish thought.

"We just thought we'd mention it so it would give you some more options," Harriet said, smiling at her.

"It's always good to have choices," Melvin added.

CHAPTER 35

*T*hat night the wind was blowing. Things around the house were bashing and cracking so loud that Cherish wondered if the house would blow away. Then she hoped the animals were okay.

Finally, Cherish must've drifted off to sleep because a loud crash woke her.

Then she heard the screams. She jumped out of bed and ran to see what was going on.

Melvin opened his bedroom door, and called out, "The roof's fallen in."

Cherish moved further into the room and looked up and saw the rain pouring in from the sky. In an instant, everyone was there in the hallway, staring upward while Harriet was sobbing on her husband's arm.

"Are you all okay?" asked Wilma.

"I think we're fine, aren't we, Harriet?"

"Yes," Harriet responded through sobs.

Malachi took charge. "I've got something in the barn that'll cover the hole. Simon, come help me."

"Sure."

Simon and Malachi ran out into the rain. Cherish watched out the window. All was darkness except for the flashlight Malachi carried. Then jagged lightning lit up the dark sky.

"We won't know the damage until morning," *Mamm* said as she gave Melvin and Harriet towels to dry themselves.

"I'm glad neither of you were hurt," Favor said.

Melvin said, *"Gott's* grace protected us."

"Amen," Harriet uttered. "We could've been killed. We should leave as soon as we can, Melvin. All our clothes would've gotten wet."

"We can dry them by the fire," Wilma suggested. "And you can borrow ours until yours dry."

"Thank you, Wilma. But we've been here as long as we can. We'll leave in the morning."

Somehow, Malachi and Simon managed to get a tarpaulin anchored down over the house to stop the rain from coming in.

Mamm gave up her bed for Harriet and Melvin, and she slept in the bedroom with Cherish and Favor. Cherish didn't come to bed for a long time because she was in the kitchen, crying over the roof.

"It's just a roof, Cherish. It'll be fine," Malachi said, trying to console her. Simon had already gone to bed and he hadn't even noticed how upset she was.

"I don't have money to fix it."

"I've got plenty of material in the barn. I'll get some men around in a day or two and we'll fix it as good as new."

"You can do that?"

Malachi laughed. "I can."

Cherish sniffed. "Thank you."

"Go to bed. I think it might be a big day tomorrow cleaning up the farm. I heard a lot of things out there blowing around."

Cherish looked down at Wally. "At least we know Wally is safe."

"Yeah." Malachi looked down at him too.

When Cherish woke the next morning, she was surprised to see the Koppels were packing things into their neighbor's truck.

Mamm saw her looking out the window. "They were up before daylight and they called their friend to come and get them."

"Oh, I didn't mean to sleep in this long."

"You needed it after last night's upset."

"I'm too sad to look in the bedroom."

"Don't even look at it. Malachi said he'd fix it all."

"I can't let him do it all. The bed would have to be thrown out and everything in there would be ruined."

"Let him handle it. He's your manager. Let him manage."

"Okay. You're right, *Mamm*. Are they going to say goodbye at least?"

"I'm sure they will."

"I'll go out and see them."

Simon saw her coming out the door and ran over to her. "We're going in a minute, Cherish."

"But, you haven't had breakfast."

"I know, but Ma's keen to get home."

"Is she still upset about the roof falling on her?" As soon as Cherish said it she realized how crazy that sounded. "Sorry, of course she would be."

"Yes, she's a little shaken."

Cherish looked over at them and saw Favor was there, talking to Harriet. Harriet saw her and waved. "Good morning, Cherish."

"You're leaving already?"

"We are. I'll just say goodbye to your mother."

The three guests walked into the house and everyone said their goodbyes. Simon lingered to say goodbye to Cherish. "I'll write to you."

"Okay and I'll write back."

Favor sniggered, but Cherish ignored her. Then Simon walked out the door.

Now there were only the four of them.

THE DAY they were going home, Cherish was up early helping with feeding the animals. "I'll have to do all this on my own one day."

"Not if you're married."

Cherish giggled.

Malachi stopped what he was doing and looked up at her. "What's funny?"

"The thought of being married."

"Don't you wanna be married?" he asked.

"Some day, I guess."

"Looks like it's not gonna be Simon."

Cherish smiled and said nothing.

"Maybe you could marry me and I could help ya here. We could create a good life together."

Cherish froze on the spot. A feeling rushed through her that she didn't recognize. She looked up at him and it was as though she saw him for the first time. Wispy brown hair swept across his face in the breeze. His features were plain, but they all fitted together perfectly. She did the only thing she could, she took a step closer.

The corners of his lips lifted upward and he too came closer.

Then Cherish gave him an almighty shove, nearly knocking him into the pig pen. He managed to grab hold of the fence and he pulled himself back to his feet. He laughed. "What was that for?"

"That was for saying something silly."

"So are you saying no?"

She stomped away without saying a word. Did he like her or did he just want to stay on the farm? He had nowhere else to go and he admitted that.

"Wait up." He caught up with her.

She stopped and put her hands on her hips. "Why did you say that just now?"

"I like you, that's why. Thought you would've understood that."

"Like? You're not supposed to ask someone to marry you if you just like them. You like Annie, so have you asked Annie to marry you too?"

"Nope. I told ya, she's just a friend."

She stared at him again, waiting for him to say something. Then an odd thing happened. She had an incredible urge that she wanted him to put his arms around her. "You're ridiculous." Cherish bunched the sides of her dress in her hands and ran to the house. When she got there, she turned around to see him

433

walking away. As usual, Wally followed him. He seemed so sad, so downcast.

Cherish got inside and closed the door behind her.

She couldn't like him, she couldn't!

He was so unsuitable. She huffed and hit the door hard with her open hand. Now she had to apologize to him for calling him ridiculous. It wasn't nice.

"There you are, Cherish. Go and pack! The driver's coming at ten."

"Okay."

"What's wrong with you?" *Mamm* came closer to her.

"Nothing."

"You're all flushed."

"I just ran from the barn, that's why"

"Just get packed will you and tell Favor to do the same."

CHERISH HAD breakfast in her room, alone. She told the others she was saving time by doing that as she was still packing. As she ate, she thought about what she'd say to Malachi. He had been serious in what he said so she shouldn't have reacted that way.

THE CAR ARRIVED EARLY and *Mamm* made sure everyone had everything and they weren't leaving anything behind.

"Now where's Malachi gone? We have to say goodbye. Go find him, Cherish."

Cherish gulped. "Me?"

"Yes. Now go."

Cherish walked toward the barn. She'd been avoiding him ever since he'd mentioned marrying him.

"Run!" *Mamm* yelled out.

Once Cherish opened the barn door, she saw Malachi polishing the brass bits of his horse's harness. "We're going now."

"Already?"

"Yes. The car's here early."

He dropped the cloth onto the harness and wiped his hands on a damp cloth.

"I'm sorry for what I said to you before," Cherish said.

He walked over to her. "Sorry for which thing you said? You say a lot of things."

"I said you are ridiculous, but I... you're not."

Malachi smiled. "I hope you'll be back soon, Cherish. I love it when you visit."

Tears stung behind Cherish's eyes. She didn't want to go. Didn't want to leave the farm, and maybe, just maybe, she didn't want to leave Malachi.

"Are you crying?" he asked.

"No."

He stepped forward and wiped a tear as it trickled down her cheek. She felt her chest rising and falling as her heart fluttered at his closeness. Then his finger tip traveled down her cheek and went to her chin. He lifted her chin.

She looked up into his eyes as he lowered his head, her eyes closed, and she savoured the moment when their lips touched.

Then the barn door was flung open and they jumped apart.

It was Favor.

"Oh, I'm sorry." Favor turned and hurried away.

"Wait!" Cherish had to catch up with her before she told *Mamm.* She'd never be allowed back to the farm if her mother found out.

"Don't tell *Mamm,*" Cherish whispered when she caught up with Favor.

"We'll talk about this later."

Cherish had never seen Favor so annoyed.

"What are you both doing? Where's Malachi?" *Mamm* asked when they were back at the car.

Cherish turned to see Malachi walking out of the barn. "He's coming."

Favor went to get in the car and *Mamm* told her to wait and say goodbye to Malachi.

The driver was already in the car waiting to go.

"Goodbye, Malachi. Thank you for having us. Are you sure you'll manage that roof repair?" Wilma asked.

He smiled. "It'll be fine, Wilma. I'll have some men come over and it'll be fixed in no time, as good as new. We've got plenty of spare roofing material in the barn. Thanks for coming. Do come again soon."

Cherish noticed that Malachi spoke well when he was speaking to her mother, so he could do it if he wanted.

Wilma gave him a lovely smile. "I'm not sure when we'll be back."

Malachi looked at Cherish and she looked back at him. She wanted to turn back time and this time have Favor not open those barn doors when she did. Every fiber of her being wanted to finish that kiss that still lingered on her lips.

Now she was leaving, without exploring what her feelings were all about. It seemed so wrong.

"Bye, Malachi and Wally," Cherish said.

"Yeah, bye." Favor dove into the front seat.

"Safe trip everyone," Malachi said.

"You can get in the car now, Cherish," *Mamm* ordered.

Malachi gave Cherish a special smile and a nod. It was as though he was acknowledging their shared kiss.

As they drove away, Cherish knew she had another reason to go back to the farm. That reason was Malachi. There were so many things she didn't like about him. He was untidy, he couldn't write properly, he couldn't even talk properly half the time. But, he had just as many good points. He was reliable, he was hardworking, and he was unique and he kept her interested.

As the car's movement lulled her into sleepytime, she allowed herself to dream about what a life with Malachi would be like.

CHAPTER 36

Once they were home, Cherish played with Caramel for a bit before she checked on her birds. Then she saw Favor carrying her bags up the stairs so she followed Favor into her room. "Don't say anything to anyone," Cherish warned.

Favor sat on her bed, heavily. Then her mouth fell open in an exaggerated manner. "Just tell me, what was that?"

"It was just a kiss."

"So, you like him? How long has it been going on?"

"There's nothing going on." Cherish sat down on the bed with her. "It was just… a goodbye kiss."

Favor laughed. "No it wasn't. I know a goodbye kiss when I see it. That was no goodbye kiss."

Cherish huffed. "Just please don't say anything, especially to *Mamm* and don't say anything to Krystal either. I know you probably tell her everything."

"I won't. I'm just in shock. I never thought of the two of you together."

"Why? What's wrong with him?" Cherish bit her lip, waiting for her sister's reply.

"He's just your farm manager. I guess there's nothing wrong with him. I just didn't expect it. That's all."

"I didn't plan to kiss him." Cherish kept quiet that he'd mentioned marriage. He probably wasn't serious anyway.

"I'm envious. I wish someone kissed me. What was it like?"

Cherish couldn't keep the smile from her face. "I can't explain it."

"I'm going to wait until I'm married before I kiss anyone."

"Me too."

Favor giggled. "Too late."

"Well, I was. That's what I planned. Oh, now I feel awful."

"Don't. At least now you know what it's like to kiss. Now get out. I've got to unpack."

Cherish stood. "Thanks for keeping quiet about this. Please, you must or *Mamm* won't let me go back to the farm."

"Yeah. You'll owe me one."

"I figured as much, and that's okay." Cherish walked out of the room, quite willing to do Favor anything she asked as long as she kept her mouth closed. For Favor, that wasn't going to be easy. She was the one who caused Adam and Bliss to break up because she revealed a secret. Had Favor learned her lesson?

Cherish walked into the kitchen to see Ada and Wilma with their heads together talking.

Ada was delighted that everyone was back. She told Wilma, "Debbie and I have organized a big family dinner for you tomorrow night. Everyone's coming. Adam, Andrew and Krystal will be there too."

"Oh. That'll be a lot of fun. Did you say Krystal?" *Mamm* asked.

"Yes. We found out that Krystal had something to do with getting Adam and Bliss back together. We're not sure what. We think she had a talk with him."

"Then I'll be glad to have her here for a meal. I'll be sure to thank her for whatever she did, or said."

THE NEXT MORNING, Fairfax had given Cherish the job of checking the northern fences. She left that to sneak off to visit Florence. It would be safe to confide in Florence and tell her what had happened. She needed a woman's opinion on what was going on in Malachi's mind.

When she climbed through the fence that divided the two properties, she saw Carter and Florence about to get in the car. Iris was the first one to see her and waved and pointed.

That's when Florence looked over and saw her hurrying toward the car. "Wait up."

They all waited for her to get to them.

"You're back from the farm already?" Carter asked.

"I am."

"How did it go?" Florence asked.

"Dreadful. It was so crowded. We had Simon and his parents. Bliss came with us too, so we had Bliss and Favor."

"Sounds like a crowded nightmare," Carter said.

"That's not the worst of it. The last night Simon and his parents were there, the roof over their bedroom fell in."

"What?" Florence gasped.

"It's true. There was a huge storm and it just fell in on top of them."

"Oh no. Were they hurt?"

"No. Only the roof was hurt, but Malachi is organizing that to be fixed. He's so capable, so good." With Carter there, there was no way she could talk to Florence. She'd have to come back another time. "It was awful having Simon and his parents there, and I think you were right, Carter."

"Right about what?"

"I don't like to say Simon is a mamma's boy, but they are involved way too much in his life."

Carter chuckled. "I told you so."

Cherish laughed.

Florence shook her head. "I'm so sorry, Cherish."

"It's okay. I won't hold you up. I just came over to tell you that we're all back."

"Thanks for letting us know. We're just heading into town to do some shopping. Do you want to come with us?"

"I do, but I'd better not. *Mamm* will have so many jobs lined up for me. I better go back and finish checking the fences."

They said their goodbyes, and after Cherish gave Iris a special cuddle, she walked back toward the orchard.

CHAPTER 37

*A*t the big family dinner that night, nearly the entire extended family was there.

"What else has been going on since we were gone?" Wilma asked.

Ada touched Joy's foot under the table, telling her it was time to speak.

Joy cleared her throat and nudged her husband's elbow.

Isaac looked at her and then put down his chicken leg and wiped his hands and face with a napkin. "Shall I tell them?" he asked Joy.

Joy smiled back at him and nodded.

"Somebody tell us," *Mamm* said.

Isaac took a deep breath. "Joy and I are having another baby."

"What?" *Mamm* leaped to her feet. "That's great news. The best news I've heard so far this year." *Mamm* ran over to the other side of the table and hugged both Isaac and Joy. Then everyone else congratulated them too. When Wilma sat back down, she looked at Ada. "You don't seem very surprised."

"I'm not." Ada sat there looking satisfied with herself.

"Did you know before me?"

"Sorry, *Mamm,*" Joy blurted out. "I couldn't keep quiet about it. I wanted you to be first to know, but I couldn't keep it in."

"It's fine, Joy. I know what it's like to have news that you can't hold in." *Mamm* gave Joy a reassuring smile.

"Well, since everyone's here at the table, Adam and I have some news." Bliss couldn't stop smiling.

"Yes. We know you're back together. We're not stupid," Favor said.

"Yes, we are back together," Adam said.

"Thanks to me, I'm told." Krystal smirked.

"It was the mule," Ada said. Everyone frowned at Ada, whose comparison with the story from the Bible was lost on them because she didn't fully explain it. Just as well because Krystal wouldn't take kindly to be likened to a mule. Ada then shook her head. "Don't worry."

"Are you saying I'm stubborn, Ada? Stubborn as a mule?" Krystal asked.

"No. I don't think you're stubborn."

"Then a mule is also someone who smuggles drugs." Krystal pouted. "I've never done that."

Ada gasped. "I didn't know a mule meant that too?"

"Yes."

"I'm sorry. Just forget my comment. I don't know what I was saying." Ada hung her head.

"Bliss and I have news too," Adam blurted.

"Out with it," Levi stared expectantly at Bliss and Adam.

444

"Bliss has agreed to marry me."

Both Wilma and Ada leaped up and squealed with delight. "You didn't know this too?" Wilma asked Ada.

"No. I didn't. They kept it from me."

"Are you happy, *Mamm* and *Dat?*" Bliss asked.

Everyone got up and hugged Bliss and Adam.

"We most certainly are happy for both of you," Levi said. Then he shook Adam's hand. "Welcome to the family."

"When's the wedding?" Wilma asked. "Is it going to be soon? Most weddings are held at the end of the year, but we won't mind if you break with that tradition."

Adam said, "We are planning on the end of the year. We'll have to see the bishop and work out an exact date."

Mamm sank into her chair. "That's excellent. It gives us plenty of time to plan things."

"And plenty of time to finish some quilts," Debbie added.

"Oh yes. We shall."

Bliss said, "I knew Joy's news and she knew mine. We kept each other's secrets until today."

"*Wunderbaar,*" Samuel said. "Anyone got anything else to announce?"

Matthew just sat there, scratching his thumb.

"What about you, Matthew?" Ada asked.

Matthew looked up. "No. Nothing's going on with me. I'm not having a baby or getting married."

Levi chuckled. "That's good to know."

"No job news?" Samuel asked.

"No. You all know my job news."

Bliss giggled. "Cherish, do you have news about Simon?"

"Like what?"

"Are you and he dating after you both had some time together?" Levi asked.

Cherish was shocked that Levi would ask such a thing. From the look on *Mamm's* face, she was shocked too. "No. No, we aren't. Nothing like that."

"That's too bad," Ada said. "He's such a nice boy. I mean, a nice young man. I did hear a whisper that he got along well with Annie."

"Who did you hear that from?" Favor asked.

"Can't say." Ada gave a little chuckle.

"Probably just a rumor. Rumors aren't always true." Favor hung her head.

Levi said, "I'm just happy everyone's home."

Fairfax agreed, "And we're going to start the year with us all working hard on the orchard. Yes, I am the boss of you all if any of you were wondering."

"You'll keep them on their toes." Wilma laughed.

"I want us to have a better season than last year, *Gott* willing."

Cherish looked around at everyone. The people missing were Florence, Carter and baby Iris. They never came to family events.

Christina and Mark were missing too. They had been invited, but found it too hard to leave the house very often with their newborn twins.

Fairfax and Hope, the newlyweds, looked delightfully happy and so did Joy and Isaac. Bliss and Adam kept looking at each other with lovey-dovey eyes, and Cherish was so pleased they were back together.

Favor sat there looking glum, even though her best friend

Krystal was sitting next to her. Favor was obviously missing Simon and she made no secret of her crush on him. As far as Cherish was concerned, she could have him. Her sister was welcome to Simon and his parents. All this love and together-ness forced Cherish to think about Malachi. It wasn't fair their kiss had been cut short and then she had to leave right away.

"I'm so happy we have another wedding coming and another *boppli* is on the way," *Mamm* said.

"Don't forget more twins are coming, Wilma," Ada reminded her.

"I'm not forgetting about Miriam and Earl's twins. How could I? I thank *Gott* every night for them having *kinner* with her being so old. It's a miracle."

"We'll have to visit them and help when the babies are born. Miriam has no family nearby does she?"

"I'm not sure."

"Earl doesn't." Ada pushed out her lips.

"I know that," *Mamm* said. "And they'll be born in the next few months. She won't give us an exact date but I'm sure of it. I did the sums."

A hush fell over the room as everyone wondered what sums Wilma was talking about.

Cherish said the only thing she could, "I'm coming too."

"Oh no," Fairfax said. "You're working on the orchard." He wagged a finger in front of her face. "No getting out of work when I'm in charge. Everyone must do their share."

Cherish's mouth fell open at her new boss's reaction.

"To be fair, I think it would be a good idea if Cherish came with us," Ada said.

"Unfair!" Favor yelled out.

Wilma turned to Ada. "Why do you think Cherish should come with us?"

Ada's eyebrows rose so high that they nearly reached the edge of her prayer *kapp*. "Have you seen how many dirty diapers twins can create?"

Everyone laughed.

Matthew said, "Looks like you're going to be the diaper changer, Cherish."

"I agree. You can come with us as long as you do what we say." Wilma gave a nod.

Fairfax was still insistent. "I say she can't go. There's work to be done."

Hope put her hand on Fairfax's arm, and whispered, "You'll never win against Ada and Wilma."

As visions of masses of dirty diapers floated in front of Cherish's face, she wondered if she should've kept her mouth closed just this once.

Thank you for reading Amish Farm Mayhem.

THE STOLEN AMISH WEDDING

BOOK #27 THE AMISH BONNET SISTERS

CHAPTER 1

*C*herish washed the dishes at the kitchen sink, looking out the window at Levi. He hadn't been well these past couple of years. Everyone was worried about how lethargic and pale he was. It was as though he'd aged fifteen years in the past three.

It was because of Levi's health that Cherish couldn't leave the orchard and move to her farm. The timing was off and, lately, Cherish had been wondering if the timing would ever be right.

It'd been three whole years since Cherish had been to the farm. It wasn't fair.

The last time she'd been there was when Simon and his parents had visited. That visit had only served to bring Favor and Simon together—so much together that they were getting married in just one month.

Cherish didn't really mind that Favor had stolen Simon away. It had annoyed her at the time though, especially when

Favor had flirted with him even before Cherish had admitted to Favor that she was no longer interested.

Somehow, *Mamm* knew how Cherish had felt and often reminded her that she had done the very same thing with Jonathon before he married Honor. Cherish accepted that, but she'd been young and silly back then so that was her excuse. Favor was much older, so she had no reason to behave like that.

Simon and Favor's courtship had lasted two and a half years. It was a long time and Cherish figured Simon had been waiting for his mother's approval before he asked Favor to wed. Simon never did anything without his mother's say-so. Simon's mother was just one of the reasons Cherish knew she could never marry into that family.

As Cherish washed the breakfast dishes, she saw Samuel had joined Levi outside and they were both doing something with the horses in the yard. Her mind wandered back to the time Simon and his family had visited the farm.

Simon and she had no alone time between Favor inviting herself places, and Simon's parents doing the same. It was so rude of Favor, but Favor didn't care. She was too in love with Simon to care about her sister's feelings, and she even loved Simon's parents. Just as well because they'd be in her life forever once Simon and Favor married.

Ada walked into the kitchen. "What are you doing, Cherish? Daydreaming again? That's all you ever do these days."

"I was just thinking about Favor and Simon."

"So the answer to my question is yes. I've never seen a girl daydream as much as you do." Ada gave a small chuckle. "I knew Simon would be good for either you or Favor. It's wonderful. I hope you're not upset that he chose her."

Cherish turned away from the sink, trying to hold in her laughter. That wasn't how it had happened, but who cared how Ada saw things? It didn't bother Cherish one bit. "I'm just happy for Favor."

Ada sat down at the table. "I know you say that, but deep down you must feel odd being the only one out of your sisters that isn't married or who has plans to marry. You're twenty one now."

"Hmm. Thanks for reminding me. It's fine. I'm okay with it. I'm not in a rush. I might not marry at all."

"Oh, that wouldn't do."

Cherish giggled at Ada's horrified expression.

"Do you even like anyone?" Ada asked with her eyes bugging out.

"Not at the moment. Why's it awful to be unmarried? I think it's a good choice." Cherish wasn't going to share her feelings with Ada. She pulled out the plug, shook the water off her hands and sat down with Ada. "I just want to get to the farm."

"Get to the farm, get to the farm," Timmy said, parroting her.

Ada and Cherish looked at each other, then looked at the two budgies in the cage and laughed.

Cherish covered her mouth with her hand. "Oh, I didn't realize I say it that much that Timmy has learned to say that."

"You do, so there you go. He is a clever bird."

Cherish stared at Ada. "Do you like Timmy now?"

"I never said I didn't. It's your mother who doesn't take kindly to pets."

"Oh."

"Your mother and I don't need to agree with everything, but

I do agree with her feelings about the fact that you can't leave your family now. Everyone needs you—everyone."

Cherish sighed. "That's the problem. I can't go, can I? Levi's too sick. He says he's okay, but everyone knows he's not."

"Do you mean to just visit the farm or to go there for good?"

Cherish sighed. "I guess just to visit for now would be *wunderbaar.* I know *Mamm* would be too upset if I left for good. Especially with Favor already being at the Koppels' house."

"It's your duty to stay here."

"Is it, Ada? Or is it my duty to live my own life?" Cherish could no longer hold in her frustration. "They've had their lives. My life is and always has been the farm. It's calling out to me. I can hear it whispering to me, telling me to come home."

Ada put her hand on Cherish's arm. "I know how hard this is for you, but that's the way things have to be for now. We'll be visiting your farm very shortly when we go to Favor's wedding." Ada turned her gaze to the ceiling. "It's so odd that she's already moved to the Koppels' farm. And so odd that she's agreed to have the wedding there rather than here, her childhood home."

"I know. The whole situation is very weird." Cherish slumped into her chair. The place wasn't the same without Favor. Even though they didn't always get along, she'd grown up with Favor. They'd been each other's special friend when they were growing up.

"Cup of tea?" Ada asked.

"No thanks." Cherish shook her head. "I don't feel like one. I've just had *kaffe.*"

"I mean for me. I'd like a cup of hot tea when you're ready."

"Oh, sure."

Ada *would* come in for tea when she'd just finished cleaning the kitchen.

There was no use complaining. No one would listen. As Cherish made the tea, she continued thinking about the farm. "Debbie's here so *Mamm* and Levi wouldn't be alone."

"Debbie is busy with her stall at the market. Anytime now, she'll be off marrying Peter. I'll guarantee it. No man courts a woman for that long if he doesn't want to marry her."

Cherish filled the teakettle with water. "Why is Debbie's market stall more important than me moving to my farm?" Cherish popped the kettle on the lit stove.

"Because Debbie's older and she has a child. Besides, Levi and Wilma aren't her parents. A person has a duty to the people who raised them."

"I know." Cherish shook some tea leaves into the pot, thinking that she'd raised herself for the most part. She wasn't about to say that aloud and risk a lecture from Ada.

Ada looked on in horror at what she was doing with the tea leaves. "I've given up telling you to use a spoon for that."

"Spoons are all different sizes anyway. I've never heard you complain before."

"You never listen, that's why." Ada smiled. "Don't worry. You'll get to live on your farm."

Cherish took a deep breath and sat down. At this stage, she couldn't see how. If Levi got worse and died, then *Mamm* would fall apart and then she'd never get away from the orchard. Unless she took *Mamm* to the farm when that day came. No. *Mamm* would never be that far away from Ada or the home that held so many memories. Wilma had lived at the orchard for most of her life, and she'd been friends with Ada for even longer. That wasn't the answer.

Cherish was trapped there forever.

She put a cup and saucer down in front of Ada, then poured the hot water into the teapot.

"I feel like I'm never getting away from here."

Ada's eyes bugged open. "Oh, you poor thing. Never getting away from this beautiful large house with the most luscious apple trees at your door, with food always on your table, surrounded by a loving family." Ada paused to draw a quick breath and then continued, "Open your eyes and see the beauty that surrounds you every day. Anyone would love to be standing in your stockinged feet, Cherish. You've got a lovely family. You have everything you should want and need at your stubby fingertips."

Cherish frowned and looked down at her fingers. "They're not stubby. I just know I need to be at the farm—to live there. That's my real home, not here."

"Don't let your mother hear you say that. She'd be heart broken," Ada whispered, even though there was no one to over-hear them.

"She knows how I feel, but I've kept quiet about it since Levi's been sick. I haven't mentioned the farm once. Well, maybe once or possibly twice." The worst thing for Cherish was seeing no way out. Since Aunt Dagmar had left the farm to her, she'd visited it once each year, with the exception of the past three years. Every day of those past three years, Cherish had remembered with longing the brief shared moment between Malachi and herself when their lips had touched.

Did he ever think about it too?

He never mentioned it in all the letters he wrote or the calls he made to her from the phone in the barn.

"It's been quiet here since Favor left," Ada said.

"I know, and we'll notice one person less when it gets busier around harvest time."

"But when you eventually get to your farm to live permanently, Favor will live close by. That's good for you."

"That'll be great, but it'll be too far for her to go there and back in the same day with the horse and buggy. She'll have to come and stay for a couple of days. She'll be married by then so she can bring Simon with her."

Ada shook her head and looked down.

"What did I say? Oh, you mean I should've realized that Favor and Simon won't be allowed to go anywhere without Melvin and Harriet? Favor will never be able to shake the in-laws off. They'll be stuck to her like glue." Cherish giggled. "She knew what they were like before she agreed to marry him. That's one reason I changed my mind about him."

Ada shook her head and her cheeks wobbled. "That's not nice. Harriet is my dear friend and that was unkind. That's the problem with you."

Cherish frowned. "I'm just saying the truth. Is that a bad thing?" The truth was that Cherish used humor to cover up how depressing it was being trapped. What she really wanted to do was spread her wings and fly. Fly away from the orchard, away from feeling like a child, and away from people who smothered her. Why couldn't she say what was on her mind without being judged for it?

Ada continued, "You need to adjust your attitude about Simon's parents. They're some of the loveliest people I know.

And yes, they're close to their son and why wouldn't they be? He's all they have. Harriet wasn't blessed with loads of *kinner* like your *mudder* and I were. We could spread our love among our *kinner*. Their love is concentrated on Simon."

"It's okay if we don't always agree. You have your opinion and I have mine. My idea is that you raise your children and there comes a time when you have to let them go. Let them make their own mistakes, and let them be who they're meant to be. I think that's the best way to be a good parent." When Cherish saw Ada was unconvinced, she went on. "Look at birds, they push their baby birds out of the nest when it's time. They don't follow them around checking on them until they have babies of their own."

"Then that's what you can do when you have your babies. You can push yours out of the nest to fend for themselves and never give them another thought."

"I will." Cherish sighed.

"Did I say something that upsetting?" Ada asked.

"No, why?"

"You sighed. You've been doing that a lot lately."

"Oh. I didn't realize. I'll try not to sigh."

"Exactly. In everything give thanks. That's what we're told to do."

Cherish nodded. "I'll give it a go. I am grateful I'll be at the farm soon. And I'm grateful you'll be there with me. You've been so kind over the years accompanying me to the farm. I'm thankful for that."

"I do what I can." Ada chuckled. "Now you can pour. I can tell you this, Cherish, sometimes in life things don't go as planned. You have to ride out the storms. It'll be good for you to have some hardships. I'm not saying that the orchard and living here is a hardship, it's anything but."

"You're right about things not going as planned. Look at Favor and Simon. Who would ever have thought that would've happened? Well, it hasn't happened yet I suppose. There's still time for Favor to change her mind."

"Sour grapes." Ada picked up the teapot and swirled it. "You missed out. You had your chance with him. I know you said you didn't like him anymore, but maybe you only said that because you knew he was going to choose Favor."

"That's okay if you want to think that." Cherish smiled. She'd had a lucky escape from Simon and his clinging parents. They reminded her of a vine that grew up and covered a tree. The vine covered the tree so much that the tree withered because the vine was cutting off the light and the air. If that's what Favor wanted, she was welcome to them. Everyone had warned her, everyone but Ada, who saw nothing wrong with Simon being attached to his folks.

"Nothing to say?" Ada asked.

"I'll have to be quicker next time when a man shows me the slightest bit of interest."

"Yes, you will." Ada poured herself a cup of tea. "You're not having a cup?"

"No. I've got to get the room ready for Miriam and Earl, and two more rooms for the children. Then I've got to clean the house."

"Just sit and talk with me until Wilma gets back from visiting Joy. She won't be long. There's plenty of time. They're not due here till just on dark. I hope they can stay a long time."

"I'm not sure. They said maybe a day or two. I think they're

visiting all their relatives and staying a day or so at each place."
Cherish was eager to see Earl, her older half brother, and his
family. As much as she was keen to get her work over and done
with, it seemed Ada wanted to talk. She felt a bit sorry for her
for some reason. "I hope Joy feels better."

"We'll soon find out. If she hasn't recovered from her cold,
Wilma will have to stay there longer." Ada took a sip of tea.
"Who would've thought Miriam would've had twins, and then
triplets a year later?"

"I know. It's amazing. Just as well we've got a big house for
when they visit. I wonder if they'll have any more."

"They very well could. They have five children now and your
mother and I were worried about her having none. We thought
Earl and she would be childless, given Miriam's age."

Cherish couldn't help smiling. "How does that make you
feel?"

"Well, it's not nice to be wrong. I'm happy to be wrong this
time though. Five children in three years is pretty good."

Cherish laughed. "I know. It's a miracle. I can't wait to see
them all." Then Cherish heard the phone ringing from the barn.
She looked out the window and saw that Samuel's buggy was
gone and Levi was nowhere to be seen. They'd probably gone
somewhere together. They often did that without telling
anyone.

"You'd better run if you want to get that," Ada told her.

Cherish left Ada and ran out, hoping it would be Malachi.
He called her at least once a week. Cherish picked up the
receiver just as it rang one more time. "Hello, Baker Apple
Orchard."

"Cherish, where's Favor?" It was Krystal.

Cherish was disappointed. "You know where she is. She's staying with the Koppels."

"I'm sorry. I didn't mean to say where's Favor. I don't know what's gotten into me. My head's all of a muddle and I'm going mad. I wanted you and I need to see you now. Can you meet me at the quilt shop?"

"Well, we've got Earl and Miriam coming later today and—"

"Please, Cherish? I need to talk with someone."

Cherish knew Krystal must've been hugely upset by something if she'd reached out to her. She sounded awfully shaken up about something. "Would it be possible that you could come here?"

"Oh. Yes. I didn't think of that. I can come before the shop opens. I'll see you soon."

Before Cherish could answer, Krystal had ended the call. The dial tone hummed in Cherish's ear.

CHAPTER 2

W hen Krystal arrived, she helped Cherish make the beds for the guests.

"What's so important?" Cherish asked, as she tucked the sheet in at the corners.

"I'm leaving."

Cherish stood up. "You're leaving? What... You mean leaving the community?"

"Yes. I talked to the bishop and he wasn't okay with me writing a book."

Cherish covered her mouth and sat heavily on the bed. After all this time, Krystal had fooled them. Here she was, openly admitting her wrongdoing. She'd said she wouldn't continue with the book, and then she'd joined their community. "Writing a book?"

"It's written."

"It's written?" Cherish asked.

"Cherish, you're just repeating everything I say."

Cherish closed her mouth when she realized it was gaping open. "I'm more shocked about you leaving than about the book. What about the quilt shop, and what about Gertie? She's come to rely on you so much."

"I know, but it is what it is."

Cherish frowned. What type of an answer was that?

"I'm not looking forward to telling Gertie. Will you come with me?" Krystal asked.

"No."

Krystal grabbed Cherish's arm. "You have to. Favor's gone, she was my only friend and you're her sister."

Cherish shook her head. "Let's take things back a little. Why did you suddenly write a book when you said you wouldn't?"

Krystal hung her head. "I'm sorry, but..." Krystal heaved a huge sigh. "Okay. I'll tell you the truth. It doesn't matter anyway now, I suppose. Years ago when I had to leave here, I shopped my idea around and then I found an agent. The agent got me a book deal. But when I submitted what I'd written up to that point, they didn't like it. They suggested I get more entrenched into Amish life, become one of you and then rewrite it with a different take on things."

Cherish nibbled on a fingernail. She hadn't seen this coming. "This was all a trick?"

"People have to suffer for the sake of art. Art is often about suffering. Writing is an art form."

Cherish's face scrunched up. "So everyone has to suffer so you can write? Or are you saying that you have suffered by being one of us?"

"It's not about you, it's about me. The book is about my experience of not only living with the Amish, but actually *being*

Amish. There are plenty of books out there from people who've visited the Amish, so I found out. My book will be better because I became one of you and lived as one of you for years."

"So you went through all this, got baptized and everything for nothing?" Cherish asked. "You lied to the bishop and to *Gott?*"

"No it's not for—"

"No, that's right. It's for art and your own selfish reasons. What about *Gott?* You mocked us. You became one of us and we gave you our trust."

"I believe in God. Of course I do. At the time, I was thinking of *not* writing the book at all. I was going to give back the advance the publisher paid me."

"You got paid… money?" Cherish asked.

"Oh, yes."

Cherish shook her head. This was why she'd never trusted Krystal, but she had gotten used to her. "I was right about you all the time. What are you going to say about us in your book?"

"It's not only about you and your family. It's about how the whole community works. Their attitudes, beliefs, and lifestyle."

"Their? You're one of us."

"Not for much longer. Don't worry, I've only said lovely things about you and your family. I have such great memories of living here at the orchard."

Cherish folded her arms. "That's the only reason you came back here all those years ago?"

"That's right."

Cherish shook her head. "So, does the bishop know?"

"Yes. I just told you that."

"I didn't take that in. I'm in shock. What did he say?" Cherish asked.

"He didn't like it. He seemed a bit upset with me. He said I'd have to make a choice. He told me to pray about it, and I have."

"So, he hasn't kicked you out or anything?"

Krystal sat on the half made bed. "No. I haven't been shunned or excommunicated, but I have to leave. He's given me a couple of weeks before I give him my final decision."

"Where will you go?"

"Anywhere I want. I've invested the advance they gave me and when the book sells, I'll get even more money."

Now Cherish started to feel a little sorry for her. "Have you got friends outside of the community?"

"I've got Eddie and his folks."

"Is that it?" Cherish asked. Eddie and his parents were beekeepers that lived close to the orchard, and they were *Englishers.*

"Yes, but it doesn't take long to make friends."

"Are you and Eddie secretly dating?" Cherish had been suspicious of that for years.

"No. We liked each other at one point, and then it fizzled because we couldn't see each other that much. Besides, he's too in love with his bees. I didn't want to compete with insects for his attention."

"Forget the book, Krystal. Just stay. You've become part of this community. People rely on you now. Look how you helped Debbie get her tea onto that website."

"Yes, I did set up a website for her. It's not hard when you know what to do."

"And you've helped a ton of other people as well."

Krystal adjusted her prayer *kapp*. "It's not as though I can't be replaced. Tons of people can do what I do. Anyway, what do you care? You've never liked me."

Cherish had to say what she felt. "It's not about liking, it's about trust. I've never trusted you and now I know why."

"Well, I'm sorry things worked out this way. I'm sorry I deceived everyone, but it's what I had to do to get the book finished."

"Where did you find time to write it?"

"There was nothing else to do at night. I can't go out and there's no TV. I wrote it all longhand in a notebook and when it's not busy at the shop, I transferred it to a file on the computer. It's already off being edited."

"Wow. I have no words." Cherish leaned against the wall.

Krystal smiled. "How about congratulations?"

"I don't think so. Are you going to tell Levi and Wilma?"

"No. I've already told Favor and she was fine with it. I'll send her my address when I get to where I'm going. I'll go up and stay with mom for a while. So will you come with me?"

"Where?"

"To tell Gertie. She'll be upset. She'll worry about who will run the shop for her. She's come to rely on me for everything. But it's not as though I'm not replaceable. Someone else can run the shop for her."

"I feel sorry for her. She believed in you. She always said such nice things about you."

"Has she?" Krystal's eyebrows shot up.

"Yes."

"We really get along. She's like the grandmother I'll never

467

have. I'll miss her. I'll miss a lot of people. I could've been very at home here if things had been different."

Even though Cherish and Krystal weren't close, Cherish couldn't imagine what life would be like without her around. "Cancel the book and stay. You've got a life here. You're one of us now."

"How many years have I been here? I don't know, six years or something?"

Cherish nodded. "That's right, about six or even more."

"Six years and I have no husband. No one's interested in me. I don't want to be alone forever. All the good men are married."

"No they aren't."

"Who's not married? You tell me."

Cherish guessed she was leaving because she saw no prospects of marriage. Maybe it wasn't about the book at all. "Andrew Weeks. He's perfect. He's a good friend of Adam Wengerd, Bliss's husband."

"I know who Adam is, silly." Krystal gazed up at the ceiling. "I never thought of Andrew like that."

"He's hard working and he's nice," Cherish added. "And there are others. I just can't think of them at this minute."

"If Andrew liked me, he would've made it known by now."

"So, you'd be willing to get to know him better?" Cherish asked.

Krystal pressed her lips together and appeared to be deep in thought. "No. I've sent the book in. My bridges are burned. The bishop probably hates me and I told him I'm leaving."

"He doesn't hate you and you don't have to leave. You said he gave you time to think about it."

Krystal's cheeks flushed and she looked as though she was

about to cry. "I know, but he's disappointed in me. Thanks for trying to make me stay. It shows me you do care about me a little bit."

"I do." Cherish was surprised to hear herself admit that. "You've changed a lot from the selfish girl who'd arrived at the apple orchard, pretending she was someone else."

"Thanks." Krystal giggled. "We did have some fun times, didn't we?"

Cherish smiled thinking about all the good times and the bad. "Just think about staying, would you?"

"I've given it a lot of thought. I'm leaving tonight. Eddie's coming to collect me from Gertie's house after I shut the store. I'll stay the night at his parents' house and they'll drive me to the bus station as soon as I book the ticket."

"You've got it all planned out," Cherish said.

"I do."

"Was any of it real, Krystal?"

Krystal laughed. "You're sounding like a boyfriend I'm breaking up with. Sadly, my life has gone by without experiencing any kind of courtship. There was only my brief flirtation with Eddie."

Typical Krystal. She hadn't even answered the question. "Have you told Favor yet?"

"Yes, I told you I did. She wasn't even shocked. She was too busy talking about Simon to want to talk about me and what's going on in my life. I can't believe she agreed to marry him. She won't listen to me."

"You told her *not* to marry him?"

"Not in so many words. I tried to get her to see what everyone else sees. Simon needs to cut the apron strings and

move away from his parents' farm. Favor should tell him to do that before she agrees to marry him. But it's too late for that."

"Yes. It's already going ahead. Simon's mother is planning it. Hopefully, Favor will get a say."

Krystal twirled her *kapp* strings around her fingers. "It's always at the bride's house. I can't believe Wilma agreed to have it at Simon's house."

Cherish recalled how upset her mother was when Favor announced she was moving to Simon's parents' house ahead of the wedding. And not only that, Favor announced she was having the wedding at the Koppels' farm. "Well, Simon's mother can be very forceful and now with Favor already living there, *Mamm* didn't really have a say."

Krystal shook her head. "I don't know what Favor's thinking. She'll wake up one day and realize she's made a dreadful mistake. Then what is she going to do?"

Cherish was shocked to hear Krystal speaking so forthrightly. "That's exactly what I thought, but she gets on so well with Harriet. Maybe she's fine with the way Simon is—"

"Ruled by his parents? I wasn't going to say something as strong as that, but I think they run his life. Now they'll run Favor's life. I guess it's her choice if she wants that. I'm just sad she's gone. We used to be so close, but she's hardly even talked to me since Simon came into our lives."

"Favor will want you there at her wedding. You two have been so close for so long. You're still her best friend. Why don't you stay for the wedding and then make up your mind about leaving after that. You could meet someone at the wedding."

Krystal shrugged her shoulders. "I doubt it."

"She's been a bit withdrawn from all of us, but you should go to the wedding."

"She talked about me being an attendant ages ago, but she hasn't mentioned it lately. I think Harriet told her I shouldn't be one because I wasn't born into the community."

"No, she wouldn't have done that." Cherish shook her head, but once she thought about it some more, Harriet *might* have suggested that.

"I don't know. So, will you come with me to tell Gertie?" Krystal stared at Cherish with hopeful eyes.

Cherish swallowed hard. It was the very last thing she wanted to do, but lately she had a hard time saying no to people. "Okay. I'll come with you. That doesn't mean I'm pleased about the book."

"It's not a bad book. I say nothing mean about anyone. You'll have to read it and see for yourself."

"I'll have to take your word on that. I don't want to read it."

"You should."

Cherish shook her head. "No thanks. I'll give it a miss."

"I'll meet you at Gertie's place? I'm going there now to tell her. Then I'll work in the quilt shop for one last day. We'll have to leave now or we'll be late."

"Okay. I'll follow you there, but I can't stay long. I'll have to be here when Earl and Miriam arrive. They're meant to be here at six."

"Six! You've got all day."

"I know but I've got a lot to do before they get here. There's no one to help me."

The girls went downstairs to find Wilma back from Joy's

house. Cherish told her she had to go somewhere with Krystal and she wouldn't be long.

As Cherish climbed into her buggy, she wondered if she was going there simply to pick up the pieces. There was a good chance that Gertie could break down. She hadn't been well and this might destroy her. Cherish knew Krystal was right, Gertie had come to rely on Krystal for pretty much everything. Now Gertie would be one more person the family would have to take care of.

CHAPTER 3

*C*herish stayed behind Krystal as she walked to the front door of Gertie's house where Krystal had lived for the past few years. Krystal hesitated when she put her hand on the door handle.

"There's always time to change your mind," Cherish whispered. "You don't have to leave. You've become like family. I can't imagine the community without you." Cherish didn't want to say it, but it felt like another of her sisters was moving away.

She looked over her shoulder at Cherish. "It's too late. The book's out of my hands now. I really have to leave."

When they walked in, the house was dark and all the curtains were drawn. Krystal opened one of the curtains. It was then they both saw Gertie sleeping on the couch.

"Do you want me to wait until she wakes up?" Cherish asked, worried about the time.

Krystal looked over at Cherish. Then she had a closer look at Gertie.

And right then, Cherish had a dreadful feeling.

Krystal moved closer to Gertie and touched her shoulder. Gertie's arm slid off her chest and just hung there. Gertie didn't even wake up. Krystal whipped her head around and looked at Cherish.

Cherish stuttered, "Is, is she...?"

"Gertie. Wake up." Krystal touched Gertie again on her shoulder and Gertie didn't move.

Cherish rushed over. "Is she breathing?"

Krystal picked up Gertie's wrist and felt for a pulse. "I can't feel anything. You try."

Cherish stepped back. One look at Gertie's pale face and she knew that she was dead. "No. She's gone, Krystal."

Krystal slumped in front of Gertie and wept.

Tears streamed down Cherish's face as she backed away and then leaned against the wall. It reminded her of when Aunt Dagmar died. She was alive and talking one minute and then gone the next.

"What will we do?" Krystal asked through her tears.

Cherish took a deep breath. "We'll call the bishop. Where's the nearest phone?"

"I don't know. I can't think." Krystal cried harder still.

"Let's both go over to the bishop's house."

"We can't just leave her here."

"She'll be fine."

"You go, Cherish. I'll stay here."

Cherish got to the bishop's house and found out the bishop was out, but due back any minute. Cherish told Hannah, the bishop's wife, what had happened and went back to Gertie's house to wait with Krystal.

Half an hour after Cherish had gotten back, the bishop pulled up outside Gertie's house.

"Here's the bishop. This is awful. I hope he's okay with me being here," Krystal said.

"Of course he will be."

Krystal felt pangs of all kinds of anxiety as Cherish opened the door for Bishop Paul. "Hello, Cherish."

"Hello."

"Hannah is feeling poorly. She wanted to come, but I told her to stay home."

"That was nice of her. I'm sorry she's not well."

"Thank you. She'll be fine." He walked through the door and said hello to Krystal.

Krystal nodded. "Hello."

"You found her?" he asked as he walked over to look at Gertie.

"Cherish and I did."

"I called the funeral director and he'll be here shortly."

Krystal told him, "I'm sorry for what I said to you before and about the book."

"You have to do what you think is best."

Krystal licked her lips. "It was a hard decision."

The bishop sat down. "I'll have to contact her relatives. I'll do that as soon as I get home."

"Yes, of course." Krystal sat down too and so did Cherish.

Then there was an awkward silence.

"We just found her like that," Krystal said.

"She was old, in her nineties. *Gott* called her home," the bishop said.

"Ninety is old," Cherish commented. "When will the funeral be?"

A tear trickled down Krystal's cheek.

Cherish wished she hadn't said that. "I'm sorry. I didn't mean to upset you."

The bishop answered, "It'll depend on what her family wants. They're all in Haven."

"All in Heaven?" Cherish asked.

The bishop frowned at her. "Haven County."

"Oh, Heaven County?" Cherish asked again.

"They live in *Haven* County, Cherish," Krystal told her.

"Oh, sorry. Heaven County sounds like such a nice place. It would, if it existed. There's probably no place with that name in all the world." Cherish wished she hadn't even opened her mouth. "How about I make some hot tea?"

"That would be nice," Bishop Paul said.

Cherish stood up, and then Krystal offered to help her. Once they were both in the kitchen, Krystal whispered, "This is awkward with him waiting around. I just told him I'm leaving and now I see him again."

"I know, but I'm glad he's here." Cherish filled the tea kettle while Krystal organized cups and saucers.

Krystal wiped away another tear and then blinked hard. "I'm glad she never had to find out I was leaving. She would've been so upset, and then who would've been here to look after her?"

Cherish shrugged her shoulders. "Don't think about all the what ifs. They'll drive you crazy."

Krystal grabbed the teapot. "This was hers. She loved this teapot."

Cherish blinked back tears of her own. It was so sad.

"How will I get over this? I was about to leave her," Krystal whispered.

"You will get over it. You won't forget, but it will get easier as time moves on. When Aunt Dagmar died, I just went out of the house to do something and I came back and she was gone. Just like that."

"I remember that, but you weren't about to leave her."

"I guess not." Cherish sighed. "At least we'll see them again one day. They aren't really gone, they're just not here."

"Well, if they're not here, then they aren't here."

Cherish hoped Krystal hadn't lost her faith in God. Or had that been a lie too?

BEFORE THE FUNERAL DIRECTOR ARRIVED, Eddie pulled up outside the house in his pickup truck.

Both Krystal and Cherish looked out the window and saw him. Krystal said, "Cherish, can you tell him what's happened? I can't even talk about it. Tell him my trip will be delayed and I'll talk to him later."

"Sure." Cherish headed out the door. Eddie saw her and got out of the truck to meet her.

"Hey, what's going on? Where's Krystal?" he asked, glancing over at the house.

"Gertie has just died."

"No." His mouth fell open and he placed his hand on his forehead.

"Yes."

"Oh, I'm so sorry. I knew she was getting frail. How's Krystal holding up?"

"She's too upset to talk to anyone. She asked me to tell you that her trip is off and she'll contact you later."

"She's not leaving anymore?" he asked.

"I think she's still going, but I guess she'll stick around for a while, at least for Gertie's funeral."

"Oh yes. There'll be a funeral." Eddie looked over at the house once more.

"Are you still in love with her?" Cherish asked.

Eddie rubbed his nose. "You can tell?"

"I can."

His eyebrows rose just slightly as though he was still hopeful. "I'm not in her plans. All I can do is be there for her. Anyway, that doesn't seem important with Gertie passing away so suddenly."

Cherish was happy to talk about something other than death. It was too upsetting. "Does Krystal know how you feel?"

"I try to tell her, but she changes the subject or makes a joke about it. I've done all I can think of to do."

"I think you two would be good together."

"Yeah, well, try telling her that." He rolled his eyes.

Cherish didn't want to get his hopes up. Perhaps she'd already said too much. "I've been trying to talk her into staying."

Eddie hadn't heard a word she'd said. "I guess she was always out of my league."

"I don't think that's true. It's probably just a timing thing."

He looked back at the house for a third time. "Tell her I'm thinking of her."

"I will, Eddie."

Eddie got back into his truck and lowered the window. "I'll see you later, Cherish. It's about time I delivered you some more honey."

Cherish smiled. "My mother will love that. We all will."

Eddie gave her a nod, and the window closed. Then he reversed his truck down the driveway. Cherish stood there and watched him leave. Now she had to go back into the house and wait for the funeral director.

When the funeral director arrived in a large white van, Cherish and Krystal huddled in Krystal's bedroom while the bishop talked to him and sorted out some details.

"I feel so guilty," Krystal whispered.

"Don't. You didn't cause this."

"I know, but I was leaving her. I didn't realize how sick she was."

"She might not have been that sick. It was her time to leave. She's gone home to be with *Gott*. That's good for her, but not so much for everyone who's left."

"Yeah, I know."

"Do you believe that?" Cherish asked.

"Of course I do. I believe in God, and even more so now that I've been living in the community. Don't give me a lecture, not now."

Cherish kept quiet and a few minutes later, the bishop called out to Krystal. They both left the bedroom and walked back out to the living room.

"He's taken her. I'll call the family. Do you have somewhere to stay tonight, Krystal?"

"I'll stay here. I'll be fine. I was leaving soon anyway. I'll just stay and mind the house until some relatives of Gertie's arrive."

"Denke. At least the house won't be empty." The bishop said a quick goodbye and then he left.

"Come back to the house with me. You can stay there until you figure out what you want to do."

Krystal shook her head. "I'll be fine here, thanks."

Cherish looked around. She couldn't imagine staying in the quiet house where Gertie had just died. "Just stay with us for one night. You don't want to be on your own after the shock you've had."

"Um." Krystal looked up at the ceiling. "No. I'll be okay."

Cherish tried a few more times but she still couldn't talk Krystal into coming home with her.

CHAPTER 4

By the time Cherish got back to the house it was late in the day and everyone was there. Earl came out of the house to greet her. "Cherish, I heard what happened. I'm so sorry."

Cherish rushed into his arms and sobbed. She needed her big brother. Even though they were far apart in age, he'd always been there whenever she'd reached out with problems. "I was with Krystal when she found her."

"I know. Someone called Wilma on the phone and told her everything. Everyone's been waiting for you so we could all eat together."

Cherish stepped back and wiped her eyes. "It's so good to see you."

"It's good to see you too. You've grown up."

Cherish smiled. "It had to happen."

"Come in and see our babies."

Cherish glanced at the horse. "I have to unhitch the buggy first and—"

"Matthew said he'd do that. He'll be out in a minute."

"Okay."

Earl put his arm around her shoulders and together they walked inside. "Miriam is upstairs putting the babies to sleep."

Cherish walked faster and then raced up the stairs ahead of Earl. She walked in to see the twins for the first time. The three year old boys were sleeping in the same single bed. "Oh, they're asleep already." Cherish crept in and had a closer look. Both boys had thick dark hair and creamy skin.

Earl whispered, "That's Rory, near the window and this one's Ramon."

"I don't know how you tell them apart."

"It's easy. Not so easy when I see them from a distance."

"Can I see the girls?"

"Sure."

Earl and Cherish headed to the bedroom that had been designated for the triplets. Ada and Wilma had managed to find three cribs for them. When they entered the room, Cherish saw Miriam. She had one baby in her arms, and the other two were fast asleep.

"Hi, Miriam," Cherish whispered.

"Hello, Cherish. I'm so sorry about Gertie."

Cherish nodded. "Thank you. Look at your beautiful babies."

Miriam smiled. "We've been very blessed."

"You have." Cherish looked at the sleeping babies and then stared at the one who was awake. "Can I have a hold?"

"Of course you can. This one is Tamika. She's always the last to go to sleep." Miriam handed Tamika over.

Cherish looked down at the baby in her arms. "She's so small. She's looking at me like she knows everything I'm saying."

"She's very alert. Nothing gets past her."

Earl was still in the room, standing behind Cherish. "This one over here is Tara, and that one is Tilly."

"All names starting with T," Cherish said with a smile.

"They're all names I liked over the years. I never thought I'd get to use all my favorite names."

"They're all so beautiful. You must sit there and stare at them all day."

Miriam laughed. "If only I had the time. Five babies are an awful lot of work."

"I know. I remember how it was with Christina when she had the twins. Someone had to always be there to help her in the early days. You have triplets as well as twins."

"I have a lot of help. The other ladies in the community have been wonderful."

Cherish looked down at Tamika. She'd been rocking the little girl from side to side and now she was starting to close her eyes.

Earl said, "You've got the right touch. She's almost asleep. Now we'll be able to eat in peace. I'm starving."

"You two go. I'll put her to sleep and I'll be down in a minute." Miriam took the baby from Cherish and Cherish and Earl headed downstairs.

When Cherish stepped into the kitchen, Wilma and Ada barraged her with questions.

All of which Cherish answered, even though she didn't want to talk about anything. It had been awful waiting in the house until the funeral director came and took Gertie away.

"Where will Krystal live now?" *Mamm* asked.

Cherish was a little shocked that *Mamm* hadn't already heard on the grapevine that Krystal was leaving. "I don't know if she has plans. It's only just happened."

"Oh, you didn't leave her in the house by herself, did you?" Ada asked.

"I asked her to come a bunch of times, but she said she preferred to stay there."

"By herself?" *Mamm* asked.

Cherish nodded.

"No." *Mamm* shook her head. "I'll have Matthew fetch her. She can stay here until she finds somewhere else."

"I'm sorry, *Mamm*. I wasn't thinking straight. I asked her but I guess I didn't *insist* on her coming here."

"And neither was Krystal thinking with her right mind. She needs to be around people at this time," Ada said.

"I totally agree." *Mamm* nodded.

CHAPTER 5

$\mathcal{M}$atthew did what he was told. He didn't mind going to fetch Krystal. He'd been fond of her for the longest time. She was just one of the women he'd been pining after. Unfortunately, none of the young women ever noticed him or took him seriously.

He stopped the buggy outside of Gertie's house. He knew he couldn't take no for an answer about her coming back to the orchard. If he turned up alone, Ada and Wilma would blame him.

He knocked on the door. Krystal opened it almost right away. "Hi, Matthew."

She looked almost unrecognizable. Her eyes were red rimmed and her face was all puffy and pale. "Hello. I'm sorry about Gertie. I know you were close with her."

"Thanks. Um, do you want to come in?"

"I'm here because Wilma has insisted you stay at her house.

Ada's insisting I bring you back too. No one wants you to be alone."

"They sent you to fetch me?"

"Correct."

A smile spread across her face, making her look more like her pretty self. "Come in and sit down."

They moved into the living room. "You're always there aren't you, Matthew?"

"Always where?"

She sat down on a chair while he stayed on his feet. "Always there when anyone needs any help with anything."

Matthew shrugged his shoulders. "I'm just trying to help out where I can. Wilma is the one insisting you come back with me to stay at her place."

"Insisting, you say?"

"Yes."

"That's kind of Wilma. I suppose she hasn't found out yet."

"Found out what?" he asked.

"I'm leaving. I'm moving on. Leaving the community all together. Cherish knows."

He tilted his head to one side. "Why would you do something like that?"

"I'm surprised Cherish didn't tell everyone. I'm writing a book about my stay in the community. I've actually already written it. It'll be published sometime soon. I'm not sure when."

Matthew sat down on the couch. "You don't have to leave, do you?"

Krystal remained sitting and nodded to where he sat. "That's where we found Gertie when we came home."

Matthew jumped up and looked down at the couch. Then he moved across and sat on the chair next to Krystal. "What's to stop you from staying?"

"The bishop. He wasn't happy with me writing a book. I tried to explain what kind of a book it was. It doesn't say anything mean about anyone, but I could tell by the way the bishop spoke to me that he was very upset. I think he thought I was the worst person in the world."

"No, he wouldn't think that. Anyway, why don't you at least come back with me for a meal and then think about whether you'll want to stay there at least for tonight?"

"I am hungry and I don't feel like cooking now. Thanks, Matthew. I'll grab some things and just stay there for the night. I was kind of dreading being here alone."

"Good. I'll wait right here while you pack a bag."

IN THE BUGGY on the way back to the orchard, Krystal asked, "So what have you been doing lately, Matthew?"

"Just keeping busy, doing my job."

Krystal looked out the window. It was getting dark now and soon she had to face everyone at Wilma's house. "I don't know if I feel like talking. I hope people don't ask me too many questions."

"No. I'm sure everyone will be more thoughtful than that."

"I hope so. I don't want to be around people and yet I don't want to be alone." Krystal started sobbing. Tears were falling from her eyes and she couldn't stop them.

Matthew looked over at her and then he pulled the horse

and buggy off the road and brought the horse to a halt. "I'm so sorry, Krystal."

"She was like a grandmother to me. At least I didn't get to tell her I was leaving. That would've really upset her." She looked across at Matthew. "Do you think someone told her before I got there?"

"No. Not at all. She was an old lady. That's why she died. She wouldn't have known, would she? I mean who knew besides you?"

"No one I guess. Only the bishop. Thanks, Matthew, for keeping me calm." Krystal picked up the end of her apron and wiped her eyes. "You can go now. You didn't need to stop."

Matthew moved the horse and buggy back onto the road. "I'm not used to people crying."

"Now I wish I'd never told the bishop I was leaving."

Matthew asked, "Were you leaving because he didn't want you to write the book or something?"

"No. I thought it was time to leave. I only planned to stay to get writing material for the book. Do you think less of me now?"

"No. I'm just shocked that you'd be thinking of leaving. Everything was going so well for you. That's what it looked like to me."

Krystal didn't want to tell him the real reason. It would be too embarrassing to tell him she was having trouble finding someone who wanted to marry her. It wasn't about the book. "Sometimes appearances can be deceiving. For the most part, everyone accepted me. But I wonder if deep down they really did. I think I got a surface acceptance."

Matthew glanced over at her. "I'm very sad you feel that way."

"Are you? Do you really care?" Krystal asked him.

"Of course I do."

Krystal buried her face in her hands. "I'm sorry. Don't worry about me. I've just had the worst day of my life. I shouldn't take it out on you."

"Everyone cares about you, Krystal. You should know that. I had the biggest crush on you a few years ago. You're a big reason why I stayed here instead of going back home."

"Really?" That made Krystal feel a little better. Someone liked her—a male.

He laughed. "It's true."

"I had no idea. Well, maybe a little bit, but that's so sweet that you told me."

"I wasn't the only one."

"You mean someone else liked me?" Krystal asked.

"Yeah. Every man I know, just about."

"How come I didn't know about this?"

"Because everyone thought you were too good for them. I mean, look at you. You're not half bad to look at."

Krystal was shocked. "They thought I was too good? I thought none of the young men liked me at all. I kind of thought it was because I wasn't born into the community and wasn't raised Amish."

"Well, some might think that, but not everyone. Not me." He glanced over at her and at that moment she knew that he still liked her.

This changed everything. Matthew was a decent man. He was only a little younger and she'd always thought of him as way too young for her. Over the past few years, he'd matured. If someone saw the two of them together, they'd never guess that Matthew was younger. "Thanks for being so kind."

"I'm just doing what I can to help. Here we are."

She looked around. They were at the orchard already. Now she had to face everyone. "I don't know if I can go in. What will everyone think of me? They'd know by now that I wrote a book. Cherish would've told them everything."

"I don't think she would've. She didn't say anything when I was there. Of course you can go in. No one's thinking about that. They're just sad for you because they know how upset you'd be about Gertie."

"Is that right?" She stared into his eyes and found some comfort.

"That's right. We'll go into the house together if that makes you feel better."

"I'd like that." Krystal got out of the buggy and walked around to meet Matthew. He gave her a beaming smile and together, they walked into the house.

Ada and Wilma met them at the door and both ladies made her feel at home right away. Matthew had been right. No one cared about the book, at least, not at the present time. Once she was settled, Matthew left her and went outside to tend his horse.

There were so many people sitting at the long table. Earl and Miriam were there and also Debbie's boyfriend, Peter.

From the conversation, Krystal realized that Cherish hadn't told anyone that she was leaving. Also, no one had mentioned she was writing a book. If only she hadn't told the bishop. Now, since she'd done that, she really had to go.

CHAPTER 6

$\mathcal{W}$hen Cherish was alone in the kitchen, washing up, Krystal walked in and picked up a tea towel.

"Hey, you don't have to do that."

Krystal moved her *kapp* strings over her shoulders. "It's okay. I like to keep busy. Thanks for keeping quiet about me leaving and about the book."

"It's your news to tell, not mine."

"It's nice of you."

Cherish stopped washing up and looked at her. "You don't have to go."

"I really do. How can I stay once the book comes out with the bishop not approving of it? He doesn't approve of the book and he doesn't approve of me."

"Cancel the book."

"It's too late for that. I've signed a contract. I've committed to it. They're reading it now."

Cherish kept trying to talk her into staying, but Krystal

wasn't really listening. It went in one ear and out the other. Once Krystal had finished helping in the kitchen, she went back to the living room and noticed Matthew was heading out the front door. "Are you going now, Matthew?"

He turned around and stared at her. "Um. I'm going soon."

Krystal glanced over at everyone gathered around the fire, then looked back at Matthew. "Let's go outside for a moment."

"Okay." He opened the door for Krystal and she walked out.

She saw the two white porch chairs and sat down in one.

Matthew sat in the other. "It's a nice night."

"I guess so. I haven't really noticed."

"I'm sorry. It was a stupid thing to say." He shook his head. "It's not a nice night."

In the semi-darkness, she looked down at the boards that made up the porch. "You're right. It's one of the worst days of my life."

"Life can be so hard sometimes."

She appreciated his sympathetic words, but she was sure he hadn't had one hard day in his whole life. "Did you know you wanted to work in an orchard when you were growing up?"

"No. Did you know you were going to write a book about the Amish when you were growing up?"

Krystal gave half a laugh. "No. I never even knew about Amish people back then."

"I just didn't want to work on the farm. The orchard's similar but a lot better. I've grown to love it."

"Good for you. I've never found anywhere I belong. I thought I'd found that here, but then the book got in the way. Now Gertie's gone, there's not much point in sticking around."

"Forget the book. Just live here at the orchard. Debbie

moved here. They took her in. I'm sure they'll do the same for you."

Krystal shook her head. "No. Debbie's Levi's niece. That's why they've done that. I'm sure I've worn out my welcome to stay with Wilma and Levi for anything longer than just a few days. They're not the society for taking in lost souls."

Matthew laughed at her comment. "I hardly think you're a lost soul. That's extreme. Maybe you could stay with Ada. She's got plenty of spare rooms."

"No. I'll stay here for a day or two and then I'll go back to my mother for a while. Actually, I'll stay until Gertie's funeral."

"Maybe you'll change your mind after that."

Krystal smiled at him. "We'll see."

CHAPTER 7

Three days later, they were at Gertie's funeral. After the burial, the crowd gathered at the bishop's house. All Gertie's family were there.

Gertie's grandson, Noah, caught Krystal's eye. He was thirty, single, and according to Ada, he was 'a little on the wild side.' To Ada, that meant he didn't fit in. To Krystal, that meant he was intriguing.

When Noah looked at her, she looked away. He came over. "You're Krystal?"

She turned around. "Yes."

"I'm Noah."

"Hello, Noah. You're Gertie's grandson."

"Yeah. One of them."

Krystal couldn't even recall Gertie talking about him. "I've been living with her for three years and you never came to visit."

"I didn't want a lecture, that's why."

Krystal was intrigued. "About what?"

Noah grinned. "This and that."

"Is it so bad that you can't say?"

Noah chuckled and looked down. "Not that bad. Everything was bad according to my grandmother. I should've visited her more often. I regret that now. Seems odd that I made the effort to come to her funeral. I should've made the effort to see her when she was alive. That would've made more sense."

"Where are you from?" Krystal asked.

"Up north. I hear you helped my grandmother a lot."

It gave Krystal a sense of peace that everyone acknowledged how helpful she'd been to Gertie. "I did. I ran her store and I lived with her."

"Where will you live now? My father said he'll probably sell the house."

"I was moving away anyhow."

"Where to?"

Krystal just shrugged her shoulders. If he could be evasive, so could she.

"Just going where the wind blows you?" Noah asked.

"Possibly."

"You've got no family?" he asked.

"I only have a mother. I suppose you know I wasn't born into the community."

"I heard that. Everyone seems to know."

"So, I don't really fit in. Just as well I decided to leave."

"You don't have to rush off, do you?"

She looked into his dark brown eyes. "I'm not going right this minute. I'm staying at the Baker Apple Orchard for a day or two."

496

"Is that so? Maybe I'll visit you tomorrow or before I leave." He grinned as he adjusted his black hat.

"If you want. There's not much else to do."

Noah laughed. "What do you do around here for fun?"

"Not much. What do you do where you're from?"

"We go sledding in the snow or we swim in the waterhole."

Krystal laughed. "That sounds a bit tame."

"It's not. We swing off ropes into the water, and we do harness racing and that can be quite dangerous. Anyway, I want to thank you for looking after my grandmother so well."

"It was nothing. She looked after me too. She took me in when I had nowhere to go. I'll miss her dreadfully."

"We all will." Noah looked down at his feet. Then he looked back up at her. "Can I get you a soda?"

"Yes please." She waited there while he went to get her a drink, then Wilma walked up to her.

"Who's that?" Wilma asked.

"It's Noah. Gertie's grandson."

Wilma looked over at him. "He's grown up. I would never have recognized him. Now, Krystal, are you sure you won't stay? I've had a talk with Levi and he's quite happy if you live with us for as long as you want. Favor has gone and there's plenty of room now. We can even give you some work on the orchard."

Krystal shook her head. "That's so generous of you. Thank you, but I feel it's time to move on."

"I heard about the book," Wilma blurted out.

"Oh yes. I guess you're upset with me."

"No, I'm not."

Krystal was amazed to hear it. "That's a surprise. I'm sure everyone else is."

"We just don't want you to go. You'll be sadly missed. It seems everyone is moving away or moving on. Favor left and Gertie has gone now too. Now you're talking about going and it's a bit upsetting. Levi and I consider you part of our family. I know things haven't been smooth all the time between us, but that doesn't mean you're any less important."

Krystal didn't know what to say. Tears stung behind her eyes. If they wanted her to stay, maybe she did have some people who resembled family. It touched her heart that they were willing to forget the past.

Noah came back and handed a glass of soda to Krystal. He smiled at Wilma. "Hello, Mrs... Bruner."

"Hello, Noah."

"Would you like a drink of something too, Mrs. Bruner?"

"No. I'm fine, thank you. It's nice to see you again, Noah."

"And you."

"I'll leave you young people to it." Wilma walked away, and said over her shoulder, "Please consider what I said, Krystal."

"I definitely will."

"That was weird," Noah said. "What's she leaving us to?"

Krystal laughed. "That's just the way she talks." Krystal took a mouthful of her drink and swallowed. "Thanks for this."

"You looked thirsty."

"I was. It's a bit overwhelming. I was about to tell Gertie I was leaving and I found her there."

"Oh, you were the one who found her?"

"I was. I had my friend Cherish with me. I needed someone with me while I broke the news."

"I don't blame you. Gertie's a bit scary. I mean, she was."

"No. I wasn't scared. I just didn't really want to tell her. I was just nervous. I thought she might break down or something. Then she'd talk me into staying. I should've stayed to look after her. I'm so selfish all the time."

"You are?" Noah asked.

Krystal nodded and then moved to set her drink down on a nearby table. Why was she saying this to someone she liked? "Not really. I'm trying not to be. I want to be the best person I can be, but it's not always easy."

"Why were you leaving? Care to tell me?" Noah asked.

"I don't think so."

He laughed. "Come on. It's easy talking to a stranger." He pulled out a chair and sat down.

She looked around and sat down with him. "I've never fitted in anywhere."

"I know what that's like. I'm pretty much the odd one out wherever I go. When I was growing up I wasn't paid much attention even though I was an only child. My mother cared more about the unfortunate people in the community. She was always doing good deeds, ignoring me and my father. I left the community when I was sixteen, went back when I was eighteen and left again. Obviously, I'm back now. Everyone's always looking at me as though I'm about to leave." He chuckled.

"And are you?"

"Maybe." Noah laughed again. "Anyway, you were telling me about yourself. Stop me if I'm talking too much. Okay, now it's your turn to say something."

"I've done some things I'm not proud of. Apart from that,

I've been writing about my experiences in the community, and I'm about to publish a book."

His eyes opened wide. "For real?"

"Yes."

"Hey, you should've interviewed me for your book. I've got a ton of scandalous stories. Some of them, you wouldn't believe."

Krystal laughed. "I'd like to hear about them sometime. Anyway, I've written a book and I deceived people and that's why I have to leave. I thought you should know."

"Ah, so this book was written in secret?" Noah asked.

Krystal felt awful that she had to tell him it was. "Yes."

"My grandmother didn't even know about it?"

"No. We were close, but I kept that from her. She would probably be very disappointed in me just like everyone else."

"I don't think so. The word on the street is that she thought very highly of you. When someone's on her good side, they can do no wrong."

"I hope so. I'd like to think that she thought that way. I wish I could have just one more minute with her. I'd thank her and I'd tell her how much she meant to me." Krystal blinked back tears. "Just one minute, that's all."

"Maybe she'll hear you from where she is with God."

"Do you think so?" Krystal was enjoying his upbeat personality. He was so different from anyone she'd ever met.

"I wouldn't be surprised. And I'm sure she'd want you to stay."

"I can't stay now. Didn't I tell you the bishop's upset with me?" Krystal asked.

"Where I come from, the bishop's always upset."

"And everyone else will be too when they find out about it."

"It's none of their business."

Krystal liked that he was taking her side. "It is kind of, if I've mentioned them in the book. I don't say anything bad about anyone, not one person. It's mostly just telling my experiences. Telling about the lifestyle. I think people will be interested to know from an insider's point of view."

Noah shrugged his shoulders. "I don't see any harm in it at all."

Krystal was delighted to hear that. "I guess people want their lives to stay private."

"You could change their names. Or do you have to use their real names?"

"I've already changed their names," Krystal said.

"Maybe they'll make it into a movie."

Krystal laughed. "I've got to get it published first. It's mostly fiction that gets made into movies. This'll be non-fiction except for the part about the name changing."

"So what else can you tell me about yourself, Krystal?"

At that moment, Krystal realized that he was interested in her. This was the first time she'd felt genuine interest from an Amish man that wasn't Matthew. "There's not much to tell."

"I bet there's a lot more you can tell me."

There was, but it was mostly all things she was ashamed of. "You tell me something about yourself first."

"I already did."

"What did you do when you left the community?" Krystal asked.

Noah adjusted his hat. "Fell in with the wrong crowd, and ended up in jail."

Krystal gasped. "Really?" She was delighted that he wasn't

perfect. He was someone who also had a past. She might have a chance with someone like him.

"I was only in jail for a night, but that was enough to shock some sense into me."

Krystal laughed.

"What was the worst thing you've ever done?"

"I can't tell you that. I don't know you well enough." Although she said it in a joking manner, that was the truth. Where would she start anyway? The worst thing she'd done was come to the Baker Apple Orchard, pretending she was Caroline. She then prolonged her stay, lying about the family house burning down.

She never would've done that now, but back then, she was desperate to have a loving home with a normal family. Her mother had never been a maternal kind of person. The only person who paid her any attention was her best friend, Caroline. Then Caroline died in a horrible accident. Now it occurred to Krystal that the two people in the world who believed in her most had both died.

"Tell me the second worst thing you've ever done, then," Noah said.

"No. I prefer to concentrate on positive things."

He laughed. "You're right. I know one good thing you did and that was look after my grandmother. I appreciate that."

"You're welcome. How come you hardly saw her? There must be more to it than what you told me."

"My father wasn't talking to her."

"Why?"

"He was annoyed when he found out she was telling people

she never had any children." He gulped a couple of swallows of soda and then put the glass down.

"I have no idea why she would do that. Do you think her memory was failing?" Krystal asked.

"No. She was pretty sharp, wasn't she? That's what we heard from people in this community who knew her."

"Yes, she appeared to be okay, but I thought maybe her long term memory was affected. She actually never talked about her family and I never asked." Krystal felt bad about that now, realizing that she was mainly talking about herself when she'd been with Gertie.

"My father thought she was being mean. Who knows?" Noah lifted his hands in the air.

"I don't know."

Noah asked, "She never mentioned my father, or me?"

"No. We talked about other things. She didn't ever ask me about my family and I didn't ask her about hers."

"What about your family? Tell me about them." He leaned back in his chair.

"It's just my mother. I haven't seen her or talked to her for years. I did talk to her the other day, but apart from that, not for years."

"So the community is your family?"

"I guess they've become my family. I had a good friend, Favor, but she's moved away. She'll be married soon. I haven't talked to her recently either."

"She abandoned you?" he asked.

"I guess that's what it feels like."

"Yeah. I've had friends do that to me too when they get

married. They want to spend all their time with their wives. It's so selfish." He offered a crooked smile.

A giggle escaped Krystal's lips. "Totally selfish." The more she talked to Noah, the more handsome he became. She'd stay in the community if she could marry a man like him.

"Come and meet my father," he suggested.

Krystal had already heard Noah's mother had died. "Okay. I'd like that."

Noah took her to a man with a long gray beard. She'd seen him hours before at the graveyard. She had expected he'd be a little younger. He was sitting down with his hands over his large belly. "Pa, this is Krystal."

The man's face lit up. "Hello, Krystal. You're the young lady who took good care of my mother."

Krystal smiled. "She took care of me too. I think that'd be fair to say. She gave me a place to live and a job."

He stood up. "I'm Amos."

Krystal stared up at him. He was well over six feet and nearly as wide. Noah looked nothing like him. "Hi, Amos."

Noah chuckled. "I'm hopeless at introductions. I didn't even tell you his name."

"It's fine. You did a good job," Krystal told him.

"I understand you were living in the house?" Amos asked.

"I was. I'm staying with the Bakers for the moment. Ah, I mean the Bruners."

Amos rubbed the side of his face. "Could you move back to the house until we decide what we'll do with it? You'd be helping us out."

"Really?" Was this an answer to prayer—a sign that she should stay in the community?

"Yes. I'll be staying in the house for another week, but you can move back after that. And if you wouldn't mind staying on at the quilt store until we can find a buyer that would help us out too."

"Sure. I'd love to."

"You'd be paid, of course. Whatever you're getting now. We'll close it for another week and then you can reopen it."

"If that's what you want," Krystal replied. "I'm willing to fit in with whatever you want. I can help you with anything you need."

"That should do it for now," Amos said. "Noah can take care of all the details. He'll be staying on a little longer and figuring out some things. He'll go through the books at the store. He's great with numbers."

Krystal stared at Noah. "Oh? Where will you be staying?"

"With some friends. Jack and Frannie Yoder."

"Okay. They're not far from Gertie's."

Someone came up to talk with Noah and Amos, so Krystal moved away.

CHAPTER 8

The next day.

Cherish went into the barn to find out if Krystal had any clothes that needed washing. She was going to wash some of her clothes and there was room left in the gas-powered machine. She was a little shocked to see Krystal talking on a cell phone.

When Krystal looked up and saw her, she quickly ended the call. "I wasn't calling in the house. That's okay, isn't it?"

Cherish nodded. "It's fine." It was fine since she was leaving, but you needed to give the bishop a good reason if you wanted a cell phone. Such as you needed it for work only, or you were a midwife and you needed it for emergency calls.

"I've got so much to say. Firstly, Amos, Gertie's son, wants me to go back to the store and still live in the house until they figure out what to do. Not now, but soon."

"Perfect. Who was that on the phone?" Cherish asked.

"It was my agent."

"The book agent?"

"Yes. It's not good news." Krystal lowered her head. "They said my writing was dull and uninspired. It needs a complete rewrite. I'm so embarrassed. I asked them to let me out of the contract and they are refusing. They suggested I collaborate with one of their established authors."

"You don't want to do that?" Cherish asked.

"No. Then it wouldn't be mine any more. It wouldn't be my story. I wrote what I wanted to say. I know it's good. I don't know why they're saying it isn't."

Cherish felt so sorry for her. "That's dreadful."

"They paid me an advance so I can't walk away. But collaborating wasn't in the contract, so I'm refusing to do it. The contract works both ways, I'm guessing. Unless there was some fine print that I didn't notice."

"Can you give them the money back?"

Krystal gasped. "Give them back the money?"

"Yes."

"I don't know. It never occurred to me." Krystal bit her lip. "I could ask them about it."

"Do it," Cherish urged. "Things are falling into place if Gertie's son is letting you stay on at the quilt store."

"That's what I thought. It's only temporary, but I do feel it gives me hope. I'll call the agent back tomorrow when I carefully think through what I'm going to say."

"How are things going with you and Noah? You looked pretty friendly yesterday."

Krystal looked up at her in shock. "What do you mean?"

"He seems to like you."

"Do you think so? Like, as in *like* or, like as in, he's just being nice?" Krystal asked.

"I think he genuinely likes you. He could be another good reason to stay."

Krystal smiled. "We're not supposed to stay for love."

"You wouldn't be. You'll be staying because you love it here. This is where God wants you. He brought you Noah so you wouldn't leave the community."

"Do you think so?"

"Of course. It's obvious. I could tell how much Noah likes you because he kept looking at you."

"How was he looking at me?"

"Like he adores you."

Krystal looked down. "Yeah, but once he finds out all the terrible things I've done, he won't like me."

"That's all in the past. You wouldn't do those things now. You've changed. Even I can see that."

"No. I wouldn't, but people think that if you've done something once, you'll do it again. I don't want him to think that I'm that kind of person."

Cherish believed that Krystal had changed. Well, she thought she'd changed before Krystal told her she was still writing that silly book. That had been a real shock. "If he's the man God has for you, he won't care. He won't hold it against you."

"You're right. I do like him. I don't know much about him, but I want to know more. I'll see if I can get out of this book thing. The thing I've spent the last five years of my life on."

"If that's what you choose."

"Oh, Cherish, you're not saying he likes me just to stop me from moving forward with the book, are you?"

"No. I'd never do that."

"Well, give me a minute and I'll make a call and see what I can do. They don't like it anyway and I don't want to spend the next five years rewriting it."

"Aren't you going to think about it and call them tomorrow?"

Krystal bit her lip. "No. They've upset me. I don't want to do it anymore. Everyone here has been so nice. I do feel I belong here. I'll say a quick prayer and I'm sure God will turn things around for me and they'll let me out of the deal."

"I'll wait outside and pray too."

"Thanks, Cherish."

Cherish left her alone to make her call. Then she paced up and down outside the barn, praying for Krystal. That phone call was going to decide the direction of Krystal's life.

A minute later, Krystal burst through the barn doors. She didn't look happy.

Cherish rushed to her. "What happened?"

"They said they'll get their head person to look at it and then they'll decide if they'll let me out of the contract. Then she said if they let me out, I'll have to pay back the money."

"That's great news."

Krystal didn't look so convinced. "I'll have to wait and see what they'll say."

"When will you know?"

"I'm not sure. I think I'll go lie down for a bit if that's okay. I think best when I'm half asleep and I've got a lot of thinking to do."

"Sure."

"I think, at the moment, I would like to stay. I just hope the bishop will look kindly on my repentant heart."

"I'm sure he will. It's not like you killed anyone."

Krystal looked thoughtful.

"Well, you didn't, did you?"

Krystal grinned. "Of course I didn't."

CHAPTER 9

*a*s Cherish sat chopping the vegetables for the stew, Matthew came in and sat down in front of her, landing heavily on the chair. "So, how do you feel about Favor getting married?"

"Good. If that's what she wants to do."

"Are you sure you're fine with it? The rumors are that you and Simon were friendly once."

Cherish put the chopping knife down and stared at him. He was trying to stir her and she wasn't in the mood to take the bait. "Don't say that please."

"Why not?"

"It'll ruin it for them. I did like him a little, but then it turned out that Favor was better suited to him."

Matthew chuckled. "Yeah."

Cherish started chopping again. "What's funny?"

"Nothing."

Cherish rolled her eyes. "If you've got something to say, then say it."

Matthew leaned back in the chair and crossed one leg over the other. "Seems to me you have a need."

"I have a need?" Cherish knew what he was about to say. She should marry him because his two older brothers had married two of her older sisters. "It's not going to happen, Matthew, so just forget it."

"I like it that you think you know what I'm going to say."

"I do. You've always wanted to marry one of my sisters or…"

Matthew coughed, and made a gagging sound. "You think I want to marry you?"

She stared at him. She couldn't say she did, because that would sound like she was vain or something. "Well…"

"No!" He pushed out his lips and shook his head.

"Well, what's my need, according to you?" Cherish asked.

"You need a friend because Favor's gone."

"I do need a friend sometimes, but I'm blessed because I have Debbie as a stand-in sister."

"She's busy all the time. I hardly ever see her when I'm here. She's either off selling her tea or she's out with Peter."

"So are you going to be my new best friend?" Cherish couldn't help but laugh.

"Forget it, Cherish. You're always so prickly. You'll never get a man if you don't lose your spikes. Just calm down." Matthew leapt to his feet and walked away.

Cherish laughed harder. He was going to suggest that he be her friend, or something more than a friend. What he needed to do was grow up. He was always acting so needy and that was off-putting to any woman.

Ada walked into the room. "Where's he going so fast?"

"Away from me, I think."

Ada sat down with her. "What did you do to him this time, Cherish?"

"I upset him about something. It's not hard to do lately."

"Were you teasing him again?"

"Oh, Ada, would I do something like that?"

Ada picked up a piece of carrot and popped it into her mouth. "You should go easy on him. You know he's got the biggest crush on you."

Cherish couldn't keep the smile from her face. That was the first time she'd heard Ada use the word crush. "He's got a crush on everyone."

"You and I will have to do something about that. Who can we match him with?"

Cherish shook her head. "Hey, I've got enough problems to deal with."

"What about your friend, Fenella? She's not married yet, is she?"

"She wouldn't be interested. I haven't heard from her for ages. I wrote two times recently and she hasn't written back. I'm not sure what her problem is."

Ada's lips turned down at the corners. "Friendships are diffi-cult sometimes. You really have to make an effort. It's not like having sisters. You can't get away from sisters. They're always with you. Maybe Fenella needs to learn that lesson."

"Sisters aren't always with you. Favor moved, and so did Honor and Mercy."

"*Jah*, but they'll always be your sisters. When you see them again it'll be like no time ever passed."

Cherish sighed. "I guess so. I don't know when that'll be though."

"Now back to Matthew's future wife. Who is there for him?"

Cherish couldn't think of anyone. "Don't you think he needs to grow up a bit first?"

"No I don't. He's twenty four. That's old enough. The right woman would cause him to grow up. I think you're still seeing him as younger than he is. Everyone grows and changes. Look at yourself. You're not the impulsive headstrong girl you once were."

"Do you really think it's a good idea to match him with someone?"

"I've been holding off for years. Now his mother is getting anxious. She wants more grandchildren. Four aren't enough for her and she's getting impatient."

"Just know it's not going to be me if that's what you're hinting at."

Ada stared at her and blinked her eyes a few times. "You could do worse."

Cherish couldn't stop laughing. "He's not for me. He's a good friend, but that's all he'll ever be."

"He might grow on you."

"That's not good. Mold grows on things."

Ada chuckled. "Just help me, would you?"

Cherish didn't want to say no. "How about I keep an eye out for someone who might suit?"

"Thank you and so will I. Between the two of us we're sure to come up with someone. And what about yourself? Anything happening with you and Malachi?"

Cherish stared at Ada. How did she know she was fond of him? "No."

"I'm sorry to hear that. He'd be as close to perfect for you as anyone could be."

Cherish's mouth fell open. She had no idea Ada felt that way.

"Don't you think so?" Ada asked.

"I really don't know." Now that Ada thought he was good for her, Cherish wasn't so sure. She'd always imagined that Ada and *Mamm* wouldn't approve of the man she chose.

"Well, don't leave things too long or he might find someone else."

"I'm not even sure if I want to marry any time soon. I don't feel I'm old enough. I still feel like a kid."

"I blame your mother for that. She babied you for way too long."

Cherish knew Ada didn't mean any harm with anything she said, but Cherish was tired of being called spoiled or the baby just because she was the youngest. If anything, she had less attention than the others. "It's just how I feel."

"You might not have met the right man yet. Or maybe you have met him and don't want to admit it. It's okay to let someone get close to you."

The last thing Cherish needed was to get a lecture from Ada. "Do you want a cup of hot tea?"

"Always."

Cherish stood up and filled up the teakettle. "Where's *Mamm?*"

"She's over with Christina, visiting. Joy's there too with Faith and baby Audrey."

"Why didn't you go?"

"I was going to, but by the time I got ready and did all my chores, I thought I might as well just come here and wait for her. I've also got a bit of a headache and children are so noisy. Audrey's going through the squealing stage."

Cherish laughed.

"I know, you would think that's funny, but I'm not as young as I used to be."

"So you took an extra-long time with your chores today and used that as an excuse to come straight here?" Cherish teased her.

Ada covered her mouth and laughed. "You're a funny girl, Cherish."

"Not a girl, a woman."

"That you are. You've grown into a lovely young woman. Your mother spent many years worried about you and how you'd turn out. She thought you'd run away and get into some bad things. So did Florence, but you're perfectly fine. I knew you would be."

Cherish stopped herself from rolling her eyes. Ada told her about her past nearly every second day. "Thanks, Ada. I think that's the nicest thing you've ever said to me."

Ada wagged a finger at her. "Don't get used to it."

"I definitely won't."

Cherish made a cup of hot tea for Ada and sat down with a cup of Debbie's latest concoction for herself – vanilla and lavender tea. "All I want to do is move to the farm."

"No, Cherish. You can't go now. You'd break your mother's heart. Levi's not well and then she's losing Favor."

"She's not losing Favor, she's gaining a son," Cherish said.

Ada pushed out her lips. She clearly didn't think that was correct. "Between you, me and your two birds over there, I don't think Wilma would've picked Simon for Favor or for you. It's no secret that she doesn't exactly get along with Harriet and Melvin. I can't work out why because I simply adore them."

"I know that. Harriet and Melvin don't stop talking about the time they visited my farm and the roof fell in on them. Anyone would think we deliberately did something to the roof and prayed for the storm to come."

Ada chuckled. "Oh, I shouldn't laugh. I know it's not funny, but I can't help it when I picture the roof coming down. I'm glad they weren't hurt. Imagine lying in bed trying to sleep and the roof falls on you."

"It was such a shock. They left the next day. Then Malachi fixed the roof as good as new."

"He's quite handy. He's the perfect farm manager for you. That's why you don't have to hurry off to your farm. Let him look after it."

Cherish stared into her tea. It was her life, but she felt like she was living it for the convenience of everyone else. Now she knew how Florence must've felt when she ran away to marry Carter. Florence would tell her to live her own life.

"Wouldn't you agree?" Ada asked.

Cherish looked up. "What?"

"I said you don't have to hurry to your farm."

"Well, I'm not there now. If I was hurrying, I would've gone there years ago."

"Exactly." Ada smiled as though they were agreeing, but Ada had no idea how Cherish felt. No one ever saw anything from her side.

"Nice having our little talk." Cherish stood up to go, but sat back down again when Ada opened her mouth to speak.

"I have something that might put a smile on your face."

"What's that?" Cherish needed something to be happy about.

"Annie Whylie is getting married."

"She is?"

"*Jah.* That means I can take you to the farm earlier than we planned so the two of us can go to Annie's wedding. She's getting married about a week before Favor. Then Wilma and the others will come a few days before Favor—"

Cherish flew off her chair and hugged Ada, causing Ada to chuckle.

"I thought you'd be happy about that," Ada said.

"Have you cleared it with *Mamm?*"

"Oh, yes. She said it's fine."

Cherish was delighted with the news. That meant that Malachi was right all those times when he told that he and Annie were just friends. "I'll have to call Malachi. I wonder why he didn't tell me. I'm not surprised though. He really writes a lot of nonsense in his letters. He gives me no real news."

"He calls you often enough. I would have thought he would've mentioned it since he's close with Annie."

"He doesn't call that much."

Once Ada finished her cup of tea, Cherish raced to the barn to call Malachi. She pushed the double barn doors open, and made her way to the phone in the back. As usual, it was covered in dust. Hardly anyone used the phone. She brushed the dirt away with her fingertips before she dialed the number she knew by heart.

Malachi answered almost immediately. "Hello."

"Malachi, it's me. Why didn't you tell me about Annie getting married?"

"Who's this?"

Cherish huffed. "It's me. Cherish."

He chuckled. "I know it's you."

"Well?"

"I didn't tell you she was getting married because you never asked me."

Cherish stamped her foot on the barn floor. "Are you kidding me?"

"Nope."

"Well, we're now coming there earlier than planned so we can go to her wedding, if that's okay with you. Is it?" She wanted him to be pleased that she was coming sooner—wanted him to celebrate the moment with her.

"It's your farm. Do as you want."

He didn't sound pleased or excited and that bothered Cherish. "I'm only asking to be polite. You're the one living there."

"Sure you can stay. I'll look forward to it. I always look forward to your visits."

He said he was pleased, but he didn't sound like it. She couldn't question him about the tone of his voice because she'd sound like she was crazy. "Thanks. Who's Annie marrying?"

"Gus Waltham."

"That doesn't tell me much. Who is he?" Cherish asked.

"He's from our community. He's a little older, but neither of them cares about that."

Cherish couldn't recall anyone with that name. He must've been new to the area. "How much older is he?"

521

"Dunno. I never asked."

"I should know better than to ask you for details, Malachi. You never tell me anything."

"I'm sorry. Next time I see either of them, I'll ask a whole bunch of questions so I can give you more information."

"Thank you. That would be great. At least then we'd have something to talk about," Cherish said. "My family will ask me and I'll have to tell them I don't know."

He laughed. "You know I'm not like that. I just take people for how I see them."

"That's exciting that Annie's getting married."

"Yeah. She's pretty happy. Only thing is, I haven't seen much of her since she's been dating. She hardly ever visits anymore."

Cherish smiled. If Annie had liked Malachi, she'd probably given up waiting for him to do anything about it. Caramel came up to Cherish wagging his tail and sat down beside her. She leaned down and patted his head. "I wonder if I can bring Caramel with me this time."

"Depends if you've tried him out with any geese yet."

"I'll do it before I get there."

"Make sure he's okay. Just one bite from a dog and it'd be all over for Wally."

"I've been meaning to take him to the park and introduce him to a goose."

"Yeah, you've been meaning to do that ever since I got Wally."

Everyone was always telling her off. She didn't need to hear it from Malachi too. "I've been busy. My life is not one of strolling along past the apple trees plucking off an apple when I feel like it. I have a lot of hard work to do. I've got orchard work and community work, not to mention all the chores around the house which have doubled since Favor just up and left."

"I have a lot of work too, but I seem to get everything done."

Cherish didn't want to sound like a complainer. "I'll take Caramel tomorrow."

"Good. Let me know how it goes. You know I can't have him here if he's goin' to chase Wally."

"I know that. I won't let that happen. I don't know if Ada will be okay with him in the car either."

"When are you coming? The wedding's in just two weeks."

"I'm not sure. I'll have to ask Ada. I guess we'll be there a day or two before Annie's wedding. Ada will need a full day to recover from the long drive."

"That'll be good."

She smiled at the way he was sounding more enthusiastic.

"I'll talk to you tomorrow, Cherish. Make sure you take Caramel to that park and introduce him to some geese."

"I will. Bye, Malachi."

"Bye." He ended the call before she did.

Cherish heard the clunk of the receiver hitting the top of the phone. She replaced her receiver.

"Who are you calling?"

Cherish turned around to see the silhouette of her mother standing in the light of the open barn doors. "I was just talking with Malachi. Ada just told me Annie Whylie's getting married, and Ada's taking me to the farm earlier. Hey, I wonder how she found out about Annie before me?"

"From Harriet I suspect."

"Oh, yes, Harriet." Cherish walked toward her mother.

"I'm happy for you that you'll be leaving here even sooner."

Cherish detected something in her mother's voice. "That's all right, isn't it?"

"*Jah.* I already said it was okay. We'll have to work out what's going to happen with Favor's wedding regarding who's going and such. Our plan is for Ada to take you ahead of time so you can both go to Annie's wedding. The rest of us will come in time for Favor's."

Cherish heaved a sigh of relief. "Is everything okay, *Mamm?*"

All of a sudden *Mamm* wrapped her arms around Cherish. Cherish was shocked, her mother being one who rarely showed affection. Something was going on.

"Are you sure you're okay, *Mamm?*"

"Why wouldn't I be? Just because everyone's deserting me..."

"I'll stay home with you then if it's going to make you that upset. I don't need to go to Annie's wedding. I'll just go with you to Favor's." Cherish looked down at Caramel, who was now sitting at her feet. She really wanted to go to the farm as soon as possible, but she felt bad for her mother.

"I don't mean that." *Mamm* sniffed. "Favor's already gone. Once she's married, things will never be the same. She'll never be back here to live. You're all I've got left."

That's not what Cherish wanted to hear, not when she was trying to move to the farm. "Debbie's here and Levi, also Ada and Samuel are over here nearly every day. Hope, Bliss, and Joy are only minutes away."

"It's not the same. They're all busy with other things. You'll only know how my heart feels when you've had children of your own."

Cherish bit her tongue. She was tempted to point out that if she had to stay at the orchard forever, she would never get married and therefore never have any children. "I'm still here."

"I know you'll have to leave one day. I just want to hang onto you for as long as possible." Wilma gave Cherish another squeeze. "Just go early with Ada and we'll see you the day before Favor's wedding."

Cherish had to laugh. "Easy, I can barely breathe. Let's go inside and you can help Ada and me plan the trip."

CHAPTER 10

Weeks later...

Cherish sat in the car with Ada as they were driven in the hired vehicle. Caramel wasn't able to come to the farm with them because he hadn't been at all nice to the geese at the park. All he wanted to do was chase them. Cherish wasn't sure what he would've done when he caught up with one of them. Just as well she'd kept him on a tight leash.

Cherish looked over at Ada who was nodding off to sleep. If Ada slept, she'd have no one to talk with. The driver had earphones in, listening to music. "It's so lovely of you to come with me, Ada."

Ada jumped a little then opened her eyes. "Are we there already?"

"No."

Ada looked over at Cherish. "Did you say something?"

"Yes. I said thanks for coming with me."

"Well, I had to. Who else was going to play chaperone and keep you behaving?"

"You didn't have to," Cherish said.

"Didn't I?" Ada's eyebrows rose. "Well, how about we turn around then? I didn't know I didn't have to."

Cherish laughed. "I am grateful. You've come with me so many times now."

Ada patted Cherish's hand. "You don't need to keep thanking me. I know how much it means to you."

"Still, it's not like you're my mother or anything. You don't have to do stuff for me."

Ada chuckled. "All Wilma's children are like my own. It also gives me something to do. I like going to different places."

Ada eventually fell asleep about one minute before they arrived at the farm. When the car stopped, she opened her eyes.

"We're here," Cherish said.

"Finally."

The afternoon sun warmed Cherish's skin as soon as she got out of the car. She closed her eyes and took a deep breath. The air was so different at the farm.

"Where's Malachi?" Ada asked.

"He'll be around somewhere."

The driver got their bags out of the trunk.

"Leave them there," Ada told him. "Thank you for the safe journey."

He nodded. "You're welcome." He'd already been paid so he got into the car and zoomed away.

Cherish followed Ada toward the house, feeling more than a little anxious to see Malachi.

Birds chirped loudly in the trees and butterflies danced around the daisies that lined the walkway to the front porch. Malachi had been busy planting flowers since the last time she was there.

"Good day, ladies."

Cherish looked up to see Malachi walking toward them with Wally waddling close behind. As was always the way, Malachi had dirt all over his clothes and his face was also smeared with dirt.

"Hello, Malachi, Wally," Ada said as she patted Wally on his head before stepping onto the porch.

He looked at Cherish and she said, "Good afternoon, Malachi. How has your day been?" It came out far too formal, but it was too late to take back her words.

"It was good." He smiled and came closer to her. "Better now that you've arrived."

Cherish felt her heart beat fast. Was he flirting with her?

"Thank you," Ada said. "And we're better now that we're here. Could you please grab the bags and meet us inside, Malachi?"

"Sure thing." He brushed past Cherish, touching her shoulder ever so slightly. It sent tingles throughout her body.

Cherish then noticed Ada smirking so she tried to avoid making eye-contact with her. She continued walking past Ada and opened the front door. She untied her black traveling bonnet as she walked into the kitchen. Placing her bonnet on the table, she noticed Malachi had laid out fresh ham and cheese sandwiches for their arrival. Ada followed her into the kitchen and put the kettle on to boil.

"I heard what he said, you know." Ada opened the pantry and reached for the cups.

"I don't know what you're talking about," Cherish said, sure that she was blushing.

"You know exactly what I'm talking about. *Better now that you've arrived...*" she said, mimicking him.

"Oh, Ada, we're friends. Don't go getting ideas just because you want to marry me off."

"Oh Cherish, you're so naive! And you're not getting any younger either! Malachi is a fine man and your poor *Mamm's* waited long enough for you to wed."

"Last thing I heard, she wanted me to stay. Has she said something different to you? If she's that hungry to get rid of me, I'll pack up and move here as soon as I can."

"She probably wants you to stay, you're right. If I were Wilma, I'd want you to marry as soon as you can, so you'd give me grandchildren." A giggle escaped Ada's lips.

Cherish rolled her eyes and walked to the cupboard to grab some plates for the sandwiches. "Can we talk about this at a different time please?" She didn't want Malachi to walk in and hear them talking about him.

"No, and I saw that eye-roll! Time is ticking. Tick tock."

"Time is ticking for what?" Malachi asked as he walked into the kitchen. Cherish froze, not knowing what to say. She looked at Ada who didn't seem to care that she'd been overheard.

"Time is ticking to eat these delicious sandwiches you've made for us, Malachi." Ada laughed awkwardly as she sat down at the table. "We don't want them getting cold."

"Um, all right then." He sat down with them.

The kettle started to whistle and Cherish was relieved for the distraction. "I'll get that!"

"No, I insist I'll take care of the tea." Malachi got up and walked over.

"Fine man you are, Malachi," Ada said as she patted him on the back. "That's what Cherish and I were just talking about. Fine man indeed." Ada sat down next to Cherish.

Malachi poured them some tea and sat down across from Cherish. Cherish handed him a plate. They caught each other's gaze for a moment and smiled at each other before grabbing some sandwiches to put on their plates.

Before the meal was even finished, Ada stood up. "I am tired. I'll have a lie down for a while."

"I've got a meal ready for later. I just have to heat it."

"Thanks, Malachi," Ada said.

Cherish rolled her eyes at Ada once more. She knew exactly what Ada was trying to do. "You've hardly eaten anything yet, Ada."

"I shall take it with me. Don't be a pest, Cherish. Thank you kindly, Malachi." Ada picked up her tea and her plate with the half a sandwich and started walking. She then stopped and turned to Cherish. "And I saw that eye-roll again, Cherish!" Ada turned her head back and kept walking. Malachi and Cherish looked at each other and laughed.

"So…" He looked at her again and folded his arms in front of him. "You two were talking about me?"

Cherish got nervous for a moment and didn't know what to say. "Oh you know what Ada's like, always giving someone a hard time about something."

"Is that right?" he asked, smiling at her.

Cherish felt her face go bright red. She wanted to talk to Malachi about their kiss, but he hadn't said anything since, and she didn't want to embarrass herself. Surely by now, if he was interested, he would've said something.

He licked his lips. "I've got a few things to tell you."

Maybe he was going to talk to her about it now? "I'm listening."

"There's another section of fence that's come down. I've been working on it all day. I had to move the sheep to the other paddock for now." He took another bite of his sandwich.

"Okay." She tried not to sound too disappointed. "Is that all you wanted to say?"

He shook his head and then swallowed his mouthful. "There's more. It's been a rough few days. A strong wind knocked over a tree, smashing it onto one of the wood sheds. I've been working on removing it. The tree, that is. The shed's will be okay once the tree's gone."

"Oh, I hope all the animals were all right," Cherish said, concerned.

"They were fine."

Cherish was starting to get annoyed. Why had he kissed her in the first place if he wasn't going to do anything else about it? She did her best to put the whole kissing incident out of her mind because he'd certainly put it out of his.

At that moment, Cherish decided she wouldn't attend Annie's wedding unless Malachi confessed that he was interested in her. It would be awful to go to the wedding only to be surrounded by happiness when her own life was muddled. She'd tell Ada and Malachi tomorrow that she wasn't going.

CHAPTER 11

On the third day at the farm, Malachi still hadn't mentioned anything about their shared moment from three years ago. Now she had escalated from annoyed to agitated. "Why do you sometimes speak properly and sometimes you don't?"

"I dunno. I can do what I want and speak how I want. The problem is, you think you're better than me."

"No, I don't."

"You always have," Malachi said.

"That's ridiculous."

"Now I'm ridiculous and you're still better than I am."

"No. I didn't mean that." She huffed.

"Didn't you?" He lowered his head and looked up at her from under his dark lashes.

"We used to get on so well. What happened?"

He made a noise from the back of his throat. "I think Simon happened."

"Simon?"

"Why do you seem so surprised?" Malachi asked.

"You mean the Simon, who's marrying my sister?"

"He wasn't interested in her when he and his folks came here that time."

He was still annoyed that she'd briefly liked Simon. Surely he couldn't think she liked him now, could he? Or were his feelings hurt? "Don't be silly, Malachi. I was never going to marry Simon. You knew that back when he and his parents were here."

"I'm not so sure about that. We must remember things differently. Him being here showed me a different side of you."

Cherish just needed some answers and she needed them now. They kissed after Simon and his parents had left and he wasn't cranky back then. "Will you just be honest with me and tell me how you feel?"

His eyes widened. "How I feel about what?"

She hadn't wanted to be so forthright. He should've been the one to raise the subject. "About me."

"You're the best boss I ever had, also the only one."

Cherish was upset that he was making a joke. This was serious. "Now I feel like an idiot. I've been an idiot for three years." Cherish walked away, frustrated. Now she'd have to forget him. She'd wasted three years of her life thinking fondly about him. If he wasn't man enough to say how he felt, he wasn't man enough to deserve her affections.

Cherish sat on top of the hill. It was her favorite place on the farm. It would've been a great place to build a house, but Aunt Dagmar had said it wouldn't be sheltered from the storms. Now with everything going on in her life, Cherish felt like her life was in the midst of a life-storm. Otherwise known as a crisis.

"Cherish."

She turned around to see Malachi walking toward her with Wally, his constant companion, not far behind.

"What's wrong?" he asked.

She didn't feel like talking. She'd already said too much. If he didn't know what was wrong then he didn't know her at all. "Nothing."

He sat down next to her. "It's beautiful, isn't it?"

"It is."

"I'm gonna hate to leave this place," Malachi said.

"You'll probably be here forever and I'll be at the orchard forever. You might as well make this your permanent home."

"You've never said that before. You always said you were moving here. Why are you giving up?"

She stared at him. Hadn't he been listening at all?

He looked away when she didn't answer. "I suppose you're talking about Levi being sick."

"Yes. That's mostly it."

"Well, isn't Debbie there?" Malachi asked.

"Yes, but she's off doing her tea thing every day."

"What does she do with her kid?"

"Jared stays with us or sometimes she takes him with her. I can't rely on Debbie, she'll probably marry Peter and move out. That could happen at any time."

"Have you talked to your mother about this?" Malachi asked.

"No. I don't want to make her feel bad." Cherish took a deep breath.

"She'd tell you to do what you have to do. This is your life. They've had their life, you're only just starting out."

Cherish let out a sigh. That was her opinion exactly and if she ever had children, she'd encourage them to each follow their own path. She wouldn't hold them back. Obviously, *Mamm* didn't see it that way. *Mamm* was always someone who needed a person to rely on. It was Cherish's father, then it was Florence. After that, *Mamm* relied on Levi. Who would be the person her mother relied on when Levi died? Cherish knew it would be her, simply because she was the last one to leave home. Cherish stared straight ahead. "I wish it was that simple, Malachi."

"It can be. You're just complicating it. Maybe you don't really want to move here at all."

She jumped up and looked down at him. "How could you say that? Moving here is all I've wanted for years."

"Calm down and let's talk it through. C'mon, sit back down."

Cherish knew she'd overreacted. Malachi never meant any harm. He was always on her side about things. She did as he said and sat down. "Okay. Let's talk and I hope we can find some kind of solution."

Malachi stretched his legs out in front of him and leaned back on his elbows. "Just tell 'em you're moving. Give them a date that you're going so they can get organized. I mean, your mother has Ada and plenty of friends."

"I know, but it's not the same as having someone right there, living at the house. I don't think my mother has ever been alone."

"Joy lives close by, and what about Hope and your step sister, Bliss ?"

"Yes, I know." Cherish was impressed that he remembered their names.

"I think you're worrying about nothing. If something did happen to Levi, she's still got Debbie there and her other daughters are close by. Old people are often left alone when one spouse dies. They've got to expect that."

Malachi didn't realize *Mamm* was not like a regular person. "I guess I just feel responsible."

He laughed.

Cherish stared at him. "What's so funny?"

"You're so different from the carefree girl I met years ago."

"How so?"

"You seemed a bit selfish, and definitely spoiled. Now you're caring about your mother."

Cherish smiled. "I guess I've changed a little bit, but everyone cares about their mother."

"Especially Simon."

Cherish dug Malachi in the ribs while stifling a laugh.

"If you move here, how about I try to stay close by?" Malachi suggested. "If you need to go back and visit your mother often, I'll be here to look after the place for you."

Cherish was touched that he'd organize his life around her. "You can't make a promise like that."

"Sure I can. I can do anything I want. I don't have anyone to answer to. It's not as though I'm married or anything."

Cherish wondered if that was why he was so standoffish with her. He wanted to stay free. Marriage would give him someone he had to answer to. "Thanks anyway, but you don't know where life will take you when you leave here."

"Um, I'm pretty sure I'm steering the ship, God willing, of course." Malachi chuckled.

Cherish looked back out over her property once more. She'd daydreamed about them living on the property as a young married couple and raising their children on the farm.

"Are you sure you don't want to come to Annie's wedding tomorrow?" he asked.

Cherish shook her head. "No. You and Ada go. I don't like to leave the farm with no one on it."

He laughed. "Why? It's not going anywhere."

"I know but... the truth is I'm really not in the mood for a wedding. Or to look at the sea of gingerbread houses that would be at the wedding. Ada saw them all yesterday at Annie's place and she can't stop talking about them." Cherish bit her lip. That sounded like an awful thing to say and she regretted it.

"You've never liked Annie much, have you?" Malachi asked.

Cherish laughed but only because she was totally surprised at his question. "Don't be silly. I like her. It's just that she gets along better with Ada, so I guess I let the two of them be friends."

"People can have more than one friend you know."

"I know that. Ada is more friendly with Annie's mother so it makes sense that she goes. Years ago, I thought you might like Annie as more than a friend."

"No. I've always told you we were just friends. Did it take her getting married for you to believe me?" Malachi asked.

Cherish nodded and smiled at him. "I know that now, but people always say that they're friends when they want to keep their relationship secret for a while. It's something I'd probably do. I mean, you don't want everyone giving their opinion on the person you're dating until you know how you feel about them yourself."

"Sounds like you've put a lot of thought into it."

Cherish shrugged her shoulders. "Not especially."

Malachi plucked a blade of grass and put the end of it in his mouth. "You sound like some kind of an expert."

"No. I'm not."

Malachi pushed his hat back slightly. "How many boyfriends have you had?"

Cherish guessed he hadn't had any girlfriends. He'd never spoken about any so he can't have been too involved with anyone. "I've had about as many boyfriends as you've had girl-friends."

Malachi laughed. "Wow, you've had that many? You *must* be an expert by now."

"Why? How many have you had? You haven't told me about any."

He gave a low chuckle. "You seriously want to know?"

She nodded. "Just tell me. I won't be shocked."

He looked out over the paddocks, and said in a soft voice, "None."

"Oh. That's what I thought." She stared at him when he kept quiet. He wasn't even looking at her. She had to ask the next question on her lips. "Why not?"

"Because the woman I want is a bit tricky." He still wasn't looking at her.

She narrowed her eyes. Was he talking about her? Could she be the woman he wanted? "Tell me about her."

"Nah. There's too much to tell and we're trying to sort out your problems at the minute, not mine."

Cherish wasn't going to let it go. Not if there was a chance he could be talking about her. "My problems can wait. They're not going away anytime soon. Now tell me about this woman. What's the best thing you like about her?"

A smile hinted around his lips. "The way her cheeks flush red when she's embarrassed. The way she talks too much when she gets flustered. The way she blurts out things without thinking and then regrets it later. There are other things too but they can't be said with words. They have to be felt."

Cherish could feel her cheeks burning as hope overflowed within her body. "And why isn't she your girlfriend?" Cherish's heart pumped hard against her chest, hoping he'd admit she was the one.

"It's complicated. I'm not sure how she feels and I don't want to ruin things between us. I have to wait and see how things go."

"But don't you have so much more to gain by saying something?" she asked.

He moved his mouth to one side. "It's risky."

Cherish pushed a little further. "Is she worth the risk?"

He gulped. "She sure is."

With the worst timing in the world, Ada called out from the house, "Malachi, Cherish, I've made soup. It's on the table. Hurry up or it will get cold, and take your shoes off, Malachi. I've just washed the floor."

Malachi smiled at Cherish as he stood.

She wasn't going to let him off the hook. "To be continued," she said as she got to her feet.

He didn't comment as he started walking toward the house. She caught up to him. It had taken ages to get him to the point of talking about dating and women. What if she wasn't the woman he liked? What if he was talking about some other woman? Thanks to Ada and her dreadful timing, she might never find out.

"Well, say something." They were nearly at the house and Cherish couldn't take the silence any longer.

He raised his eyebrows. "Ada's been busy cleaning and making soup."

Cherish gave up. If he didn't want to talk about 'them' then neither would she. "I know. She said she's making up for visiting Annie yesterday. I'm a little shocked she was willing to go to Annie's by herself. She hardly ever takes a horse and buggy out alone these days."

"It's different here. There's hardly any traffic."

"I guess. What are you wearing to the wedding tomorrow?" Cherish asked.

"I have a suit."

"You do? I've never seen you in one."

"There's a first time for everything. You'll see me tomorrow. Are you sure you won't come?"

"No, thanks. I'll stay here with Wally. I'm sure he'll keep me company." Cherish glanced behind her at Malachi's faithful goose.

"He will. I just wish I could take him with me."

Cherish laughed. "You can't do that. It'd be a weird sight."

Ada opened the front door and once they'd taken off their boots, Ada ushered them through to the kitchen.

"Smells delicious as always," Malachi said as he sat down at the kitchen table.

Ada smiled like she always did when someone complimented her cooking. "It's just a simple meal of corn and chicken soup."

Malachi looked over the various salads and other vegetables on the table. "Looks like a feast to me."

After they said their silent prayer of thanks for the food, Cherish ate her corn and chicken soup, thinking about the men who'd been interested in her over the years. Then she looked over at Malachi. Some of the other men had been better looking, and had more going for them, but there was always something missing. That 'something' had prevented her from getting too close to them.

"This is really good, Ada. Thanks," Malachi said.

Cherish mindlessly agreed, "Yes, it is."

"I offered to help at the wedding, but I was told I should rest. They don't know me if they think I'll just sit around at the wedding and not help in the kitchen."

"No, they don't know you very well, Ada." Cherish said.

"Well, they'll soon get to know me."

"Are you sure you won't come with us tomorrow, Cherish?" Malachi asked.

"No. I'll stay here with Wally."

"I was seriously thinking of taking him," Malachi said.

Ada turned to him, horrified. "You can't take a goose to a wedding. One of the cooks will think he's the main course. He'll be in the oven faster than you can blink."

Cherish's mouth opened in shock. "Don't say that in front of him, Ada."

Ada's eyebrows rose. "Say it in front of Malachi or Wally?"

"Both. Either."

Malachi finally agreed. "Okay. I'll leave him here for Cherish to look after."

"That'll be fine. We get along well. I mean we would if you weren't here, Malachi. He might even follow me."

Ada chuckled. "I'm glad we've got that sorted out. I don't know what the pair of you would do without me around."

Cherish looked over at Malachi and they exchanged a smile.

Ada happened to catch a glimpse of their shared moment. For years, Ada had thought Cherish and Malachi would make a good pair, so why were they taking so long about it? Ada knew that if she pushed Cherish a certain way, it wouldn't be appreciated. All Ada could do was watch and pray, wait and hope.

One day, Cherish might see that Malachi was the perfect choice for her. As her farm manager, Malachi was in a difficult position if he showed his feelings and they weren't returned. Ada was certain Malachi was in love with Cherish. It was obvious the way his eyes softened when he looked at her.

CHAPTER 12

$\mathcal{W}$hile Malachi and Ada were at Annie Whylie's wedding, Cherish sat with Wally on the hill, eating a cheese sandwich.

If Malachi liked her, he'd have to do something about it. She was through with giving him hints. She'd done that yesterday and nothing had come of it.

"You know him best, Wally? What advice can you give me?"

Wally just made himself comfortable, tucking his legs under himself as he lowered his body to the ground. Every so often, Cherish would break off tiny pieces of bread and feed it to Wally.

"I guess it'll be lonely if I ever do move here. I won't have you because you'll be wherever Malachi is, but I'll have Caramel, and Timmy and Tommy. They're good company. I once thought that I'd move here with Bliss or Favor. Bliss is married now and Favor will be married soon. I'm all on my own."

"You don't have to be." It was Malachi's voice. He was back.

Cherish jumped up in fright, dropping what was left of her sandwich. "Oh, Wally just ate the rest of my cheese sandwich." She turned to see Malachi was standing there in a suit, looking like the most handsome man on the planet. He completely took her breath away. She hadn't seen Ava or Malachi leave because she'd slept in and they'd left so early. When she realised her mouth was gaping open, she closed it, but she still couldn't take her eyes from him. "What are you doing? Why aren't you at the wedding?"

"I had somewhere more important to be," Malachi said.

"Where?"

A smile tickled the corners of his lips. "Here with you."

Heat rose in her cheeks. "But isn't Annie your best friend? She'll want you there."

"She's a friend. I wouldn't say she's my best friend. You seem upset about something and I don't like to see you like this," Malachi said.

"I feel bad that you missed the wedding, Malachi."

"I didn't miss the whole thing. I do have to go back and get Ada. When I return, I'll grab something to eat there, and no one will ever know I left. Hey, you can come too if you want."

"Won't all that going back and forward be too much for the horse?" Cherish asked.

"I'll hitch the other horse. There's no problem I can't solve." He placed his hands on his hips.

Cherish burst out laughing. Mostly, she was nervous about what he might say. This was the first time they were completely alone together on the farm. There was no Ada to interrupt them. "I still don't know why you came back."

"I thought you might've changed your mind about going," Malachi said.

"I was just sitting here, thinking."

He moved closer. "About Annie's wedding?"

"No. This and that. Life in general. I suppose I should've gone to the wedding. It's a little rude of me since I'm here, so close, and everything."

"You can still go. Let's do it."

Cherish looked down at her clothes. "I'll need to change."

"You look fine to me," Malachi said.

"Give me two minutes. I'll change."

"Okay. While you're doing that, I'll unhitch the horse and hitch the other one."

Cherish bunched up the sides of her dress in her hands and ran to the house. Her mood was greatly improved seeing that Malachi made the effort to come back to see her. Could he have missed her?

After she changed into her Sunday best, she headed outside. Maybe on the drive there, he'd mention something about that kiss.

Malachi was leaning against the buggy, waiting for her. He'd already closed Wally in the barn. He had to do that or Wally would try to follow them.

Cherish glanced down at her dress as she asked Malachi, "Hey, what do you think of this dress? It's new."

"Looks lovely to me, but I can't say I know much about clothes."

"Well, you look nice in your suit. You should wear it all the time."

He laughed as he opened the buggy door for her. "Let's go. Right now, we have the end of a wedding to attend."

Cherish giggled as she climbed into the buggy. "I could do with a piece of cake or two."

"You're always thinking about food." He jumped into the driver's seat.

She slapped him playfully on his shoulder. "Am not."

"You are." Malachi laughed as he moved the horse and buggy away from the farm.

"I just eat because I need to eat. Everyone does."

"Yeah, but you don't have to eat cookies and cake all the time. That's all you ever eat."

"That's because they taste good."

"I can't disagree with you there."

"I am getting a bit hungry. I hope there's some food left when we get there." Cherish looked over at him.

"I saw you eating just now. You were having a sandwich."

"That's right, but it wasn't that tasty. Thanks for coming to get me. You didn't need to do that."

"I thought about you being all by yourself. It was odd because you normally love being around people. You've been acting distracted."

"I've got a lot going on."

"Levi and your mother?"

Cherish nodded. "Yes, and other things. Things that I don't want to talk about." An anxious feeling gnawed at Cherish's stomach. Did he like her or not? The last thing she wanted was to end up getting hurt. "It's a wonder Favor and the Koppels didn't go to Annie's wedding. It's not that far for them."

"Who knows their reasoning. Why? Do you want to see Simon again?"

Cherish stared at him to see if he was joking. He wasn't. "No. Of course not."

"Well, you liked him once. That's why you brought him to the farm."

Cherish twisted to face him better. "Can you stop talking about me and Simon? It's really quite annoying. He's marrying Favor in a week. I'm not sure what you're trying to say."

"I can stop talking altogether if it suits you."

She could tell by Malachi's clenched jaw and the way his knuckles were gripping the buggy lines that he was annoyed.

Cherish wanted a man who was easy going and good natured. At this time, Malachi was showing her that he was neither of those things if he'd suddenly gotten into a dark mood.

Maybe her judgment was off, and it had been 'off' for the past three years.

CHAPTER 13

*A*s soon as they arrived at the wedding, Cherish wished she'd been left at home with her thoughts. "Thanks for bringing me here."

"You've already thanked me," Malachi muttered, as he jumped out of the buggy.

Before he could help her down, she got out too and walked into the crowd. With the mood he was in, she didn't even wait for him to tend to his horse.

Looking around, she saw a couple of people she recognized. She didn't know that many people since she hadn't been to many of the meetings for Malachi's community over the last few years.

Then she spotted Ada with an armful of dirty plates. This was a rare time she was pleased to see her.

Ada looked up and smiled as she walked over. "You came?"

"*Jah*. Malachi came back and got me."

"I won't ask why or how that came about. Seems like a jolly waste of time, and the poor horse must be worn out."

"Malachi swapped horses when he got home."

"Collect all those dishes on the table and follow me inside." Ada nodded at a table.

Cherish was a little shocked. She hadn't volunteered to be one of the helpers, but she was grateful to have something to do. The last thing she felt like doing was talking to a bunch of strangers, trying to think of something interesting to say.

She joined Ada and a bunch of other women in the kitchen. A buzz of several conversations met Cherish's ears. The women seemed to be talking all at once as dirty and clean dishes were passing from hand to hand. Ada came up to her and took the plates from her and piled them on one side of the sink.

Then Ada sidled up to her. "You missed the whole thing, you know."

"Yeah, I thought I would."

"Go out and congratulate the happy couple. Then come back here and help."

"Sure." Cherish headed out of the kitchen to find the newlyweds, but something in the living room caught her eye. There was a table full of cakes and desserts, and then there was a second table with people gathered around it. She moved closer and saw the second table had four gingerbread houses on it.

That didn't surprise Cherish at all. She knew she couldn't escape being at Annie's house without seeing or hearing about gingerbread houses.

They drew her in. Annie's mother's cakes were always detailed and fabulous. The first cake Cherish saw looked like it had small children outside in the yard. They were made out of candy. Or were they made out of hard frosting? Hmm.

When a couple of people opposite her moved away to look at the next table of cakes, Cherish couldn't resist snapping off one of the babies.

She popped it in her mouth before anyone saw.

Then she had her answer—hard frosting.

She moved onto the next one and took a piece of candy from the side. That too went into her mouth. She also took pieces off the next two. By the time she got to the desserts, she didn't feel like any. Then she went outside to find the happy bride so she could offer Annie her best wishes.

The first thing she spotted was Malachi talking to a young woman at one of the tables. They were both eating cake. The sight sent pangs of jealousy right through her. Who was that woman and why was he talking to her and smiling? He hadn't been smiling during their buggy ride.

Cherish decided to forget him and found Annie and her husband at the top table. They were both talking to people. Cherish came close and waited. When Annie saw her, she flew out of her chair and ran to her.

"You came."

"Of course. I wouldn't miss it."

"Malachi thought you'd be feeling better. I told him to go fetch you."

Cherish wasn't happy to hear that. "You told him to get me?"

"Yes, and just as well because here you are, all better."

"That's right. Congratulations on being married."

"Thank you. You'll have to meet my husband." Annie

giggled and covered her mouth. "Oh, I just can't get used to saying that. My husband," she said again and another flurry of giggles followed. When Annie turned around, her husband was gone. "I don't know where he is. He was just there."

"I'll meet him soon. How long have you known him?"

"Three or four years. We only started dating six months ago and we both knew."

Cherish was looking at Malachi out of the corner of her eye. "Knew what?"

"We knew we were meant to be together." Annie sighed. "Love is just wonderful. You just wait, Cherish. You'll find out."

"I'll have to take your word for it."

"What are you looking at, Cherish?" Annie followed her line of vision.

Cherish bit her lip. She didn't know she was making it obvious. "I'm looking for all the cakes and gingerbread houses. I've been looking forward to seeing them. Malachi said your mother made some special ones."

"Oh, Cherish. You won't believe how delightful they are. Come and see them." Annie looped her arm through Cherish's and led her into the house.

On a table in the living room were the four gingerbread houses. Annie explained at length what each cake represented. One was a representation of Annie's childhood and it even had a representation of Annie and the two cats she was raised with —made out of hard frosting. The next one was Annie over the last ten years. The third was for Annie's wedding, and the fourth was for Annie's future and had many tiny candy babies.

"Oh no!" Annie gasped.

"What's the matter?"

Annie pointed to the babies playing in the green yard. "A baby's missing."

Cherish felt dreadful. She'd eaten Annie's baby! "You mean those little things are not for eating?"

Annie sighed. "No. Everyone would know that. Why would someone do that?"

"I have no idea. That's awful." Cherish touched her lips, hoping she didn't have any remnants around her mouth.

Annie leaned over one of the gingerbread houses. "Oh, and look. Something's broken off this one too."

"That's awful. Don't worry. It would've been someone who didn't know they couldn't eat them. Perhaps one of the children did it."

"You're right. It must've been one of the children. I mean, they are for eating, but the ones for eating today are on another table. I don't know when we'll eat these."

"Your mother has a talent for doing these."

"She does. Most of all she's been a great mom. Come and meet some people. You'll have to get to know everyone when you move here. Best you start to get to know them now."

"Okay. Great!" As they moved toward some people, Cherish reflected on how awful she'd been to Annie over the years. Now Cherish felt awful about ruining the gingerbread houses. What a truly awful person she was. No wonder Malachi was talking to another woman. Why couldn't she be more good-natured like Annie, or even Bliss? Bliss would never have snapped off one of those babies.

Forcing a smile, Cherish let Annie take her around and introduce her to everyone at the wedding.

CHAPTER 14

*A*da and Cherish stayed at the farm for a week before Wilma, Debbie and Jared arrived. On the day of their arrival, Ada was unbelievably excited. She'd spent most of the day in the kitchen, cooking. Cherish tried to help her, but her talents in the kitchen weren't up to Ada's standards. The closer it got to evening, the more edgy Ada became.

"Not like that, Cherish. Here give it to me." Ada ripped the spatula from Cherish's hand and nudged her to the side with her hip. "You must whisk gravy quickly, like this or it all sticks to the saucepan."

"Okay Ada, I'll set the table. You can do the gravy."

"I'm trying to teach you. If you don't look and listen you'll never learn."

Cherish turned away from Ada and rolled her eyes before she grabbed some plates from the cupboard. *Mamm*, Debbie, and Jared were arriving any minute.

Cherish walked to the table and set the plates down. She

glanced out the back window and saw Malachi walking in from the barn. Wally followed close behind. Then Malachi played with Wally by running in circles and zig zagging. Wally spread his wings and stuck out his long neck, and then his wings flapped with excitement. Cherish laughed to herself.

Ada suddenly spoke. "I think I hear a car. Quickly! help me get the pork out of the oven." Ada tipped the gravy into a jug.

Cherish walked toward Ada and put on her oven mitts. Cherish opened the oven door and took hold of the baking tray.

"Quickly, they'll be walking in any minute!" Ada barked, causing Cherish to jump. The pork fell to one side of the tray.

Scalding fat splashed on Cherish's wrist. "Oh! Ouch!" Cherish yelled as she jumped back watching in horror as the tray fell to the floor. Cherish then looked down and saw hot juices and vegetables strewn all over the floor.

"Are you okay?" Malachi appeared in the kitchen and ran toward her.

"Oh my… Cherish you're so clumsy. I spent hours chopping those vegetables! Everything is ruined!" Ada quickly leaned down and started picking up the food. "Luckily the meat stayed in the tray." She grabbed a dish towel and picked up the tray of meat and set it on the stove.

"I'm fine thanks, Malachi." By now, Cherish was fed up. She had listened to Ada complaining all day about this and that, and picking on every little thing she did. It was worse than being around *Mamm* on a bad day.

"No, you're not okay, Cherish. Look at your arm." Malachi pointed at Cherish's arm.

Cherish looked down. "It is a bit sore, but it's okay."

"Some burns can hurt for days after." Malachi grabbed her

hand and walked her over to the sink. Cherish watched as he ran her arm under the cold water. She felt his fingers, lightly touching her skin to observe the damage. She looked at his face, still covered with dirt from the day's work. He was genuinely concerned about her. This was the same warmth and tenderness she'd felt from him three years ago. He did care!

"Hello! We're here," Wilma announced as she walked through the front door. Debbie and Jared followed close behind. "Malachi, will you be a dear and get our bags?" Wilma called out.

"Of course, Wilma," he replied as he walked toward the front door. Malachi turned back to Cherish. "Keep your arm under the cold water for a few more minutes."

"Oh, what's happened?" Wilma blurted when she saw Cherish at the sink.

Ada got in first. "I'll tell you what happened, it all landed on the floor. All of the vegetables, everything but the meat."

"Oh, never mind about my arm," Cherish said.

"It's still there, isn't it?" Ada snapped. "It's good that I made macaroni and cheese as well, or we'd be eating only pork and bread tonight. I do look forward to eating my vegetables in the evening." Ada plopped the bowl heavily on the table.

"I'm sorry I burned myself and spilled the vegetables, but don't worry I'm okay," Cherish said, sarcastically.

"It was an accident, wasn't it?" Wilma asked.

Cherish turned off the tap. "I surely didn't do it on purpose."

"Are you okay, Cherish?" Debbie asked.

"She burned herself while spilling all our vegetables on the floor," Ada told her.

Jared grabbed the forks and started banging them on the table.

"Don't do that, Jared." Debbie took the forks from him and picked him up and put him on a chair. "Don't touch anything," she warned him. "The food smells delicious, Ada."

"Well, it's just pork now and macaroni and cheese. Most of the deliciousness will be ending up in the trash." Ada shook her head.

"The animals will eat them," Cherish said, hating to see anything on the farm go to waste.

"Everybody to the table," Ada announced. "Sorry there's no vegetables tonight. Cherish was clumsy and dropped them on the floor." Ada shook her head.

Cherish frowned. "Yes, everyone knows that by now, Ada."

Debbie noticed Cherish looking defeated. "Sit next to me, Cherish."

Cherish sat down next to her.

"It looks delicious, don't you think, Jared?" Debbie asked.

"No!" Jared screamed as he reached over and stuck his small hand in the middle of the large bowl of macaroni.

"Stop! No!" Debbie jumped out of her seat to catch his hand. It was too late. The macaroni went flying across the room, straight into Malachi who was walking around the corner into the kitchen.

"Whoa!" Malachi said as he jumped back in shock. Macaroni hit his shirt and fell onto the floor.

"Jared, say you're sorry to Malachi now," an embarrassed Debbie said.

"No, I'm not!" Jared screamed.

"I'm so sorry, Malachi," Debbie said. "He's overtired."

"Don't be concerned, it's just a bit of food. I liked to throw food too when I was young." Malachi walked to the table, giving Jared a smile before sitting down next to Cherish.

"I'll clean it up after dinner," Cherish told Debbie.

"Is that all you have to say or do about it, Debbie?" Ada asked. Ada then asked Wilma, "Wilma, are you going to say something?"

Wilma stood, looking quite shocked about all the mess. "Shall we clean the floor before we eat?"

"No. Leave it so we can be reminded it's a mixture of Cherish's error and Jared's behavior. What Cherish did was an accident so I suppose we can't blame her, but what Jared did wasn't an accident."

Debbie didn't want to start her few days away like this. Coming to the wedding was the first vacation she'd had since Jared was born.

Why did Ada have to pick on Jared so much? Debbie already felt like everyone was judging her as a bad parent. She couldn't raise a hand to Jared. Not after all the strappings she'd endured throughout her childhood. Ada was always telling her Jared needed a belting.

"Oh, Ada, he's just a boy," Wilma said. "Do you know what I'm more concerned about? The fact that Harriet manipulated Favor and Simon into having the wedding at their farm!" Wilma sat heavily in the chair. "Thanks for this food. We're so hungry. We didn't stop once on the way because we knew you'd have cooked us something special."

Ada eyed Cherish.

"I spilled the food. I'm sorry. Ada took a long time preparing the food. Sorry I ruined it." Then Cherish couldn't hold back her thoughts any longer. *"Mamm,* Favor didn't have a choice. You know what Simon's like. She will end up doing whatever Simon's mother wants for the rest of her life."

"Cherish! That's a dreadful thing to say. They are a loving family." Ada glared at Cherish.

Cherish didn't even look at Ada. She knew Ada was just saying that because Simon's mother, Harriet, was a good friend of hers.

"Put it behind you, Wilma, or you won't enjoy the wedding. It's already been decided," Debbie said.

"Yes, yes, I know," Wilma said dismissively as she buried her head in her hands.

"I'm going to ignore the food and the grease on the floor and suggest we all do the same until after we eat. Let us give thanks for what the Lord has provided," Ada suggested. "And we'll ignore what happened to the macaroni or we'll have little to eat tonight."

"I'm sorry," Debbie said.

"Did anyone notice that Cherish burned her arm badly?" Malachi asked.

"We did. How is it now, Cherish?" *Mamm* asked.

"It's just a little burn." She showed her mother her arm. "But now it's starting to hurt."

Mamm had a close look. "It doesn't look too bad."

Cherish didn't say anything, but now it was starting to sting as well.

"Let's give our thanks before the food gets colder than it already is," Ada suggested.

They all closed their eyes and said their own silent prayer of thanks for the food.

CHERISH WAS grateful when dinner was finally over. It was embarrassing to have all that drama going on in front of Malachi. But it wasn't the first time he'd been amongst it.

Ada had gone to her bedroom. Cherish and Debbie washed the dishes together while Wilma and Malachi sat by the fire, talking. Jared had gone to bed early after he spat at Ada when she'd looked at him unkindly during their dessert of cream and fruit salad.

Debbie washed the dishes while Cherish stood with her back leaning on the sink, drying the dishes when Debbie passed them to her.

They stood in silence as they did the cleaning, both in their own minds. Cherish overheard Wilma laughing at something Malachi had said. She couldn't help but wonder what they were talking about.

During the meal, they'd managed to stay off the subject of the Koppel's stealing the wedding somewhat, but as soon as they walked into the other room, Wilma did nothing but complain about the Koppels.

CHAPTER 15

When Debbie and Cherish finished cleaning the kitchen, they joined Malachi and Wilma in the living room. "How are you feeling now, *Mamm?*" Cherish asked.

Wilma's mouth pulled down at the corners. "How would I be feeling? I think Favor's too young to marry. Besides my doubts about that, they stole my wedding from me. Levi won't be able to see Favor get married. He's upset. He doesn't say anything though. I told him he shouldn't make the trip."

Cherish made a suggestion. "As Debbie said, the decision's already been made. Let's look at what good things are happening. At least Samuel's watching over Levi and looking after the animals."

"I know. It's nice that we have good friends." Wilma looked around. "Where's Ada?"

"She's gone to bed already," Debbie said.

"Oh. She didn't even say goodnight."

"I think she was very tired." Debbie did her best to cover a yawn with her hand.

"I hope I didn't offend Ada with the things I said about Harriet. Cherish, you're the only one of Favor's sisters coming. Well, Florence is coming with Carter and Iris, but they have enough money to do anything they choose. Everyone else would come if they could afford it. Favor should have been more thoughtful about where she agreed to have the wedding."

"Favor will be so happy that they're coming," Debbie said, trying to introduce some positivity.

"If they had it at home, at our orchard, everyone would've been able to come." *Mamm* pouted, puffing out her cheeks.

"I know, but that's not what Favor chose. We have to respect that," Debbie added.

"Never! I'll never agree with Favor's choice. The wedding is always held at the bride's home."

"Not always, *Mamm*," Cherish said.

Mamm narrowed her eyes. "Always, in our family."

"Florence eloped. Are you forgetting that?" Cherish asked.

"I'm not counting her. She left. She wouldn't have expected to have her wedding at our house after that choice."

Cherish could tell how upset her mother was and she couldn't blame her. Harriet, Favor's mother-in-law-to-be, was forceful when she wanted her way about something. In Cherish's opinion, *Mamm* was right to be upset. Harriet did steal the wedding from *Mamm*.

But Cherish kept her opinion to herself knowing *Mamm* might become even more distraught about the whole thing. Besides all that, *Mamm* grumbling to Malachi was embarrassing.

He was sitting there listening, looking like he'd rather be anywhere but in the middle of this conversation.

"Tomorrow is Favor's special day and it's odd to be going to it, rather than hosting it. Can you see that, Malachi? I'm sure you can."

Malachi looked up. "I can understand how that would make you feel. I don't know the answer."

Mamm sighed. "There is no answer. Thanks for listening, all of you. I know I've probably been annoying, but it's upsetting for a mother. If I totally approved of the man she chose, that would lessen my anguish."

Cherish gasped that her mother would say such a thing in front of Malachi. Although, her dislike of the Koppels was probably already obvious.

Debbie whispered, "Don't say that in front of Ada. She loves the Koppels, and thinks it's a wonderful match. I don't have an opinion either way. He seems like a nice young man. I just say it's Favor's choice. She's happy so we can all be happy for her."

Wilma nodded. "Yes. We can all be happy. We have no choice. Tomorrow, she'll be married. You are coming with us to the wedding aren't you, Malachi?"

"Yes. I am, if that's all right."

Cherish said, "Ada ordered a vehicle big enough to take us all."

"Ah good. Now, I'll keep quiet," Wilma said. "I'll hold my tongue forever. What else am I to do? They'll be joined in the sight of *Gott*. I can't speak against that."

Debbie put her hand lightly on Wilma's shoulder. "How about a nice hot cup of tea?"

Wilma nodded. "I'd like that. I'll just put out of my mind

that I had nothing to do with the wedding plans, making the wedding clothes or even the food. I'll also put out of my mind that I'm not sleeping in the same *haus* as my daughter who's getting married tomorrow."

Debbie was on her way to the kitchen, and said over her shoulder, "At least she didn't elope or marry in secret. You'll get to be at her wedding."

Wilma nodded, and murmured, "There's always someone worse off I suppose. I'll count my blessings."

CHAPTER 16

*A*t the Koppel house on the morning of Favor's wedding, tears flooded Favor's eyes. She yanked and pulled at the dress Harriet had finished sewing the night before. Favor's stomach churned when she saw her reflection in the window pane.

All the guests would be arriving soon, and the dress was awful. She'd told Harriet she wanted a blue dress. The color was so dark that it wasn't blue at all. It was such a dark shade of blue that it was almost black.

Apart from the dreadful color, so unsuited to a wedding, it was way too big. The sleeves hung down past her fingers, and instead of ending just below her knees, the dress ended at her calves, not far above her ankles.

The fabric was so awful and scratchy that Favor was sure Harriet used cheap material she'd had stored away in a cupboard for the past twenty years. That notion was reinforced by the horrible, musty odor.

How had she let it come this far?

Favor knew she should've put her foot down with Harriet a long time ago, but if she'd done that, Simon might've broken up with her. She couldn't risk that.

The door opened and Favor was delighted to see Cherish. "There you are," Cherish said, smiling from ear to ear. "It's your wedding day! I just saw Carter and Florence downstairs. They look so excited to be here. Have you seen them yet?" Cherish put out her arms to embrace Favor, but Favor just stood there, looking down at her dress.

"Oh, Cherish. Look at this."

Cherish's gaze fell on the awful dress. "Is… is that what you're wearing?" Cherish stuttered. The hesitance in her voice made it obvious to Favor that yes, it was that bad.

"*Nee*, I cannot wear this dress. It's horrible. It doesn't even fit me right!" Favor threw herself onto the bed. Her mind filled with doubts. Would she be able to deal with Simon's parents forever? She felt Cherish sit next to her.

"Come on, Favor, it's your wedding day! Cheer up, it's not the ugliest dress I've ever seen."

"It's black!"

"I can see that."

"I don't know what to do." Favor sat up to face Cherish, tears still falling down her face. "You don't understand, it's horrible here at the farm. Simon can't say no to his parents. They're so demanding. What will my future look like here? Will he still listen to his mother over me when we have children of our own? He really can't say no to her."

"I know, we all know." Cherish said as she wiped a tear from

Favor's cheek. "You don't have to marry him if you don't want to, you know? It's not too late to change your mind."

"Don't be stupid, Cherish, of course I won't back out. This is the life I chose. I hope I can cope though. It's hard seeing him asking his mother's opinion on everything and ignoring mine. Sometimes he agrees with me and then switches when he finds out his mother has a different opinion. Even things to do with the wedding and it's *my* wedding. It's not his mother's."

"Well, we all knew what he was like from the beginning. We also knew that you'd probably end up marrying him anyway."

"What's that supposed to mean?" Favor grabbed a handkerchief from her bed and held it over her eyes.

Suddenly the door swung open, making them both jump. They turned around to see Ada and Wilma walking into the room.

"Favor! What's wrong?" Wilma exclaimed. Then Wilma's eyes fell on the dress. "You can't wear that, Favor. Stand up."

Favor stood and turned slowly in a circle.

Wilma shook her head. "It doesn't fit you right at all! Is this some kind of a joke?"

"I know it's bad!" Favor turned away from them.

"Shh, *Mamm*, let's not be hasty, I think it's fine. Let's not make matters worse today." Cherish passed her sister another handkerchief.

"Favor, is that your wedding dress? Why aren't you wearing the one Harriet made for you?" Ada asked.

"This is it!" Favor almost yelled.

"My. Truly?" Ada's eyes bugged out as she looked more closely at the dress.

"Yes. It's true," Cherish said.

"Oh dear. The first thing that comes to my mind when looking at the dress is, where's the funeral?" Ada stepped forward, picked up the hem and studied the stitches. She dropped the dress and shook her head.

"It's ugly. She can't wear a black dress." Wilma shook her head.

"It's a little late for that, Wilma," Ada said. "Anyway, Harriet's feelings would be hurt if Favor didn't wear the dress that she lovingly sewed."

"It's ugly! I'm sorry, but it is. What about your Sunday best dress?" Wilma suggested.

"Maybe. I'm not sure." Favor knew her Sunday best was her only option now. "How can I do that to Harriet? She would be offended, she wouldn't forgive me. Things are already tense between us ever since I insisted on having some particular food items for the meal after the wedding."

While everyone stood there in silence at her outburst, Favor knew the real problem wasn't Harriet. It was Simon. If Simon would understand, she might consider wearing something else, but she knew he would be upset with her if she didn't wear the dress his mother made. Favor felt her emotions overflow inside of her. This was supposed to be the happiest day in her life, but it was turning out to be the worst.

Cherish grabbed at one of Favor's sleeves. "Maybe we could tuck these up. Fold them back so at least your hands are showing."

Favor moved her hand away. "I don't think I can do this! What will my life be like here? It's so far away and all Simon does is whatever his *Mamm* wants! She sets the rules and he abides by them, even over me! I didn't want her to sew me a dress, and I didn't want to have my wedding here. I've always wanted to be married at my home, at the orchard. It's all about what *she* wants, I can't do this!" Favor broke down into tears once more. *Mamm* stepped in closer and Favor fell into her mother's arms and sobbed.

Ada took on her no nonsense tone. "Listen to me, Favor." Ada walked over to her, then adjusted Favor's prayer *kapp*. "You can always go back to the orchard, but we didn't travel all the way here just to watch you destroy a young man on his wedding day. This sounds like something you should have thought about before you made your loved ones travel halfway across the country. What will everyone think of us and you if you change your mind on today of all days?"

"Ada, come on now. You can see she's upset. She can change her mind and come home with us if that's what she wants," Cherish argued.

"It's true. You can," *Mamm* said, agreeing with Cherish over Ada for probably the very first time—ever. "Pack your bags and we'll leave."

Favor felt Ada's disappointment, but it made her think for a moment. She really did love Simon. The thought of losing him made her feel sick. He was so good to her, and he just wanted to do right by everyone. He was just being a good son when he agreed with his mother. Maybe when they were married, he'd do what she wanted.

"You two are making me feel awful. It is true, Favor, you don't have to marry him if you don't want," Ada said. "I'll support your decision, Favor. I'll even go and break the news to everyone now."

"*Nee*, I won't go home. I do love him." Favor wiped the tears from her eyes and then sniffed. She looked at herself in the reflection of the window pane once more. "I want to spend the rest of my life with him which is why I am making these sacrifices now. Things will get better. He loves his mother and that's why he agrees with her. When we're married, he'll agree with me. Our love will grow deeper."

"Trust in God and he will pave the way on your journey," Wilma said as she patted Favor's back.

"And wear your Sunday best dress." Ada said. "As much as Harriet is one of my dear friends, she can't sew. And I say that with much love."

"*Nee.*" Favor turned around to face them and lifted her chin. "I will wear this dress with confidence, for Simon."

"Okay Favor! All he cares about is making his mother happy anyway," Cherish blurted out. When everyone stared at her, she said, "What? I'm just agreeing with what she said."

"Are you in here, Favor?" someone said through the closed door.

"That's Florence! She'll be able to fix your dress, Favor," Cherish said.

Wilma was closest to the door, so she flung it open. When everyone had greeted her, Florence stared in horror at Favor's dark dress.

Florence pointed at the dress. "What's that?"

Favor looked down at it. "Harriet made it for me, and I've decided to wear it. I know it's awful, but that's just how it is."

"Can you fix it?" *Mamm* asked.

Everyone stared at Florence.

"How much time have I got?"

"Half an hour probably," Ada said.

"I can bring it in quite a bit." Florence moved forward and held the dress at the sides.

"Could you? Oh, Florence, that would be so wonderful, and Harriet would never know because she's never seen me in it."

Florence frowned. "You didn't try it on while she was working on it?"

"No. She only finished it last night. She wouldn't even show me the fabric. I just said I wanted blue."

"That's black," Florence said, frowning.

Ada said, "It's blue according to Harriet, but let's not waste time debating. Favor, grab a needle and thread and get that dress off so Florence can save the day. Everyone else can leave the room!"

"You've saved my life, Florence. Look at the *kapp,* though. It's so large and horrible. Perhaps I should just wear my everyday one."

Florence smiled. "Did Harriet make that too?"

"Yes."

"Well, I have brought with me a present from Christina."

"No!" Favor covered her mouth and happy tears filled her eyes. "She made me a prayer *kapp?*"

"Yes. Carter's got it downstairs. And you can tell Harriet it was a wedding gift, so you had to wear it."

"That's *wunderbaar* and Harriet won't mind a bit."

"I'll fetch it now," Ada said as she was halfway out the door.

Favor hugged Florence tightly. "Thank you for coming. Thank you for being the very best sister ever."

Now tears welled in Florence's eyes. So many times over these past years she missed being at the farm with all her half-sisters. She'd been like a mother to them and they'd relied on her for everything. It'd been a hard and busy life back then, but there were many moments of joy and family togetherness that she'd hold close to her heart forever. She knew it was now time. It was time for her and Carter to add a second child to their family, God willing. Iris needed to experience growing up with a sibling just the same as she'd grown up in a bubbly and lively household.

CHAPTER 17

*A*t the ceremony, the bishop had to yell as he read, the heavy rain outside making it hard for anyone to hear. The room was filled with the scent of freshly baked goods that lined the table at the back of the room. Along with the baked goods, Favor caught a whiff of the pleasant fragrance from the flower petals spread along the floor.

The flower petals were Favor's idea and she had to fight Harriet to get them. In the end, she had to settle for dried flowers rather than fresh, but Favor was pleased with the win, however small.

Favor sat on the front bench with Simon, listening to the bishop's words. She was thankful that her wedding dress now looked like a dress, instead of the sack that it was before Florence came to her rescue. The *kapp* from Christina was just perfect, as she knew it would be. Both Christina and Florence had been given the gift of excellent needlework skills. Favor silently thanked God that Florence and Carter had gone out of their way to come to her wedding. Florence hadn't forgotten their family when she'd moved on with her life outside of the community.

Favor looked out the window at the pouring rain that had forced them to marry inside.

Was this a sign from God that all wouldn't be well with their marriage?

Favor had wanted the ceremony in the garden seeing it was a Spring wedding rather than the usual wintertime one.

The room was filled with guests who stood shoulder to shoulder as there wasn't much room for many rows of benches inside the house.

As she turned and caught Harriet's eye, her mind flooded with doubts once more. Had her almost-mother-in-law created the awful dress as an attempt to embarrass her?

Suddenly remembering what she'd looked like in the dress, she felt her chest tighten and her face go bright red with embarrassment at what might have been.

I can't do this, I can't do this!

Favor took a deep breath and closed her eyes. Turning to face Simon, she opened them to see his handsome, smiling face. Suddenly, it didn't matter that she was getting married in a dress so dark that everyone thought it was black. It didn't matter that she looked like she was going to a funeral rather than a wedding. And it didn't matter about his mother.

A wave of relief rushed over her body as she felt the love and devotion coming from him.

She was doing all of this for him and she'd surely be rewarded somehow. She'd be rewarded for putting up with

Harriet, and trying to go along with everything that was so odd in comparison to the family she'd been used to.

Maybe she'd even be rewarded for wearing the dress to save anyone's feelings from being hurt. Perhaps she'd also be rewarded for going through with the wedding when part of her wanted to run.

She could go home, but what would she be going home to? Simon wouldn't be there, and that didn't even make sense. Sitting here with him now, she realized she was where she belonged—with the man she loved.

"And now I'd like to welcome Malcolm to sing for us," the bishop said, interrupting Favor's thoughts.

She watched as Malcolm stood up. He looked around at everyone and then took a deep breath in. Then out of his mouth came his deep voice that was surely a gift from God. She was sure heaven would be full of such wonderful voices. Everyone in the room had to feel close to God whenever Malcolm sang the Godly words of praise and devotion.

Wilma watched on, feeling a little disheartened. Almost all her children had gotten married and left home. She felt grateful Cherish was still at the house. She had Debbie too, but she would soon be marrying Peter. They hadn't yet talked of marriage, but she knew it wouldn't be long. Harriet was seated directly in front of her. Wilma considered it quite rude she hadn't asked Wilma to sit with her. She'd been ignored from the moment she'd walked into the house hours earlier.

Then Wilma spied Florence and Carter with little Iris. They were standing at the side of the room with some other *Englishers*. It pleased Wilma that she was there. Florence hadn't entirely abandoned her girls. She was interested in more than managing the orchard and that was comforting.

Ada nudged Wilma, urging her to look at Harriet who was sniffing and wiping away tears. Wilma smiled, but she didn't feel like doing so. She should be the one crying, and they wouldn't be tears of happiness. Then a wicked thought occurred to Wilma. Maybe Harriet was crying because she saw someone had fixed the dress that she'd forced Favor to wear.

Harriet got everything her way. It'd been that way from the start of Favor and Simon's relationship. Favor was made to wed there at Harriet's farm and now look what happened—the rain and the awful dress. Wilma was sure God didn't approve of Favor marrying at the Koppels' farm and was showing His disapproval. It was good to know that God was on her side.

If they'd married at the orchard, the weather would have been beautiful. She looked over at Favor and hoped she hadn't given her the wrong advice. Should she have been more forceful in suggesting Favor change her mind and leave? Should she have encouraged her to flee? Flee from the Koppels? It was so hard to know what to do in certain situations.

When Malcolm finished his song, the bishop stood again.

All of a sudden, Ada leaped off her seat and then fell to the floor. Then Wilma noticed Jared had slipped out of Debbie's arms. Ada had been trying to catch him as he ran to the bishop down the aisle made by the two rows of benches.

"Stop! Stop!" Ada hissed as Jared gathered speed, followed closely by Debbie.

Then Debbie tripped over someone's feet, and Ada managed to pass her.

Jared threw his leg in the air, trying to kick the bishop. Just before he could reach him, Simon scooped him up in his arms. Simon then handed him back to an embarrassed Ada.

Wilma couldn't help but think… was this disruption another sign from God? Was her daughter's marriage doomed before it even began?

"Naughty boy, Jared! No supper for you tonight. I can't believe you just did that!" Ada yelled at the top of her lungs, clearly not caring that a peaceful wedding ceremony was happening. Jared was screaming and crying as she pulled him to the back of the room, scolding him the whole time. By this time, Debbie was back on her feet, walking quietly to the back of the room.

"We shall continue," the bishop said, in a calming way.

The next several minutes were a blur to Favor as her head pulsated and her vision blurred. She felt she was passing out, and had to fight it all the while. Then she heard the bishop say that they were now married, they were husband and wife. Relief washed over her, and she looked over at her husband and smiled.

They were married!

Simon was finally her husband.

He'd listen to her from now on. She'd be the main woman in his life now, and not Harriet.

It was done. She could relax.

Simon mouthed 'I love you.' A tear ran down her cheek as all her worries lifted from her. She mouthed back the same words and she knew at that moment that everything would be okay.

Everyone moved forward to congratulate them.

After she and Simon had greeted all the well-wishers, she

noticed how the room was set up. Harriet had done a great job, and the food smelled amazing.

Now she felt bad about having doubts and for saying horrid things about Harriet, who was now her mother-in-law.

She hitched up her sleeves that had fallen over her hands. Then she noticed her mother, alone, standing in the corner. *Mamm* probably wouldn't eat anything at all out of protest for not having the wedding at the orchard. *Mamm* had cooked for all of her children's weddings and had organized and planned what food they'd have. She'd been totally left out of this wedding. She left Simon and went over to talk with her. Favor thought it was time to thank her for being such a good mother.

Cherish didn't notice her mother looking sad at all. She was too busy eyeing her favorite Dutch apple dumplings, soft pretzels, shoofly pie, along with all the different varieties of smoked cheeses, and cured meats. The hot meats were on a table of their own. Cherish noticed the pork chops, ham and roast beef, but she was more interested in the desserts on the table next to them. As she went to grab a plate, still looking upon the food, she felt a hand brush into hers.

"Oh sorry!" she said as she turned and saw Malachi smiling at her, also reaching for a plate.

"Not at all, I was just grabbing this plate for you because I saw you fixated on the food," he said with a hint of a smile around his lips.

"*Ach*, thank you." She was a little embarrassed. "It's been a rough morning and I haven't eaten since last night!"

"What did you think of the wedding?" He stepped closer once again, brushing his hand over hers to reach for some bread. Her tummy filled with butterflies.

"I mean, it's a bit sad about the weather especially since Favor didn't want to have the wedding here at all, so having to have it indoors I think made her a little upset."

"Hopefully your wedding goes a little smoother than this." He started loading up his food onto the plate. "Do you want to get married soon?" he asked, deliberately avoiding her eyes.

Why is he asking me? She made a joke of it. "Is that a proposal?"

He laughed. "I didn't mean to marry *me*. You wouldn't want to do that."

"Cherish! I did it! I'm married," Favor exclaimed as she walked toward them. She was like a different person from the one who'd been crying about her dress earlier that day.

"Congratulations, Favor. You look beautiful. You look just like a proper bride."

Favor wedged herself between them. "Malachi, it's good to see you two talking!" Favor elbowed Malachi and gave Cherish a cheeky wink. "You know, I thought one day you two would get together!"

Cherish felt her cheeks burn.

"Really?" Malachi said, intrigued. "Why would you think that?"

"Oh come on, Malachi, you know I saw you two in the barn that time, kissing. You were both so close that a blade of grass couldn't fit between you."

"Favor, don't you need to say hi to your wedding guests?" Cherish gulped and added, "They've traveled long enough to be here." Cherish couldn't even look at Malachi with all the heat rising in her cheeks. She knew her face must've been beet red.

CHAPTER 18

"The barn?" Malachi replied, genuinely looking confused.

Favor hit his arm. "Oh come on, Malachi, don't pretend you don't remember! I saw you two share a kiss in the barn a few years ago. It was the first time I was at the farm. Cherish was bright red for days. Much like she is now." Favor giggled before she continued, "And she threatened me to never mention it. I never have until now, but you both know about it so where's the harm, hmm?"

Cherish was now looking at Malachi. Was he serious? How could he not remember? Did he go around kissing women all the time? She surely didn't want a man like that! And how could he forget such a moment? Her mood escalated from embarrassed to offended.

"I honestly don't recall. I'm sorry!" Malachi held his plate of food with one hand as he smoothed back his hair that had fallen across his face.

"Oh well, it mustn't have meant much then!" Cherish took her food and went to walk away.

"Wait, Cherish, you remember? What? We did?" He followed her.

She turned around to face him. "Yes, we did, but obviously it wasn't that big a deal for you or very memorable. No harm done!" Cherish walked away in a huff, taking a full plate of dumplings with her.

Favor took a couple of steps until she was level with him. "Wow, Malachi. You ruined that. Great work." Favor turned and hurried to catch up with her sister. "Cherish, wait up!" Favor yelled as she ran to catch up to her.

Cherish stopped and turned to face her. "Shh, Favor, don't embarrass me."

"Okay, but that was rude! Who else would he have kissed?" Favor asked as they sat down at the end of a large table.

"I don't know, but if he doesn't remember, I don't want to remember either!" Cherish shoved a whole Dutch apple dumpling into her mouth.

"I know you've had a thing for him since then, Cherish, I'm here if you need to talk."

"You better go back to Simon. You should be at your special wedding table with him." Cherish looked over at the table and saw Harriet sitting where Favor should've been. "You go back to Simon. I'll be okay," Cherish repeated. "This is your wedding. I don't want to ruin it for you."

"Are you sure you'll be all right?" Favor asked.

"I'll be fine." Cherish pulled the plate of dumplings closer. "As long as I can eat these I'll be fine. Go." Cherish bit into another one.

"Okay. Come and say goodbye before you go, okay? Don't forget."

"I will. We'll be here all day."

Favor gave her a hug and then left her. Cherish was a little surprised that Favor showed such compassion. Or was she so tragic at this moment that even someone as selfish as Favor was sorry for her.

Then when Cherish looked back at Simon, she saw Malachi still standing by the food, now speaking with *Mamm*. She noticed him looking over her way and when their eyes met, he deliberately looked away.

***

Later that evening, when the crowd had thinned, *Mamm* decided it was time to leave. "Everyone out the front in five minutes or you'll be left here." Wilma scurried around the now half-empty house. The sun was beginning to set as more people left. Cherish stood in the kitchen, watching Favor and Simon as they said goodbye to their guests at the door. It was nice to see Favor now in good spirits, much happier than Cherish had ever seen her. She was like a new woman.

"We should go too," Carter said, holding Iris's hand.

Florence added, "Iris has had a big day." Iris was shy and stepped behind Carter when Wilma tried to hug her goodbye.

"Another bonnet sister is married. That only leaves you, Cherish. You'll be next."

"Um, what did you call us?" Cherish asked.

Florence playfully slapped Carter's arm. "Don't mind him.

He has funny nicknames for people. He thinks they're funny even if other people don't."

"Hmm. I'm not sure I like what you just said, Carter." Ada raised her eyebrows, staring at him. Carter just laughed.

Cherish didn't care. She swooped behind Carter and grabbed Iris, causing her to giggle. Then Iris hugged Cherish. "Goodbye, Iris. I'll visit you soon after we get home. And remember, I'm your favorite aunty. Who's your favorite?"

"Aunt Cherish is."

"That's right."

"You're brainwashing her, Cherish," Carter said.

Cherish rose to her feet. "I'm just telling her the truth. She didn't allow anyone else to cuddle her, did she?"

"I guess not."

Favor moved forward with Simon to say goodbye to Florence and her family.

"Car's here!" Wilma hollered, not caring that there were other people in the house. "Debbie, Ada, Jared, Cherish, and Malachi out the front now!" she continued, as she pushed past Cherish nudging her along the way.

"We will come outside and wish you farewell." Harriet pulled her husband by the arm, leading him out the front door.

Cherish and everyone else followed them. The rain had finally stopped and Cherish breathed deeply in the fresh air. It had been so stuffy in the house with all those people. The cold breeze on her cheeks was so refreshing. She felt a certain peace listening to the wind rustling through the trees. Then she knew why. That sound reminded her of the orchard.

Looking back, she saw Carter, Florence and Iris getting in

their car. At the house, she saw Favor hand-in-hand with Simon. Right next to Simon stood Harriet and Melvin.

She continued watching as Malachi said his goodbyes and headed towards the car. He hadn't stopped looking at her since their conversation. Did he realize how obvious he was making it?

"Thank you for the lovely quilt you all made. It's so beautiful. It'll always remind me of home." Favor said as she hugged Wilma, who was clearly eager to leave.

"The pleasure is ours. Be sure to come back and visit us as soon as you're able. You can all come. Harriet and Melvin too." Wilma patted her firmly on the back before turning to Harriet. She gave Harriet a quick hug and a kiss before getting into the car.

"Thank you for having us, the wedding was beautiful, and the food was delicious," Cherish hugged Favor goodbye.

"Yes the food was absolutely delicious, Harriet," Ada said. "You did a wonderful job."

"And you, little one, come and give Aunty Harriet a kiss." Harriet signaled for Jared to come closer. Just as Harriet came closer, Jared swung his arm back and went to punch her.

Debbie leaped forward just in time and grabbed Jared's arm before it met Harriet's tummy. "Jared! No!" She picked him up and took him over to the car. Jared was squirming and screaming the whole way.

"I'm so sorry, Harriet," Ada said. "That boy will have to learn some good manners. Thank you again, it was a beautiful wedding," Ada hurried toward the car.

When Malachi reached the car, there were two seats left. One right at the back next to Jared and one facing Cherish. She secretly hoped he would sit at the back, eager to avoid any awkwardness.

She still didn't know how to feel about him denying their kiss.

For a moment there, she thought he might like her too. But she must have been wrong. Surely he would have done or said something by now if he liked her, but he hadn't.

Sure enough, he jumped into the car and buckled himself into the seat directly across from her.

As the car drove away, Ada was still harping on. "I told you, Debbie, that boy is no good! He needs a firm hand. When are you going to get married and allow a man to discipline him properly?"

"I wanna get out!" Jared screamed.

"Jared, the car is moving so you must sit still." Debbie sounded totally defeated.

"No!" he screamed through tears as he balled his tiny hands into fists.

The driver glanced around at him. "You must stay seated."

Jared covered his face with his hands after kicking both feet in the air at the driver.

"You know, I've had boys and none of them would even dare think about punching someone or kicking someone," Ada said.

"He's just a little boy, Ada," Debbie replied

"Where are we?" Jared yelled out. "I can't see out."

"We're going to Aunt Cherish's farm, Jared. I told you that already. It won't be long. Just be patient," Debbie replied.

"*Jah*, be patient or I'll smack your bottom." Ada said, causing Jared to burst into tears once more.

"Ada, please," Debbie said.

Ada just shrugged her shoulders. "When are you going to marry Peter, Debbie? Or maybe you need to find someone tougher who will discipline Jared. He'll end up in trouble and in jail. I don't know what's wrong with that boy."

"Nothing is wrong with him. He's a child." Debbie was now clearly offended.

Cherish sat there, not knowing what to do. She should've said something to help Debbie, but she was too nervous about the way Malachi was staring at her.

CHAPTER 19

*A*da wouldn't let up. "Nonsense, no child of mine would ever behave like that. A tough man that would knock some sense into him is what you need. Wilma, why are you so quiet? Don't you think something needs to be done about his foul behavior?"

Debbie stared at Wilma, who clearly looked annoyed at the situation, yet she remained silent. Debbie had become close friends with Wilma and Ada, but now she just wanted Ada to stop.

Finally, Wilma spoke. "He's barely out of being a baby, Ada. He'll grow out of this."

"Rubbish, Wilma! Absolute rubbish. You never kicked anyone when you were a boy did you, Malachi?" Ada asked.

Looking a little embarrassed, Malachi took his time to respond. "I'm sure I did when I was his age. Boys can be hard to handle."

"That's why Debbie needs a father for Jared. And I don't

believe for a minute that you were like this at his age. A good man like you... I don't believe it for a second." Ada pursed her lips.

Cherish had mentally blocked her ears. She was quiet as she again contemplated her and Malachi's kiss from years ago. Now she was embarrassed that the incident meant so little to him.

Had their kiss been that bad?

Did she have an unpleasant body odor or had there been something else disagreeable about her back then?

It kept playing over and over in her mind and she couldn't dull the noise of her own questions. He forgot it, and now she wished she could forget it.

The drive back to Cherish's farm felt like it took a lifetime. Malachi hadn't said a word to her, and she was glad. She was sure he would notice she was upset with him.

It was dark outside as the car came to a stop.

Cherish watched as Malachi jumped out of the car and helped Wilma and Ada step down from the eight-seater vehicle. She suddenly felt that feeling she had before—churning in her stomach. Malachi was so caring and mindful of others. For a moment, she was far less annoyed with him.

Wally made a noise and waddled over to meet them.

"Wally, how did you get out of the barn?" Malachi asked.

"You'd better check it for holes, Malachi," Ada told him.

"I'll do that later. Right now, I'll prepare supper for us."

"I'll do that, Malachi. We don't need much as we all ate way too much. Well, I know I did," Wilma announced as she made her way toward the house.

"I'll feed the animals, then," Malachi told no one in particular.

"I'll help you," Cherish said.

He put up a hand. "No, it's fine. Go inside where it's warm. It won't take me long." Rather than wait for her to reply, he and Wally walked off toward the barn.

Good, Cherish thought. She didn't want to help if he didn't remember their kiss anyway.

The house was cold as she followed the others through the front door. Cherish hung her coat on the hook behind the front door and walked into the living room. Wilma immediately started the fire while Ada went into the kitchen.

Exhausted, Cherish slumped down onto the couch while Debbie talked softly to Jared about his recent, unsatisfactory behavior.

Then Cherish must've fallen asleep because the next thing she knew Debbie was announcing that Jared was finally asleep.

Debbie sat on the chair next to her. "Sorry, did I wake you?"

Cherish sat up. "Oh. I must've fallen asleep. That's weird. I never do that."

"I don't blame you. I'm exhausted too," Debbie replied.

"What a day!" Cherish shook her head.

"You've been quiet. You hardly said a word in the car. Is everything alright?" Debbie looked worried as she sat staring at Cherish. Wilma had successfully started the fire and was now in the kitchen talking loudly with Ada.

"I'm sorry I didn't stand up for you when Ada was being mean," Cherish whispered.

"It's okay. You would've put yourself in the firing line as well and besides, it wouldn't have helped. Do you think Jared is that bad?"

"He's just lively. And—"

"Discipline, Wilma, he needs discipline!" Ada said at the top of her lungs, making Cherish and Debbie turn around while Ada kept shrieking, not caring she was being overheard. Cherish looked over at Debbie who seemed defeated.

"Does it hurt you the way Ada talks about Jared?" Cherish asked.

"Yes, it really does. It makes me wonder if there is something wrong with him. Am I a bad mother?" Tears welled up in Debbie's eyes.

"Of course not, Debbie! You're the most amazing mother I have ever known. You know what Ada's like. Always looking for something or someone to pick on. Jared is just an easy target." Cherish took Debbie's hand in hers. "Don't be upset. Things were different in Ada's day. Besides, every child has their own personality. Jared is just unique. And he's not going to go around kicking people when he's an adult, is he? People don't do that, and neither will Jared."

That made Debbie laugh. "I guess you're right about that. I am worried about him though. He was violent twice today. It makes me think maybe he does need a father figure in his life. Perhaps I need a husband and then things might be different for Jared. Maybe he senses how upset I get sometimes."

"What do you get upset about?"

Debbie huffed. "My parents, John's parents and the stupid decision I made. If only I'd stood up to John."

"It was all meant to be, Debbie. If you'd done anything different, you might not have Jared."

"I know, but sometimes I get so tired. When I get tired I start to have regrets. And what if everyone thinks the same as Ada and they're just not telling me?"

"He's only three."

"Nearly four as Ada keeps reminding me."

"I don't think you have anything to worry about. Don't let her put bad thoughts into your head. We'll pray for him."

"Thank you, Cherish. Now what's been up with you all afternoon?" Debbie asked leaning in closer so Wilma and Ada couldn't hear her answer.

"Well, it's about Malachi." Cherish was a little nervous to tell her.

"Malachi?" Debbie asked, seeming confused.

Cherish took a deep breath. It would feel good to unburden herself and get Debbie's opinion on what had taken place. "Yes, Malachi. A few years ago, we shared a kiss in the barn as I was leaving to go home. Favor caught us and ran out." Debbie looked shocked and didn't say anything. So Cherish continued, "Then today Favor brought it up, but Malachi said he didn't remember."

CHAPTER 20

*D*ebbie was silent while she got her head around
what Cherish had just said. "I guessed it. I saw how
you'd wait to get a letter from him. You talk about him
constantly. I was right about the two of you."

"Shhh, Debbie, please don't tell *Mamm,* and we're not
dating. He doesn't even remember we kissed. So don't say 'the
two of us' like there's something going on."

"Are you sure he doesn't remember? You know what men
are like. Maybe he's scared you don't feel the same."

Cherish looked over at the blazing fire that was giving off so
much warmth. "I'm sure that's not it. Anyway, I don't even
know if I like him like that." Cherish turned away from Debbie
and slumped back into the couch.

"Oh Cherish, I know you. If you didn't like him, you
wouldn't have been dead silent the whole afternoon. You hate it
when there's silence. You're always talking. This is bothering
you because you have feelings for him."

Cherish stopped for a moment and thought. Debbie was right. She could try to ignore her feelings for him, but she was starting to realize that her feelings were getting harder to ignore.

Cherish took a deep breath. The scent of garlic, onions, and fried chicken made Cherish realize she was working up an appetite. Those Dutch apple dumplings hadn't filled her up enough to skip Ada's food.

"Dinnertime! To the table everyone," Wilma announced as she walked over and opened the back door. "Malachi! Dinner now! Come inside," Wilma screamed at the top of her lungs.

Debbie and Cherish walked into the kitchen and sat at the table. Ada was already seated, frowning at them both as they sat down. *Mamm* had heated up garlic bread and onion soup and Ada had crumbed and fried chicken legs. Malachi came in through the mud room, changed his shoes and washed up before making his way to the table.

"Smells delicious," he said as he went to sit down next to Debbie.

"Malachi. You sit here. I prefer this seat over here." Debbie got up and sat next to Ada, forcing him to sit next to Cherish.

"Ahh, okay," Malachi said as he sat next to Cherish.

Cherish frowned at Debbie. She didn't need her help. It had been a mistake to mention anything to her if she was going to do things like this.

They all closed their eyes and said their silent prayer of thanks for the food.

"The soup smells amazing, Wilma!" Ada said once she opened her eyes.

Cherish felt nervous being this close to Malachi. She had never felt this anxious being around him before.

After Wilma tasted her soup, she said, "You know, I wasn't sure about the wedding in the beginning, but it turned out to be quite all right, don't you think?" Wilma asked everyone. "I'm still not happy that Samuel and Levi weren't there to see her married. They've been close to her for her whole life."

"I know exactly how you feel, Wilma," Ada said.

"It was truly beautiful, Wilma. Much better than the wedding I had with no one I knew there except for John. I wasn't even married by our bishop—it was a celebrant. Favor's wedding was a far sight better than that."

Everyone was silent after Debbie's remark.

Debbie spoke again, "I believe there is someone for everyone. And God even finds someone for widows, like you, Wilma. So maybe I will get married again one day." Debbie waited for Ada to tell her that Peter was the one for her, but thankfully, Ada was silent on that subject for once.

Wilma nodded. "Yes, I was blessed that Levi came along. It was a rocky road at the start, but time was on our side. Now we do miss each other when we're apart."

"And *Gott* was too." Ada gave a nod.

"*Gott* was what?" Cherish asked, trying to understand what she meant.

Ada stared at Cherish. "*Gott* finds someone for everyone."

Cherish frowned, wondering if Ada had something wrong with her hearing.

"Malachi, why aren't you married yet?" Debbie asked.

Cherish nearly choked on her bread. She grabbed the glass of water in front of her and took a gulp.

Malachi looked up. "Excuse me?"

"Debbie, how rude! We don't ask questions like that." Wilma chuckled while Ada stifled her laughter.

Cherish felt her cheeks burning. One day, she'd learn to keep things to herself. No one in her family could keep a secret and now she'd found out that included Debbie.

"Well, I guess the Lord hasn't sent me the right woman yet," Malachi replied.

"Maybe your helpmeet is closer than you think," Debbie said. Cherish gave her a gentle nudge with her foot under the table.

"Maybe," he replied as he smiled in Cherish's direction, making her stomach flood with butterflies once more. She didn't dare look at him.

Then Debbie asked, "I wonder if we could stay a couple more days, Wilma. It's been pretty tiring so far. If we stayed two more days, we could relax without the usual day-to-day responsibilities. Peter is looking after my stall until I come back. I didn't even tell him a day that I'd be returning."

Wilma looked down for a moment. "I am worried about Levi, but if you want to so badly, we could stay two more days. I'm sure that wouldn't hurt."

Now Cherish was pleased with Debbie.

"If that's okay with you, Malachi?" Wilma asked.

"Sure is. I'm loving the company. It's usually just me and Wally."

CHAPTER 21

Back at the orchard…

Krystal stepped into the bright sunshine as she made her way down the front steps of the Baker/Bruner house.

It was a beautiful day. She couldn't think of a more beautiful place than the Baker Apple Orchard. It had been a blessing and a pleasure to live there. Now more than ever she was grateful for all those years she'd stayed with Favor and her sisters.

She hurried to the horse and buggy that the early visitor, Samuel, had hitched for her.

She had slept in that morning, and would be late to open the store. She climbed into the driver's seat and was in the process of turning the buggy around when she heard a voice.

"Excuse me."

She turned around to see Noah walking toward her.

"Hello there," he said.

SAMANTHA PRICE

Immediately, she got out of the buggy. "Noah, what are you doing here?" She adjusted her *kapp,* hoping she looked okay.

"Sorry, I didn't mean to frighten you. I called out a few times," he said as he came closer to her.

Krystal realized she'd been in such a rush that she hadn't seen his horse and buggy parked on the other side of the driveway.

"Ah, I'm sorry about that, I'm late to open the store this morning," She looked down at her feet, feeling a little embarrassed. She loved working at the store, and it wasn't often that she was late.

"That's actually what I wanted to talk to you about." He cleared his throat before continuing. "I wanted to ask if you wouldn't mind staying on at the shop until we can figure out what to do with it."

"Yes. Your father asked me that and I agreed."

"I know, but he meant like for a week, but now it'll be for longer than that. You'll be paid, of course. We're not asking for charity."

Krystal felt a wave of relief rush over her. She was glad to still have a job for now.

"Of course, it would be my pleasure!" She smiled as she looked down at her feet again, feeling a little shy. She was sure she was blushing for the first time in her life. Normally, she was so confident with men, but not with Noah.

"Thank you, I really appreciate it. I also wanted to let you know, you're more than welcome to stay at Gertie's house for the long term. It'll be a while before the family comes to an agreement on that. We don't expect you to pay rent or anything. Just stay there and keep it nice."

604

"Really?" No other man in the community had been this good to her.

"Of course. Gertie would have wanted it that way."

"Well, thank you. I really appreciate that. Um, I guess I should go. The shop needs to be opened."

"One more thing." He swallowed hard. "Would you like to come for a picnic with me today?"

"I'm sorry, I can't. I've got to work at the shop today."

"What about afterwards?"

Krystal thought about it for a moment. "Okay, that would be lovely." She smiled and gave him a wave as she climbed into her buggy and picked up the lines. No time was wasted having the horse move forward.

"I'll see you then!" he yelled as she passed him in the horse and buggy.

KRYSTAL FELT nervous as she sat in the shop. She was hand-sewing a quilt Gertie had started and she couldn't focus.

"Ouch!" she cried out aloud as the needle pricked her finger. She'd never be great at sewing. It was different for the Amish women who'd been raised to sew. She moved to the back room and held her hand under the running water of the sink. As she did so, she thought about what she'd talk about with Noah.

He knew she wasn't born in the community, but exactly how much did he know about her? He'd shared with her that he had a shady past, so perhaps that meant he'd excuse hers?

She would have to be honest and tell him all the bad things about herself. But when? She didn't want to get to know him and fall in love, only for him to leave when he found out the truth. But if she told him too early, she'd scare him off.

She turned off the tap and dried her hands. Then she opened the first aid kit and started to bandage her finger. It wasn't easy to do that one-handed.

The more she thought about it, the more she came to the conclusion it would be the best thing to tell him upfront. If he got scared off then that simply meant he wasn't the right man for her.

Then she heard the rain come pelting down.

Would there be a picnic at all if this kept up?

One thing she knew was that her day would be quiet. Barely anyone came into the store when it was raining.

Just as well she'd had hardly any customers because all day Krystal had trouble focusing on anything but her past. Besides a couple of lookers, she had some people stop by to see her. One pair of visitors was Levi and Samuel.

By the afternoon, the rain had lessened. When she saw Noah's horse and buggy pull up outside the store, a wave of excitement rushed over her. She waited until he got out and came in to see her.

"Is it that time already?" she asked as he walked through the front door.

"I believe it is." He smiled and stood there with his hands on his hips, looking ever so handsome.

"Why don't I close up and meet you out front?" Krystal folded the quilt she was still working on. Trying to sew with only nine fingers had helped take her mind off things.

"Okay," Noah said as he turned and walked out the door.

She walked around the store, turning off the lights. She

grabbed her string bag and adjusted her prayer *kapp* before walking out to meet him.

"Was it a good day for the store?" he asked as she locked the front door.

"Not so much thanks to the rain," she said as he gestured for her to climb into the buggy.

"Where's your buggy?" he asked.

"Samuel stopped by with Levi today. I told them about the picnic. Levi had the idea to drive the buggy home and Samuel followed in his."

"That was a risky move. What if I hadn't turned up at all? You'd be stranded here."

"I knew you would. Why? Was there a chance you'd not come without telling me?"

He laughed. "Don't worry about me. It was a silly thing to say. I guess... you make me nervous."

She looked over at his handsome face. "Oh careful," she said when a bike pulled out in front of them.

"I saw it!" he spat out. "Sorry. I didn't mean to yell. It's just that I dislike those bike riders. They think they own the road. They make up their own rules."

Krystal was a little shocked at his outburst and didn't know what to say so she kept silent.

It was a short trip to the park. As he pulled up the buggy, Krystal saw a picnic blanket sprawled over a table in the center of the park.

"Grass is wet," he said as he smiled at her.

"You already came and set this up?"

"Yep. Let's go!" He was in a much better mood now. He

jumped out of the buggy and raced around to open her door. He held her hand as she stepped down to the ground.

He had done this, all for her. She felt nervous but excited as they walked toward the table.

"No one has ever taken me out on a picnic date before," she said as they sat down. She looked at everything on the table. There was fresh cheese and grapes, croissants and fresh pumpkin pie and pickled vegetables. For drinks there was a choice of orange juice and soda.

"So this is a date then?" Noah teased as he passed her a plate and poured her some orange juice.

"Oh, I mean, no, I..." Krystal felt a little silly.

"I'm just kidding. The pleasure is all mine, and I find that hard to believe. A pretty girl like you? I'm sure half the men in town are lining up for you."

Krystal felt a lump in her throat. This was her opportunity to tell him. She wanted to say something but couldn't bring herself to do it just yet. "You are very kind. I'm very appreciative of you showing me such generosity."

"Of course. I'm told my grandmother spoke very highly of you. She would want you to be taken care of."

Hearing this made Krystal start to tear up. Gertie had always been there for her. She missed her so much at that moment. She'd been a fool to think she could walk out on Gertie, and turn her back on the community that had welcomed her with open arms and open hearts.

"She was a dear friend to me," Krystal said as she wiped a tear from her cheek. She felt herself freeze as Noah leaned in close. Was he about to kiss her? He pulled a tissue from the picnic basket and dabbed her cheeks with it. Her heart raced.

Before she could say anything, rain began to fall, and fall hard. They jumped to their feet, quickly grabbing everything off the table. Then with the picnic basket under Noah's arm, they ran back to the horse and buggy.

They laughed when they were both sitting in the buggy, looking at each other, soaking wet.

"That came out of nowhere," she said.

He reached behind him and grabbed a towel and handed it to her.

"Thank you."

"Well, that didn't go to plan," Noah said. "I guess we better make our way home then."

Krystal wondered why he didn't suggest that they'd eat in the buggy. It just made sense. Since he didn't mention it, she didn't want to.

"Haiya!" he yelled at the horse as they moved away from the park.

He whistled as they drove along. They each caught one another's eye every so often and smiled. Krystal didn't mind the whistling, but it made having any kind of conversation difficult.

Out of nowhere a man riding a bike nearly ran into the side of the horse. Noah had to move the horse and buggy off the road to avoid him. Suddenly, the horse and buggy came to a halt, jolting them both forward. The bike rider didn't stop.

"Whoa!" Krystal screamed.

"Are you okay?" Noah asked, looking worried.

"Yes, I'm fine."

"Something's not fine. I'll go take a look." Noah jumped out of the carriage and into the rain. "Agh, come on now!" Noah yelled.

Krystal turned around and looked out the back buggy window. She saw him throw his hat violently on the ground, still yelling. Then he walked up to her window. "We're stuck in the mud." He threw his hands in the air. "I can't believe this."

Krystal was frozen in shock. She had never heard an Amish man lose his temper like this before. The more Noah shouted, the more uncomfortable she became.

Was this because he had spent so much time away from the community and picked up bad habits?

She started to feel sick. She had only thought of staying in the community because of him. Now she wasn't so sure that was the best idea.

Suddenly, a horse and buggy pulled up beside them. She watched as a tall man jumped out of the buggy and ran into the rain toward them. It was Andrew Weeks. Andrew was Bliss's husband's business partner. Then she remembered someone had suggested he'd be a good match for her. All was not lost.

Andrew said a few words to Noah before they unhitched the horses. Noah walked toward her side of the carriage.

"This man will help us. We'll need to be outside the buggy so he can pull the buggy out." He looked at the ground. She noticed how much his demeanor had changed, even towards her. He seemed cold. She took his hand and jumped out of the buggy.

Andrew gave Krystal a nod as he connected the buggy to the rear of his buggy.

"Thank you, Andrew," she said, yelling over the rain that was now falling a little more gently.

Andrew gave her a wave before he got back into his buggy.

Krystal was intrigued. Andrew seemed so nice, and energetic. She'd noticed how strong he was as he did all the work himself with ease while Noah stood there, watching.

"Okay, step back!" Andrew yelled from inside the buggy. His horses moved forward and as they did so, the buggy was pulled out of the mud.

Krystal clapped her hands and jumped up and down. "It's out."

Noah laughed. "It is. You get back in the buggy now, out of the rain."

Krystal did as he said. She watched as Andrew and Noah hitched the horses onto the buggy.

Noah said, looking a little embarrassed, "A bike came out of nowhere and I had to get off the road or hit it. That's the only choice I had."

Krystal noticed Noah hadn't thanked him. "Thank you, Andrew!"

"You're welcome. You two stay warm now! All the best." He turned and headed to his horse and buggy and then he drove off.

"You okay?" Noah asked Krystal as he got back into the buggy.

She realized she had been staring into space, watching Andrew's buggy drive off into the distance. "Yes."

When he moved the horses forward, he said, "Sorry about that. I lost my temper and that wasn't okay."

She was pleased that he saw he was in the wrong. If he could see that, then there might be some hope that he could change. She wasn't about to judge him. "It's fine, don't worry about it."

"When will you move back to Gertie's house? My father's gone now and you did tell him you'd stay there for a while."

"Very soon. Thank you, and thank your father for me." She'd much rather stay at the orchard, but now she felt obligated to stay at Gertie's house. "It was good that Andrew came along when he did."

"I would've been able to get us out."

She tried to be positive and show him she wasn't someone to dwell on the downside of life. "The rain ruined our picnic, but I still had a fun time."

He gave her a wide smile. "I'm glad."

When they got to the orchard, she asked, "Would you like to come in?" She hoped he'd say no. Right now, she just wanted him to be far away from her.

"No. I should go."

She smiled. "Thanks again for everything."

"No problem, Krystal."

Krystal was delighted that he wasn't coming inside because she wasn't used to being around people who had so much pent-up anger.

She walked toward the house, listening to the clip clopping of the horse's hooves moving away. Krystal stepped up onto the porch and then sat on one of the chairs. She had to process what just happened.

Noah had a basket full of food.

What was he going to do with it?

Why didn't they eat?

Why was he so upset by bike riders?

And, why hadn't he thanked Andrew for pulling them out of the mud?

CHAPTER 22

$\mathcal{I}$t was two days after Favor's wedding. She was lying in bed listening to her husband and his mother talking in the kitchen. The walls in the house were thin and it didn't help that Favor and Simon's room was right next to the kitchen. It made sleeping in awfully hard with the way Harriet clanged the pots and pans about. She even cracked eggs abnormally loudly.

"I'm taking her a cup of coffee. Just like I always do," Simon said to his mother after she'd questioned him regarding where he was going with the mug of coffee.

"Yes, but you're married now. She should be looking after you," Harriet said. "Wives take care of husbands, not the other way around."

Favor listened hard. What would her new husband say? She hoped he wouldn't agree with his mother as he always did.

"I don't mind. You know she's not good at getting up in the mornings."

"Humph. I thought that would change once you were married. There are responsibilities. We should all get up early and feed the animals."

"There's no need, Ma. Just relax. She catches up on work through the day. She told me so."

"We'll all have a talk this afternoon. Call it a family meeting."

"Talk about what?" Simon asked.

"Favor's duties. She'll have to improve."

Favor was annoyed. She always worked hard, much harder than she'd ever worked on the orchard. To hear her mother-in-law say that about her was just hurtful.

Simon opened the bedroom door and walked through. "Sorry, I'm late. I hope it's not too cold."

Favor sat up in bed, acting like she'd just woken up. She stretched her arms above her head. "Thank you. I'm sure it'll be fine."

"Ma stopped me to talk. That's why it might be a little cold." Simon put her cup on the nightstand. "She's upset about you sleeping in."

"It's hard to wake up so early. That's why I need the coffee. I mean, is it even necessary to get up at dawn?"

Simon chuckled. "I don't mind, but the animals get hungry."

"But the three of you do it, so why do I need to be there? I'd just be watching you. Your mother likes to do everything herself anyway."

"I'm just telling you what she said."

"I heard it." Favor reached for her coffee. "I don't know why she can't talk to me directly. Why does she tell you to tell me things?"

Simon sat on the bed. "I guess she doesn't want to say anything to upset you. I don't mind if you sleep in."

"Why don't you tell her that?" Favor sipped her drink. "I mean, did you tell her?"

"She's probably wondering what will happen when they're no longer here."

Favor looked up. This was great news. His parents were going somewhere. Then Favor and Simon could finally have some alone time. "Where are they going?"

"Nowhere. I mean when they go home to be with God."

"Oh." Favor looked down. Would she have to wait that long to be alone with her husband? "When that time comes, I'll get up early because I'll have to."

Simon smiled at her. "I know you will."

"Simon, if you don't mind that I sleep-in, why don't you tell your folks that?"

"I will." He gave a reassuring smile.

Favor was doubtful since he hadn't done that one time when he was talking with his folks. "Really? For sure? You'd stand up to them and tell them you're okay with it?"

He laughed. "It's not really standing up to them. It's just giving my opinion."

Favor was delighted to hear it. "Thank you. When I sleep-in in the morning, I get more done through the day because I'm well-rested. That's reason enough for not getting up before the sun rises."

"I've got to help pa with some things."

She grabbed his arm. "You will say something to them, won't you?"

"Yes. I sure will."

"Okay. I'll get up soon."

He leaned over and kissed her forehead and then left the room.

Favor finished her coffee and then slowly got dressed. Once she had pulled on her dress and stockings, she brushed out her hair. Her mind drifted to her wedding. It was over so quickly and she didn't know when she'd see her family again. But then again, she had an entirely new family now. A new family that came with a new set of problems. Favor had decided a long time ago that she wouldn't be pushed around by Harriet once she was married.

She had to stick with that. She'd dig her heels in about everything if she had to. No, she'd let Simon do it for her. That's what marriage was all about; it was a partnership. She'd let Simon stand up for her.

Favor braided her hair, and then fastened her braids before she placed her prayer *kapp* on her head. Then she tied the strings under her chin. Now she was ready to face Harriet.

When Favor walked into the kitchen, she saw Harriet busy at the stove, standing with her back to her. Favor leaned against the wall and said nothing.

Her thoughts raced away with her. Most young married couples woke up in a house alone, with privacy. When she'd been a young girl dreaming about being a bride, she never imagined this was what her early married life would look like.

"Good morning, Harriet," Favor said as she sat down at the table.

Harriet whipped her head around. "Good *afternoon*, Favor."

"Err, it's *morning*."

"Is it? Well, it might as well be afternoon with all the work Melvin, Simon and I have done, and all before you woke up."

Favor thought it was best not to confront Harriet directly. It was best to let Simon tell Harriet later that she could sleep in. "I'm sorry. I'll get better at this."

"I certainly hope so. You know we live on a farm. We've been waiting for you to realize you have to pull your weight. We're having a family meeting later today."

"Okay. It's always a good idea to have family meetings." Favor couldn't help smiling, thinking about the look on Harriet's face when Simon put his foot down about his wife sleeping in.

"Yes. It certainly is good to have a time when we can talk about what's bothering us." Harriet put eggs and bacon on a plate and placed it in front of Favor.

"Thank you."

Harriet sat down with a cup of coffee. "One day, you might be making me breakfast."

"I cook. Don't make it sound like I don't." Favor pouted. How could Harriet speak to her like that when she was trying to be nice to her?

"I know you do, but I don't think it's fair that you sleep in. You could—"

Favor couldn't take it anymore. She jumped up and ran out of the room. When she got to her bedroom, she closed herself in. Then she sat on her bed and cried.

Harriet burst into the room. "Favor, you didn't let me finish speaking."

Favor sniffed back her tears. She'd have to get a lock put on the door. "I just got married. I just need some time to get used to the routine."

"But you've lived here for months in the spare room and you've always slept in. What's going to change?"

Favor pressed her lips together. She needed Simon here now to stand up for her. "Let's wait for the family meeting. We'll get everyone's opinion."

"They have the same opinion as I do. Now come out and eat your breakfast or I'll feed it to the dogs."

Favor was hungry, so she got up and walked back to the kitchen with Harriet following close behind.

"I'm sensing you're upset," Harriet said.

Favor bit her tongue at Harriet's odd comment. Of course she was upset! "I'm better." Favor sat down at the table.

"I want us all to get along. You're my daughter now."

That comment made Favor homesick for the first time since she'd been there. "I know and we will all get along."

"That's good. We should have a fresh start today."

Favor looked down at her breakfast. "Thanks for this." To make Simon happy, Favor was going to make a big effort to get along with Harriet. "I'll try to get up earlier tomorrow."

"You will?"

"Yes, but I don't know why I have to. You're all doing things and I end up just standing there."

"When you learn what to do, you'll be able to do it."

"Couldn't I have a different job? I'm not that good with animals. I never even had a pet of my own."

Harriet gasped. "You poor child. Simon had a whole host of pets. Birds, tadpoles, cats, dogs and so many other creatures and that's not including all the farm animals."

"I just wasn't interested. They're dirty and they're unpredictable. You never know what they'll do next. That's why I don't like horses because they can do anything to you, and they're so big and scary."

"If you treat them right, they'll treat you right."

Favor cut her fried egg into two pieces. "Hmm. I don't know about that."

"Don't worry. You'll grow to love all our animals." Harriet gave her a dazzling smile.

Favor forced a smile back at her.

CHAPTER 23

*A*fter the evening meal and before their nightly Bible reading, the Koppel family sat in front of the fire in the living room.

"Ma wants us to have a family meeting." Melvin's tone was awkward, as though he didn't entirely agree with his wife. Even if he didn't, Favor knew he was never going to admit it.

Harriet nodded. "That's right. It's about Favor having trouble waking up in the morning. If we all pitch in, we will all have less work to do."

"Not only that," Melvin said, "we'd finish our chores a lot faster."

"Yes. What can we do about that? Anyone got any suggestions?" Harriet looked at Simon.

When Simon didn't say anything, Favor was forced to speak. "I said earlier today that I'd try to get up a little earlier,"

Harriet sighed. "You must do it, not *try* to do it."

Favor looked at her husband, who was seated beside her. He still wasn't saying anything. "What do you have to say, Simon?"

Simon looked at her. "They make some good points."

Favor couldn't believe it. He just went back on everything they'd talked about. She wasn't going to let him get away with it. "Why did you tell me just this morning that you don't mind me sleeping longer?"

"Did you say that?" Harriet asked Simon.

"Yeah, but I guess I didn't think it through."

Favor wanted to scream at him. "Well, do you mind or not? You told me you didn't mind and then you were going to tell your mother that. Now you're here, you say something totally different."

He wriggled uncomfortably in his chair. "It's not like that. I can see your point of view and I can see Ma and Pa's point of view."

Harriet wasn't happy with that. "How do you see Favor's point of view, Simon? Your problem is that you keep taking her coffee in the morning. That's why she thinks it's okay to sleep for longer. You're encouraging her."

"I feel that everyone is picking on me. I said I'd try and no one's happy with that." Without the support of her new husband, Favor felt so alone.

"Trying is good," Melvin said. "I think we can all agree that we've had a productive meeting."

Harriet folded her arms. "As long as she *does* try and knows how important it is."

"She said she would, Ma," Simon said.

Favor sat there with her arms crossed, mirroring Harriet's pose, not saying anything at all.

"Now, I think we can start our Bible reading unless anyone else has anything they want to say." When no one said anything, Melvin opened his Bible and started his readings from where they'd left off the previous night.

Favor couldn't listen. The words didn't even enter her mind or her heart. She was too upset. She sat through the whole thing just waiting until she could go to bed.

When bedtime came, she said goodnight to everyone and went straight to her room. Simon came in behind her.

"How could you do that to me?"

"Do what?"

"You didn't back me up. You let me down," Favor whined.

"Shh. Keep your voice down. They'll hear you."

"We need our own place." Favor put her head on Simon's shoulder and he put his arms around her.

"Our own place would be ideal, but you know that's not a possibility. I told you that from the start."

"We need privacy, Simon. We're newlyweds." Favor flung herself onto the bed, buried her face in the pillow and cried. Simon sat down next to her and put his arm around her once more.

"I'm sorry, Favor. I don't know what to do."

She sat up with tears streaming down her face. "Why did you let me down?"

"I didn't mean to. It's just that Ma made sense with what she said."

"You're just impossible. All you had to say was what you said to me this morning."

There was a knock on the door. Harriet said, "Is everything okay in there?"

"It's fine, Ma," Simon told her.

From behind the door, Harriet said, "Someone sounds upset."

"It's okay, Ma. I can handle it."

Favor whispered, "This is why we need our own place. How am I supposed to live like this? You can't agree with them. You have to agree with me because I'm your wife. I'm the most important person in your life, not them."

Simon opened his mouth in shock. "They're my parents. They've done so much for me. They work so hard on the farm so they've got something to leave me."

"Tell them you don't want it. If we move back to Lancaster County, I'm sure we could both work on the orchard. Or we could both find some different work."

He shook his head. "No, Favor. It's not going to happen. We discussed all this before we married. You agreed to us living here. We're staying on the farm—our farm."

"I agreed before I knew what it was like. We need privacy. I love your parents, but I don't want them listening to everything."

He sat down with her and held her hand. "Things will get better. You're just adjusting to life here."

She looked at him and knew that he was worth it. She flung her arms around him and put her head on his shoulder.

"We'll make it work. Everything will be great, you'll see," Simon said.

Favor knew everything would be great if they moved out. That's what they needed. That's what most other newly married couples enjoyed. She thought back to when Joy and Isaac first married. They were living at the orchard in the main house, but they didn't like it either. Then they got a trailer that they put behind the barn. Joy and Isaac lived there for over a year before they moved out.

Favor pulled away from him and sat up straight. "What if we got a trailer and put it on the property somewhere? We'd still be here, but we'd have our own space."

Simon frowned. "Are you serious? Why would we do that when we've got a comfortable home here?"

"One word—privacy."

"It's not worth it." Simon yawned. "Let's talk about this tomorrow."

Favor wasn't going to give up until Simon stood up to his parents and until they had their own private place. That was the only way Favor would stay sane.

CHAPTER 24

Back at Cherish's farm...

"I can't believe you're all leaving tomorrow."

Cherish was finally alone with Malachi as they sat in front of the fire. Everyone else had gone to bed. "Me either. It's been great being able to be here for so long. I mean, two weeks isn't too long since it's been three years since I was here last. Does that make sense?"

"It does. You make sense most of the time."

Cherish smiled. "Thanks, I think. So, tomorrow I'll be back at the orchard. Any last things you want to talk about? I mean with the farm of course."

"Like what?"

"I dunno. I just thought you might have some questions for me."

He shook his head. "There is something I've been meaning to talk to you about. I've been working up the courage."

Cherish frowned, pretending she was angry. "What have you done?"

He didn't even smile. "It's the fact that I'm a coward. I've not told you the truth."

"About what?" Cherish hoped he wasn't going to say he was leaving the farm. Or worse, that he *did* have a girlfriend.

He stared at her. "I remember that kiss."

Cherish couldn't believe it. "Our kiss? Why did you pretend you didn't?"

"I just didn't know where things would go."

Cherish took a chance. "Where do you want things to go?"

"Truthfully?"

She nodded.

"Well... I'd like you to be my girlfriend."

His unexpected response made her breathe heavily, making her chest rise and fall. Now she didn't know what to say.

"What do you think about that?" he asked.

She couldn't stop from smiling. "I'd like that too."

He grinned and moved closer and put his arm around her. Cherish rested her head on his shoulder. Then he said, "I've longed to hold you like this for so many years."

"Why didn't you say so?"

"I couldn't risk losing you. You're not the easiest person to get along with at times."

She couldn't stop smiling. "That's not so."

"I think you know it's true."

She didn't say any more. She just enjoyed the closeness.

"I thought if we dated and it didn't work out, I'd have to leave the farm and I love the farm. Almost as much..."

She looked up into his eyes. Was he just about to say he

loved her? Their eyes locked and then slowly, his gaze fell to her lips. Cherish closed her eyes and waited for his lips to touch hers. When they did, it was the most magical moment she'd ever experienced in her life.

Everything was perfect.

As soon as the kiss ended, he whispered, "I shouldn't have done that."

"Yes, you should've."

Then he kissed her again, just briefly before he held her tighter. "This day couldn't get any better. Hey, did you just agree to date me?"

"Yes."

He laughed. "My prayers have finally been answered after all these years."

Cherish was a little lightheaded. "This would've happened sooner if you'd stopped giving me mixed messages."

His lips twitched. "It would've happened sooner if you'd been easier to read."

"Don't blame me, it's your fault," Cherish teased.

"Okay. I'll take the blame. I don't mind."

"Neither do I," Cherish said with a laugh.

"Do you want to keep this whole thing a secret?" he asked.

Cherish didn't want to keep it quiet. "What do you want?"

"I think secrecy is best until we get to know one another."

"We know each other very well already," Cherish said.

"I know that, but not in a relationship way."

"Ah, I suppose you're right." Cherish sighed inside, wondering if they were going to have a ten year courtship? Then Cherish remembered she couldn't leave the orchard, so what was the point in dating Malachi at all?

"I'm always right," said Malachi.

Cherish laughed. "So, how do you see this working since I hardly ever get to come here? Are we going to date through letters?"

"Letters and phone calls. We can do that."

That wasn't enough for Cherish. "Okay."

"Unless you want to take a leap in faith and marry me right now."

She put her head on his shoulder and he pulled her closer. "Things are complicated at home." His comment made her glad to know what his long-term intentions were.

"If you weren't there, I'm sure they'd figure it out. Your parents have a lot of friends, and you said before that they can employ more people for the orchard."

"I know. It's Fairfax who would be employing them, he's the manager now, but I'd just feel so guilty if I left." Cherish pictured how old and frail Levi was.

"They'll work it out. Or do you want to be like Simon's parents in reverse?"

"What do you mean?" Cherish asked.

"You want to stay with your mother forever, joined at the hip?"

Cherish laughed. "You're so mean. I can't believe you said that about Simon's parents."

He laughed too. "I've never hidden how I feel about them. Not about them, but about the way they act with Simon. He's a grown man. Cherish, you'll have to leave the nest sooner or later."

"I know."

"So, is that a yes?"

"I will come here again soon. It's hard because I need someone to come with me. They can't spare me at harvest time."

"You're not answering my question. I said, is that a yes?"

"A yes to what?" Cherish asked.

He grabbed hold of her hand. "Cherish Baker, will you marry me?"

She couldn't help smiling. "We haven't even started dating yet."

"We've been dating for five minutes, and we could be getting married too if you'll have me."

"But you said—"

"Forget what I said. I was trying to be sensible and practical, but now I don't want to be tied to anything that makes sense."

Cherish giggled. "So I don't make sense?"

"You make perfect sense. You and me make perfect sense together."

Although that was what she'd wanted for a long time, she couldn't give him an answer. Not with what was going on at home. "I don't know. I'll have to think about it."

"Sure. Do that. I'm sorry. The last thing I want to do is put pressure on you. Maybe this whole thing is moving too fast. I always rush in and regret it later."

"Everything *is* happening fast."

"It might feel like that to you, but I've been thinking this way for years."

Cherish was a little surprised to hear it. "You have?"

"You must know that I've always liked you."

Cherish shook her head. "No. I thought... maybe, but I didn't know."

"I was worried you'd reject me. You could do so much better. I have nothing to offer you. That's why I haven't come forward to tell you how I feel," Malachi said.

Now Cherish understood him a little better. "There's nothing I need. I don't need money and I already have a farm, and I'm a part owner of the orchard."

"I'm so happy you said that. We only need God and each other. We can figure out the rest day by day."

"That's true. I've got a few things to figure out." She'd never forgive herself if she put herself in front of her mother. *Mamm* was so fragile sometimes, and if anything happened to Levi, *Mamm* would quickly fall apart.

"Take your time," Malachi said. "I'm not going anywhere."

"Thanks for understanding."

"I'm an understanding guy. Just remember that."

Cherish smiled. "I will."

"Just tell everyone about us when you're ready to tell 'em. I know you've got a lot to think about. Maybe you'll get home and change your mind."

"No, I won't."

He gave her a smile which calmed her. "I know you have to think about your family, but just remember you have to consider yourself too."

"Something will work out."

"Yeah, if it's meant to be, God will make a way."

"He will," Cherish said as she rested her head on his shoulder once more.

~

EARLY THE NEXT DAY, Cherish was disappointed to see the eight-seat vehicle arrive to drive them home. She'd stayed up with Malachi, talking into the early hours of the morning.

She held back tears as Malachi joined them all outside, carrying four suitcases.

"Cherish, you sit in the front," Ada ordered. "Debbie and I will sit in the back with Jared in between us. Wilma can sit opposite. Hopefully, we'll keep him calm for the journey."

"He does get bored," Debbie said.

Ada tilted her head to the side. "If he starts to pinch me again, I'll have to swap places with Cherish."

"What? So he can pinch me?" Cherish asked.

"I bruise badly. You're young. You can handle it."

Cherish noticed Debbie looking sad. It must've been awful for her, trying to control Jared's outbursts. "It's okay, Ada, you can sit in the front the whole way."

Ada grinned. "Do you mind?"

"Of course not. I'll help keep Jared occupied," Cherish said.

"Oh, you're a dear girl."

Cherish laughed and Debbie thanked her.

When all the bags were in the trunk, Cherish walked over to Malachi. She rubbed Wally's neck and then looked up into Malachi's eyes. "Goodbye, Malachi." She couldn't even hug him or allow him to give her a quick kiss.

"Bye, Cherish. I hope to see you soon." He gave her a nod.

She took a deep breath and got into the car.

"All aboard!" Ada yelled out. "We all ready?"

Mamm laughed. "We're all ready to go home."

Cherish didn't know why they were so chirpy, leaving the farm. The car moved away and she turned around and looked out the back window at Malachi and Wally getting smaller and smaller. It was awful to leave Malachi.

She faced the front.

Now she had so many things to think about.

Firstly, she needed to consider what she wanted and even whether Malachi was truly the right man for her. She'd seen how in love Favor was with Simon and how she'd ignored so many things around her. Favor had blinkers on and didn't see what other people saw about how awkward her life with Simon's parents could become. Was there anything that she couldn't see about Malachi right now?

Cherish had to make sure she was considering all her options before she gave Malachi a 'yes.' Either way, she'd move to her farm like she'd planned.

Then of course there were the logistics of making a move to the farm with so many people back home depending on her.

She'd need to get *Mamm* used to the idea that she was leaving. But... how was she going to do that?

Thank you for reading this Amish Bonnet Sisters Omnibus, Volume 9.

www.SamanthaPriceAuthor.com

THE NEXT SET IN THE SERIES

Amish Bonnet Sisters Omnibus
Volume 10
Includes books 28, 29 and 30.

A Season for Second Chances - Wilma is recovering from the wedding while Favor deals with doubts that have crept into her mind about getting married. Cherish is left wondering if it's time for her to pursue her own happiness, but can she cut loose the ties that bind her to the orchard?

A Change of Heart - Cherish gets a surprise visitor, who changes her life forever. That's not the only change for the Baker/Bruner family when tragedy strikes. Can Wilma allow the entire extended family to come together to overcome the challenges they face?

The Last Wedding - Cherish Baker is delighted she'll be getting married at the orchard, but her wedding planning is interrupted when she needs to protect her mother from poten-tially devastating news.

Wilma does her best to come to terms with recent changes and hopes the last of her daughters' weddings will bring the family together.

ABOUT SAMANTHA PRICE

Samantha Price is a USA Today bestselling and Kindle All Stars author of Amish romance books and cozy mysteries. She was raised Brethren and has a deep affinity for the Amish way of life, which she has explored extensively with over a decade of research.
She is mother to two pampered rescue cats, and a very spoiled staffy with separation issues.

Samantha loves to hear from her readers. Connect at:

samantha@samanthapriceauthor.com
www.facebook.com/SamanthaPriceAuthor
www.instagram.com/SamanthaPriceAuthor
Twitter @AmishRomance
www.pinterest.com/AmishRomance

Samantha Price
www.SamanthaPriceAuthor.com

ALL SAMANTHA PRICE'S SERIES

Amish Maids Trilogy
A 3 book Amish romance series of novels featuring 5 friends finding love.

Amish Love Blooms
A 6 book Amish romance series of novels about four sisters and their cousins.

Amish Misfits
A series of 7 stand-alone books about people who have never fitted in.

The Amish Bonnet Sisters
To date there are 28 books in this continuing family saga. My most popular and best-selling series.

Amish Women of Pleasant Valley

An 8 book Amish romance series with the same characters. This has been one of my most popular series.

Ettie Smith Amish Mysteries
An ongoing cozy mystery series with octogenarian sleuths. Popular with lovers of mysteries such as Miss Marple or Murder She Wrote.

Amish Secret Widows' Society
A ten novella mystery/romance series - a prequel to the Ettie Smith Amish Mysteries.

Expectant Amish Widows
A stand-alone Amish romance series of 19 books.

Seven Amish Bachelors
A 7 book Amish Romance series following the Fuller brothers' journey to finding love.

Amish Foster Girls
A 4 book Amish romance series with the same characters who have been fostered to an Amish family.

Amish Brides
An Amish historical romance. 5 book series with the same characters who have arrived in America to start their new life.

Amish Romance Secrets
The first series I ever wrote. 6 novellas following the same characters.

Amish Christmas Books
Each year I write an Amish Christmas stand-alone romance novel.

Amish Twin Hearts
A 4 book Amish Romance featuring twins and their friends.

Amish Wedding Season
The second series I wrote. It has the same characters throughout the 5 books.

Gretel Koch Jewel Thief
A clean 5 book suspense/mystery series about a jewel thief who has agreed to consult with the FBI.